THE EAGLE'S WING

THE EAGLE'S WING

THE GARDENS OF THE WEST, PART ONE

Francis Jarman

WILDSIDE PRESS

For Robert Reginald (1948-2013)

Published by Wildside Press LLC.
www.wildsidebooks.com

I

MARA OUT ON THE PLAIN, BUT NOT ALONE

✴ *The great northern plain.*

Mara first noticed the horsemen in the late afternoon, as the sun finally weakened. It had been hot out on the plain, where there was no shade. She had picked some broad-leaf grass to suck, to still her thirst, and later on found one of the few little streams that were still carrying water. She and the filly had both drunk gratefully.

Now it was time to go back to the camp. Her father had forbidden her to ride out—they were in a new, unfamiliar land—but the best way to make Mara do something was to say "no". It always had been, right from the days when she had first tottered about between her father's tents on stumpy little legs. Yes, he would be angry. Yes, her uncles would reproach her. But she wouldn't be beaten. The Horse People were a free folk, who rode where they wanted, without fear. Her father understood that, and would be proud of her, she hoped, even while he was shouting.

There were three riders, moving on the ridge above the low valley, and riding in the same direction that she was.

Who were they? The plain was huge. She hadn't expected to meet anyone. They looked as though they were traveling for a purpose, not riding out for entertainment as she was.

When the troops of the Citizens marched (so her father had told her), or their auxiliary cavalry rode, they used the higher ground along the crests of the hills or the sides of mountains, in this same manner. By doing so they could see danger long before it saw them, and it gave them a stronger position to defend, or a better place to attack from. Other travelers such as merchants did the same, for the first of those reasons. But three was too few for traders—sensible traders would have armed guards—and not enough for a military patrol.

The Horse People scorned such caution, and if these had been young men trying out new horses, as she had been trying out her new mount, they would have been down there in the valley, whooping and hollering, prancing, swerving, and circling. Even at a distance, Mara would have known them to be Horse People by their way of riding, and maybe even recognized them as men from her own clan.

There were few hills or valleys on the plain. She had chosen this valley, far from the camp but not too distant, so that none of the young men from the clan would see her testing the filly, and maybe laugh at her lack of skill. There was one of them, Hengilo, who had shown openly that he liked her. Her hair was now in plaits, so he was permitted to show his liking. Perhaps she liked him too. Did she? She wasn't sure. He was boastful, as was the way with young men. He talked loudly and made proud gestures in her presence, but he had made no approach to her father yet.

Anyway, who was Hengilo? She didn't have to take him. There were as many men to choose from as there were strands in a horse's tail. She was a chieftain's daughter, and would one day be a beauty—or so the other girls told her, giggling behind their hands as they discussed who might one day go with whom. Her mother said that she was still growing. She was now taller than some of the young men. She hoped that her legs wouldn't grow more. They already seemed too long to her, which made her stand awkwardly when people were looking.

She didn't want the young men to see her and laugh at her, especially if Hengilo was among them, although usually she quite liked it when the young men looked at her.

The three men on the ridge were not Blood-Drinkers either. She could tell that, too, from the way they rode. And what would Blood-Drinkers be doing south of the Great River? Let the evil ones stay where they were! Because wherever they went, they brought death.

Even her own clan had only come south a few moons ago, settling either side of the river and almost as far as the Amethyst Sea. They did so without permission from the lord of the Citizens, but there had been no violence. Her father had warned the young men to be respectful, there had been no clashes with the soldiers, and they were tolerated by the Citizens at Fanum Fortunae, who bought horses from them and sold them metal pots and pans.

No, these were not Blood-Drinkers. Blood-Drinkers would have stalked her cunningly, before striking, swooping on her like hawks with the sun behind them, riding her down. When *they* appeared, they appeared suddenly, usually in overwhelming numbers, and they were fast and deadly.

Or so she had been told. Fortunately for her, she had never actually seen a Blood-Drinker, at least not a *living* one—just the mangled body of a scavenger who had been cut off from his raiding party and left behind. The young men of the clan had trapped him up in the hills, and then wisely sent a rider back to the camp to fetch more seasoned warriors to deal with him.

In front of the young men, the warriors' pride would not allow them to pick him off with arrows, which would have been wiser. What were they if they were not warriors? And warriors sometimes had to prove that they deserved the honor of that name. So they went into the gully with drawn swords, to face the Blood-Drinker like men. Although he was hopelessly outnumbered, the fight was long and fearsome, with many wounded. Afterwards, the creature's body was dragged back to the camp behind a horse, to be a suppertime treat for the dogs. Mara remembered the eyes best of all. Even in death, they were like those of a devil, slitted, heavy-lidded, and red.

The filly was tired. It had no name, and never would have. The Horse People gave no names to their horses, because they were not for petting. But everyone who counted as someone had a horse. If you said "the horse" it could only mean one thing: your own horse.

If you were speaking of another horse, you would give its owner's name, or say "the brown mare with white ears that was foaled when the snow thawed" or "the fierce gray stallion that leaves no mare in peace". All the horses of the clan, their appearance, their strengths and their weaknesses, were known to all the clan's members. Mara's was still only "Mara's horse". Perhaps, to a few of her friends, it would one day become the "the stubborn, pretty one".

It wasn't so different with women. Their names weren't used very much. Mara had a name, but mostly she was "Corvo's girl", or "Haimo's son's girl", and when she married she would be "so-and-so's woman". "Stubborn" and "pretty" might fit her, too, some would say, but the Horse People talked far less about women than they talked about horses.

Horses were more interesting than women, but the Horse People didn't mate with them (as some foolish people believed). Even the Blood-Drinkers didn't do that, though they were reputed to drink their horses' blood, and use it in their rituals, hence their name. There were also certain darker stories, involving blood magic, about how they came to be called "Blood-Drinkers". Mara shuddered—just thinking for too long about the arts of darkness invited evil into your life.

The gentler tribes that lived north and south of the Great River, form-ing the loose confederation of clans known as the Horse People, might not mate with their horses, but they loved and understood them.

Mara had ridden her new horse fiercely, and decided that she would keep it. Her father had told her that she could give it back and have another one if the filly wasn't good enough—but not if *she* wasn't. She would be testing it, but it would also be testing her. Let her show that she could make the filly her own, however long that might take.

And it had taken a hot summer afternoon. It was a good, strong young horse, and mostly obedient, though now it was tired. There was still some distance for them to go before they reached the settlement.

Why were these men going the same way? This was not a trading route. If they were traveling to see her father, perhaps to bring him a message, why had they not called out, or signaled to her? If they had seen her, yet not made themselves known to her, as was the custom among the peoples of the plain, their intentions could not be good ones.

There was a way to find out.

She turned the horse about, and set off back in the direction they had come from and away from her father's camp. The filly reacted clumsily. It was tired, and unwilling, and it wanted to go home. Mara gripped its mane tightly. No, you do what I want! I'm tired, too, but we need to do this. Trust me, we're going back soon. I'm hungry, really hungry, and I can't eat grass like you.

She dug in her heels so as not to slip off. Her legs were sweaty, as was the horse. She was riding bareback, of course.

Saddles were for chieftains, to announce to the world that they were great men.

They were for pregnant women, and very old people, if they could afford them.

They were for the Citizens, who hated horses and only rode them when they had to.

And saddles were for warriors in battle, so that they could sit more firmly as they wielded their weapons.

Saddles were beautiful, and expensive. No-one should be allowed a saddle before they had proved that they could ride without one—not even a chieftain's daughter. That was why Mara hadn't wanted the young men to watch her break in the filly, near the camp, in case it had thrown her.

Mara looked up at the ridge. The three riders were still there, but they had changed direction too.

She turned the horse again. She needed to get back to the camp, quickly. With an exhausted mount, she couldn't outride the men, but she could trick them. They would stay on the ridge for as long as they could, because while they were up there they could see exactly where she was. But she could see them, too, and to catch her they would have to come down.

Less than half a league further on the valley widened out, before losing itself in the flatlands of the plain. There were several streams, and the ridges ended in crumbling scree and boulders. If they stayed up on the ridge until then, she could gain distance on them as they maneuvered their horses downhill. And then it would be a dash across the grassy plain. Wouldn't their horses be tired, too? Perhaps there would be men from her clan riding out beyond the camp, doing who knows what? That would be her best chance.

A glance upwards at the ridge confirmed that the riders had turned once again. They were hunting her. So be it then, she told herself.

Her plan nearly worked. The filly, though tired and reluctant, did what Mara asked of it. The riders remained up on the ridge, as she had expected they would. Occasionally she lost sight of them, as they wove between the boulders. With the sweat in her eyes it was hard to see them clearly, but they were riding as fast as she was, and two of them with saddles. If they were Citizens, she was confident she could trick them. It would be disgraceful if she couldn't.

But who was the third rider, riding skillfully without a saddle? He was riding like one of the Horse People.

When she reached the first of the streams the strangers were no longer in sight. It was almost empty of water, but there were mossy pebbles in the bed of the stream that caused her horse trouble. She urged it up a small incline and down into the second gully. She could now hear her pursuers.

Ahead of her the great plain shimmered out in all directions. Somewhere there, not far away, but hidden in the afternoon haze, was the camp—and safety!

Horse and rider lurched down into the third stream. Blinded with sweat, Mara could barely see where to direct the horse. At the wrong moment, she looked back to see where her pursuers were. The twisting movement of her body must have irritated the filly as it negotiated the uneven, stony bed of the stream, causing it to slip and stumble. There was a sudden jolt, and then both of them were thrown down into the shallow water.

Ouch! She felt her knee crack against the boulders in the stream, and the breath shaken out of her body. The filly was quicker on its feet, though not before giving its owner a kick in the ribs that left her gasping. Then it was off and away, and Mara never saw it again.

She too staggered to her feet, and then fell again as she was rushed from behind. What must have been a coarse sack was thrown over her head, and she was held face down in the riverbed, choking and sobbing with fury. There was a man's weight on her, a man who was breathing awkwardly. He must be an older man, heavy rather than physically strong. He stank, but not with the rough, sweet, familiar smell of the Horse People, the smell of herbs and hay and animal sweat.

The man seized her hands and bound them behind her back. He did it surprisingly quickly—as though he had done it many times before.

Then she was jerked to her feet, and held upright in a tight grip.

"Gotcha, my beauty!"

"Watch out! Don't damage her too much."

"Don't be an old woman. I know what I'm doing. You just do your job, and I'll do mine."

She heard two voices, distinctly different, both speaking in the Citizens' Tongue.

"What about the horse? Shouldn't we go after it?"

"Don't bother about that."

"It'll run back to her camp. And then they'll come looking for her."

"Yes, but we'll be long gone. We've got what we want, haven't we?"

To her disgust, she felt a hand caressing her thigh. Then, still pinioned, and barely able to breathe, she was pushed forward, her captor steering her across more level ground, carefully, so that she didn't fall.

Only two voices had spoken. The third man remained a silent presence in the background.

II

AULUS IS CONSIDERABLY DISPLEASED,

AND NOT WITHOUT GOOD REASON

✴ *The house of Senator Lucius Pomponius Atticus, in the City.*

"My mother has written," said Aulus Atticus, falling back onto the couch with an exaggerated groan.

He had already spent most of the afternoon recumbent and feeling sorry for himself. It was a sturdy, well-constructed couch, made softer with woolen blankets and cushions. Aulus had become rather fond of it, and this couch, in this comfortable town-house, was as good a place as any to spend a warm summer afternoon in the City.

The capital of the western half of the Empire had never had and didn't need any other name than "the City". Despite its venerable age and glorious past, it could be unbearable in the summer. Sticky heat became trapped in the alleyways of the slums, and vile smells and vicious buzzing insects ruled the streets. But only the heat reached the home of Senator Lucius Pomponius Atticus, Aulus's uncle, a large and comfortable house that was furnished with conservative good taste and located on a hillside in the richest quarter of the City.

Decimus tried to look sympathetic.

"Oh dear," he said.

"She wants me to marry. No, she *demands* that I marry. My fate is sealed. I am finished. What you see before you is a finished existence. My life is as good as over."

"Is that the letter?"

Decimus pointed to the scroll that his young master had thrown onto the refreshments table some moments before. He had thrown it with such vigor that a bowl of nuts and dried fruits had tipped onto the floor, luckily not breaking, but scattering its contents everywhere. A slave had already been summoned to clear up the mess. The young master wasn't going to do it, and Decimus, as a freed slave, wouldn't be expected to.

"No, no. Those are some poems by Placidus. The great Placidus. They're beautiful, as they always are, but I'm not in the mood right now."

"Placidus?"

He would need to explain: it wasn't a name that the freedman would naturally associate with poetry.

"*Sextus* Placidus, of course! Who else? You are such an idiot! Can you in a thousand years imagine any of the *other* Placidi wasting their time on literature? Why, even my poor dear mother would be more likely to write a love poem that any of *that* lot!"

And as if suddenly reinvigorated by the unlikely thought of his mother composing erotic verse, Aulus jumped to his feet and adopted a declamatory posture. The effect was slightly spoiled by his standing on and noisily cracking open a nut with his leather sandal.

"Now how does that last one go? It has that typical Placidian intensity." With head leant back and eyes closed, he tried to remember the poet's words. "I love the opening lines—

> *The flames of Love consume my limbs.*
> *Love's eyes flash fire that stirs my heart.*
> *I toss and turn throughout the night*

And, um, what's the next bit? Ah, yes:

> *As lust burns in my every part.*

No, that can't be right, surely? He wouldn't repeat the metaphor of burning from the opening line, would he? 'As lust eats up my every part'? Or maybe 'devours'? No, that sounds silly. Oh, I can't remember, though it was definitely about lust *doing* something to him. But did he really write 'my every part'? That's so suggestive it's almost vulgar. Well, I don't know. Anyhow, it continues much in the same vein, and I must say that it does get rather steamy:

> *Our bodies twine till break of day.*
> *As hardness enters, softness yields...*

That's much more sensitively phrased, don't you think? Decimus? Are you listening? I can see that you're bored, so I'll spare you the rest. It would be wasted on you, in any case. You have no feeling for culture."

Decimus smiled.

"I'm sure that is true."

And Aulus sat down again, with a gesture that Decimus should also sit.

"Believe it or not, I happen to know who it was that inspired those lines! I actually know the identity of the delightful creature that so inspired his passion. How about that, then? Aren't you curious?" He winked salaciously.

There was no response. Decimus, it seemed, was not curious. He was *so* out of touch.

"Forgive me for not recognizing the lines. I do spend a lot of time away on the frontier."

"And Sextus has moved on since then. A different style as well as a different muse! But I wouldn't expect you to know that either. I gather that you spend more time with *horses* and *barbarians* than with women!"

"Quite right." A pause. "Ah, so it *is* a woman that he is referring to?"

"Of course it is! Whatever did you imagine?"

"Well…"

"Oh, yes. I suppose it must seem an abnormal preference for one of the Placidi to, er…to like women, I mean."

The freedman smiled maliciously.

"Well, it's good to know that there's a Placidus who does! We wouldn't want such an illustrious family to die out, now, would we?"

Aulus had to laugh, because they both knew that there were very many people who would be happy to see the end of the hated Placidi.

An elderly cleaner slipped quietly into the room with brush and pan. Unnoticed, he made a silent gesture of deference to Aulus, the young master, swept up the debris from the mosaic floor, gathered up the scroll and replaced it on the refreshments table, Neither Aulus nor Decimus even bothered to glance at him.

It was often said that slaves nowadays were too noisy and gossipy, always rushing about in a flap and answering you back with cheeky remarks and grimaces, or provoking you with sulks or sullen behavior. But not in the house of Lucius Atticus. The slaves were well-trained, well-treated, and well-fed. They were quiet, and many of them were elderly. Like the artworks, they were discreet, but expensive. There were many other such houses belonging to members of the Senatorial class in that part of the City, but few with such a sedate atmosphere. There were no noisy, gossipy slaves here!

Almost ghostlike, the cleaner left as quietly as he had entered, leaving the two young men alone again. They were obviously friends, though equal neither in age nor in status.

The younger man, Aulus, would have been quick to admit that no stranger would immediately have identified him as the "master". The best clue would be the rather better quality of his clothes, but even that would require a closer look. Aulus dressed fancily (and that was said of freedmen, too), but he also dressed carelessly, and he didn't change his clothes quite as often as he might have done.

He no longer had a personal servant, but he knew that Beltran the footman, who had been delegated to attend to some of his needs, was often driven to despair by the over- and undergarments flung aside or left to be discovered lodged behind furniture. (Sometimes many months later.) What needed to be cleaned? Or repaired? What would the young master want to wear again? Aulus would feel deeply sorry for the footman—if he weren't too busy with more important matters.

Decimus dressed plainly, but with good taste, and his clothes were always clean. The older man was dark, bearded, and, as Aulus had to acknowledge, roughly handsome. He was tall and muscular, and naturally gifted, with skills that his different masters had encouraged him to perfect, thus greatly increasing his value. He knew how to ride, hunt, swim, fight (and kill when necessary), and he could express himself in numerous tongues, both civilized and barbarian. He had also, over the years, apparently learned how to give pleasure to women, and not merely with his conversation, and he knew how to command the attention of men. All admirable and enviable abilities, thought Aulus, with more than a twinge of envy.

When Decimus came into a room, people would stop what they were doing; when Aulus came in, they would look for a scroll to read, or a slave to shout at, or somewhere else to be.

Aulus was younger by several years, and rather smaller. He was paler-skinned, with light brown hair and beard—if the stubbly matter that disguised his slightly flabby jaw could honestly be called a beard. According to the standards by which the Citizens judged beauty he would not (as he well knew) have been regarded as outstandingly attractive.

He had none of the useful skills of Decimus, though he had attempted, at different times in his young life, to master one or two of them. Boredom had all too often got in the way. He understood poetry, however; he could speak well (if given encouragement) and listen even better; and he had a gift for making friends (but also for losing them). He wished harm to no-one, but had a knack of causing it anyway, without wanting to.

Aulus Pomponius Atticus was the son of one Senator and the nephew of another, and the youngest and (by far) the least distinguished member of a famous family. Decimus had once been his slave, and was now his friend.

Even at fourteen, Decimus had stood out among the sad merchandise of Issachar the Slaver. Castor, who ran the household of Lucius Atticus's younger brother Faustus, had been informed about the remarkable young slave, and had recommended him to his master. Soon afterwards, Decimus was purchased, at no little expense, to look after the unpromising son of the house and perhaps, by example, "to encourage him in the direction of manliness", as Faustus Atticus had put it, with characteristic pomposity.

Sadly, he had failed, as various tutors and pedagogues had also done, though by no fault of their own or through any lack of effort. Aulus was, to put it mildly, unmalleable material. It wouldn't have been surprising if the Senator had not briefly wondered whether the boy, with his clumsiness and his light coloring, might not have been fathered on the Lady Pomponia by some favorite slave.

One of Decimus's few successes in the "manliness project" had been to arrange, with great tact, for his young master to lose his innocence. In the course of doing this, he had also managed to instill in him the novel idea that women, like slaves or animals, should be treated with kindness.

Aulus had become a clumsy yet generous and considerate lover. This was soon common knowledge in the slaves' quarters, into which the young master made a number of timid forays, with mixed success, and where he was viewed with affectionate contempt (and given the nickname "Junior"). The forays soon ended when Aulus, hugely embarrassed, discovered that he was being mocked behind his back.

These activities were fortunately never brought to the attention of the boy's father, who was looking for (and would only have noticed) evidence of the more traditional Citizen virtues—qualities that had enabled the Citizens to conquer most of the known world. Kindness towards slaves was not one of those qualities. Faustus Atticus was known to be deeply disappointed in his son. He must therefore have been surprised when Aulus appeared one day in his study, demanding that Decimus be freed.

The Senator would probably have preferred to re-sell him, recouping some of his original outlay. But Aulus was insistent, and Decimus had served loyally for more than ten years. There was at the time a government scheme to reward "decurial manumissions", as they were called, so the Senator got some of his money back after all.

"I need to have you here more, Decimus. You spend far too much time on the frontier. I never ask you what you do there: I just assume that it's *his* business that you're doing. Does he make it worth your while?"

Unlike most freed slaves, who were employed by their former masters, Decimus worked for the government. Which in practice meant for

Ogilo, because it was Ogilo who was the ruler in the West, and not the Emperor. He was Master of Horse and Foot, but everyone called him "the General".

"Yes, I do a few things for him, here and there, when I'm asked to. But I don't neglect you, sir, do I?"

They spoke to each other openly and freely, as they always had done, even as master and slave. When Decimus said "sir" or "my lord" it was a sign of irony, or humor, just as it was when Aulus occasionally let slip a good-natured "lazy fellow" or "rogue". Or it was for the benefit of anyone listening who happened to have more conventional views on how freedmen and their former masters should talk to each other.

"I need your advice—this is a deadly serious matter—and how can I get your advice if you're never here?" Aulus put on a dramatic look that was intended to convey innocent suffering. "This whole abominable topic gives me a headache."

And to add to his general feeling of malaise, he discovered a piece of cracked nutshell embedded in his sandal.

"What did your lady mother write, may I ask? Did she make any particular recommendation? Did she mention the names of suitable candidates?"

"The answer to *all* your stupid questions is 'I don't know'. She wrote to my uncle, not to me. Davus"—Davus was his uncle's freedman secretary—"intercepted the letter and has kindly given me the gist of her remarks, but he held back on the details." He paused. "Damn it, this won't come out of my sandal." And then: "It's funny, though, that my *mother* should write to my uncle."

Decimus nodded—he knew the internal politics of the Atticus family almost as well as Aulus did. Lucius Atticus had a different view of the world to that of his brother, and they belonged to opposing political factions in the Senate. But the brothers were on speaking terms, and they even corresponded occasionally, though only when it was absolutely necessary, on formal occasions, for instance, or where money or property was involved.

With Aulus's mother it was quite different. Lucius Atticus was known to have no time whatsoever for his annoying sister-in-law, the Lady Pomponia, with her pieties and religious pretensions. Small wonder that Aulus preferred to live at his uncle's comfortable house in the capital, rather than with his father and his mother on the frontier at Fanum Fortunae. So, given that they detested each other, why should it be the Lady Pomponia who had written to her brother-in-law, and not Senator Faustus?

"Are you sure that it was your mother that wrote, and not your father?"

"According to Davus, yes. My father doesn't write to his brother very often, as you know, and he never, ever writes to me. He's too busy bossing all his soldiers around. And his wretched administrators. And all those stupid barbarians. So, would you believe it, he leaves it to my *mother* to tell me what to do. Not very flattering, that, wouldn't you say? Maybe I should have been born a barbarian—then I might have been granted a little more of his attention!"

Decimus disagreed.

"No no, there is hope in this. If your father had written to you, you'd now have to do something about it, wouldn't you? And with no excuses! But your *mother*... well, that gives you time, surely."

"You think so? My father will always support her, you know that, whether he agrees with her or not. She just nags him into submission. Nag, nag, nag. He always runs away from a fight with her. I wonder if he's like that in the Senate, too?"

Now that was an interesting thought. His uncle was a seasoned debater, but his father...? Aulus hated the Senate, and had hardly ever been there. The sessions were mind-numbingly dull. The old bores sat around twitching at their togas, worrying about their piles, and making speeches that no-one listened to. He had *no* wish to embark on a Senatorial career, as would normally be expected of a young man with his background.

That was something else that he had in common with Sextus Placidus, apart from poetry—and loving the same woman. Their uncles had successfully applied for each of them to be exempted from Senatorial duties: Lucius Atticus with some sadness, and only after a long discussion with his nephew; Gnaeus Julius Placidus with complete indifference.

"Even if you can't directly refuse your lady mother, you do realize that you can stall her with delaying tactics? Don't forget, sir, that you're an eligible, clean-living young nobleman. And that you're from a distinguished and wealthy family. Marriage is a matter that requires careful planning. It's not something to be rushed into!"

Aulus was amused at this portrait of himself.

"You think I'm eligible? I can't say that I've heard that from anyone else recently. Look, you're not a slave anymore, you can be honest with me." Actually, Decimus always had been, even before he was freed by Aulus's father. "'Eligible': I rather like that! Forget the 'clean-living', of course. And we're not really wealthy. Not like the Placidi."

He might have added that *no-one* in the West was rich like the Placidi. Nor many in the eastern half of the Empire either.

"Very well, then let me be honest with you. You know what you could do, O Eligible One? You could go onto the *attack*."

"How do you mean?"

And Decimus explained what he meant.

"Consider the following course of action. First, you must choose a young lady from among your circle of female acquaintances—naturally it must be someone of appropriate social standing—who is to *your* taste, but who would horrify your mother. As I remember them, *any* of your lady friends would fit the bill! Or has my Lord taken to moving in, how shall we put it, more *refined*, more *pious* circles since we last met?"

Aulus grinned.

"Does a pack-mule load its own pack? Does a Sybarite work before breakfast?"

"I thought not. So, make your choice, someone who is superficially suitable, and then, with the help of your uncle, push through the betrothal. By the time that your mother finds out, and her gossipy lady friends have told her a few things about the candidate, it will difficult to undo the arrangements without causing grave insult to the young lady's family—your father won't be keen to make more enemies in the Senate than he already has. They won't allow the marriage, of course, but it will take them ages to *un-arrange* it."

Aulus found some aspects of the proposal quite appealing, but was not completely convinced.

"Your plan has a fatal weakness. In fact, it has *two* fatal weaknesses."

"Which are…?"

But it was at this point that Senator Lucius Atticus chose to enter the room. Decimus jumped to attention and saluted the Senator, as protocol required.

"Sir!"

"At ease, Decimus. We're not on the frontier."

Aulus had risen more languidly to his feet.

"Uncle."

"I need to speak to you." Decimus made a move to leave the room. "No, please stay, Decimus. Listen to what I have to tell my nephew."

"Sir."

"You know that, unlike my brother, *I* consider you to be part of our family. And you are my nephew's friend. Yes, don't protest: a freedman *can* be a friend! I certainly regard Davus as such."

"How can I be of help, sir?"

"A problem has arisen. A *complication*. And my nephew will have to deal with it. You've always been infinitely more mature and sensible than he has. Maybe you can help him. If not, you can at least take him off somewhere to drown his sorrows. Now, sit down, both of you, and listen."

III

MARA ENCOUNTERS AN OLD

FRIEND—WELL, ALMOST

⬧ *The great northern plain.*

First she was thrown, tied and still hooded, over one of the horses with a saddle, and secured with some kind of strap. The saddle was cheap and hard, and it rubbed into her, causing bruises and soreness. They rode fast, to get away from any pursuers, she imagined. Two of the men would be sharing a horse, so they wouldn't be able to keep up that pace for very long.

She hoped that her absence had been noticed, and that the young men had been sent out to find her. When they did, blood would be spilt! Mara was sick from the bumping of the horse, and she was choking inside the sack. Only the thought of the vengeance that she was sure would soon be in hot pursuit kept her spirits up. Throughout her ordeal, although she could see nothing, she was able to hear and smell. Moreover, she could sense the horses, and what they were doing. In this way, she was aware of what was happening.

Despite her anger, she was also very scared.

Two of her cousins had kidnapped her when she was small, and carried her off in a bag, and pretended that they were going to eat her. They had made lip-smacking noises, and lit a fire. One of them had squeezed her bottom and said, "Let's cut off a bit from here! We can grill it! There isn't much meat on her anywhere else."

She had recognized their voices, so she knew it was only a game, but she had still been frightened. Perhaps they would hurt her in some other way?

Her uncle had found them, and beaten his sons with a riding-whip, although her father hadn't demanded it. How the boys had yelled!

But this was not a game. And these men *were* going to hurt her, she knew that.

They halted, and she was tipped down from the horse, ungently. She heard one of the men say that her feet should be bound together, to stop her from running off. Obviously they were still out on the plain, where was no tree or bush they could tie her to.

A man came to do this—not the smelly older man, but someone cleaner-smelling and less dexterous. Perhaps younger? He smelt more like one of the Horse People than the other man did. He was breathing loudly. Was he nervous? He fumbled with a rope around her ankles, and then for no reason put his hands between her legs, higher up, and began to touch her where he shouldn't.

No, that wasn't right. Stop it.

She heard someone shout "Get away!" in the Citizens' Tongue, and then what may have been expletives and curses, to judge from the way they sounded, in some other Tongue. A third man joined in. The man who had been tying her responded, in a younger, softer voice. She heard him say "You promised" and "It was agreed", and someone said "Issachar". Because of the sack, it was hard to hear everything that they were saying, but she could now distinguish between the three voices: there was the smelly man, the younger man, who had touched her, and the third man.

She heard more shouts, in all three voices, the sounds of what might have been a brief scuffle, with slaps and grunts, and then quieter voices, with someone (the smelly older man?) saying "You have been paid" several times. A silence followed.

After a while, one of the horses whinnied. She knew what that meant. The horse was protesting indignantly that it was going to be ridden once again that day. There was more talking, this time very indistinct. Finally there were the various sounds of a horseman leaving, but she heard no saddle-creaking, or the noise of an unskilled rider throwing himself back into the saddle, so the man who was leaving was therefore the man who had been riding bareback.

"He's gone, fuck him, and good riddance! Now let's take a look at our little princess."

The smelly man removed the sack from her head.

The cold, fresh air hit her like a blow across the face. But for a moment it was wonderful. It had grown dark. At first she could barely see anything, except that they were somewhere out on the plain. She blinked to clear her eyes, and looked at her captors. The smelly man was just as she had imagined he would be, stocky and ugly, with scars across his face. The other man was taller and thinner, younger, and much better-looking. They were both staring at her.

She wouldn't let these men frighten her, she told herself. Even though she really was frightened. They were robbers, outlaw scum, not warriors. With all the boldness that she could muster, she demanded, "Who are you?"

They both laughed, unpleasantly.

The thin man said, "Shall I hit her, boss, or will you?"

The smelly man replied, "No need, she'll learn soon enough to keep her mouth shut." He punched her shoulder. "Won't you princess?" He turned to the thin man: "Let her blab. It might even be amusing. I like a bit of entertainment before I turn in, don't you?"

Although her shoulder hurt, she tried again.

"It's cold. Why don't you light a fire?"

The smelly man found that very funny.

"Oh yes, so all your horsey friends can find us? I think not." He took Mara's chin in a large, grubby hand and turned her face from side to side, peering at her so closely that the smell of his breath made her queasy. He hadn't eaten much, and whatever it was can't have been good: something nasty, with lots of onions. "The light's not perfect, but to me you don't look much like a princess. In fact, to me you look like just another little horse-fucker slut. A commodity of which there is no shortage on the market!"

The thin man laughed.

"How many real live princesses have you seen then, boss?"

"Oh, they *all* think they're princesses till you show them what's what."

What did that have to do with her? They were robbers, so they wanted money. Her father had no money, only horses, but she couldn't say that.

"My father will pay you generously if you bring me back unharmed."

"You don't say? And who *is* your father?"

Not without pride, she told him. He should learn whom he was dealing with, and show her the respect that was due to someone of her rank. Her father was Corvo, chieftain of the Speaking Bird clan, the son of Haimo of the Council of the Horse People, and he led thirty warriors in battle. Thirty was a slight exaggeration.

The two men exchanged looks.

"Well, that's not good, is it? I would say that we've been well and truly screwed. We pay upfront for a princess, waste half a day riding backwards and forwards, and what do we end up with? A village headman's daughter!"

"Shall I ride after him, boss? And get the money back? I never liked the guy."

"No. What's done is done. We might want to use him again. Anyway, do you think *you* could catch up with him? Not a chance! Those bastards grow up living and breathing horses. He'll be back with the king of the birds long before you can reach him. And he'll be telling them to search in the other direction, I hope. After all, he won't want them to find her, will he now? That wouldn't be good for him."

And so Mara realized the shameful truth of what had happened to her.

"You paid one of my own people to betray me?"

Her shock was genuine. There was no treachery, ever, among the Horse People. How could you have a confederation of free warriors without trust? Treachery was the unforgivable crime, far worse than murder, and second only to horse-stealing.

"Oh, princess, you make me sound so wicked! I'm not a wicked man, am I?"

"No, boss!"

"And your nice friend didn't need to be persuaded. *He* came to *us*."

"It was someone from my clan, someone I trusted?"

"That would be telling, wouldn't it? But, broadly speaking, yes. Now, *there's* wickedness for you! Right, brother?"

He turned and grinned at the thin man, who grinned back.

"Too right, boss. It's a bad, bad world out there!"

"He knew we had special orders to look for interesting items, as well as the usual stuff, and so he made a suggestion: *you*. He had to convince us, though—by turning you into a princess. And we fell for it! What a bastard. Some people just can't be trusted."

"He sold me for money!"

"No, not even that. I don't think he cared much about the money. And we didn't give him very much. You know what? I think he just wanted to have first crack at your cherry."

Mara was indignant. What was his name? Her father would tear his heart out!

The thin man was delighted.

"She's got some fight in her, this one! Can we do her now, boss? You can go first, of course."

"No, keep your hands off her. Why do you think I told...*our friend*"—he had almost let the name slip out—"not to touch her?"

"I dunno."

"Oh, use your head! She's a *virgin*. She'll fetch far more intact than if she's been well-ridden. Even a dirty little horsey-girl like her. You should know that by now."

"You're right, boss."

"I'm always right. And that's why *I'm* in charge here, and not you."

Mara could hardly believe that they were talking about her. She was in the hands of slave-hunters. She was now shivering from the cold, and from exhaustion. She wanted only to sleep, and hope to wake up tomorrow back in the camp as if the whole thing had been no more than an evil dream.

"So how do we know she's a virgin, then? Maybe we should test her."

"No need! I can *see* she's a virgin."

"Howdja do that, boss?"

"Because of what our friend told us. Remember? No? You should listen more, instead of clomping around with your tongue and your dick hanging out all the time! It made a lot of sense to *me*. Look, the hair at the back. See that?"

He grabbed Mara's head by her long, fair hair, and pulled it to one side, but not roughly.

"Yeah. So what?"

"The little horsey-girls just wear it long. When they start bleeding, they put it in plaits, like these here, but they don't cut it short. When they shack up, *that's* when the women cut their hair. You've been in knocking-shops from Trebenna to Sybaris, and seen dozens of whores, right?"

Even as he replied, the thin man was leering at her as if she were naked.

"Oh, yes, boss, *hundreds*, not dozens."

"And some of the whores were horse-fuckers?"

"Yeah, quite a lot of them. I like big girls, well-built, with nice tits."

"Well, I bet you never saw one of them with long hair, did you?"

The thin man paused for thought.

"No, I never did."

"You see! As I said, I'm always right." He turned Mara's head again, and looked into her eyes. "Or could I be mistaken, princess? You haven't had a man up there yet, have you? Come on, you can tell your nice uncle!"

Mara was too shocked to speak.

"I bet our friend wishes he'd kept his mouth shut, eh, boss? Then he could've had his fun with her."

"And afterwards she'd have to cut off her plaits." The smelly man yanked at her hair, then released his grip. "Time to get some sleep! You too, princess. And don't you try any tricks in the night, or I may just let my colleague here take you for a little ride. What you've still got between your legs might make you more valuable, but not *that* much more valuable. I hope we understand each other?"

It wasn't comfortable, lying hobbled on the ground, but she had slept out on the plain often before. She had to move around, to find a position where she wasn't lying with a stone pressing into her side. And a lizard came and looked at her, very close, otherwise she wouldn't have seen it, but it wasn't one of the poisonous ones. That didn't keep her awake.

What kept her awake, although she was desperately tired, was the thought of the traitor who had sold her into slavery, and who had even tried to abuse her. May he rot in the Other Place! May She with the Talons take him, and rip out his guts! She had heard his voice…

She had heard his voice, and it was somehow familiar. Who was it? Surely it couldn't be one of the warriors? They had all sworn a sacred oath to her father. Many of them were older men, with wives and children; this man had sounded younger.

And she had heard her captors mention the name "Issachar", but there was no-one in her clan who was called that. What sort of name was that anyway? Surely there could be no-one among the Horse People with such an outlandish name?

She was still working her way through the twenty or thirty young men of her clan, the ones who were not yet warriors, remembering how they sounded when they spoke, when she finally drifted off into sleep.

IV

THOMASIUS COUNTS THEM BACK IN, AND

NOTICES THAT THERE IS ONE TOO MANY

🞳 *The fortress of Cascantum.*

It came about by chance that Thomasius the Sub-officer heard that a chieftain's daughter of the Horse People had been abducted, but it was not chance that made him go after it. He had never been good at leaving matters be—especially when they were better left that way.

That had been the story of his life, or rather the story of his career (which was almost the same thing). His friend Grassica thought he was too persistent for his own good, like those dogs that won't stop worrying at your sandals or your leather harness until you give them a kicking.

He had been standing lookout on the walls of the fortress of Cascantum, and had woken from his daydream just in time to count the returning cavalry back in. He hadn't counted them out, but he had been told the number to watch out for. They were Sueni auxiliary troops, Dream People, and the number was important.

The number was important, because they were hired by the year through a contractor, who might or might not be their commander. If some of them got themselves killed out on patrol, well, sad for them—and there would be fewer quarrelsome, unreliable barbarian "allies" left to worry about, some would say. And if they buggered off back home, so what? That, too, wouldn't be much of a loss. They weren't exactly the backbone of the Citizen Army.

Who was it who had had the idea of using swamp-dwellers as cavalry in the first place? They fell off their horses almost as often as the Citizens did. But the Horse People, who *could* ride, Thomasius gave them that, were newer to the ways of the Citizens, and to military discipline, and so they were even less reliable than the swampies were.

No, what mattered to those higher up the chain of command was simply: how many men were left in the troop, and how much did the contractor have to be paid? Deaths and desertions didn't matter; paying the contractors too much most certainly did.

From the point of view of a hardworking Sub-officer, "higher up" meant first of all the Company-commander, Decius, may Sol piss on him from a great height! Then came the pretty-boy Staff Officers, and finally the Lord Commander himself. His Mightiness couldn't be expected to do lookout duty, and the Staff Officers were a decorative waste of space. Decius, though: why shouldn't the obnoxious but otherwise broadly competent Company-commander (just once in a while) spend a happy hour or two peering out over the plain?

It wasn't exactly exciting work. From the vantage point of the fortress wall the flatness spread out to the horizon in all directions, its monotony creased rather than interrupted by low hills and the gullies of streams. The only feature of real interest was the Great River, which flowed past the northern side of the fortress. There were a handful of boats on it, presumably carrying trading goods from the north down to the ocean.

The route downriver was still reasonably safe. The Horse People had been allowed across the River to settle. Correction: they had crossed the River, and permission to do so had been granted afterwards. Now they controlled both its banks between Cascantum and the swamps where the Sueni lived. The Horse People were probably running away from the Blood-Drinkers (not that you'd ever tell them that to their faces) and so they were quiet, for the time being.

The Dream People of the swamps were supposedly the allies of the West. They even traded a bit on the River, when they had something of interest to sell. Beyond the swamps was the fortress of Gladium, where there were two full divisions of the Citizen Army (just as there were at Cascantum), and beyond that the River flowed down to the ocean, marking the border with the eastern half of the Empire, whose troops secured the far bank.

Maritima, the great trading city at the mouth of the River, and the natural entrepôt for the trade downriver, happened to be in the East. Its twin-city and rival, Trebenna, was in the West, but it was many leagues further down the coast, and few of the river-boats were ocean-worthy.

The trade upriver, on the other hand, was almost dead. The Horse People were abandoning the plain to the far north. There had always been enmity between them and their more numerous neighbors, a confederation of unruly tribes that called themselves simply the Free People; now there was also talk of huge numbers of Blood-Drinkers on the move.

Settlements had been wiped out. Herdsmen had been butchered. Such things had always happened. The Free People would rape, pillage, and take slaves, the way most conquerors did, and life still went on. Similarly, the people of the south had not forgotten what the Citizens did to their capital at the end of the Sybarite War, hundreds of years ago, yet Sybaris had become a great city once again. But the Blood-Drinkers were different. They left behind only death: scorched fields, and pyramids of rotting human and animal heads, contemptuously mixed together, where once there had been a camp or a village.

Sueni cavalry from Cascantum patrolled the near bank of the River along much of its length, but they ventured out onto the far bank only for short stretches either side of the fortress. If attacked, they could retreat across the bridge; otherwise, they would have their backs to the River, which meant swimming, and leaving the precious horses behind, or death.

There were no other bridges spanning the River until you reached Gladium, although the Sueni sometimes used canoes to cross. In late summer and autumn, when it was carrying less water, there were a couple of places where the River might be forded by a brave and knowledgeable horseman. And in some winters it froze, but only above Cascantum and near to the mountains.

The far bank was not safe, and both the soldiers and the traders knew it. The flatlands further north of the River were now eerily empty, except for wolves and birds of prey. The Free People were suspiciously quiet—were they too on the move? Beyond the horizon, anything might be lurking.

Thomasius was hungry. He could have done with a packed lunch. This was what came of not having a proper servant, rather than just a trooper who occasionally cleaned his quarters for him. He didn't have to do this duty. He could have ordered a Citizen soldier to stand watch for him, just as Decius had delegated the task to *him*. But, as everybody knew, soldiers could be bribed, unfortunately, and once the auxiliaries had ridden through the gate into the fortress there'd be no way of confirming, in the hubbub of the barracks, how many of them there still were. So if you wanted a job done well, you did it yourself.

Sub-officers were above suspicion, Thomasius liked to think. They *were* the backbone of the Citizen Army, certainly in their own opinion, though since the reforms of Maximus the Great (Sol bless his memory!) they were no longer known as "Centurions" and had lost some of their status.

Many changes had been introduced. Back then, the senior Lord Commander was normally also the governor of the province; now,

Rhaetius, Lord Commander of the Seventh Division, outranked his colleague the Lord Commander of the Fourth but had to share power in the province with a civilian, the Governor of the North. If this had the advantage of keeping too much power out of the hands of one man, it had the disadvantage of slowing down decision-making. The road between Cascantum and the nearby city of Fanum Fortunae was thus a busy one, crowded with messengers between the Lord Commander and Lord Governor Faustus Pomponius Atticus, and needing to be well protected by patrols.

Fanum Fortunae, on the Amethyst Sea! Well, more a town than a city, and more a lake than a sea. But memories of its cheerful wine shops and brothels sent Thomasius into a happy, mildly erotic reverie, so compelling that he almost missed the patrol that he had been ordered to keep lookout for. It now came clattering over the wooden pontoon bridge across the Great River and into the fortress, past children playing, off-duty soldiers fishing, and the rotting bodies of criminals exposed on the execution platform.

It was led by its Troop-commander, who was followed in by a standard-bearer carrying the garish windsock favored by the cavalry. It was brightly decorated to make it look like a dragon. The men of the Citizen Army thought the banners of the cavalry were rather ludicrous—the standard that the foot-soldiers marched behind showed a spread eagle with massive claws, not some painted mythical beast to frighten children with.

Thomasius counted them back in, and found the number to be… one more than expected. All of them had been riding freely; there was no obvious prisoner among them, no miserable specimen being dragged along behind a horse. So who was the extra man, riding in with the troopers? A new recruit?

Thomasius left his post and by means of a series of steps and staircases negotiated his way quickly down the defensive walls. He was nimble for his age, and he wasn't wearing armor or carrying any weapons, so it didn't take him long to reach the lower part of the fortress. His friend Sub-officer Grassica had been on duty at the inner gate. Perhaps he would know more.

Cascantum was a decent enough posting. There were better ones, in the south, but also some that were far worse—guarding the laborers at government quarries or mines, for example. The quarters were spacious and comfortable. They had been built before the division of the Empire, when the Citizen Army was much bigger and better manned than it was now.

The township that sprawled beyond the southern walls of the fortress hardly deserved the name. The wine was cheap and nasty, and the whores filthy: runaway Sueni girls; ugly local women who'd given away their virginity too easily and then couldn't find a husband; and raddled old tarts who could no longer make a living in the big-city brothels of the south. But Fanum Fortunae was not too far away.

A long-serving Sub-officer like Thomasius was often trusted with messages for the "capital", and could stay there overnight, when no urgent response was needed. Thomasius also had the right to a few days of holiday leave, once or twice a year. There was no family left for him to visit, and it wasn't a long ride to Fanum Fortunae, across the grassland of the Gap between the Great River and the Amethyst Sea, and then along the lakeside to the city.

Once, Thomasius had used a longer period of leave to go even further, riding north from Fanum into the Valley. This was the fertile heartland of the northern province, with orchards and lush farms tucked in between the mountains, which shielded them not only from the northern weather, but also from barbarians, Blood-Drinkers, and the like.

There were no real towns in the Valley, and so no whores. It was therefore not an ideal place for a serving soldier to forget all his cares. But it might be a good place to retire to, if Thomasius could only save enough money to get himself a reasonable-sized farm and a couple of slaves (the Army retirement settlement for a Sub-officer would buy him a small plot of land, though probably with barren soil).

Thomasius reached the inner gate while the last of the Sueni were still unpacking their gear and harnesses. Grassica, in full duty armor, saluted him cursorily and nodded towards the horsemen.

"What in Sol's name do they feed their fucking horses? They've only just arrived and they've crapped up half my courtyard!" He grinned. "How can I help you, comrade? Unless you've come to do some shit-shoveling?"

Thomasius told him that he'd counted one more man in than had left.

"So: who's the mystery man?"

"Why don't you ask the Big Man himself?" He spat. "Troop-commander Urtho I believe he's called. Swampie Number One as far as I'm concerned."

But when he spoke to him, Grassica was polite enough. The Troop-commander came across to join them, leading his horse. He was an enormous man, with fists like great knuckles of pork and thighs like tree-trunks. Thomasius felt sorry for his horse, which looked tiny beside him.

Urtho had a surprisingly good command of the Citizens' Tongue, though he also had a thick, syrupy Sueni accent.

"The other man? He's a horse-fucker. He wants to talk to Lord Commander Rhaetius."

"He's from the Horse People?"

Thomasius was curious about the Horse People. He had even started learning their tongue, helped by two men from his unit who had common-law wives from beyond the Great River. The Horse People might be unreliable as auxiliary soldiers, liable to disappear without warning to attend some clan feast or tribal ritual, but he liked their straightforwardness and honesty. He even found their tall, fair-haired women attractive—an unconventional taste for a Citizen to have.

The Horse People were now partly within the borders of the West. Whether they liked it or not, the Citizens' Army would have plenty of dealings with them in future. Citizens seldom bothered to learn how to speak to their barbarian allies, preferring to rely on local interpreters to translate everything for them. But one day, Thomasius was sure of that, there would be an urgent need for Sub-officers who had knowledge of the tongue and the customs of the Horse People. That road could open up promising avenues of promotion—perhaps. "Company-commander Thomasius" sounded good, and the retirement settlement would be much more than a Sub-officer's.

"Yes, I already said that. Can't you hear properly? A fucking horse-fucker."

There was no love lost between the Dream People of the swamps and the Horse People of the plain. Urtho glowered across to where the man in question was standing waiting, helpless and downcast. It was easy to spot him. He was slightly too old to be one of the auxiliaries, and wasn't dressed in the manner of the Sueni. Although clearly distressed, he still had a certain dignity.

Urtho snorted.

"He's a *chieftain*. Or so he claims."

"Hmm." Thomasius found himself thinking out loud. "There's no way the Lord Commander will see him, just like that, chieftain or no chieftain. And you told him that?"

"I would've put a stick up his arse, but we have orders now to be *nice* to them."

"Er, quite. And what does he actually want? Did he say?"

"Oh yes! He told us the whole story on the way in. Shouting and moaning, he was. He wouldn't shut up about it. But we had a good laugh, me and my men. You know what he wants to tell the Lord Commander? That some bastard has grabbed his precious daughter, his one and only, and ridden off with her! Not bad, eh?"

"You mean: she's been kidnapped?"

"Who knows? Who cares? One whore less, what does it matter? Look, they're all slags, right? She just slipped away for a bit of fun. And right now some lucky guy is giving little horsey-girl the time of her life! Showing her some riding tricks even she didn't know about! I wish it was me in the saddle! They're well-built, those horsey bitches. I could give her a riding lesson or two."

Troop-commander Urtho obviously didn't share in the father's distress.

"You found him on the far bank?"

"With a hunting party. First he said, Blood-Drinkers had taken her. Stupid cunt! No Blood-Drinkers anywhere. Not that we looked for them too hard, eh? Then he says: Citizens took her, so Citizens must give her back! And I say: you can come with us, but not the other horseys. Waste of fucking time."

The Sub-officers' eyes met.

"There haven't been any lost girls brought in recently, have there?"

"No, though we don't check the whore-houses. Not officially." Grassica winked. "You're off duty now, comrade, why don't *you*, er, undertake that onerous task?"

"He ought to see *someone*. We're not at war with them. I'll see what I can do. Leave him with me."

Once again Thomasius, instead of letting be, had opened the door to trouble. Urtho congratulated him ironically.

"Well done, comrade Sub-officer, and you're welcome to him! As for me: I have physical needs. I've been in the saddle for hours. You want to see the sores on my arse? First I'm going for a shit. Then I'm going for a nice juicy screw. By the way, I hope you can speak horse-fucker lingo? No? Pity, that." And as he led his horse away, he turned and called to Thomasius. "Good luck and good fuck, as they say. What a laugh, though, eh? Poor little horsey-girl! Don't it make your heart bleed?"

V

FLORIANUS IS SUMMONED TO AN AUDIENCE

WITH THE MOST POWERFUL MAN IN

THE WESTERN HALF OF THE EMPIRE

✠ *The Imperial Palace.*

Groveling before the imperial throne, Florianus the eunuch touched his lips reverently to the edge of the Emperor's purple robe, as was required of him, and to each of his red leather shoes in turn, which was not.

"Thank you, your Imperial Majesty. Thank you."

There were sycophantic sighs from the courtiers arrayed behind him, but no reply from the Emperor. No reply was expected. In turning, the gaudy imperial robes brushed against his face. He kept his eyes lowered for the time that he calculated the Emperor would need to step down from the dais and leave the throne-room. Any casual eye contact in this situation would be inappropriate. The audience was now over. His Imperial Majesty had other things to do. As did his High Chamberlain.

The dais had not been swept properly, he noticed. Someone would be made to pay for that.

Florianus glanced up, to make sure that the Sublime Presence had left the room. Those who had attended the audience were dispersing rapidly, pushing and shoving their way out into the corridors and gardens of the Palace, or already forming little circles of gossip or intrigue within the throne-room.

The political scheming and maneuvering was complex, even though only one man in the West had real power: the General. It was a pity that the major factions in the Senate didn't wear badges, or uniforms! By tradition, they each "adopted" one of the four racing teams of the hippodrome, but they didn't wear their colors, unfortunately—which would make it so much easier to follow what was going on....

Thus if Florianus were a Senator, he would be a White. The Whites were the party of the court and the adherents of the Emperor, and were also supported by those in the army who were nostalgic for the glorious days of Maximillus's grandfather, Maximus. Since there was no Purple racing team, the color white was a reasonable choice. It was the color of purity; and the Imperial Guards were famous for their white cloaks.

The Blues, the largest faction, were the team of the old-established aristocracy of the City, who had no love for the Maximian Dynasty. Blue had been the color of the nobles for many centuries, since the days when they had battled for power with the plebs. Those days were long gone—today, the street thugs of the Mob were in the pay of noble gentlemen like the Naevius family.

Green was the color of the General, the guarantor of stability, and therefore of those who wanted peace in the western half of the Empire. The wealthy merchants of Trebenna, for instance, wanted peace: they lived in constant fear for their profits. The people of the Province, the richest territory of the West, also wanted peace: they were closer to its dangerous borders than the City was, and so had good cause to fear carnage and war.

Why green? There was no special reason. This was simply the last of the factions to form, and the Green racing team had been the only one not already associated with a political group.

If Green stood for peace, Red (as far as Florianus was concerned) stood for trouble. The Red team was supported by the great landowners of the south, wealthy families like the Placidi, who scorned the Maximians and coveted the imperial throne for one of their own.

And there were other forces at work.

Some believed that the Reds were being encouraged by the rulers in the East, whose aim was to destabilize and weaken the West before bringing it under Eastern control. Maximus's historic division of the Empire between his sons would thus be undone, and the unity of the Empire restored. Florianus had no proof of this, however, except for the screamed confession of a captured Eastern agent, broken beyond repair on the rack.

It seemed doubtfut to him that the ambitious Placidi shared that aim—why overthrow the spineless Maximillus, Emperor in the West, only to replace him with his equally spineless cousin Theodore, Emperor in the East? Unless the Placidi were playing an even longer game and waiting for the moment to seize control over both East *and* West?

Florianus was pushed roughly to one side. He had almost blundered into the path of the High Priest of Sol, and his Holiness's attendants had bundled him aside. It would be inauspicious for a eunuch to touch the great man, even by accident.

Yes, let us not forget the things of the spirit! The High Priest swept majestically past, his head turned arrogantly upwards (to look for his god, or just to keep his diadem in place?). Was he any worse than the other spiritual leaders and eminent followers of the different religions now jostling and glaring at each other most un-spiritually as they made for the doors of the throne-room? Florianus had no appetite for myths, but men killed and died for them, and religious beliefs often cut across political allegiances, producing strange bedfellows and creating surprising new alliances.

Moving in the other direction, away from the doors, Julian was pushing slowly through the crowd like a lone sheep lost in a stampeding flock. Ah, Julian! Florianus observed, not for the first time, how the man shoved and glowered at the powerless while stepping aside fawningly, with bowed head, for the mighty or the potentially dangerous. How could he remember so many people, and who they were?

Julian was his messenger, his servant, his assistant, his informant, his clerk. He was invaluable—yet he was not to be trusted. A tiny purse of silver pieces would be enough to loosen his tongue. How useful to be so venal, so accommodating, he thought! Sure proof against torture: why would anyone waste time heating the fire and preparing the instruments, when everything that they wanted could be bought so cheaply?

And how good it was that he knew Julian down to his base depths, and so would never be fooled by him. There were no complicating uncertainties or scruples here. He had bought the man. Julian might on occasion be bought by others, on this or that small matter, but in the end he would always return to Florianus and tell his master what he knew.

Now he stood before the High Chamberlain, preening himself smugly like a bad actor, his fingers twitching at the decorative tassels of his costume and at the gilded medallion of office around his neck. Florianus wore a similar medallion, though his was larger, and of pure gold.

Given that he knew Julian so well, why did he still find him irritating? Florianus considered himself to be a tolerant man: every single person, man or woman, had some small redeeming feature, or, more to the point, some specific *usefulness*. (Perhaps the loathsome Placidi were an exception. And the Blood-Drinkers, of course—if they were human.) So what was it that irked him about Julian? Was it the patronizing smirk that was so often on Julian's face when he spoke to his master, the contempt of the complete man for the incomplete?

Florianus had never thought of his incompleteness as a problem. He had been cut very young. Watching how the others, the so-called "complete" men, were tormented to the point of madness by their urges, he congratulated himself that he was able to lead a calmer life. There were other, safer, pleasures that he could indulge in, like art, music, literature, food and fine wines, and he could refine and sharpen his intellectual faculties untroubled by the cravings of lust.

Or so he liked to tell himself. But there were satisfactions that he knew he was missing. To be loved, for instance, or to be desired, beyond the few moments before and during physical penetration. Nobody loved Florianus, or ever had done (he could barely remember his mother). He treated his slaves, and the Palace staff too, justly and without harshness, but none of them loved him. A dog might have loved him, but he was frightened of dogs. He had a rare caged bird, which he had taught to praise the name of the Emperor, and a clever cat that came to him, purring false affection, when it wanted a delicacy from his plate. That was behavior he could understand—but it wasn't love.

Anyway, if he loved someone, if he desired someone, what could it lead to? Nothing. Would his feelings be returned? No. "Complete" men had opportunities that he would never have, both to love and to be loved.

He could have settled the matter of his irritation by having Julian castrated. He might not be a slave, but he was a nobody, with no protector other than the High Chamberlain, and so it would be easy to arrange. But Florianus, unlike most eunuchs, had no petty spitefulness in his character—or so he believed. Besides, if Julian thought that he was irritating his master with his smugness, then that in itself could be turned to good effect. Let the man continue to draw satisfaction from it, rather than looking for some more dangerous way to express his resentment.

"My Lord."

Julian bowed, as etiquette required, and deeper than was necessary. He was good at the formalities of etiquette. Better to err on the side of obsequiousness. But did he think that it canceled out the smirk?

Florianus had the right to be addressed as a lord, though not by virtue of his birth—he had been born a slave—or because of his wealth. Yes, there was wealth, because money accrued naturally to a man in his position, yet Florianus was far less corrupt than most, and he lived comfortably but modestly, shielding his possessions from the view of the greedy or envious.

He was addressed as a lord because of his function as High Chamberlain. Nobody would bow or grovel to the flabby little eunuch—Florianus was very well aware of that—but they bowed or groveled to the glorious majesty of the god-like figure that he served and represented: Maximillus, First Citizen and Imperator, son of Maximus the Younger, grandson of Maximus the Great!

"You found me, Julian. You have been running. It must then be a matter of urgency?"

Julian was far too concerned about his dignity to actually run in his robe of office, but when he was aroused, he flushed and his skin glowed unattractively. For a brief moment, the eunuch imagined him as he might look in coitus with some frightened slave- or serving-girl, or with a desperate female petitioner hoping for some favor from him. He would look just like this, his face glistening and his eyes protruding a little. Florianus quickly banished the distasteful image from his mind.

"It is urgent, my Lord."

"Then speak."

"You are summoned to the Lord General."

How strange! The General had not been at the audience, although it was obligatory for high office holders to be there, unless excused by his Imperial Majesty. Was his absence intentional? The half-barbarian dictator could do what he liked with Maximillus, everyone knew that, but there was one thing that he *couldn't* do: he could never become his successor. It was the General's power and authority that kept the boy on his throne. The arrangement worked well. So why then draw unnecessary attention to Maximillus's weakness by humiliating him in public?

Or was the General ill, perhaps? No, Ogilo had the constitution of a Sybarite bull. He was never ill. Unless... Had the Placidi slipped some creature into the kitchens to tamper with the General's favorite mushrooms?

"To his quarters?"

"No, my Lord."

"He is not in his private rooms?"

"He is in the small audience chamber."

"You mean: he has been giving audience?" At the same time as the Imperial Audience? No, that would be unthinkable!

"My Lord, that is not for me to say." Julian knew what dangerous ground he was on. He drew closer to his master, his eyes gleaming. "But they told me that he received visitors."

"Messengers bringing information from the border? Urgent business? News from the East?"

"The last person who was seen to attend him was Senator Gnaeus Julius Placidus."

"Really?"

Despite his many years of practice in dissembling in public, Florianus had difficulty suppressing his astonishment.

VI

AULUS DISCUSSES WOMEN WITH HIS

UNCLE, AND IS GIVEN AN ULTIMATUM

✠ *The house of Senator Lucius Pomponius Atticus, in the City.*

Senator Lucius Atticus appraised his nephew with an expression that Aulus found hard to interpret. Was it contempt? Irritation? Exasperation? Could it be a mixture of all three? Or was he merely tired?

Aulus gave his uncle a lot of reasons to be tired.

That he didn't like the way that Aulus dressed—and for which he paid the bills—was a recognized problem between them, though the Senator had long ago despaired of being able to persuade his nephew back into togas. Or Citizen robes. Or even proper tunics. Many of the Citizens had turned to wearing woolen breeches in the barbarian style, since these were both warmer and more comfortable than tunics and leggings. Senator Atticus didn't consider this decadent behavior to be worthy of imitation.

Today, Aulus was wearing breeches—not of wool, though, but in a soft and expensive shiny cloth from Sybaris, which rather spoilt the "rough barbarian" effect—combined with a tunic. The tunic would hardly have pleased the Senator, however, being decorated with tiny seed-pearls and stitched with golden thread in a pattern of sunbursts. Aulus could imagine his uncle thinking: the boy looks like the owner of a brothel!

His father would have said it out loud, but Lucius Atticus was generally polite and amiable towards his nephew, whatever the situation, although there were few topics of conversation that they could easily share.

"Faustus…"

"*Aulus*, please, uncle."

His uncle sighed.

"I thought you'd gotten over that nonsense. Faustus was the name you were given, wasn't it? Faustus Pomponius Atticus, the same as your father. In fact, I can even remember a time when you were known under his roof as 'Junior'."

Aulus winced. That was a phase of his life that he preferred *not* to be reminded of. Though his uncle probably didn't know anything about the circumstances that had led to the hated nickname...

"Nobody worries much about names these days, do they, uncle? Except for a few of the great families. And you do know how our own family got its start into greatness? From the sack of Sybaris: from selling off the captured soldiers as slaves, and looting the furniture and artworks from the Sybarite palaces. Highly distinguished..."

Senator Atticus looked most displeased.

"That may be true, but don't ever let your father hear you talking like that! It's bad enough that you've rejected his given name and chosen to call yourself Aulus. You think I'm a fuddy-duddy and you talk about 'these days', and 'back then', but tell me this: who in Sol's name is called Aulus—*these days*."

Decimus couldn't help laughing. "Aulus" was not a fashionable name. The Senator glared at him.

"Oh, I'm sorry, sir, no disrespect was intended. But that's a good point that you just made."

Aulus flashed him a fierce "I-didn't-expect-*you*-of-all-people-to-stab-me-in-the-back" look. Then he explained to his uncle that he had chosen the name—old-fashioned though it might be—not to hurt his father's feelings (did the old reptile have any?) but to express something about himself. As he also tried to do in his poetry.

"Ah, yes, your poetry! Ahem. Poetry of which we have so far seen precious little. Or, to be more precise: not a single line. Now I'm not much of a literary man, but I have a feeling that the most productive poets do their best work *before* the late afternoon and the carousals of the evening? A change in your sleeping habits might do wonders for your creativity!"

Before Aulus could say anything—though what was there left to say on this sensitive question?—Decimus came to his rescue.

"I can vouch for Master Aulus, sir. Just before you joined us, we were having a long and intense discussion about matters of poetic creativity."

Which was true, more or less, Aulus told himself. (On second thoughts, less rather than more.) He decided not to follow up that particular point. It was a nuisance that Sextus was so brilliant, and so prolific. Aulus was sure that he himself was also somebody very special, and very gifted—it was just that the *area* of his remarkable talent hadn't become obvious yet. But it would. His day would come.

His uncle wasn't listening, but hopping from foot to foot as he discovered that he was treading on pieces of broken nutshell.

"Don't they ever sweep in here? And it isn't just your given name that you've abandoned—you no longer call yourself Pomponius."

Aulus defended himself. Who needed three names? And the associations of the clan-name really weren't so wonderful. It wasn't just the business with the sack of Sybaris. There had been a Pomponius who was a claimant to the throne, back in the Years of Chaos, before Maximus came along. For two weeks—until they cut his head off! There was the Pomponius who tried to join the Blue racing team, and made a complete fool of himself. And there was one who had pimped for Severian the Evil, and who had been torn to pieces by the Mob, the first time that he stepped outside the Palace without a bodyguard.

"I don't need to be part of *that* tradition, uncle."

"You father obviously does. Like it or not, it's a famous name that we bear, and your father uses it on every possible occasion. But I didn't come to talk to you about your name... *Aulus* (if you must have it so!)." He paused, for dramatic effect. "Your lady mother has written to me."

Both the young men feigned surprise.

"Uncle, how can that be? I was always under the impression that you and my mother were... well... sort of..."

"Say it: not the best of friends? My sister-in-law has religious views that I can neither share nor respect. Sol (praised be his name!) was always good enough for me. And I bless the memory of the old gods, even though I can't find it in myself to believe in them anymore. But this Slave worship, with its mad priests and murderous fanatics... It has taken over our City and many of our best families. Even my brother professes to be a follower."

Aulus gave a sniffle of contempt.

"I doubt whether my father has made any great effort to understand their beliefs."

Lucius Atticus refused to be provoked.

"Yes, my brother is not overly inclined in the direction of studying, reading, or learning. He was always more, um, the *man of action*. But he does claim to be one of them, just as most of the Senators of the Blue faction now do. And many of the Reds as well."

The Senator began to pace up and down, his head lowered thoughtfully and his hands clasped behind his back—a sure sign, Aulus knew, that he was about to say something of import. He tried to head him off.

"Uncle..."

"No, listen! It's time for you to know your mother's thoughts, Aulus. It will not surprise you to hear that she disapproves of your present way of living"—how in Sol's name could she know about any of that, who could have ratted on him?—"and that she wishes you to marry as soon as possible. The right sort of person. A virtuous young woman, from noble stock, of course."

"Yes. Well…"

"Don't tell me that you don't know any women here in the City! From what I've heard, you spend a great deal of your time with women— no doubt getting to know them *very* closely. But whether your mother would regard them as suitable is a different question."

"There are no women among them who share my mother's religious convictions, if that is what you mean, uncle."

A smile flashed briefly across his uncle's face.

"And I'm pleased to hear that too!" He paused. "Aulus, I'm an old man." He quickly held up a hand to stifle his nephew's polite protest. "No, I am, but I was young once, just like you, and the way that I spent my time failed to meet with *my* father's approval too. It was my brother Faustus who was always the well-behaved, dutiful son. I was the wild one, the tearaway. On one notable occasion, the word 'debauched' was even used…"

"No, I can't believe that, uncle!"

Aulus's surprise was genuine. Whatever had his uncle got up to back then?

"Yes, truly. Of course, those were much more innocent times than the ones we live in today. But I had gone too far. The moment came when I had to learn to behave more responsibly, or accept the consequences. And that moment has now come for you. It's your decision. I can't force you to marry. But if you choose to defy your parents, you can't remain under my roof, because I would then be countenancing your defiance. And that would tear this family apart. Do you want to lose the support of your whole family? And are you in a position to maintain yourself, Aulus, by your own efforts?"

The second question was a rhetorical one, as all three of them knew. Aulus was effectively without a copper piece to his name. His mind went blank: everything was grayness and gloom, like one of those sanctuaries of the Slave worshipers. He had no idea how to reply to his uncle. Once again Decimus tried to help.

"Sir, there are any number of suitable young ladies of noble breeding whom your nephew could choose from. Each and every one of them would be delighted to become a daughter of the House of Pomponius."

The Senator fixed Decimus with a steely look.

"I don't want a list of these female paragons. Your loyalty does both of you credit, Decimus, but I doubt whether you have been on many of his nocturnal outings." He turned to Aulus again. "Can you name an appropriate candidate from amongst all these ladies?"

"Oh, uncle, there really are so many of them. I haven't been courting any one lady in particular."

"No, please continue!"

"Er, well—"

Decimus prompted him.

"The Lady Cornelia is known to favor you, sir."

Thank you, Decimus, thank you! The Lady Cornelia, who was both plain *and* boring, was reputed to be among the most desperate spinsters in the City. She was older than Aulus. Cornelia was of impeccable birth and known to be of spotless virtue. She was an earnest follower of the Slave with a interest in metaphysical and philosophical questions—an intellectual, even, which was an obvious reason why no man had ever wished to marry her.

Better still: she and Aulus had sometimes been seen together—because she occasionally tagged along behind her little cousin Fannia. (Fannia was not to be mentioned: she had a *very* different reputation, one which might even have reached the Senator's ears.)

"Really?" The Senator seemed impressed. "The Cornelii are an excellent family, although Senator Cornelius Rufus is perhaps too friendly with the Placidi. I don't much care for that."

The Cornelii and Placidi were closely linked, to be sure. Aulus had only failed to have his way with Fannia, he liked to believe, because Sextus Placidus had got there first.

"But we shouldn't rule her out, uncle, merely for political reasons"— though Aulus was certain that his uncle had done just that. Desperate for another name, he took an enormous gamble. "There is also the Lady Lollia Maxima."

"I don't think I know that person? The family is to my knowledge no longer represented in the Senate."

Thank you for that, Sol, thank you! Lollia Maxima was indeed a young woman who only came out after dark, usually well-fortified with wine, and went about her operations under different names. If the Senator had known about even a fraction of her activities, the thought of her joining his family would have brought on a seizure.

Decimus suggested the Lady Anthemia, the daughter of Senator Anthemius Capito. Brilliant! Another harmless bore. Aulus had been to the theater with a group of giggling, flirtatious young ladies, the only one of whom he wouldn't have pleasured (given half a chance) being the horse-faced and dimwitted Anthemia.

The Senator had had enough.

"I have to respond to this letter of your mother's. I'll give you a few days to think about it, but not more than a week. And then I want a name. Or two names, if you prefer. I will be happy to approach the families on your behalf. Not the Cornelii, though." He turned to Decimus. "It was good to see you. Please visit me again before you leave. That may be very soon. I suspect that the General already has new tasks for you."

And then he was gone.

The two young men had stood politely to salute the Senator. Now, with a yelp of pain, Aulus flung himself back on to the couch, scattering the cushions.

"Demons from hell, Decimus, what do I do now?"

"I thought that we had a workable plan?"

"Do we, Decimus? Do we? I'm not going to risk tying myself to some haggard old crone like Cornelia. I'd rather die! And that frump Anthemia is even worse than Cornelia. Now Fannia…" His mind drifted happily to thoughts of the buxom little sexpot. "But I could never present her to my parents."

"You took a great risk, mentioning Lollia Maxima. Even I know what *that* lady gets up to! If your uncle should make enquiries…"

"Then I'll just say that I got the names mixed up. It's as simple as that. Maybe there's a Lollia Maximilla or a Laelia Maxima out there somewhere."

"You still need a name. So, young master, start thinking! Unless you want to join the rest of us and begin working for a living."

Aulus looked thoroughly gloomy.

"Decimus…!"

"The plan will work. Trust me! You just need to find the right person." He paused. "But your Lordliness said that our plan had two fatal weaknesses. What did you mean by that?"

Aulus sighed.

"None of my lady friends wants to get married. Persuading them won't be easy. And anyone that I would like well enough to marry would send my mother into a fit."

"Is that *one* fatal weakness, or *two*, what you just said?"

"That counts as one fatal weakness."

"So what is the second one?"

Aulus was now feeling thoroughly sorry for himself.

"However well the plan works, and even if we can find some reasonably tolerable female for me to get married to, I'm still going to end up *married*, for Sol's sake!"

A thought that plunged him back into the depths of despair.

VII

MARA IS NOT THE PRINCESS

WHO WAS EXPECTED

�֎ *The great northern plain.*

It was cold in the early morning hours. Mara, who was normally too busy doing things to worry about whether it was hot or cold, now suffered miserably. She had been woken by cramps. They had tied her up very tight, both her arms and her legs, so that she couldn't escape during the night, and so that they could sleep undisturbed. She was bruised and battered from having been transported like a sack of horse-dung. And she was also desperately thirsty.

The smelly man was still snoring loudly, while the thin man, half-awake, grunted and muttered to himself. Mara feared that he might come over and start touching her, but he stayed away.

At least the air was fresh. She dreaded the moment when they would cover her head in the sack again and throw her over one of the horses.

When the men woke, shortly before sunrise, they shared their simple breakfast with her, taking it in turns to thrust a piece of oatcake into her mouth or to give her a swig of vile-tasting water from a bottle.

Before they set off, the smelly man asked, "Do you want to piss or anything?"

She nodded. He untied the rope around her legs, pulled down her rough woolen riding breeches for her, smacked her amiably on the behind, and invited her to squat and get on with it. He then ignored her, but the thin man hunkered down opposite her, grinning and staring, so that at first she couldn't go. Only after the smelly man had noticed, and driven the thin man away, could she relieve herself.

This time, they left off the sack, and let her trot behind the smelly man's horse at the end of a rope. It wasn't far, he told her. They traveled slowly, halting several times to allow Mara to rest. Mara estimated that they must be going east, or south-east.

East, she knew, would take them to the swamps. Were these men Sueni? Why should two Sueni talk to each other in the Citizens' Tongue?

South or south-east would take them away from the Great River and deep into the southern part of the plain, where few of the Horse People had ever been before. Out there somewhere in the distance was the fabled Tower of the Sky, the home of wizards and necromancers. It was an evil place, people said. But why should they be going there?

They reached their immediate destination after only a short ride, and Mara's worst fears were confirmed. Tucked among sparse bushes at the base of a low hill was an encampment of slavers.

The smelly man brought his horse to a stop, tugged at Mara's rope to bring her forward, and then kicked her to the ground with his foot. She landed painfully at the feet of a large, grim-looking man.

He was pitch-black! Like a demon! She had known that such men existed, and that they were men, not demons, but she had never before seen one. Even Blood-Drinkers were not as dark as this. And he was wearing a flowing robe such as she had also never seen before, and a cloth wrapped around his head as if he had injured himself there.

The smelly man dismounted and saluted the black man by touching his feet. This then was the leader of the gang! They spoke to each other in the Citizens' Tongue, which the black man had difficulties with, so the smelly man had to speak very slowly and clearly.

Mara could follow almost everything that was being said, even thought the black man couldn't pronounce the "s" sound at the end of words. She learned that the smelly man's name was Orcus, which was not a tribal name. She never heard anyone use the black man's name; he was always simply "the boss".

The boss was very angry.

"The boy told *princeh*. You give him money. *My* money. We wait for you here one day, one night. Bad place. There no water here. Them patrol all the time. Fuck all soldier! That bitch princeh? Cunt! Where her princeh crown?"

He kicked at her—but to make a point, rather than with serious intention to hurt her—and missed anyway. She no longer cared: after what she'd been through, one more bruise wouldn't make a difference.

"Look, boss, she's the daughter of a chieftain. The horseys don't have princes or princesses. They're not like us. But this is what Issachar wants, isn't it?"

Issachar! Mara listened carefully.

The boss cursed. His teeth were filed to sharp points. Was he a cannibal?

"Don't say that name!"

"Sorry, boss."

"Bitch just dirty horsey cunt. We have enough of them. No? Look."

And he made a sweeping gesture with his arm that took in the encampment around them.

Mara now saw that there were dozens of prisoners, mostly women and children. Some of them may have been from the Horse People, but, if so, they were from other clans, and they were slaves or camp-followers. They weren't free folk, people she might have recognized from some past gathering of the Horse People, where there were sports and dancing and opportunities for the young men and women to meet each other. And none of the young women that she could see here were wearing plaits.

Maybe Orcus had the same thought.

"But this one's a virgin."

"Really? Virgin girl?"

Orcus had finally succeeded in catching the boss's interest.

"Yes. Look, she's still got the plaits. You'll get more money for her. There are some men who *like* little virgins. You know what I mean?"

And he leered at her in much the same way that the thin man had done, though without conveying the same feeling of lust. It was just for show, she thought, something that he was putting on for the benefit of the boss.

"You say *little* virgin? No. Too big. What man want horsey virgin? Shit! Hairy girl. Hard skin. Big feet. Afterward, what he do with her? Too ugly for hou'-work."

But Orcus now had his boss's attention, and the arguments began to flow. He wasn't prepared to give up so easily. There was money to be made here.

Mara could scarcely believe her ears: they were talking about *her*.

"Come on, boss, there's always a market for virgins. And some men have more unusual tastes, don't they? We know that. When we get to Trebenna, you can sell her to some rich old merchant…"

"You think? And how long he go bored with horsey virgin? One week? Two week?"

"Alright, so maybe he gets bored. It's bound to happen. Then he can sell her to a knocking-shop. And for a good price, too! Because those people can train her." He smiled knowingly. "They have ways to fix her, so that she stays 'a virgin' for weeks, and nobody will know. Months, even, if they're good. Pick the right customers, and you can earn a lot of money. And when she can't keep it tight anymore, so what? They can sell her again. Maybe to an old guy who likes her. Or to the plantations in the south, you know, for field work. Look, boss, she's a healthy girl. Robust. These Horse People are as strong as their horses!"

Mara was horrified. How could there be so much evil in the world?

The boss yawned, unimpressed.

"Little problem here."

"No problem! Feel her legs, boss, look at those muscles—they grip the horse with their legs, so they *never* fall off. Have you seen them ride? Now, just imagine how strong you have to be to ride like that."

"No. Little problem here. Actually, big problem."

"What problem?"

"We don't go to Trebenna."

"What?"

Ignoring Orcus, the boss turned to another of his men. He beckoned him to come over and then pointed at Mara with a surprisingly long, black finger.

"Put her with other cunt. No-one touch her. *No-one*. She stay horsey virgin."

Mara was yanked to her feet and dragged a short distance to where a group of ragged, unhappy-looking women were huddled. Only then did the man untie the rope binding her legs; her hands remained bound.

She fell to the ground, exhausted. The grass had been trampled flat, but it was still soft and inviting. She would have liked to have slept, but she felt the eyes of the other women on her.

A voice whispered, "Look, it's a fucking virgin!" and there was a titter of laughter, but very soft, so as not to draw the attention of the slavers.

Mara looked at the women around her. None of them were as young as she was. Several might be Horse People, but none still had their plaits. There were also a couple of very dirty, bedraggled Sueni.

A small, dark-haired woman leant across and fingered Mara's plaits. Then, using the Tongue, she asked her which clan she was from.

The woman had facial tattoos, showing that she had once been a slave among the Horse People. She was very beautiful, but not in the way that women of the Horse People were beautiful. Her skin was too dark. Where did she come from then? The Horse People were a free folk—they kept no slaves of their own kind, only slaves that they purchased in trade, or enemies captured in war.

"I am of the Speaking Bird clan. I'm sure you have heard of it! My father is the clan chieftain."

"Ah, so you're the famous princess we've all been hanging around waiting for. The 'special item' that Orcus and Dirty Fingers were sent to fetch."

"Dirty Fingers?"

"Yes, that's what *we* call him. He's a piece of shit. His real name is Thrasyllus. He likes to come visiting. Most of us have had a night-time visit from Dirty Fingers, haven't we, ladies?"

There were muttered comments and curses. One of the women said that he would get what was coming to him, and spat.

"But he leaves *me* in peace. Which is good for me, and good for him. He thinks I'm a witch."

"Why is that?"

"Because of my markings. You know, the tattoos. And because of my eyes."

She looked up and trapped Mara with her gaze. She had striking gray-green eyes that, set in her dark face, caught like fishermen's hooks. Mara was completely unsettled. Foolishly—because the woman must once have come from somewhere far beyond the southern horizon, and not from the north—she asked her what clan *she* was from.

"What a question! Who cares? I never belonged to one of your Horse clans—except as some man's property. I was just a slave. So nothing's really changed for me, has it? My name is Manasa. And what is *yours*, princess from the Speaking Bird clan of the Horse People?"

Mara told her. Manasa asked her what the meaning of her name was. Everyone should know what their name meant. Mara told her that it meant "happy" in the Tongue of the Horse People.

"I was born the daughter and granddaughter of chieftains, so the wise woman who birthed me said that my life would be a happy one. That's why she told my father to name me Mara."

She was an only child. If more daughters had come, they would also have been given names beginning with "Ma", because that was the way that the Horse People did these things. So she and Manasa could be sisters!

Manasa laughed.

"I think not, princess. You and I were born under different skies. And as for your wise woman, she wasn't very good at seeing into the future, was she? I was better named. 'Manasa' means 'valuable like gold'. Well, I've been bought and sold often enough, so I suppose they got that right."

VIII

FLORIANUS'S WORLD IS TURNED UPSIDE DOWN

✠ *The Imperial Palace.*

Florianus puffed and panted to keep up with Julian, who strode on ahead of him, showing no consideration for the eunuch's stumpy legs. Florianus didn't need a guide to show him the way to the small audience chamber—he knew the layout of the Palace far better than anyone else—but etiquette required that the High Chamberlain when on official business be preceded by an attendant.

Soon they were joined by a small detachment of white-cloaked Imperial Guards, huge, hairy barbarians armed with fearsome-looking spears. By ancient tradition, the Guards were recruited from the Sueni, the Horse People, the Free People, and other northern tribes. They fell in behind Julian, and did nothing to slow the pace with which the little party navigated its way through the Golden Rooms, the area of the Palace reserved for the Emperor.

Strange, Florianus thought to himself: all this fuss, with people attending him and supposedly guarding him, but what if an assassin simply crept up behind him and stabbed him in the back? All his guards were marching along in front of him, with their backs turned. Did they "guard" the Emperor like this, too? He made a mental note to speak about it to the Commander of the Guard.

The Golden Rooms contained not only the throne-room, or main audience chamber, but also the huge suite of luxurious private rooms used by the Emperor. In addition there were rooms reserved for the Empress and her attendants, for the imperial mistresses and concubines (female), for catamites (male), for close personal friends of the Emperor, for favored slaves and eunuchs, and for private visitors. Also here were the Palace quarters of the High Chamberlain, who needed to be as close as possible to his master. Since Maximillus was unmarried, and not much more than a child, and had neither brothers nor sisters, many rooms remained empty for the present, or were used for storage.

Even as a young eunuch, in the time of the present Emperor's father, Maximus the Younger, Florianus had lived in the Golden Rooms, serving—and spying on—the imperial mistresses installed there. Maximus was not a notably virile man, and his mistresses had shown a tendency to soon start looking for outside (and strictly forbidden) distractions.

The corridors were lit by torches, held in ornamental metal brackets, and were decorated with gaudy paintings and golden mosaics. Many of these celebrated the military triumphs of earlier rulers. The flames from the torches cast ugly, flickering shadows, making the lurid images of conquest, death, and subjugation seem even uglier. The art in the private rooms, on the other hand, was often of an erotic nature, or showed feasting, hunting scenes, or exotic wild life.

Florianus couldn't help noticing the missing mosaic stones and peeling frescoes, or how frayed the carpets and wall-hangings had become. Most of the artworks were badly in need of repair or replacement. But who would pay for that? The Emperor was poorer than several of his subjects were (the Placidi, for instance). And he was kept on a tight rein by the General, who controlled the finances of the West.

Ogilo raised money by taxation, and by levies on the rich trade that ran through Trebenna. He spent it on protecting that trade and maintaining peace in the West, by paying his soldiers well and hiring Sueni mercenaries. He also sent an annual tribute to the Blood-Drinkers. So there was not much left over for expensive improvements to the Palace.

There was resentment about this in court circles. Florianus was an influential figure among the Whites—behind the scenes, rather than in the public arena—and he ought to have been similarly enraged by the shabbiness into which the half-barbarian Ogilo had allowed the ancient Imperial Palace of the West to decline. But if he was honest with himself, what would he have done differently to the General?

Whites and Greens were anyhow supposed to be allies, holding off the resentful Blues of the City and the treacherous Reds of the south, none of whom had any love for Emperor Maximillus.

Now the little party traversed a series of interconnected courtyards and entered the area of the Palace known as the Silver Rooms, with the offices of the imperial administration, a guesthouse for state visitors, and the private quarters of important members of the executive; also, the small audience chamber.

When they reached it, the commander of the party of Imperial Guardsmen hammered on the thick wooden door with the butt-end of his spear. After it had creaked open, Florianus and Julian waited patiently while the officer handed over responsibility for their persons to the soldiers on duty inside, members of the General's personal bodyguard.

Florianus made an elaborate show of primping his hair and rearranging his gold chain and medallion of office.

"Will I do?" he asked Julian. "Well?"

He wasn't vain about his appearance—he knew that it would never be anything but unimpressive—but eunuchs were expected to be vain. It was always best to be as people expected you to be, otherwise they became nervous. So, let them see what they want to see…until the moment that you make your move.

The Imperial Guardsmen wheeled about and marched off, and an equally magnificent barbarian with great waxed mustaches and a powerful body odor ushered Florianus and his assistant in to meet the General.

There was no throne in the chamber, which was never used by the Emperor. Instead, there was an ornate magistrate's stool of office on a slightly raised platform, with a number of chairs positioned below and in front of it. Ogilo, however, was standing alone beside a huge table covered in maps, scrolls, and dusty ledgers.

The ruler of the West was a big man, though smaller than most of his bodyguards. He was plainly but carefully dressed, without bright colors, a style that he cultivated. His leather belt, scabbard and wrist-guard were undecorated, but of superb quality. Florianus knew that anything that the General *used* would be of the finest, and that he would make sure of that. What he merely *wore* interested him far less.

Ogilo usually had a stern and humorless expression on his face; he seldom smiled. His coloring was northern: brown hair, now turning to silver, pale blue eyes, and pale skin. He wore a sword—his favored weapon—at his side, and a silver chain of office, less elaborate than the one that Florianus wore, around his neck. Despite his many battles, his face was unscarred. His movements and gestures were slow and measured, those of a man who was used to being obeyed without question.

He gestured to the bodyguards to leave the chamber, and waited until they had done so before addressing Florianus. He thanked the High Chamberlain for having answered his summons so promptly. He knew, he said, that Florianus had had a day of onerous duties.

The voice betrayed nothing of his origins, which were the object of much popular interest. In fact, the General was the only high military commander that Florianus had ever met who spoke the Citizens' Tongue like a well-educated man.

Florianus knew more about him than most people did. Ogilo was a bastard. His father, a handsome, muscular youth, had been sent to the City as a hostage from some minor barbarian tribe that no-one had ever heard of. The court ladies had found him excitingly attractive, and he had bedded several of them. One of them, the daughter of Senator Marcus Naevius the Elder, he got with child.

It was an enormous scandal. Marriage between a barbarian and a Citizen woman of good birth was unthinkable. Naevia was ostracized by polite society, including her own family, and died in labor. The child's father rescued the baby, before Naevius could make sure that it was never seen again. He chose the daughter of a Trebennan merchant to be his common-law wife, and a mother to his son.

The Naevii did not forgive. Ogilo (as the child had been named, after the barbarian fashion) was only four when his father was lured to a meeting in a fetid alleyway in the slums. Here, a hired killer knifed him to death and mutilated the corpse. The merchant's daughter had grown to love little Ogilo. She took him to Trebenna, re-married, and brought the boy up, in the best traditions of her class, to be sensible, frugal, and practical. He became a soldier.

The Naevii did not forgive. Nor did they forget. Old Naevius was followed into the Senate by his son, now the leader of the Blue faction. The Blues resented the low-born Maximians, yet tolerated the even lower-born General, the guarantor of peace and stability and protector of their own wealth and privileges. *Most* of them did, but not the Naevii, whose feelings for the General were personal.

Senator Marcus Naevius the Younger viewed his illegitimate nephew with a deep loathing, as did Naevius's thuggish son Quintus, Ogilo's cousin. Quintus controlled the City Mob. The City police, who took their orders from the decrepit City Prefect, Lentulus, did little to keep the Mob in check.

The General didn't need a bodyguard inside the Palace; outside, he definitely did.

Only Ogilo's barbaric name and coloring revealed his origins, and nobody "knew" him. He had, it seemed, no personal life worth mentioning. He was unmarried. Did he keep a woman? Or a boy? Even Florianus, who was well-informed about such things, didn't know.

Many would have expected him to have married a princess of the Imperial house, but Maximillus had no sisters—he was the sole fruit of the miserable loins of his father—and the rulers in the East had no wish to increase the General's status by a family alliance.

His status were already great enough. It was Ogilo who had held the Blood-Drinkers at Neopolis. No-one could defeat them; they were invincible, like a huge wave or a storm or a plague of locusts. But he had dug trenches and built earthworks around the capital of the East, and then fought the Blood-Drinkers to a standstill.

Florianus made a deep bow. The General was not higher in formal rank than he was, but his power was immeasurably greater.

"My Lord, you do me honor. My duties today were not so onerous, but it was the morning of the Imperial Audience. Indeed, many were surprised that you were not in attendance on his Imperial Majesty."

Ogilo acknowledged the barb with a slight raising of his eyebrows.

"I hope that his Majesty did not take my absence amiss. It was not intended as a snub. I had urgent duties here, in the Silver Rooms. In his service."

"I was given to believe that your Lordship was holding audience here in the small chamber?"

So, that will teach that wretch Julian to make me run halfway across the Palace! Florianus out of the corner of his eye saw his assistant stiffen, his face reddening with embarrassment. Ah, that sweaty glow that he knew so well!

"No, it was nothing as exciting as an audience. Merely a few visitors, reporting to me on matters of some urgency and of some concern for the peace and safety of the Empire."

"My Lord, it was entirely my error to draw such a wrong conclusion. Forgive me."

As his assistant would have realized, the apology was aimed at Julian, too—there was no point in completely crushing the man—and Florianus (whose hearing was acute) heard a faint zishing of air as Julian breathed out in relief.

"No reason."

"But you did have a reason for wanting to see me, my Lord?"

He had two, but the first was a matter that first required corroboration. The other matter, however, was of a sensitive nature.

Florianus nodded towards Julian.

"Might it not be better…?"

"No. The boy can stay—he saw my visitor. Better to have him inside the secret, his mouth shut, than outside, talking about it. In any case, it may soon become public knowledge."

Florianus smiled. That reference to "the boy"—"boy" in the sense of "servant", not "youth"—would normally have been deeply hurtful, but now Julian would be blossoming inside at the thought of being chosen to be the bearer of an important secret. Still, better if it didn't need to remain secret for too long.

If Julian had bowed any lower, his nose would have scraped the floor.

"My Lord, I am your devoted slave. You can trust me with any task or secret. Truly. *Any.*"

The General ignored him.

"He saw my visitor, but you didn't. A surprising person to come knocking at my door: Senator Gnaeus Julius Placidus."

Gnaeus Placidus. The fat one. The degenerate. Cruel eyes and mouth. A clever debater. A sharp, legally-trained mind in a disgusting body.

"What did he want from you, my Lord? If it's not a secret. The Placidi are not known to be your dearest friends. Or ours."

And now the General smiled, a wan smile like the first shimmer of melting on a frozen lake. Then the smile disappeared.

"Good. We're talking politics. Whites and Greens. Reds. Which is what it's all about, of course. He left his attendants outside. I had to offer him a chair, because he can barely stand without support. You may wish to sit, too, when you've heard what I'm about to say. However, if you take *that* chair, clean his slime off it first. Prepare for a shock! He came to make an offer, on behalf of his brother. The hand of his niece, Julia Placida."

Florianus was indeed shocked. Yet also puzzled. His *niece*? Gnaeus Placidus had no wife—for reasons everyone knew about. But his brother Gaius had similar inclinations, it was said, if not more sinister ones, and was also unmarried.

Gaius was the thin one. The one known as "the wizard". For many, he was the incarnation of evil. Though never seen in the Senate, he was the most ambitious man in both the empires, some claimed. He could summon demons to do his work, and conjure up the dead! Had Gaius been secretly married all these years?

The General noticed Florianus's confusion.

"Yes, where does this girl suddenly come from, you may be thinking. Neither of the Placidi does anything to women that might lead to the birth of a child. Murder them, yes. *Eat them*, perhaps, in Gnaeus's case (I wouldn't put it past him). But take them to bed? No, the girl is the daughter of their dead brother, Publius."

Of course! It had slipped his mind. And Publius had also had a son, too young to fight for his huge inheritance, but old enough to be tricked by uncle Gnaeus into signing it away, in return for an allowance.

"So she is the sister of Sextus Placidus?"

"The eccentric young poet—a constant affront to his uncles, Sol bless him! But I doubt that they know each other."

The General explained that the little girl had been taken away by Gaius Placidus and brought up on his estates in the south as his ward.

"Poor child! He must have turned her into a monster. Or a witch."

"Who knows, Lord Chamberlain? They are bringing her to the City, to be *shown*. And not, I am told, in a cage."

"But how could they imagine that you would accept the girl, my Lord? They hate you, because you block their path to the throne."

Then the unthinkable happened: the General laughed out loud.

"How you flatter me! But Gaius Placidus doesn't want to give his precious ward to *me*. He can't even bear to look at me! Which is probably why he sent his voluminous brother as messenger. No, Julia is not for me—she is intended for the Emperor!"

Florianus felt as if the air had suddenly been punched out of him. Julia Placida as *Empress*? His immediate thought was that she would stab her husband or poison him on their wedding night.

That was not to be ruled out, the General conceded. But Senator Gnaeus had explained it differently. Little Julia would be a peace offering, a guarantee that the Placidi *wouldn't* try to kill the Emperor. That made some sense. After all, what was the point of endangering a ship after climbing on board and occupying the most comfortable cabins? A ship that was already sailing in your direction.

"And what would the Placidi gain from the marriage?" Florianus asked, although he already knew the answer.

"They would naturally expect certain positions of high rank and influence within the state. And when she has given Maximillus a son and heir, enriching the modest Maximian stock (his words, not mine) with noble Placidian blood, then they would truly be part of the Imperial family."

The arrangement had its charms. It would keep the south quiet, and it would infuriate the Blues. But Florianus's world was being turned on its head. New alliances would be forged, old animosities forgotten—but would it be for a short while only, or for longer?

"And where would this leave *you*, my Lord?"

"Our new friend also said to me: 'Do you really think that *we* are the ones who want you dead, General? We have no personal animosity towards you. Can the same be said of your uncle Marcus Naevius? Or of your dear cousin Quintus?' Still, it won't stop the Placidi organizing a little 'accident' to remove me from the scene, if they ever get the chance."

"Not everybody admires you, my Lord, as much as I do."

Should he take this proposal to the Emperor, on the General's behalf?

"No. Talk to no-one. Maximillus is too young to make such decisions. Whom he beds is up to him, but whom he marries is an affair of state. He has no choice in that. I haven't decided what to do yet. I need a few more days. There are people who must be consulted. Not a word to anyone, Florianus. You too, boy: not a word! Now leave me. We'll talk about this again very soon, and then we'll have to take action. You notice that I say 'we'?"

No Guards accompanied them on the way back. Florianus was no longer on official business, so according to protocol no bodyguard was needed.

There was a cold draught in the corridor. He hadn't noticed it on his way to the General, but now it made him shiver. He hadn't noticed the echoing of their footsteps, but now he did.

His mood was somber as he puzzled over what had just happened. If the General wanted to pursue a Placidian marriage for the Emperor, he would need Florianus's help, and Florianus would have to act quickly. The General was a man who was known to think long and hard about what he was about to do, and who did nothing without a good reason. Why had he then taken the trouble to summon Florianus, only to send him away after instructing him to remain silent? Something wasn't right.

Florianus was so lost in these thoughts that he barely heard Julian telling him that there had been another guest who had come to speak to the General.

"I saw him leaving. I didn't recognize him, but he had the look of the north about him. The frontier."

"Messengers and emissaries come and go. There is nothing unusual about that."

"But this one wore riding boots, caked in dried mud. He hadn't had time to clean them. And here in the City it hasn't rained for many weeks, my Lord."

IX

THOMASIUS TAKES HIS LIFE IN HIS HANDS,

AND IS SAVED BY THE CHAIN OF COMMAND

✠ *The fortress of Cascantum.*

In for a copper, in for a gold piece. Thomasius wanted to help the man. He had a kind of simple dignity and carried himself with natural grace, but he was clearly distressed at the loss of his daughter. Thomasius himself had no children, but one day he might have, and then he hoped that he would act just as vigorously if anything happened to one of them.

Unfortunately, there was no way that he could go straight to Lord Commander Rhaetius. It had to be the chain of command. So, against Grassica's good advice, Thomasius had decided to take the anxious father to see Company-commander Decius. The Lord Commander had the reputation of being a decent man. Decius, on the other hand, had the reputation of being an arse-wipe. That was the word that Grassica had used to describe him—and not as a term of endearment—but it might have come from almost anyone in Decius's company.

To make it worse, he had it in for Sub-officer Thomasius. In going to him like this, Thomasius was more or less taking his life in his hands. Sol only knew what the Company-commander might do to him!

How should he explain things to Decius? Who *was* the horsey fellow exactly? A chieftain? Of what rank? Thomasius wished that he had asked for more information from Urtho, but the giant Troop-commander had been more concerned to get away quickly to relieve himself than to pass the time of day with the two Sub-officers.

Now was the opportunity for Thomasius to test his knowledge of the man's language—for which the Horse People themselves had no special name. They simply called it "the Tongue", as if no other ones existed.

So far Thomasius had only learned the numbers, and how to say "My name is Thomasius", "What is your name?", "Where is the temple?",

"Where is the inn?", and "You are a very beautiful woman". Normally you would learn the standard phrases that were used for greetings, or upon departure, but Thomasius had not yet been able to master these: they were fiendishly difficult, because they varied according to both your own rank and the other person's.

It took him three attempts before the man eventually understood that the name of the person talking to him was Thomasius. Very well, he needed to work on his pronunciation. That hardly came as a surprise.

The next one was easier: the man's own name was Corvo. He added a whole lot of stuff that Thomasius couldn't follow, but which probably meant "son of thingie", "grandson of whatnot", "big chief number one", and so on.

Thomasius decided not to bother with the temple or the inn. Or that he thought anyone was beautiful.

Corvo took off his superb silver torque—interesting that the Sueni hadn't stolen it from him, perhaps it was too obviously a mark of his chieftainhood?—and offered it to Thomasius, with tears in his eyes. Then he offered him his silver armbands. No, Thomasius wouldn't take them. He didn't take bribes. But Decius did, so they might yet be useful.

They walked into the inner part of the fortress. On the way, they passed a group of men from Thomasius's unit, who were relaxing off-duty. After all the saluting was done, they asked him where he was going with the "interesting gentleman". Did he now have a "pet barbarian"? Or was this colorful character his new instructor, ha, ha? (All his men knew about the Sub-officer's struggles with the Horse People's funny lingo, and most of them thought it was a hilarious waste of time.)

Thomasius didn't mind being laughed at. He had a good relation-ship with most of the men in his unit, and he knew that when it came to it, when there was serious action going on, his men would trust him unconditionally, and follow him anywhere.

Except to the door of Company-commander Decius.

When he told them where it was they were going, they offered their sincere condolences. Decius! The last person that *any* of them would go to voluntarily was their Company-commander. Some of them offered opinions on the beloved Company-commander's parentage, the size or condition of his genitals, or the fate that they considered he deserved (if any of them ever had the chance to influence it); one of them grinned lugubriously at Thomasius, and made a throat-cutting gesture.

None of them knew where Decius was.

For what seemed like hours, Thomasius led Corvo to all the differ-ent places where the Company-commander might have been expected to be found, since he wasn't known to be off-duty: wardrooms, the tiny company secretariat, store-rooms, and even the men's barracks. Finally, he learned that Decius was in his personal quarters.

That was bad news. He wasn't supposed to be there while he was on duty, and he wouldn't appreciate anyone drawing attention to it. Nor would he much like being disturbed, whatever it was he was doing. Probably he was snoozing, or drinking; maybe both. He certainly wouldn't be having sex. Decius had never been able to persuade anyone to become "his girl", he wasn't one of those officers who buggered the recruits, and you didn't invite whores to your quarters, you went to where they worked.

It was quite a long walk. When they got there, Thomasius thumped on the Company-commander's door, and then opened it without waiting for an invitation to enter. There was no point in showing that you were frightened: Decius could always smell fear, and he fed off it. Even when you were weaker, or outnumbered, the frontal attack was the only way to approach this kind of enemy.

Decius was lying on his bunk, bleary-eyed but still half-awake. The table was littered with dirty plates. There was also an overturned lead cup, which, to judge by the stains and pools on the table immediately around it, had probably been used for quaffing cheap wine. There was no sign of the Company-commander's orderly: either he had slipped away the first moment he could, as his master sank into a stupor, or he had been driven off with curses and a drunken kick up the backside.

Decius struggled upright when he saw his Sub-officer, shouted at him as expected, but then stopped and goggled with outrage when he saw who was standing behind him. Thomasius began to explain who this was, and what he wanted; he didn't get very far. The Company-commander was now wide-awake, and venomous.

"Sub-officer, this time you really have gone too far! This is unbelievable. You've been traipsing round the fortress with this horse-fucking gentleman, explaining everything nicely, showing him the way around, the layout, telling him where everything is... I can't believe it! He's probably a fucking spy!"

Thomasius held his ground.

"The Horse People are our allies, sir. We have a duty to help them."

"Help them my arse! Next time the horse-fuckers go on their annual burn-rape-and-pillage, we'll have *you* to thank for it when they come rampaging through here cutting off our dicks. Let's just hope they start with yours."

Decius managed to clamber to his feet. This didn't make him more impressive; rather the opposite, in fact. He was a small man—which may have been at the root of his problem with people of even slightly more imposing build, like Thomasius. He was also decidedly ugly, with a wide, toad-like face, and a tendency to drool as he spoke.

"The Sueni troopers brought him in at his own request, sir. I thought it would be best to bring him straight to you."

"Oh, and why is that? To deliberately disturb me in the few quiet moments that I have? To upset my digestion?"

"You *are* the senior duty officer, sir."

As the words slipped out, Thomasius realized that it was a bad, bad mistake to remind Decius that he was on duty, and therefore shouldn't have been lazing about in his quarters.

"Don't you dare tell me how to do my job! You arsehole! Who do you think you are! Your own whore of a mother won't recognize you when I'm finished with you! I'll turn your guts into giblet stew! You'll wish you'd never been born! I'll—"

And then, behind Thomasius and Corvo, the door opened. The Company-commander gawped past them in amazement, and sprang to attention as best he could.

Staff Officer Petronius wafted fragrantly into the room, followed by two clomping soldiers in full gear.

"Sir!"

"Why are you half-dressed, man, and not on duty?" Decius could only gulp. "What? Speak up, man!"

Thomasius saw a way to repair some of the damage.

"Sir, permission to speak? The Company-commander was taken sick. Something he ate. I had to escort him to his quarters. He's still not well."

Thomasius's explanation seemed to satisfy the officer. Petronius was an exquisite young man, especially in his dress uniform, but he wasn't the sharpest arrow in the divisional quiver. When Sol was handing out intellect, Petronius must have been standing way back in the line. (Along with one or two other Staff Officers that Thomasius knew.)

"Good thinking, Sub-officer. You'd best take over the rest of his duty shift for him."

"Sir!"

"Now there's some story going round about a Horse People chieftain who was brought in by a patrol today. This must be that same gentleman? Good. Lord Commander Rhaetius wishes to see him at once. This way, please."

When Corvo failed to react, Petronius gingerly took his arm and began to move him towards the door.

"Sir, you might need an interpreter. Perhaps the Sueni Troop-commander who brought him in?"

"Again, good thinking! It's Sub-officer Thomasius, am I right? You'll soon have your own company at this rate! But there's no need for an interpreter. The Lord Commander speaks the Tongue fluently, I'm told. Right, let's go!"

Thomasius should have left with them. It would have been more sensible. Because if he had been hoping for a word of gratitude from Decius, he was promptly disappointed.

"That was clever, Sub-officer. Or should I say: *Company-commander*? Oh, you were lucky there. Saved by the fancy-boy! I wonder who arranged that?"

"Sir, I had better go on duty."

"Oh, yes, *my* duty. Alright, go and do my job for me, but don't get any funny ideas about taking over my company. I'll have to watch you. In fact, I'm watching you *right now*, arsehole! Now get out of my sight!"

Thomasius found out quickly enough what had happened, when he met Grassica coming off duty at the inner gate.

"As you know, comrade, our rank doesn't automatically entitle us to having an orderly, but there is a charming local lady who cooks for me, looks after my clothes, and warms my bed. I sometimes have to remind her to wash, but otherwise it's an arrangement that I can heartily recommend."

"Arrangement?"

"Well, there is a certain commercial aspect to it. But don't get me wrong: Gemma loves me deeply. She's not a whore! Of course, it's a bit more expensive than having to pay one of the men to do for you"— which is how Thomasius had always got by—"unless your tastes happen to lie in that direction, so that you actually favor that option."

"Sol forbid!"

"Quite."

"But what does all this have to do with Lord Commander Rhaetius?"

"Have patience, comrade, I'm coming to it! Now, my lady friend has a sister, Gemmella, who was looking to find similar employment at the fortress. Knowing that you prefer to save your money, I introduced her to Staff Officer Petronius. The poor boy had been looking lonely. She almost wet herself when she saw him! As you'll be aware, he's, er, a lot prettier than either of us. Gemmella herself is also quite a sweet little thing. So, he's a stupid, upper-class twat, to be sure, but now he's a *happy*, stupid, upper-class twat. And he owes me."

"You mean…?"

Grassica smiled.

"It didn't take long. While you were roaming the fortresss with your horsey gentleman, I spoke to my lady friend; she went straight to her sister; her sister spoke to Petronius; and Petronius spoke to the Lord Commander. 'Chain of command' is what it's called. It's the way we do things round here, comrade, and it works very well."

X

DECIMUS HAS URGENT BUSINESS IN THE NORTH

The road to the north.

Decimus left the City by the North Gate, mounted sedately on a riding mule. For long distances, mules were far more comfortable than horses. He would be traveling in the guise of a trader in amber, riding north to buy the "golden tears" that wealthy Citizens' wives found so appealing.

The Horse People and the Sueni bought them from traders who had crossed the mountains with sealskins, dried fish and other products from the Fish People of the icy northern shores. These, and furs that they had bought from the Free People, they traded for horses, hunting-dogs, and whatever Citizen products the tribesmen no longer needed, or preferred to sell for a profit.

The tribesmen themselves regarded amber as unlucky, but were willing to trade it onwards. The wise men of the Sueni explained that the creamy yellow pieces were dried and petrified drops of milk from the teats of the Earth Cow, while the transparent ones came from her vagina. Such dangerous objects had no place among the possessions of honest men. Let them bring misfortune on the Citizens!

A trader in amber, even a strong young man like Decimus, would not be riding a horse for such a long journey. As he was a beginner in the trade, he could not yet travel with armed servants, though if he was successful in his quest, he would hire bodyguards for the return route. In the meantime, he carried a sword. Men of ill intent would certainly think twice about tackling him. It was easy to believe that he was some kind of adventurer, perhaps a former cavalryman who had chosen a quicker way to enrich himself than by long years of service with the Citizen Army.

He was in company with several other merchants and traders, some of them with a small entourage of armed protectors. They had found each other at dawn at the North Gate, on a little square where travelers would meet and make arrangements to travel together. Only a very large robber band would dare to challenge such a group by day; at night, however, they would need to be on their guard.

Decimus had no intention of remaining in their company for long. This was his cover for the departure only, when the eyes of people who wished him (and the General) no good would be watching all activity at the City gates. Mules were too slow. He would switch to a horse as soon as he could.

The General had told him, "Your business, now, is north," and he must try to reach the north as quickly as possible. There was a chain of government rest-houses along many of the main roads, providing those on government business, and private travelers with enough money or influence to obtain an Imperial pass, with food, beds, and fresh mounts. But to take advantage of these facilities would be to draw attention to himself. Instead, he would be using the normal inns and hostelries, and occasionally the services of a small network of informal contacts. He had committed their names and locations to memory. It would be unfortunate if this information fell into the hands of the enemy.

The enemy? "Enemies", more like it. There were so many who were hostile to the General: the Reds, the Blues, the agents of the East. And could even the Whites be trusted? Then there were powerful commercial interests, who resented any intrusion into their affairs; and the followers of the Slave cult also hated the General, seeing him as a bulwark of the old religion of Sol.

The safest route to the north would have been to take the coast road to Portus and from there travel by ship to Maritima; from Maritima, a river-boat would have transported him up the Great River. But this would have been endlessly slow—as well as unendurably boring, Decimus reminded himself—and if the enemy found him, a boat would not be a good place to be cornered. Moreover, at Maritima he would have to enter the eastern half of the Empire, and his identity would be carefully scrutinized.

A second option would have been to take ship to Trebenna (where both Decimus and the General had many friends), and from there use the road through the Riverlands that led to the Stone Gates Pass. The pass itself would be closely watched, but beyond it lay the Province, whose nobles were strong for the General. Senator Terebinthian was the most effective spokesman for the General in debates in the Senate. The people of the Province still followed ancient gods like the Great Mother, the

Horned One, or the Two Riders, and they had no love for the Slave cult favored by the Blues.

This was the route that his enemies would have expected Decimus to take, and for that reason he had chosen a different one. He would stay with the little party of merchants until they reached the central mountains that shielded the City from its outer territories. Then, while his traveling companions were negotiating the passes in single file, he would endeavor to give them the slip, making them believe that he had somehow taken a wrong turning on the mountain road.

After that he would use horses, for speed. He would need to traverse the whole length of the Province, but there was a good road, the Great Provincial Road, that led to Fanum Fortunae on the Amethyst Sea. Once there, his contacts would brief him on what was happening.

According to the General, someone was stirring up the tribes, by encouraging slavers to raid the Sueni and the Horse People. They were targeting the wives of priests, or the children of powerful chieftains, to cause bad feeling against the Citizens.

"The Lord Governors and Lord Commanders of the northern provinces have been told to put a stop to these activities. Lord Rhaetius in Cascantum has been particularly energetic in his efforts; others, I'm afraid, less so."

"Lord Governor Atticus in Fanum Fortunae…"

"Whom you know well!" The General had seemed amused to be discussing the former master with his former slave. "He is a good example of what I mean. He's a stupid rather than a malicious man. But he's a Blue: he may be supporting this foolishness."

"I shall convey your best wishes, my Lord! One of my most reliable sources of information in Fanum works in his household. If I visit the house, I'll be expected to present myself and pay my respects. Do you have a message for him? He knows that I work for you."

Tell him nothing that he doesn't already know, was the answer.

He was to be careful, not intervening directly and openly in the activities of the slavers.

"Any such intervention would be interference in the property rights of the new owners. There have always been slavers at work on the northern frontier, but in the past they *bought* captives or criminals from the tribes, perfectly legally. Or they raided across the Great River into the lands of our enemies. Those activities were legitimate."

Legitimate! Decimus remembered how he himself had been taken, barely out of childhood, in just such a raid; put on sale, naked and trembling, on a whitewashed block in Trebenna; and sold onwards several times, always at a profit, as his owners realized how talented he was. He had never been abused, or beaten, so as not to break his spirit and lessen his value. Most slaves were less fortunate.

Decimus had his own views on the institution of slavery, but he had wisely kept them to himself, merely nodding in agreement with the General, and remarking, "Slavers in those days were careful not to provoke the friendly tribes of the frontier."

"Indeed. And now the Horse People are crossing the Great River into the Empire. They are putting themselves under our protection, the protection of the eagle's wing, as the Sueni did more than a generation ago. We have a responsibility towards them. We can't enslave them at will. We want them as our allies, and one day as loyal subjects. We don't want them as our enemies or as rebels. So find out who is causing this trouble."

"And send you the name, my Lord?"

"No. Send me no messages—who knows who might intercept them? I've sent no signals to the frontier regarding your assignment, for the same reason, and I'm giving you no written instructions. Whatever you find out, take the information to Lord Rhaetius, or bring it to me personally. Soon I may have to leave the City and travel north." And then the General had lowered his voice, and spoken slowly but distinctly. "If you find this man, and you are sure, and you can do it discreetly...*put a permanent end to his activities*. You understand what I mean?"

The first part of the journey went as planned. Despite the earliness of the hour, the area around the North Gate was bustling with activity. It was a wonderful hour of the day, the best time to be traveling, when the air was fresh and cool. Master Aulus, he thought to himself, slugabed under his blankets, had never experienced this time of day, except when coming home in a stupor from a drunken party!

Decimus "attached" himself to a pompous, elderly government official named Plancus, who had been ordered to attend to relatively trivial state business in the Province. Although he was of moderately high rank, no entourage had been assigned to accompany him. He was attended only by his servant, who was even older than Plancus was and distinctly timorous. Resentful by nature, the official had taken this omission as a deliberate affront to his dignity.

Decimus had noticed the servant eyeing the hefty armed attendants of the merchants, and—pointing at his own sword, "a veteran of many battles, with a sharp point and sharp edges too!"—had offered him and his master his services as a bodyguard. A meeting was soon arranged, and his offer accepted, in return for a small fee, the shared use of the servant for cooking duties, and "good company and conversation on the road". The terms were almost implausibly generous, but Plancus still took a long time to come to a decision. (Probably his normal speed of decision-making as a government official! Decimus was only too familiar with such gentlemen.)

Plancus proved to be very poor company indeed, recounting in a monotone wearying tales of petty departmental intrigue, which mostly ended with the punchline "Who does he think he is? Well, I showed him, didn't I!" Decimus doubted whether he had ever shown anyone anything, except (and then only after endless negotiation) his willy to the girl next door, when they were both five.

He was hugely relieved to get away from the man. The moment came, at dusk, on a road in the foothills. Decimus, riding at the back of the column, took advantage of the dust kicked up by the mules and the spreading shadow to slip his own mule quietly between the thorn-bushes that lined the road, setting off down a side-track that he had used before. The travelers were tired, many of them dozing in the saddle, and no-one noticed his departure.

At the next village there was a farmer waiting for him, impatiently, with a horse. By using a higher road across the hills he could overtake his former companions. After that, he would be traveling so much faster than them that there would be no danger of their catching up with him. And none of them, except Plancus, were intending to go as far as Fanum Fortunae.

He changed horses once, but only when he was probably two days ahead of them did he risk staying overnight at an inn. It was not the first of the pre-arranged locations, where there would be a fresh mount waiting for him—this was many hours further on—but he was tired and the horse was exhausted. So there was a slight change of plan.

And he had another reason.

All afternoon he had been followed by two riders on horseback, who kept at a clever distance, much as he would have done if he had been tracking them. Except that he would have done it better. They weren't on mules, so who were they? Thugs or enforcers working for some rich landlord? Robbers? Perhaps out-of-work mercenaries, sitting astride their only property? Or something more sinister?

Decimus almost hoped that they were tracking him. He preferred *knowing* that he was being hunted to strongly suspecting it, but not being sure.

He trusted himself to be able to deal with them if they attacked him directly, though they might use unorthodox weapons like poisoned daggers, tiger-claws, or wire lassos. There were only two of them. But if they aimed to jump him at night? He couldn't afford to camp by the roadside—he wouldn't get a moment's sleep. He needed to be in a room that could be locked or bolted from the inside.

The inn was not ideal. It was ramshackle and dirty, and the eating hall was crowded with ragged-clothed travelers of the meaner kind, no doubt many of them petty thieves or runaways. The innkeeper himself looked as though he might well be an organizer of criminal activities, or the regular receiver of stolen goods. He glowered at Decimus suspiciously—"You're not from here?"—and demanded an exorbitant amount for supper, which turned out to be bread and a greasy stew, washed down with beer of the poorest quality.

As for somewhere to sleep, the inn was full, and Decimus would therefore have to make do with a side-room of the kitchen that was standing empty. There was no bed, but a pallet of straw and some blankets would be provided. If he needed to piss or ease himself in the night, well, he could do it in one of the corners—a suggestion that to Decimus seemed to sum up the inn, and the level of service that it offered, quite nicely.

The maid who brought him the bedding offered to keep him company for the night. This was the customary practice in inns. She was a friendly, dumpy local girl, with plump thighs and an appealing squint, and Decimus, had he not been so tired, wouldn't have been averse to a cuddle. However, should he have night-time visitors with more evil intentions, her presence would only complicate matters.

The room was windowless, as almost all rooms were, so any intruders would have to use the door. But the door had no lock or bolt! That was a nuisance. The room did contain some standing shelving with old cooking pans and skillets that were not in regular use, and Decimus decided to move this furniture against the door. He took down the kitchenware piece by piece, shifted the shelves, and then put the pans back into place.

Loaded with so much metal, the shelves were heavy. Any intruders would eventually be able to push the door open, but it would take a considerable effort and Decimus, who was a light sleeper (like most slaves or former slaves), would be woken by the sound of metal pans crashing onto the stone floor.

He slept fully dressed, with his sword by his side. He had paid the innkeeper extra for a large oil-lamp, which he left burning in a corner, well away from the straw.

When the two men came for him, it happened as he had predicted. By the time his visitors were inside the room, he was ready for them. The taller of the two men came at him, lunging like an infantryman with his sword. Clang! Decimus pushed the sword aside. Next the man took a cavalryman's side-swipe at his target. Decimus parried the blow easily.

In the meantime, the smaller man, holding what looked like a sickle, was trying to get round behind Decimus, but caught his foot on the straw pallet and stumbled. As he fell, Decimus hacked at the side of his neck.

Sol, the man was wielding a farm implement! They had sent part-timers to kill him, not professionals. He didn't feel very flattered.

The swordsman had realized by now that he was facing an opponent he couldn't possibly beat. The third blow that he attempted was half-hearted and completely lacking in confidence. Decimus deflected it at leisure. He then plunged his own sword deep into the man's guts, pulled it out, and, with a mighty swing, as good as decapitated his opponent. It was much kinder that way—with a deep stomach wound, he would have died slowly and in agony.

The smaller man was twitching his life away, bleeding out, his neck half severed.

The room filled up with people, some holding torches. The innkeeper goggled at the scene of carnage. He may have been about to protest, but saw the sharp-edged, bloodstained sword that Decimus was still holding, and changed his mind.

"Do you often allow your guests to be murdered in their sleep?" Perhaps he did. Decimus wouldn't have been much surprised. He didn't wait for an answer. "These two"—he pointed at the bodies; the smaller man had now stopped twitching—"need to be buried, and where they won't be found. If they *are* found, you'll be blamed, so do it well. And clean up this mess, it's like a charnel-house in here. You can sell the horses, if they're not branded. That'll pay you for your pains. If they've got owners' brands, and you don't know how to remove them, kill the horses too. You can offer your guests horsemeat ragout for a month! If anyone asks you, say that the men rode on after me."

He thought of adding: "in the direction of Trebenna". But why bother trying to confuse them? Whoever had spotted him, and sent the killers, knew which direction he was going in. They didn't know *who* he was yet, otherwise they would have sent better men to hunt him down.

He must now be very careful. He must try to stay ahead of his pursuers. Next time that they closed in, it would be with professionals, not clowns. And next time, the odds would be against him.

XI

MARA IS MADE MORE CLOSELY AWARE

OF THE FAR-FLUNG COMMERCIAL

ACTIVITIES OF ISSACHAR OF MARITIMA

✠ *The great northern plain, and the forest.*

Manasa was the natural leader of the group of women. Perhaps as a former slave it was easier for her to accept the situation she was in? She was the only one who wasn't obviously frightened, weepy, or depressed.

Mara had nothing else to do but watch. At first, the trampled grass had been so inviting, but now she felt her bruises, and she wasn't used to sitting around like some toothless old woman grinding corn.

One of the slavers came over to them with some food. Manasa joked with him, and he joked back. She asked him for more food—*and she got it*. He even untied the women's hands for them so that they could eat together. Manasa shared the food with the other women. Mara resolved to watch her carefully. Had she taken this man as a lover? Could this be how to survive until she was rescued by her clan?

"I know what you're thinking, Mara. No, I didn't sleep with him."

"Is he frightened of you as well?"

"Why should he be? He only sleeps with men. But he comes and talks to me, because he's got no-one else to talk to. The other slavers don't like him—they're frightened that he might, well, you know, give them a quick one up the backside when they're not looking!"

Mara asked her whether she had seen a third man with Orcus and Thrasyllus, and could she describe him? Yes, Manasa had seen the other man, but only from a distance.

She gave Mara some good advice.

"Don't boast about your daddy the big chieftain. You're not the princess they were expecting, so that stuff doesn't count. The only thing that counts with them is that you're still a virgin. And because of that, you'll get an easier ride from here to the slave market—no night-time visits from Dirty Fingers for you! That's good news, surely?"

"I heard them talking about me, like cattle to be taken to the market and sold!"

"Yes, because that's what you are now, and what's going to happen to you. So get used to it. And when we reach the market, beg whatever horsey gods you pray to to give you a kind master. Beg them from the bottom of your heart. Because if they don't hear your prayer, your life is not going to be good. You'll be beaten and fucked, and fucked and beaten. And when they don't want to fuck you anymore, they'll work you to death. You'll have only one chance. If you use all your skills as a woman, you can make your master *your* slave. If you know how to do that." She paused. "*Do* you know how to do that?"

"I don't know."

Manasa laughed. "Then obviously you don't!" Then, more kindly: "These are things that can be learned, though. You know how to control a horse with your body, don't you? There are ways to control a man, too. You can make your new master very happy. In the meantime, you belong to Issachar of Maritima. Get used to it!"

Mara asked her who Issachar was, and said that the black man, the "boss", had told Orcus not to speak his name.

How long had Mara been on this earth? And she didn't know Issachar? Anywhere where people were being hurt and frightened, Issachar wouldn't be far away. Which meant that he was *everywhere*. But Mara would find out soon enough.

The women were tied up again and told to sleep until dusk. After that they would be marching, probably for most of the night.

Mara had heard correctly: they were *not* going to Trebenna. Trebenna was the greatest slave market in the western half of the Empire—that was something she *did* know. But Manasa's friend had explained to her that soldiers had been sent out from Cascantum to stop the activities of the slavers. The Lord Commander was angry with them. Those slavers who were caught were put to death very cruelly. The whole area south of the Great River was now swarming with patrols.

Word had been sent that they should go west, to Fanum Fortunae, and sell the slaves there. The merchandise wouldn't fetch so much in the little provincial town, but the journey would be shorter and safer, and fewer slaves, if any, would die on the way. In Fanum, the Lord Governor ruled, not the Lord Commander—and the slavers' activities would not be disturbed.

Mara was so jubilant that the other women had to tell her to keep her voice down. One of the women pinched her viciously and told her to shut up.

But it was good news! If they went west, they would pass by her camp, and the camps of other clans too…

No, said Manasa, they wouldn't be doing that. Because if they went due west, they would have to pass almost under the walls of Cascantum. Also, they would have to cross the Gap between the fortress and the Amethyst Sea, and a major highway as well, before they turned southwest to Fanum.

Unless the slavers were very stupid they would take a safer route. They would follow the wooded southern bank of the lake, marching parallel to the shore, and then turn northwards, going round the lake to reach Fanum on the northern bank. The trees would hide them from patrols, there would be fresh drinking water—the Amethyst Sea was fed by rivers running off the northern mountains—and the slavers might even catch some forest game to supplement the rations. But it would be several days, a week even, of hard marching.

As if that wasn't enough to dampen her spirits, Manasa added that Mara might not easily find a buyer in Fanum.

The Citizens didn't like blondes. In Trebenna, she might have been a novelty, but in Fanum horsey-girls were two for a silver piece in the brothels.

"Some dirty guy will buy *me*, though. I'm what they dream of, hot, dark and sweet, and I know how to make a man's weapon talk." Noticing how downhearted Mara was, she added, "Don't worry, on the way to Fanum I'll tell you all those things about men that virgin princesses need to know!"

The two women cuddled together to sleep for a few hours, for warmth, but also because they'd decided that they liked each other. Mara was sad that, after they reached the slave market at Fanum, they would be going different ways.

They were woken soon enough, and the slavers and their merchandise set off westwards in the direction of the Amethyst Sea. The plan, Manasa said, was to cross the open plain under cover of darkness, camp for the rest of the night just inside the forest, and then continue onwards the next morning. A long march through the forest at night, even if they had the shoreline on their right to guide them, was not practicable. The slaves would be roped together, and in the near darkness the ropes would constantly be snagging in the bushes. Mara didn't quite understand that last bit.

She had never seen a slave caravan before. She had always imagined that there would be shouting and weeping and cracking of whips, and terrible acts of cruelty, and women being abused, but instead both guards and captives marched for the most part in silence, and when a woman did fall down, exhausted, the slavers helped her.

Occasionally Orcus called a halt so that everyone could rest. This was not done out of kindness, Manasa explained: they were goods, to be brought to market in Fanum in the best condition possible, and nothing should be lost on the way.

The "boss" was nowhere to be seen. Manasa's friend told them that he was taking the other, faster, route, past the towers of Cascantum, on his own, to prepare the slave-merchants at Fanum for the arrival of the new merchandise. Orcus, forgiven for the disappointment over the "princess", had been put in charge of the caravan.

There were gasps of relief when they finally saw the tree-line looming up in front of them. They followed it, for no great distance, until they reached the shore of the lake, and then they entered the forest and made camp. The slavers even lit small fires.

Mara had never seen more than two or three trees standing together. But here there were hundreds and hundreds of them, and between the trees there were bushes and undergrowth, and even strange little flowers that were unfamiliar to Mara, who liked flowers. It was a wonderful place, huge and majestic like the grasslands but in a different way. Despite being tired and frightened, she couldn't help but be amazed by the forest.

There was no danger here from patrols—the Citizens disliked the forest, and seldom went into it, except for small hunting parties during the day-time.

Nor were there likely to be any encounters with the forest-dwellers. The little bowmen were shy, and avoided contact with the outside world. They lived further south, in the dense heart of the forest, and kept away from its northern fringes, which were too close to Famum Fortunae and the bustling highways built by the Citizens.

"How do you know all this, Manasa?"

Mara for her part knew only the plain, the Horse People, and the Great River. She'd seen a dead Blood-Drinker, but not close up, and a few Citizen traders and soldiers. And she had seen Sueni. Once, when she was very young, and they still lived far north of the River, her father had taken her with him on the long journey down to Cascantum, to barter horse-dung for Citizen goods that they needed. She had seen the great fortress, an object of wonder, and the bustling market. But these few memories made up all that she knew of the world.

How could Manasa, who was only a slave, know so much more than she did?

Because she hadn't always been a slave of the Horse People, she said. She came from far away, and had been bought and sold more than once, in different places, and had had different masters.

"But none of that matters. All that matters is watching and listening. And we slaves get to do a lot of that."

"What do you mean?"

"Do you worry much about a cooking-pot when you're not using it? Or do you just forget that it's there? Because that's what our masters do. You know, for them we're just like a table or a cooking-pot. But tables and cooking-pots don't watch and listen. Tables and cooking-pots don't *learn*."

"And you've been with lots of men?"

"Oh, most definitely, princess! And sooner or later, some man is going to put his thing in *your* little hole, too. Since you're now a slave—sooner, I imagine."

Mara was shocked, but Manasa told her that it wouldn't be the end of the world. There were far, far more terrible things that could happen. But she didn't want to talk about stuff like that in the dark of the forest. She said that she wanted to sleep, and yawned and turned away from Mara, but let her snuggle up to her.

Mara thought: she said "You're a slave"—is that really what I am now? I'm a captive, yes, a prisoner, until I'm rescued. I've been kidnapped. But I'm not a slave! No! I can't be that! Then sleep took her.

They woke suddenly. It was still very dark. It was too early! What was happening? Something was snorting and rustling near them. A wild boar, perhaps? The young men had told Mara how dangerous they could be. But then there was a human-sounding screech, and shouting.

"Fuck off! Go away!"

Dirty Fingers?

"Mara, keep still."

One of the Sueni women was cursing loudly in her own Tongue. Maybe Dirty Fingers had stumbled over her, or fallen onto her when another woman pushed him away. It was too dark to see what was happening, or who was involved.

There were grunting sounds. More women woke and started complaining.

"Hey! Leave her be, we're tired."

"There's a long march tomorrow."

"Bastard! Go away and use your hand."

"Give her some coppers and do it quickly! I want to sleep."

Then Orcus was there, holding a torch lit from the embers of one of the fires. The light of the torch revealed Dirty Fingers, his breeches around his ankles, lying on top of one of the older women, whose clothes he had opened to allow him to get at her.

There was something about the expression on the woman's face that made Mara think that maybe he wasn't forcing her. But he had probably trodden on several other women in his eager search for this one. Or had he just thrown himself onto one of the women at random?

Caught in the act, Dirty Fingers and his partner blinked into the flickering light of the torch.

Orcus was not amused.

"Shit! You can't leave them alone, can you? If we lose any of them tomorrow, I'll take it out of your share. Now, put that thing back in your breeches, get back to the men, and let these women sleep."

"Sorry, boss."

"Why can't you wait till we get to Fanum? With what you'll earn, you can *buy* yourself one of these women! Two of them, probably, the way prices are now."

"Sure, boss."

Dirty Fingers pulled up his breeches, to the accompaniment of unflattering remarks about his physical endowments. Then he disappeared back into the darkness.

Orcus helped the woman with her clothes—she was still partly bound, so she couldn't do it on her own. The night was cold, and it wouldn't be wise for her to sleep half-naked. He said, "Good night, ladies", and went back to his own improvised bed. With the torch gone, it was dark once more. The women settled down again, but Mara was troubled by her thoughts. She prodded Manasa.

"What do you want? What *I* want, princess, is to get some more sleep. If you don't mind."

"Don't you think it's strange?"

"What?"

"Orcus is so ugly, and so crude. And he stinks. I think he looks like a pig. But he isn't a cruel man, is he? He's doing his job, that's all, and he doesn't try and hurt us deliberately."

"Yes. So what?"

"Well, Dirty Fingers is quite good-looking. Compared to Orcus, anyway. But he really *is* a pig. I wonder if Orcus has a family? I'm sure that Dirty Fingers hasn't!"

Manasa laughed softly.

"Well well well, the princess is growing up! That's quite a useful discovery that you've made there."

"Do you think so? What discovery?"

"The discovery that people aren't always what they look like. Anyway, now that you know it, don't you ever forget it."

"Was he forcing her? I don't think he was."

"Why don't you ask her, then? No, leave her alone. Look, forget it. I'm tired. Tomorrow will be a hard day. Go to sleep."

There were no more disturbances.

XII

AULUS HAS VISITORS, WHO ARE

RUDELY KEPT WAITING

✠ *The house of Senator Lucius Pomponius Atticus, in the City.*

Aulus had barely finished his breakfast when visitors were announced.

Normally, visiting at breakfast-time would not be regarded as socially acceptable. However, it was no longer breakfast-time. It was closer to the hour when most Citizens would be considering interrupting their work, with a good conscience, to seek some well-earned midday refreshment. But for Aulus it was still early: he had taken his uncle's rebuke to heart and was making an effort to start his day more promptly.

He was not in a good mood. His breakfast had been served, as usual in the summer months, on the terrace. Normally he liked sitting there, or lying, stretched out on a couch, recovering from the evening before and letting the tasty food set him up for the rigors of the evening to come. The terrace caught the sun rather nicely, especially at the late hour that Aulus tended to breakfast there.

This was too early, though. The terrace was surprisingly chilly, and his food had been served by the lady's maid Sinica, and not by the footman Beltran, or by someone presentable from the kitchen.

Why did it have to be Sinica?

She had previously belonged to his father, until she earned the displeasure of his dear mother and was bartered for a crystal vase that Lady Pomponia coveted and her sister-in-law had no use for. He remembered Sinica from his nocturnal visits to the slaves' quarters many years before. She had been older than he was, a friendly, mature young woman from the south. Their encounters had (from Aulus's point of view) been shamefully unsuccessful.

At the time, she hadn't made fun of him, as some of the other girls had done. Now, older, broader-hipped and more placid—she had turned into a typical member of the Lucius Atticus household!—she probably *did* laugh at him behind his back, and recount old stories about "Junior" to her friends among his uncle's house-slaves.

He still suffered agonies of embarrassment whenever she waited on him. He found it hard to meet her eye (not that slaves were allowed casual eye-contact with their masters, of course, but these things did happen, didn't they?) and often he thought he detected her trying to suppress a quiet smile when she was in his presence.

His uncle was out of the house. He had been called to the Senate for a committee meeting, or so Davus had told him. Yet another reform of the coinage was apparently under discussion, which in practice would mean another debasement of the gold coins. The silver ones had already been reduced to copper with a thin silver coating, a plating which soon rubbed off. They fooled no-one, and were popularly known as "Maximians", because, like the dynasty, they constantly declined in quality. Most merchants demanded to be paid in "real" silver.

For once, Davus hadn't gone with him. He was sick, with the back pains that so often troubled him, and Beltran was therefore attending the Senator.

Why oh why did it have to be Sinica? Was there really no-one else available? Had all the rest of the house-slaves been given a day off? Were they in hiding? Had they mutinied, or run away to join the bandits in the mountains? Why Sinica?

Sinica had served the Senator's wife for several years, waiting on her, doing her hair, listening to her complaints about her husband, and taking care of her wardrobe. After the mistress died, no-one was sure what to do with her maid. There was no longer a lady in the house for her to serve. The widowed Senator might have sold her, or taken her into his bed—she was still attractive enough, in a bland way—but Lucius Pomponius Atticus was not that kind of man. He still pined for his wife, and his wife had trusted and liked her maid.

So Sinica remained in the household of Senator Atticus, but without clearly defined household duties. She had an easy life, serving wherever extra hands were needed, and in any part of the house. Aulus would have freed her long ago, and set her up in a little shop somewhere—preferably in a different city!—if only to spare himself the embarrassment of seeing her and having to talk to her.

Now, having cleared away the remains of his breakfast, she returned to announce to Aulus the arrival of visitors.

"Well, who is it then?"

Aulus never quite knew how to talk to Sinica, so whatever he said usually came out sounding much ruder than he wanted it to sound.

"Sextus Julius Placidus, Master."

"Yes, well, send him in then."

There was a pause. Was that a giggle? No, surely not? Aulus was once again letting her presence unsettle him. For Sol's sake! He braced himself and gave the maid what he hoped was a look of masterful authority.

"Forgive me, Master. I can't."

"What? Explain yourself!"

The maid stiffened, but kept her eyes lowered.

"My master the Senator gave orders that no visitors should be permitted to enter the house until his return from the Senate."

This was said in the low, emotionless undertone that slaves always adopted when they had to pass on something that you didn't want to hear.

"Oh, this is ridiculous! Sextus Placidus is from a family of Senators, and you are keeping him waiting in the street like a delivery boy!"

"The master your uncle gave orders…"

"Damn it, fetch Davus, even if you have to carry him here!"

She saluted him, and went back into the house.

What a stupid business. It was obvious to Aulus what his uncle was up to. He was to receive none of his young friends, men or women, until he had fulfilled his uncle's demand and supplied him with a name, or two names, to be sent to his mother. The week was nearly up, and Aulus had not been able to think of any.

Was he being punished? Or simply shielded from distractions, so that he could make up his mind more quickly? How dare his uncle treat him like this! But what could he do about it? He had no way to fight back. He had no money, he had no slave of his own, and he desperately needed his uncle's support.

At such a moment, Decimus would have been useful. But Decimus had been called away to the General almost immediately after their last meeting, and given marching orders.

Stiff-backed, and with great, almost theatrical, dignity, and the usual serious look on his face, Davus stepped out onto the terrace. Instead of announcing the secretary, as she ought to have done, Sinica remained by the door, watching from a safe distance.

Aulus apologized for having had him dragged from his sick-bed. He looked fit and sprightly enough, but that could be misleading. This was a man who had devoted his whole life, as slave and freedman, to serving his master. He would never give any indication that he was unable to fulfill those duties, however cruelly he might be suffering. And he would have gone to the Senate with his master, too, but over the years Lucius Atticus had learned to spot the tiny clues that meant that his secretary was in pain.

"Thank you for your kindness, sir. How may I help you?"

Actually, Davus had already helped him massively by warning him about the contents of his mother's letter.

In public, the secretary frequently looked at his master's frivolous nephew with an expression of worried disapproval—and what was there *not* to disapprove of in Aulus? Privately, as Aulus knew, the freedman liked him and would always help him if he could, provided that it didn't require him to betray his master.

Was it because the Senator had no children, and Aulus was the nearest thing to a son that Lucius Atticus would ever have? Davus realized it, even if his master didn't.

Aulus asked him why it was that a man who was the son of one Senator (albeit a Senator who had died many years ago) and the nephew of two others (who were among the richest and most powerful men in the Empire) was being kept waiting abjectly at the door? And Davus phrased his answer in a way that Aulus hadn't expected. Instead of referring to the Senator's orders, he pointed out that young Sextus Placidus belonged to a family who were his master's bitter enemies (which was undoubtedly true). How could such a man be allowed entry into the Senator's house without the Senator's express permission?

"Oh, come on, Davus… Sextus hates his uncles just as much as we do. And he has nothing to do with their schemes and plots. This is a social visit. He's been here often enough before. He's come to discuss his poetry with me!"

That was an appeal to Davus the man of letters, but the freedman's face registered nothing.

Help came from a most unexpected quarter.

"Master, have I your permission to speak?"

He had almost forgotten that Sinica was still there.

"Yes, if you really must."

Damn, there it was again!

"There are *two* visitors, Master. Lord Placidus, and the Lady Fannia of the Cornelii."

"Oh!"

Fannia. Aulus should have felt deeply offended that Sextus was flaunting his conquest in front of him: the same Fannia that Aulus had so much set his heart on. But on this occasion, it was perfect that Sextus had not come on his own.

"You see, Davus? A *social* visit! It's completely harmless! Sextus would hardly bring his girlfriend with him if he wanted to talk politics, would he?"

Aulus had noticed how the secretary had pursed his lips at the mention of Lady Fannia. Word of her reputation had clearly reached Davus long ago. It was not a reputation based on any activities of a literary or a political nature.

Davus made one last attempt to prevent the visit.

"The Cornelii are *also* supporters of the Reds, sir. They too are no friends of your uncle's."

"But nor are they his personal enemies. Unlike the Placidi. The *other* Placidi, of course," he added quickly, to exclude his notorious but unpolitical friend Sextus, "you know what I mean?"

"Yes, sir."

"Senator Cornelius Rufus"—Fannia's boring uncle, the father of the boring Cornelia and the head of the whole Cornelian clan—"is a man of impeccable integrity, who just happens to have different political opinions to those of my uncle."

How can I be so pompous, Aulus thought, surely Davus won't take me seriously? But he seemed to take the bait.

"That is true, sir."

"Opinions that are also different to my own, it goes without saying."

Do I *have* any political opinions? He realized that that might have been a step too far. Davus wouldn't be fooled, and he didn't want to get into a discussion about politics with the erudite freedman. Davus could run rings around him on almost any serious topic. No, on *any* topic. But now the secretary showed that he was willing to cooperate a little.

"Senator Cornelius Rufus has been a guest in this house. He expressed his condolences upon the death of your lady aunt, both in writing and personally, and he was received by your uncle with great courtesy. The Senators have also been known to exchange formal greetings in public."

Ah, you see! It's not so hard.

"Yes, I was just going to mention that. Naturally I will take full responsibility for Sextus Placidus and the Lady Fannia entering the house in my uncle's absence. If he asks, I shall say that you were in your quarters, resting, and that the house-slaves"—he nodded in the direction of Sinica—"were not aware of the visit. Except for the gatekeeper, Servo, of course. Let me think… Ah, yes, I met my guests outside on the street, and invited them in. I overruled the gatekeeper's objections. Please speak to him, Davus, and make sure that he will confirm this story if asked."

The gatekeeper was huge but slow-witted. It would take several attempts before he understood what was required of him. Let Davus do the hard work before returning to his sick-bed!

"I will make those arrangements, sir, and the maid can show your visitors to the terrace. But I would humbly suggest that, in the interests of propriety, she remain in attendance."

And to spy on me too! Oh well, if that is the price that Davus demands of me...

"Agreed. Show them in, then, and arrange with the kitchen for some refreshments to be provided. Sextus is picky, but he likes figs in honey. And fresh fruit. And nut-biscuits. The Lady Fannia has a voracious appetite—she'll be satisfied with anything that is on offer."

Oh dear, *that* didn't come out quite as he had intended.

Aulus felt a desperate need to talk to someone sympathetic about his situation. In the absence of Decimus, Sextus would have to do, but could he speak openly to him with Fannia hovering in the background? Fannia, who was renowned for her loud mouth and rude, cynical way of talking to people.

Before the death of the Senator's wife, she could have been taken to meet the lady of the house, but now there were no ladies for her to be presented to. She could hardly be left in the entrance hallway, or told to visit Davus.

Actually, you didn't *tell* Fannia to do anything, unless she already wanted to do it.

And the maid would be lurking in the corner, listening intently, and remembering every single interesting tidbit of gossip. These would be retold later, with humorous embellishments, in the slaves' quarters, especially if Fannia had humiliated him with some memorable witticism.

This was not going to be an easy meeting. But at least his uncle wouldn't be there.

XIII

FLORIANUS DOESN'T HAVE TIME TO FINISH DEALING WITH THE PAPERWORK; SOME DECISIONS WILL THEREFORE HAVE TO WAIT

✠ *The Imperial Palace.*

The messenger from the General found Florianus at work at his desk. There were Palace accounts to be checked and double-checked, a request from the Commander of the Imperial Guards for repairs to be done to the roof of the Guardsmen's quarters—and who, Florianus asked himself, would pay for that?—and a complaint from the Chief Steward that Guardsmen were relieving themselves at will in some of the courtyards, rather than using the privies. But they were barbarians: what did the man seriously expect them to do?

There were punishment orders to be confirmed, overruled or commuted. Florianus, who was in charge of the Imperial Household, always gave these orders careful attention. He liked to err on the side of magnanimity, if only in the interests of staff morale: the Palace servants, he felt, were being badly demoralized by the capricious punishments being handed out by the Emperor.

Bestowing mercy also made him feel good. And it gave him influence and popularity. Those who benefited would later come to *him* for help or with information, rather than go to one of the other wielders of power within the Palace walls. In this way he had been able to build up a network of informants around the Emperor.

It was not that Florianus was squeamish. Far from it. He had thoroughly enjoyed watching the flogging of an insolent butler who had occasionally looked at him with that same "I am a complete man" sneer on his face that Julian sometimes had. (Come to think of it, that might be a better way to settle accounts with Julian, once his usefulness had ended, rather than by castrating him. Why be so excessively brutal to a man that he despised anyway?)

An assistant cook had been caught stealing expensive spices from the pantry. Not for his own use, but for resale. There was a spices market temptingly near to the Palace. The Palace was a major customer for spices, and many of the great nobles had town-houses nearby. For all that anyone knew, the same spices might have been bought by the Palace kitchen several times without ever being used.

This time, the thief had been caught red-handed. Literally: black-handed, with his hands covered in expensive black pepper. He was a slave, and so had to be punished. However, assistant cook was a more senior rank than it sounded—the man in question might be responsible for a significant part of the kitchen's output, cooked vegetable dishes, say, or puddings. The order was to cut off his right hand and then sell him. Extreme punishments for slaves had been outlawed many years before, at a time when the followers of the Slave cult completely dominated the Senate, but the Imperial Prerogative was not bound by the laws of the Empire.

Who would benefit if the man were punished like that? He was a highly trained specialist. How long would it take to replace him, or train one of the junior kitchen staff up to his level of skill? And even if only the first part of the sentence were carried out, what use would the man be in the kitchen if he only had one hand?

Florianus was mulling over possible milder punishments—stealing on this scale couldn't be ignored completely—something like a severe flogging, perhaps, with the loss of certain minor rights and privileges—when the Guardsman told him that the Lord General requested the honor of his presence in the Silver Rooms.

It might not have been phrased like a command, but Florianus knew that it was one.

He locked away only the confidential papers, leaving the rest on his desk, and was soon on his way. To his surprise, they took a different route into the Silver Rooms, walking through a part of the Palace that was apparently open even to daily visitors, and down a long corridor lined with punishment platforms and stocks, and with hooks, chains, and manacles set into the walls.

The Emperor's famous grandfather had never used these facilities. He was a choleric but also generous man, and the punishments that he ordered within his household ranged from immediate execution to tearful admonition (followed by forgiveness), with very little in-between. Standard punishments, like floggings, or servants being shamed by being made to stand with a board around the neck specifying their particular misdemeanor, were seldom carried out.

His feeble son had left these matters to be dealt with by the High Chamberlain, at least where members of the Imperial household were concerned. Which was sensible: punishment should be systematic and predictable, inexorable but tempered with mercy, where mercy was due.

Maximillus took a more personal interest, however. Attached to hooks on the wall was the drooping, naked body of a miscreant. There was a board around his neck, but instead of spelling out his crime it simply invited passers-by to remove a large or small part of the man at their pleasure; knives, saws, pincers, and gouging instruments were laid out on a table beside him. Florianus noticed as they walked past that several fingers had already been taken, and the stumps cauterized with a hot iron. He couldn't remember having signed any such order of execution.

The meeting was not in the small audience chamber. Instead, Florianus found himself in a tiny side-room with no windows, containing only an unlit brazier, a small table (on which there were several parchments and scrolls), and two simple camp-stools. The light came from slow-burning torches in functional-looking wall-brackets, and from a single oil-lamp suspended over the table. The General was alone, without servants or attendants. This was reportedly how he housed when he was on campaign. Was he deliberately reconstructing his favored work environment, cold, plain, and uncomfortable, amidst all the luxuries of the Palace?

This would be a working meeting, the General announced, and a brief one too. He invited Florianus to be seated, and then took the other camp-stool, sitting on it with much greater ease and comfort than the eunuch could manage. Florianus was soon aware that this was an item of furniture designed for muscular military backsides, and not for broad, flabby, unmilitary bottoms like his own.

"We won't be disturbed here, my Lord, and you can talk freely. There will be no record of our meeting, and I wish you to be frank with me. You are High Chamberlain, and Controller of the Imperial Household. The safety and well-being of his Imperial Majesty are in your hands! To the best of my knowledge, he trusts you implicitly. As I do too. You also have the opportunity, no, the *duty*, to guide him in many areas of his life. And, although in public you are not a leader of the Whites, and as a eunuch never could be, behind the scenes you wield political influence in no small measure."

Florianus struggled to find a suitable response. The General's little speech had not been expected, and had caught him off guard, but he had to admit that it was a fair assessment.

The Whites were an uneasy mixture: older military commanders who remembered Maximus with affection; priests of Sol, which had been the state religion and unchallenged until the rise of the Slave cult; and toadying courtiers and functionaries who owed their positions to the Maximian Dynasty. There was no recognized leader of the White faction in the Senate—they were either young nonentities, or elderly bores, and they took their orders from the Palace. The role of Florianus in coordinating these disparate elements was considerable, though seldom acknowledged in the way that the General had just done.

It was gratifying to be appreciated for once.

"My Lord, you flatter me! And you do exaggerate my powers. I'm just a working eunuch, a freedman. I have numerous everyday tasks to carry out, and a household to run."

It sounded plausible. For a brief moment, Florianus thought of the assistant cook, whose fate was suspended until after this meeting was over.

"When we last met, I referred to two matters that you need to be informed about, if Whites and Greens are to work together to keep the Empire safe."

"The matter of Julia Placida…"

The General made a dismissive gesture with his hand. They would come to that. The other business was of greater import, and the information that the General has received had now been confirmed from a further source. He tapped one of the parchments with his finger. It was a map.

"The Blood-Drinkers are on the move. They have pushed the Sueni back into their swamps, and the Free People deeper into the mountains and into the lands of the Horse People. This movement is forcing the Horse People across the Great River. Indeed, many of them have already crossed."

"Meaning that there will be panic in the north."

No, the northerners had backbone. There would be far more panic in the City. The news could not be kept secret for long, and then Naevius would have the Mob out on the streets, to put pressure on the General.

His finger went to the map again, but this time pointing.

"Here is the Great River. As early as in the time of Maximus, small groups of Horse People were allowed to cross it and settle within the Empire, provided that they swore loyalty to the Emperor. But soon the whole federation will be south of the River, many thousands of warriors with their families, and there they will find themselves under the protection of the eagle's wing. Whether they like it or not. The alternative to that—"

"A free kingdom within our borders?"

"—is unthinkable. The Empire in the West would begin to break up. The southerners, the Province, the Sueni, the merchants of Trebenna… But an *arrangement* with the Horse People could work."

"Such as we have with the Sueni?"

"Yes, the Sueni have been under the eagle's wing for years, and many of them serve in our armed forces. If the Blood-Drinkers come in great numbers, and not merely as raiders, we shall need the support of *all* the other tribes to hold them back. And they *will* come: because just as we pay them an annual levy"—Florianus noticed how he avoided using the word "tribute"—"to persuade them to stay where they are, someone who must be formidably rich is sending gold across the River to encourage them *not* to."

"No!"

Florianus pretended to be surprised, although his informants had recently informed him about these secret payments, without being able to tell him from whom they came. The Placidi, he suggested, were obvious candidates. Or the Emperor in the East.

"Or both of them, perhaps? And there is another worrying development. Someone, perhaps the same troublemaker, has sent slavers to ravage the frontier, abducting women and children from among the tribes, and *we* are being blamed. This is against my express command. The Sueni are under our protection, by treaty. I have given my word to the Horse People—and once the Senate has debated it formally, there will be a treaty with them too. The effect of these depredations could be to turn the tribes against us, and at a time when we may soon need their active support. So I have put measures in place to deal with this problem."

Florianus thanked the General for taking him into his confidence, and, almost with a sigh of relief, got up from the camp-stool.

With a sudden movement, Ogilo reached out and thrust him down again, so that Florianus bruised his bottom painfully on the wooden frame of the stool. There was still the other little matter, he said: the marriage offer from the Placidi.

He needed information that only the High Chamberlain could give him. Florianus had a lot of day-to-day contact with the Emperor, did he not? Florianus laughed in what he hoped was an appropriately dignified and un-eunuchlike manner.

"True, my Lord, but do I guide and influence him? Why should a young boy on the threshold of manhood listen to a pathetic old eunuch like myself?" Florianus was conscious of how unconvincing he must be sounding. He tried, and failed, to suppress a giggle. "Especially when it comes to those things that most interest a healthy young man of his age!"

There it was, the very question on which the General needed his advice. He jumped to his feet, but gestured to Florianus to remain sitting. Then he began to pace up and down in the small room, not unlike the mangy tiger in its cage in the Palace bestiary.

"A young boy on the threshold of manhood, those are your words. But until he reaches manhood, I am the person entrusted with responsibility for the affairs of state and with the defense of the West. And perhaps for even longer than that, if he should prove to be weak-minded, like his cousin Theodore. As you know, that decision was taken by a Regency Council appointed by Maximus the Younger, the boy's father, on his deathbed. As you will also know, the Regency Council has been disbanded, and the Imperial Council, which might guide and advise the Emperor, exists in name only and never actually meets."

"Oh, you are in charge, my Lord, everybody knows that." He added, apologetically, "You asked me to be frank!"

The General stopped his pacing, and fixed Florianus with an unfriendly glower.

"This is hard, eunuch, but I must ask you something—and what both of us say remains in this room. Is that understood?"

Florianus was stiff with terror. Would they be talking treason? He had no wish to be crucified, or torn apart by horses, or given to the Mob for their amusement—all fates that had been met with by prominent rebels in the not so distant past. The General's laughter had not helped: if anything, it made him appear even more sinister.

"My Lord…"

"You see a great deal of his Imperial Majesty, don't you? Far more than I do. So—how does the Emperor spend his time under your supervision, Florianus? I mean, his private time."

"Like any other boy of his age, my Lord. With boyish pursuits."

Even as he spoke, Florianus realized that this was nonsense. No child had ever had so much so much opportunity to indulge any casual whim, however spiteful or degenerate. And Maximillus *did* indulge himself, in ways that the eunuch often found distasteful.

"I have heard certain… *stories*. Of unusual cruelties, and unorthodox punishments. There is an example in the punishment corridor, as you will have seen. I instructed them to bring you here by that route. Was that *your* work, my Lord Chamberlain?"

"No, my Lord. It was done without my knowledge."

"Interesting. But what interests me more is what his Majesty gets up to in his private rooms."

"Little amusements, my Lord, for the most part. Like pulling the wings off flies. That sort of stuff. He'll grow out of it."

"Pulling the wings off flies? And not off slave-girls?"

"Oh." The eunuch was surprised that the General knew, but also momentarily amused by the image that he had chosen. He responded stupidly. "I didn't know that slave-girls *had* wings!"

"Or slave-*boys*, then?"

Florianus shrugged his shoulders, trying to make the gesture look casual. No Citizens were harmed. Only slaves were involved.

"And nothing ever goes beyond the Golden Rooms."

The General looked at him sternly.

"Obviously it *does*, otherwise I wouldn't have heard about it, would I?" Florianus felt the General's words like a whip across his shoulders. "Does his Majesty participate actively in these 'boyish pursuits', or does he just watch?"

"His Majesty gives orders, but he is seldom present when they are carried out. He is a sensitive boy, as his father was. His feelings are delicate. His stomach, too—he is easily brought to vomiting. He does like to see the results of his orders, though."

The General looked puzzled. What pleasure could the boy derive from that?

Florianus explained that the Emperor probably only wished to satisfy himself that his commands had been fully obeyed.

"Hmmm. That is a very small satisfaction to be harvested from so much... drastic activity."

The eunuch smiled.

"It is our duty to satisfy his Majesty's wishes, not to question them. He is closer to God than you or me, General." His voice dropped. "He wields great power—"

The General's eyes flashed.

"No, eunuch, *I* wield great power!"

"Of course, my Lord, I am sorry."

Again, Florianus felt that he was walking close to the edge of a chasm that might at any moment swallow him up. But how should he tread, to avoid toppling into the depths? There was something here that he didn't yet understand. He didn't know what to say, but the General helped him.

"But he *believes* that he has such power, my Lord Chamberlain, since everything is done in his name! And because none of you, I imagine," he added drily, "ever tell him otherwise. But do continue with what you were telling me."

"It pleases his Majesty greatly to see the terror that he creates. So there is no need for him to actually witness the carrying out of his commands."

"And he takes no direct, er, *physical* pleasure from these encounters with slave-girls? Or slave-boys?" He paused, and laughed. "Or flies?"

"No. His Majesty is very fastidious. And he has a horror of being touched."

"Even when he is alone with them?"

"I don't understand, my Lord."

"Come on, man! You were once a eunuch of the women's quarters, weren't you? Does he *use* them? Does he do things to them? Or maybe he prefers that they do things to *him*? Is he physically ready? He has *got* a prick, hasn't he? There is no stunting of his development, no medical problem that I need to know about?"

"No, my Lord. But perhaps shyness holds him back?"

"Then he takes after his miserable father, rather than his grandfather. Maximus was quite disgustingly potent. He's a weird little creature, our Maximillus! How that family has degenerated."

Florianus coughed, and looked nervously around the room, as if the walls might have ears—as the Palace walls sometimes did. If anyone should be listening to them…

The torches flickered. Florianus felt a sudden draught.

"I didn't quite hear that, my Lord. Did you say something, your Excellency? I didn't fully catch what you said. We are all concerned for his Majesty's well-being."

"Oh, I said nothing, Florianus. Nothing that needs to leave this room. And this room is secure." There was a pause. "So—do you think he can be normal with a woman? With Julia Placida, say? Or would he try to pull *her* wings off, too?"

"I don't know, my Lord."

"I am asking this with his Majesty's best interests in mind. It would be very dangerous for all of us if he *damaged* her. Don't you agree? The point of this proposed union is to bring the Reds closer to his Majesty's cause, so to speak. Not to unleash their fury against him. Do you know the girl?"

"No, my Lord. The Placidi aren't in the habit of cultivating me socially!"

"Nor me, my Lord Chamberlain."

"She's young, that's all I know. And she's quite pretty, I'm told." He giggled. "I'm obviously not a good judge of feminine attractiveness. She'll do what's expected of her, though nobody will ask her whether she wants to be an Empress or not."

"Or whether she wants to be Maximillus's wife. Yes, she'll spread her legs if her revolting uncles tell her to, Sol help the poor child. By the way—find out whether she is still a virgin."

"There is a required ritual, my Lord, in such situations. Her uncles have no choice but to submit her for inspection."

"Good man! I knew that you would be well-informed about the necessary formalities." He smiled coldly. "More a eunuch's line of business than a general's."

"My Lord."

"Let the Senators know that if their offer is accepted this ritual may be expected of her. And say nothing to his Majesty yet—there are still a few aspects of this offer that I need to consider." He paused. "I wonder whether she is still intact? She is a Placida... I'd hardly expect it!"

Florianus coughed.

"There are procedures for *reconstituting* virginity in such cases. And his Majesty would hardly notice anyway."

"Thank Sol I'm not a woman!."

XIV

AULUS DISCOVERS THAT HE AND

SEXTUS PLACIDUS ARE IN THE SAME

BOAT, METAPHORICALLY SPEAKING

⊞ *The house of Senator Lucius Pomponius Atticus, in the City.*

Sextus Placidus propelled himself onto the terrace before Sinica had any chance to announce him, with Lady Fannia of the Cornelii snapping bad-temperedly at his heels like an underfed terrier.

"Look, I don't want to make a fool of myself, Fannia."

"Oh, be quiet, I know what I'm doing!"

"I don't think that you do. We can't drag Aulus into this. It wouldn't be right."

"And why not? Why not give it a try?"

"People will be laughing at us."

"Aulus can help, he always does! Don't you, Aulus?"

"Of course! Always! Do I?"

Aulus was grateful to be noticed at last, although he had no idea what his guests were talking about. He invited them to be seated, but Sextus had already flounced onto a couch, while Fannia paced angrily up and down. Perhaps she was annoyed at having been kept waiting at the door?

When they came in, Aulus's attention had at first been fixed on Fannia. What a gorgeous creature she was! She wasn't tall, and some might find her slightly too fleshy, but everything about her was so rounded and protuberant, in the most charming way, with hints of exquisite physical delights awaiting the explorer of the dimples of her plump cheeks, the curve of her breasts, the recesses nestling between her thighs and buttocks. And, damn it all, it was Sextus, not Aulus, who had explored there! And told the world about his discoveries, in memorable verse!

But it wasn't easy to ignore Sextus Placidus for long. And he didn't like being ignored.

There was, first of all, the perfume, which would have made itself apparent right across the width of the Great Arena. Not that Sextus had ever been to the Great Arena: the screams of the dying swordfighters and the bellowing of the wild beasts would have been an unbearable affront to his senses, or so he said. And now the followers of the Slave in the Senate had managed to get the traditional games suspended in any case.

And then there were the clothes: breeches of dyed silk, and an over-garment—it was hardly a tunic—consisting of cascading layers of fine material in different colors, decorated with little stars and moons pricked out in golden and silver thread. Unlike Aulus's ensemble, however, the items formed a harmonious whole.

Sextus was very aware of clothes.

"Aulus, you must give me the name of your tailor! That tunic is simply breathtaking!" Aulus was wearing his favorite tunic, the one with the sunbursts. "And the breeches are silk from Maritima, let me guess!"

"No no, it's some kind of material from Sybaris. Expensive enough, though."

"From the south. So, one way or the other, silk or Sybaris, my uncles will be making money out of you."

"But where does your top come from? I've never seen anything like it, it's so…so absolutely…"

He was unable to finish. Fannia stormed in-between them, and glared from one to the other.

"If you two could only hear yourselves! Why don't you form a mutual admiration society? What a pair of moon-struck sweeties you are!"

Sextus looked annoyed, but Aulus squirmed with embarrassment. What must that wretched woman Sinica be making of all this? She'll be fighting hard not to laugh, and what a feast she'll turn it into later in the slaves' quarters! He didn't dare to look at her, but he also didn't dare to send her away.

Sextus now switched to his "hurt" face.

"Fannia, you know that *you're* the only person I love. My poems are the proof of that!"

"Demons from Esbus, have you no sense of humor? But tell him now, please." She turned to Aulus. "We need your help. I'll let my *lover* explain it all. Ah, food!"

Slaves were bringing in bowls of snacks and placing them on the low table that Aulus had used for breakfast. One was a kitchen slave with a huge strawberry blotch across her face. Aulus hoped that Sextus wouldn't be offended by being served by a slave with an unsightly deformity. He was such an aesthete. The girl was pleasant enough otherwise, and very clean (for a kitchen slave). She was only serving because Beltran had accompanied his master to the Senate, and Sinica was on watchdog duty.

Fannia grabbed the bowl of figs in honey just as Sextus was reaching for it.

"Hey!"

"No, *you* talk, *I* eat. If you're well-behaved, I'll leave some for you."

But instead of talking, Sextus tucked into the biscuits. A slave brought out a pitcher of wine diluted with water, and some expensive crystal glasses.

"What is it that you need to explain?"

"Oh, nothing in particular, it's just the usual ups and downs of life…"

"*Sextus!!* Grow some testicles, man!"

Sextus put on the "hurt" face again. Fannia must have been giving him a battering long before they arrived.

"Oh, very well. My uncles are bullying me."

So, what was new about that? Aulus often felt sorry for himself. He had a father who was impossible, a mother who was even worse, and an uncle who was admittedly helpful, but permanently disapproving. Still, Sextus's problems were on another plane: he had no parents at all, and two uncles who, if they weren't themselves demons from the realm of evil, were probably in league with them. Poor Sextus…

"Say it!"

"It's nothing much, just everyday family stuff. It'll soon blow over."

"No it won't." She turned to Aulus again. "You know, for a man who considers himself a writer, Sextus is pretty useless at expressing himself about anything that actually matters." She paused. "He has this teeny-weeny problem: his uncles have told him to marry."

Aulus didn't know whether to laugh or to cry. Sextus too! It must obviously be the time of year for persecuting innocent bachelors.

But why should that be a problem for Sextus? He had a perfectly acceptable allowance; his uncles would probably add a financial sweetener to encourage him to settle down and start a family; and he was already courting someone related to the Cornelii, who were his uncles' principal allies in the City, and the leaders of the Red faction in the Senate.

He made these points to Sextus. What he *didn't* say was that the very thought of Sextus marrying Fannia, as far as he was concerned the most desirable woman on the face of the earth, made him want to cry.

And he couldn't resist taking a dig.

"You know, you're a bit older than me, so you've had your run of freedom, most people would argue." And he added, "Besides, what a bride," imagining himself blushing as he said it.

"Well, thank you, Aulus, that's very sweet of you." His insides almost melted. But the moment didn't last long. She turned to Sextus, and said, in a very different voice, "Your friend doesn't understand, does he? He doesn't understand that this is not a marriage that they'll support."

No, Aulus didn't understand it.

"Oh, come on! Why shouldn't they support the marriage? Fannia, you're one of the Cornelii!"

If Aulus should by some miracle ever become betrothed to Fannia (O blessed thought!), that might bring on heart attacks among the older members of *his* family. But why should the Placidi, who tortured little boys and drank their blood, dug up corpses, and sacrificed babies (or so it was rumored), be worried about their nephew marrying a girl who had never done nothing worse than, how can one put it, *enjoy herself a bit socially*? Why should they care?

Fannia soon put him straight. Her father was dead, her deluded mother had given away the family fortune to the Slave cult—buying herself a good time in the afterlife at her daughter's expense—and there was thus no reason why his uncles would gain anything from having *her* in the family.

Aulus insisted that his friend was an adult Citizen of independent means, who was free to marry anyone he chose. As he said this, he would have liked to have beamed encouragingly at Fannia, but he couldn't quite bring himself to do so. He did manage a modest smile—and received a withering glare from her in response.

"Aulus, you don't seriously believe that? Look, fat uncle has threatened to screw up his allowance for him with legal tricks if he doesn't cooperate. And thin uncle…well, I won't tell you what *he* is capable of doing. I'm a broadminded girl, but Gaius Placidus is not a person you want to cross."

"She's right, Aulus. My uncles have no children of their own. They've only got me, and a ward that I've never seen, Julia—who is my own sister, incidentally! They need both of us for their political tricks and games. Do you honestly think they'd let me marry for *love*?"

Fannia gazed at him with surprising tenderness (not an expression often seen on her face). Aulus was bleeding inside. Would she ever look at *him* like that? He tried to remain calm. He wasn't aware that Sextus had a sister. Well, he was now, Sextus snapped at him, and Sol only knew what nasty little marriage they were planning for *her*.

The time had come for Aulus to tell them.

"I know what you must be going through…because my family are doing the same to me! They want me to marry someone, *anyone*. But it's going to be someone whom I don't love." Because he could only love

Fannia, though he didn't say that. "They've even given me an ultimatum. One week to choose a bride—and that week is now almost up. What am I going to do?"

Sextus and Fannia looked at each other in a rather peculiar (knowing?) way.

"So *both* you boys are being forced to marry someone you don't love. Well, well." Aulus heard her say the words, but why was she purring so? "This throws a new light on things, I would say."

"Does it? How?"

"Fannia, stop it, we can't ask him."

"Why not?" She turned to Aulus. "Have they named any young lady that they specifically approve of?"

"No, they haven't." He tried to change the subject. "Sextus, have they told *you* whom they want you to marry? It would have to be someone from a Senatorial family, I suppose, and there aren't that many Red Senators with eligible daughters, are there?"

Applying his own (and Sextus's) personal criteria for what constituted "eligibility" in a young woman, the answer to that question would be: not a single one. Most of the Reds were adherents of the dreadful Slave nonsense, even if it was the more orthodox Eastern version (Blues like Aulus's parents were followers of the breakaway Western school). Piety and feminine abstinence, the very qualities that the two young men found least attractive in a young woman, would be impressed on the Senators' daughters' minds from the earliest age.

Fannia was a glorious and rebellious exception.

"Aulus, listen carefully. His fate is sealed. They already have a candidate, and do you know who it is? My dear cousin Cornelia! Can you imagine Sextus and Cornelia humping away together?"

Aulus preferred not even to try, although lurid coital images had been flashing through his mind: Fannia with Sextus, Fannia with himself (oh, if only)…

"Her father is the leader of the Red faction in the Senate, but is that supposed to make me lust after her? I *know* which woman I love—"

"Oh, Sextus!"

"—and I *know* which woman I am going to marry!" That was somewhat out of character, so he added: "If and when the time comes."

"*When*, darling."

"Yes, of course—when."

"Which brings us back to you, Aulus. *Sweetie*. Sextus knows whom he loves, and whom he's going to marry. Do you?"

"No. Obviously not."

He couldn't talk about his love for her in front of both of them, and with Sinica listening and silently laughing behind his back.

"That's *good*. Isn't it, Sextus?" Aulus had no idea what she was talking about. "Look, with your help, we can solve both these problems: yours, and ours."

"How?"

"There *aren't* many eligible young ladies out there who would meet his uncles' requirements—except for Cornelia. So if we could take Cornelia off the market, we would gain a breathing space. And who knows what might happen then? Perhaps we could even win his uncles round to accepting *me*…"

"Could that be done?"

Sextus's voice trembled with hope. Aulus had had the same thought, but for him it was cause more for despair.

Fannia was now bubbling over with enthusiasm.

"Why shouldn't it be possible? Cornelius Rufus is my uncle. If I could gain his support, so that he spoke to the Placidi… I can hear him telling them, 'Fannia may not be Cornelia, but she's also part of my family, and close to my heart. If she married Sextus it would be as good as an alliance betwen our two families'. Surely it's worth a try?"

Sextus looked skeptical, but it was Aulus who spoke.

"Why should Senator Rufus agree to it? He would be sidelining his own daughter."

Fannia scoffed at him.

"Why should he agree to it? Because, you dimwit, he doesn't want a Placidus in the family! Who would? Would *you*, Aulus?"

"But you're forgetting that he wants to marry his daughter off. And if the marriage to Sextus doesn't work out, who is going to take Cornelia off his hands?"

Fannia had a strange glint in her eye.

"Well, the answer is obvious, Aulus—it's *you*! She's crazy about you. Why do you think she follows me around? It's to see *you*!"

Oh dear. Aulus poured himself a large glass of wine and drank it down in one draught. He noticed that his hand was shaking.

Sextus glared at Fannia.

"I told you it wasn't a good idea! How can you ask him to sacrifice himself like that? And she's awful! She almost as old as his mother."

That was a huge exaggeration, but otherwise Aulus completely agreed with him. How could Fannia even dream of such a thing?

"For all your poetry, and your clever talk, you boys can't *think* properly! Listen—both of you. If you give Cornelia the *slightest* encouragement, Aulus—some words, a look, your bodies by chance brush against each other casually, you wouldn't even have to kiss her, though a quick kiss would clinch it!—she will dig in her heels and say, 'No! I'm not going to marry that vile Sextus Placidus, that philanderer, my heart belongs to another.' Her father won't force her—he's a kind man, gentle, and dignified. *And the marriage will be off!*"

Aulus was still in shock, and not at all convinced.

"*His* marriage will be off, but mine will be *on*. I'll be left married to Cornelia the Pious!"

Fannia treated him to a radiant, wicked smile.

"No you won't. This is the beauty of my little plan. Cornelius Rufus *might* accept the marriage of his daughter to a debauched layabout, who is the son of a Blue and the nephew of a Green, just to get her off the shelf. (That's you I'm talking about, by the way, Aulus.) Or he might not. But *your* family would never accept your marrying someone so close to the Placidi. Even if your father didn't, Lucius Atticus would veto it. And you would never go against *his* wishes, would you now?"

Aulus noticed how, when she smiled, dimples opened in her plump cheeks. He loved her. Now he was certain of it. He loved her so much that it hurt.

Was it his imagination, or was Sinica laughing?

XV

DECIMUS PAYS HIS RESPECTS TO HIS FORMER

MASTER, AND IS SHOWN THE DOOR

The house of Lord Governor Senator Faustus Pomponius Atticus, in Fanum Fortunae.

Returning to the place where you were once a slave can be a harrowing experience, but Decimus had been freed long before Faustus Atticus was appointed Lord Governor of the North. He therefore had no memories of the house, though many memories of those who now lived and worked in it.

The huge wooden door squeaked open. The gatekeeper, an unsympathetic Sueni, broad of shoulder and low of forehead, was not familiar to him, and was very skeptical about what he wanted. He had opened the door, but now he blocked it, grunting in response to Decimus's request to be allowed entry.

"Why should I let you in? Who are you?"

Decimus had no letter of introduction, or even a seal that the gatekeeper recognized, and the man was unwilling to leave his post to fetch the steward.

"And who *is* the master's steward these days?"

Phoenix, he was told. Decimus remembered Phoenix as an earnest, humorless footman-cum-clerk. My, he had certainly come up in the world!

"In my day it was Castor, and it is Castor that I wish to see. Also your master the Lord Governor, if that is possible, so that I can pay him my proper respects as his freedman."

But anyone could say that, apparently, and it was more than the gatekeeper's job was worth to allow a vagabond stranger into the house.

Decimus was sorely tempted to plant the stupid man on his backside, despite his size and the huge spear that he was carrying. Sueni were enthusiastic rather than accomplished fighters. But that way of gaining entry to the Lord Governor's mansion wouldn't endear him to the Lord Governor, and Decimus had been instructed to be careful and tactful.

Their conversation must have been loud, because it was heard by a footman, who came to see what was going on.

"Leon!"

Here was a friendly person who would remember him!

The gatekeeper—whose name was Togulus—still refused him entry, but could be persuaded to allow Leon to fetch permission from the steward for Decimus to enter the house.

When Leon returned, it was to say that the visitor could be escorted to see Castor. Afterwards, he was to report to the Lord Governor.

Leon steered him down the corridors and across the courtyards of what was plainly a very large house. But it doubled as an annex to the Lord Governor's headquarters, the footman explained, and the Lord Governor preferred to work where he had access to the creature comforts of his private establishment.

"Also," he muttered, "the mistress prefers him to work here, where she can keep an eye on him!"

Decimus remembered the Lady Pomponia only too well, and he hoped *not* to have to renew their acquaintance during his visit.

The footman pointed out a gilded, inscribed plaque honoring the Lord Governor's appointment—he had liked it so much that he had had it removed from where it was supposed to be hanging and re-erected inside the mansion. He also pointed out what could almost be described as a shrine proudly displaying the Lord Governor's insignia of office.

Faustus Atticus hadn't changed....

Castor was delighted to see him. He too had been freed, and was no longer steward to the Lord Governor—

"Phoenix?"

"An obvious choice. He is hardworking, and honest. He had been in this household a long time, and had served as my assistant. He can read and write, and do the numbers. I recommended him. And who else was there?"

"But you could have continued to serve as steward as a freedman, couldn't you?"

Castor explained that when the Senator became Lord Governor, he wished to have a secretary whom he could trust, and not some corrupt scribe appointed by the General who would both cheat him *and* spy on him. Then he lowered his voice.

"Little did he realize that his new secretary was already in the employ of the General! Though less openly employed by him than you are, my friend. I don't cheat him, however."

And they both laughed. Castor had been a good source of information for many years.

A young boy of ten or eleven entered the room and ran over to Castor, who pinched his cheek and tousled his hair.

"This is Phrygillus, my little assistant, and friend, and—"

He gazed lovingly at the boy. There was no need for him to finish the sentence.

"Greetings, Phrygillus!"

The boy scowled back at him.

"Is the man staying long?"

His voice was shrill, and unbroken. Phrygillus was a child of quite remarkable beauty. In fact, Decimus had never seen such an exquisite catamite. He had the satiny skin and dark locks of the south, and looked not unlike one of the angels that the Slave followers believed danced in attendance on their god. His features were delicately beautiful, though for the moment spoiled by the petulant expression on his face.

Decimus had no time for boy-love. It was the most unequal of all the many forms of love, he believed, and the "pedagogic" excuses sometimes made by its practitioners didn't convince him. Decimus had been a good-looking slave-boy himself, and knew how lucky he had been not to be abused or exploited. He had been fortunate in his masters. It was Castor who had bought him for the Atticus household, but by then he was already at an age when he must have lost any girlish appeal that he might once have had, and the steward, as he then was, had never made any physical approach to him.

He had to admit that little Phrygillus was strikingly attractive. And Castor was probably very lonely. It was not for him to judge the man.

"Don't be rude, my sweet. This is Decimus, an old friend. He is no danger to you. *Your* place in my heart is secure forever."

The boy threw himself onto the cushions by his master's side, and gazed up at him adoringly.

"Sorry," he whispered.

His master kissed him on the cheek, and pinched his thigh.

"My little finch…"

Phrygillus's pretty face lit up with affection, making him even lovelier. Sol, he must have been expensive!

Castor guessed what he was thinking.

"Yes, he wasn't cheap, but he is worth every gold piece that I paid for him. And the price was a very fair one. I had been saving for a long time, and I had good contacts among the slavers—I had been doing business with them for many years, on the master's behalf. *You* were one of my purchases, don't you remember?"

Castor sent the boy to fetch sweetmeats from the kitchen.

"I don't eat sweets," Decimus protested.

"But Phrygillus and I both do. And what you and I have to discuss is better discussed without him. The girls in the kitchen will pet him, and try and kiss him. He likes that. It will be a while before he returns."

And so Decimus was able to tell the secretary what he had been instructed to find out. Castor promised to make enquiries in the city, and to visit the slave-market and see for himself what kind of merchandise was on sale there.

Decimus must leave for Cascantum, to consult the Lord Commander, who was a loyal Green. He would visit again soon, on his way back to the City.

"Good. By then I may have discovered something of interest. But Lord Rhaetius may also have some interesting news for you. Walk with me, now: I'll bring you to the Lord Governor."

Before they left, Decimus gave him a large purse with heavy silver coins—not Maximians. Outside the Senator's office, Decimus was passed on to a footman, who announced him to his master.

The "office" was more like a luxurious living-space, and was decorated with garish images of the Slave, of angels, and of eminent priests, sages, and holy men of the "Lesser Worship". There was a lot of gold-leaf, and figures gazing heavenwards in improbable rapture, their arms stretched out to their godhead. Decimus recognized in these adornments the hand (and the appalling taste) of Lady Pomponia.

There were no obvious signs of work, such as he might have expected—the strewn parchments, maps, and tablets, the writing implements and inks, the seals, the new-fangled light-sticks known as "candles", the little stove for heating the lead. Instead, the room was equipped with comfortable furniture, and on the tables were the remains of a large meal, plates of expensive tidbits, and goblets of wine.

Senator Faustus Pomponius Atticus, reclining on a couch and wearing a toga befitting his rank, was just as Decimus remembered him. He hadn't changed at all.

Reclining next to him on a second couch was a slimly built and extremely handsome young man, probably a Sybarite from the south. His hair was finely dressed, and he had a showy gold brooch pinned to his long-sleeved robe. This was how Phrygillus would look fifteen years from now! He could almost be the boy's older brother. But what was a southerner doing so far north, and as a guest in the house of the Lord

Governor? Faustus Atticus had no known love for Reds, or for the heresies of the Slave cult that were practiced in the south.

The Senator soon made it clear to Decimus that he was not wholly pleased to see him again.

"It was you that made the decision not to remain in service with your master after your manumission—a disrespectful decision, in my opinion. And you chose to take service with the General, knowing that I disapprove of many of his policies. So why you have to keep turning up in my house, like a cheap counterfeit coin, I really don't know!"

Decimus assured the Senator that it was important to him to pay his respects to his former master whenever he happened to be in the vicinity.

"And you are doing your new master's work, I don't hesitate to doubt!"

"Some routine business has indeed brought me to the north, my Lord, yes."

"And you have already pestered Castor, I hear, distracting him from the far more important work that he does for me. Oh, never mind, just get on with it and be off with you!" He added, not unkindly, "You can eat in the kitchen before you leave."

Decimus dropped to his knees in front of the Senator and slipped his outstretched hands between those of his former master in the common gesture of fealty.

The young man had all the while been observing Decimus, with more interest than the Lord Governor had shown.

"Decimus? I've heard of you. Your reputation goes before you! The General is fortunate to have such loyal slaves."

Decimus started.

"Sir?"

"Oh, sorry, you are now a freedman of course. My mistake! I wasn't listening carefully. Such loyal *freedmen*. The slave trade is my business, so slaves are constantly on my mind. Please forgive me. But my visit to the Lord Governor and to Lady Pomponia is strictly personal."

"As my own visit to his Lordship is not business, sir, but a gesture of respect."

"You haven't told us about this 'routine business' of yours. You didn't come all the way to Fanum Fortunae just to pay your respects, I imagine?" He smiled sweetly. "Or is it a desperate secret?"

"No, no secret, sir. His Lordship has already been informed, I was given to believe."

The Senator glared at him.

"Informed of what? Pray tell us what business of state the General has been discussing with my ex-slave behind my back!"

"The matter of the slaving raids among the frontier tribes, my Lord, and the harm that they may be causing."

"Oh, *that*. I don't think that needs to be taken too seriously. Or have you been poaching Sueni virgins again, Victor?"

The Senator and his guest seemed to find that hilarious.

"Oh, would that I could, my Lord! But is there such a thing as a Sueni virgin? Do they exist? Above the age of ten or so." More laughter from the two men. Then Victor turned to Decimus. "But I would certainly know if any men in my employ were breaking the rules. Still, I do hope that your master the General is not intending to curb my business activities. One hears rumors. And I have a living to earn."

"I am not privy to his plans, sir, but I am sure that he has no intention of interfering in legitimate trading activities."

"Blessed be the Slave! That's a relief to hear! Of course, you can meddle in the commercial activities of my *competitors* as much as you like!"

"I'll bear that in mind, sir. The Lord General gave me clear instructions, and I'll do my best to carry them out."

"Oh, praiseworthy loyalty! I wish you Godspeed, then, and may the Slave watch over you. And, who knows, it may happen that our paths cross again."

It was nuanced slightly more than it should have been. Quickly, Decimus sought the man's eyes—the eyes betray the heart, as they betray reason too—but could read nothing in them. Behind their sparkle was a depth, or a deadness, that hid all meanings.

The Senator added his own fulsome appeal to the Slave for protection and guidance in all of life's manifold and burdensome undertakings. He was presumably referring to his own undertakings, since he didn't mention Decimus.

XVI

MANASA HAS BEEN TO A SLAVE-

MARKET BEFORE; MARA HASN'T

✠ *The slave-market in Fanum Fortunae.*

The worst thing was the smell of food.

The little slave-market at Fanum Fortunae occupied a small corner of the main market. Apart from the newly arrived merchandise, there were a few slaves still unsold after many days on the blocks because of their price, deformities, old age, or their unattractive appearance. All around them, in the rest of the market, food produce was on sale, including fruit and vegetables from the Valley, and fresh and salted meat and fish from the frontier lands, the Great River and the Amethyst Sea. Also on display were more exotic items from the East, which had been brought up from Maritima by boat and transported across the Gap on wagons. There was also a small livestock market: the animals, sitting or standing waiting for a buyer, looked, Manasa thought, if anything happier than most of the slaves did.

To cater for the needs of the market people and their customers, re-freshment stalls offered drinks and snacks, while in some of the taverns you could sit down to a full-scale meal. Each of the slaves had been given water, an apple, and some foul biscuits, and then nothing else for the rest of the day. They were there to be turned into money for the slavers, not to consume it in the form of food. The quicker they were purchased, the better for everyone. The smell of roasting meat, grilled fish, and fresh baked bread wafting around them soon became a torment.

Manasa looked at her new friend. She had been pretty stupid, she told herself, to make friends with horsey-girl, to cuddle up to her in the night, and explain everything to her. Very soon they were going to be split up, and they would most likely never see each other again.

There was no great shortage of blonde barbarian girls in Fanum, especially in the brothels, so who would buy Mara? The Horse People weren't too far away—later on, she might even be able to smuggle a message to her relatives, so that one night they would come calling, looking for her. Any potential buyer from Fanum would be aware of that risk. Mara's best chance of being bought would be if some easy-going Valley farmer bought her, as his only female slave, to cook, clean, and share his bed with him. If she gave him healthy children, he might even free her and take her as a common-law wife.

Mara would be desperately unhappy and lonely in her new master's home. She was physically strong—and despite her age, she was already somewhat taller than Manasa—but her spirit would be weak, now that she realized the full awfulness of what was happening to her. On the road, Manasa had tried to give her some useful advice, without much success: she was too downhearted to listen properly.

Now, as they stood on a white-washed platform, waiting to be bought, Manasa was still whispering to her. She told her to try to look more wide-awake and high-spirited, even if she didn't feel that way, and to stand up straight.

"Why should I bother? Who cares?" was the answer.

"Orcus cares. The slave-merchants care. They want you to fetch a good price. And if you don't liven up, they'll send someone to push a piece of ginger up your bottom. I'm sure you'll enjoy that! If you're lucky, it might even be your friend Thrasyllus."

After that, Mara made more of an effort to look like a good bargain. They hadn't seen the loathsome Thrasyllus since they stopped just outside Fanum, to be taken in small groups down to the lakeside, where, under heavy supervision, they had to strip off their clothes and wash themselves in the fresh water of the lake. Then they were marched through the outskirts of the city and into the market square, naked.

At the slave-market they would eventually be given clothes, but only after someone had bought them, or if they were to be taken to the sheds in the evening, to be offered for sale again the following day. On the slavers' blocks there would be no need for clothes.

Perhaps Thrasyllus had been sent on ahead to meet the boss, whose intention had been to reach Fanum much earlier to confirm the arrangements with the slave-merchants. The goods would be sold on their stands, in return for a handsome commission, since the slavers themselves had no license to sell the slaves within the city limits.

The market was noisy, and not only because of the throng of market-goers. The slaves also chattered among themselves, though not very cheerfully, and the slave-merchants had no objection to that, since it showed that their merchandise had life in it, and that the slaves were not sick or pining.

Manasa remembered her own first time on a slavers' block, at the great market in Trebenna, and told Mara that the Fanum slave-market was a much pleasanter place.

Mara looked at her as though she must be deranged.

"*Pleasanter?* What could be worse than *this*?"

And so she told her.

For instance, at Trebenna more than half the slaves were normally sold in cheap bulk lots. They were sent off to work in gangs as field-hands on the plantations of the Placidi, or as laborers in the government mines and quarries. After they were purchased, they were branded with a hot iron. The brand showed either the name or symbol of the plantation, or the crest of the government mining company.

The mines and factories were the worst fate, except for the galleys, but no women were ever bought as rowers. Conditions in the brick-making and iron-working factories were terrible. Even the bonded workers in the government factories were branded, Manasa said, because although by law they were free men they weren't supposed to run away from their place of work.

The agents who came to Trebenna to buy laborers in bulk brought their own branding-irons with them, and the slave-merchants did the branding for them as a free extra service. That way, if a slave escaped while he was being marched south, the ownership question could be resolved immediately when he was recaptured.

The slaves would be branded in batches, late in the afternoon, when there would be loud screaming, Manasa said, and a constant stench of burnt flesh.

How can you tell the difference, Mara asked, between that and the roasting meat smell?

Oh, believe me, you can. But don't worry, Manasa told her, that won't happen to you. Some of the older men might be unlucky, though... She hoped that there would be no branding in the market at Fanum.

You prayed to your gods: let me be bought as a house-slave! Then you wouldn't be branded, just tattooed perhaps. In earlier times they used to mutilate one of your ears as well, but that practice had died out.

Mara stared at the tattoos on her friend's face.

"Yes, your nice horsey people did that to me. These are my last master's designs. Very artistic, don't you think? The Horse People put this stuff on your face, so that everyone can see that you're a slave. But if a Citizen buys you to serve in the house, they want you to look smart, so your tattoo would have to be somewhere more discreet."

And then there were the booths.

"What booths?" Mara asked. "I can't see any booths here. Or do you mean those little stalls selling food?"

No, Manasa said, she didn't mean them. She meant the little curtained booths which trusted regular customers were allowed to use to *try out* a possible purchase in privacy. A young woman, perhaps. Or a pretty twelve-year-old boy.

"What do you mean: try out?" Then it dawned on her. "Oh!"

"Only regular customers, naturally. If any passing layabout could do it, the market would be like a free brothel. But there are no booths here: this is a respectable provincial town, not the big city. And you wouldn't be in danger anyway—you're a *virgin*, aren't you? Your owner will have to pay for you and take you home before he can test you!"

That didn't seem to cheer up Mara particularly.

Manasa had been sold several times. There was something about her that men liked, as bears are attracted to honey, or mice to cheese, and that certain something made her valuable.

Men couldn't keep their hands off her, but it wasn't as though she had brought her masters much luck. Her first master was skewered by a wild boar in a hunting accident, her second died of old age, and another was suddenly eaten up inside by worms. Each time, she was passed on to a relative of the dead man, who could choose between keeping her in the family or turning her into silver. Perhaps even gold. They always chose the money. One was a woman, who sold her immediately. The other two were men—they played with her for a while, until their wives complained, and then did the same.

The shabby board that hung from a rope around Mara's neck said, "Virgin." It wasn't having much effect. Her virginity would soon be gone, and after that who would want a coltish horsey-girl who couldn't do much that would be of any use in a household? She was still growing, and if her owner wasn't rich she'd probably eat him out of house and home. And there was also the matter of the exaggerated price that the slavers were asking for her.

Manasa smiled inwardly. The whole camp had waited, a day and a night, while Orcus and Thrasyllus were sent off, on the word of some slimy renegade, to catch a "princess". Some princess! Now the boss wanted a financial return for their efforts. But that wasn't how the business worked. You might have the goods, but there had to be a demand for them. One of Manasa's owners had been a trader; she had learned about such matters.

She guessed that, for the first few hours, Mara had wished that the board were bigger, so that it would hide more of her nakedness. That was how Manasa had felt too, the first time. Whenever a man looked more closely at Mara, she blushed bright red. Manasa was too dark to do that, and there weren't many things that made her blush anyway. A couple of the men leered, as Thrasyllus had done, but most appraised the women coldly, as if they were inspecting a mule.

Manasa herself had no board around her neck—her charms were obvious. Lots of men came and admired her, and some tried to touch her, but the slave-merchants' salesmen wouldn't allow them to. She was expensive, exorbitantly so, and the groping would make her tired and nervous.

Less interest was shown in Mara. She was good-looking, but she had the wrong color hair, her skin was too pale and rough, her thighs and arms were too muscular, unlike Manasa's svelte limbs, and there was too much hair on her body. She had not been depilated—there hadn't been time.

They heard the slavers and the slave-merchants arguing about the prices (and about the slave-merchants' commissions).

The goods that weren't sold on the first day would need to be locked up and guarded, which also cost money. It would be better to set lower prices, the slave-merchants argued, yet they weren't willing to move from a fixed sum in commission per item sold, which was the going practice in Fanum (where turnover was modest and the merchants liked to be sure of a guaranteed daily income).

The slavers would have preferred the commission to be an agreed fraction of the price achieved, say one-twentieth, which was the way things were done in the big slave-markets in Trebenna and Maritima. The lower the prices were, the less commission they'd have to pay.

The slave-merchants disagreed. Who wanted to sit around all day making those calculations? And they had the final word. If the matter needed to be arbitrated, the market superintendent would always take their side.

By midday, the slaves were exhausted from standing. They were only permitted to squat down for a few moments if there were no potential buyers nearby, which was seldom the case, even though that part of the market was far from crowded.

Mara now looked completely indifferent to whether someone was staring at her or not. Good, Manasa thought, she's getting used to being a slave. She's withdrawing inside, and the bad things that would soon be happening to her would therefore hurt her spirit much less.

One of the older Sueni women was the first to go. She was, it was said, an excellent cook. Another woman, who had been priced very cheaply because of her deformed foot, was bought by a toothless farmer.

He led her away, looking very pleased with his bargain. And two small boys were sold, to an elderly couple. Had they been bought as slaves, or would they be adopted? Their mother wept bitterly as she saw her children disappear.

Otherwise, business was pitifully slow, and when Manasa's friend from among the slavers looked by, bringing her a bread-roll with some cheese (which she shared with Mara), he told her the reason.

The slavers themselves were not the only people who had heard that the Lord Commander at Cascantum was trying to stop their operations. The news had also reached Fanum. Some potential buyers had been put off by the thought that anything they bought at the market might soon be confiscated as "stolen goods". The boss had therefore made a decision: the asking-prices would be drastically cut, so that the merchandise could be sold quickly and be off the streets before the soldiers arrived. The master would not be happy, though.

Mara had just begun to ask Manasa who "the master" was when the salesman prodded her on the hip and told her to shut up and stand still. A customer was looking at her, fairly intently. This might be a buyer!

He was elderly, with white hair and a beard, and plainly dressed. Manasa noticed details that Mara wouldn't. His hands were soft, his body flabby, and his movements gentle, so he wasn't a farmer. When he spoke to the salesman, asking where the "virgin" came from, it was in a quiet voice, and he spoke the Citizens' Tongue so gracefully that he couldn't possibly be a trader.

His ear was clipped, so he had once been a slave, but his dignified bearing and manner suggested that he no longer was. He had no attendants with him, showing that he probably wasn't wealthy. Perhaps he had once been the tutor to some rich man's son, and after being freed had set up his own school? Or maybe he was a freedman in government service?

He spoke to Mara.

"The man says that you are from the Horse People, and that you speak the Citizens' Tongue. Is that true?"

When Mara didn't answer, the salesman smacked her with his cane. (Whips were not allowed in the market, in case a customer accidentally got hurt.)

"Speak!"

"Yes, it's true."

Mara's voice was very small. The salesman bellowed again, but didn't hit her.

"Sir! You say 'sir'!"

The old man turned to him and made a conciliatory gesture with his hand.

"There's no need for that. You're frightening the girl, and I can't hear what she's saying." Then, to Mara: "Who taught you?"

"My father, sir."

"And who is he?"

"One of the Horse People, sir."

Good, Manasa thought. She wasn't starting any of that nonsense about her father being Big Chief Whatnot. That would be asking for trouble.

"Your father taught you well."

The salesman intervened.

"And may I point out to you, sir, that this handsome specimen of young womanhood is a virgin! You wouldn't credit how hard it is, getting them to market intact, what with all those stiff pricks running around looking for a nice hole. But we guarantee that this one is *unblemished*."

The old man gave him a cold smile.

"Unblemished, you say? Apart from the bruises and cuts, you mean, and the mark you've just made on her with your cane?" He raised his hand. "No, don't answer that. But I have to say that her condition of virginity—or otherwise—doesn't much interest me."

The salesman seemed slightly offended.

"She is definitely a virgin, sir! We've been in this business a long time, and we have a reputation to lose—"

"I'm sure you have."

His tone was distinctly ironic.

"Believe me, sir, the condition of this particular lot is indeed as described," and the salesman pointed with a grimy finger at the word on the board, "namely, *virgin*, and that will be guaranteed by us in the bill of sale. But if you'd like to examine her for yourself, we can arrange something with one of the tavern-keepers. As a special favor. We are offering the item at a most attractive price, sir. A price you won't regret!"

The old man ignored him. To Manasa's amazement, he now switched to the Tongue of the Horse People.

"What is your name?"

"Mara," this time in a louder, firmer voice, as if being able to talk in her own Tongue had momentarily liberated her. "My name is Mara."

"So, shall I buy you, Mara? Are you healthy? You look healthy enough. Do you have some sickness that they don't want me to know about?" Manasa noticed that his use of the Tongue was old-fashioned and ungrammatical, yet almost fluent. He sometimes chose the wrong word, but Mara clearly understood what he was trying to say. He smiled at her. "Don't worry, I'll still buy you. I just want to know."

She told him that she had been riding, without a saddle, only a few days before.

"If I was sick, I wouldn't have been out riding, sir."

The word "sir" sounded unnatural in the tongue of the Horse People. Manasa herself had never been asked to use it. She had always addressed her master by his name.

"I know a little about your ways, Mara. You have plaits, so you have already bled, but you are still a virgin. Am I right?" (What he should have said was, "Is rightness with me?") "Unless one of the slavers...?"

"No, sir."

He turned now to the salesman, and reverted to the Citizens' Tongue.

"Well then, young man, tell me: what is this price that I won't regret?"

Damn it, thought Manasa, horsey-girl's going to be bought before I am!

"The price is five hundred silver pieces, sir, of the old kind, but I can give you a special discount and reduce it to four hundred. Three hundred and twenty if you pay in gold."

The old man laughed, but humorlessly.

"Three hundred and twenty... That's what someone might pay for a well-trained house-slave from the south. Whereas this is a rough barbarian. Unless my eyes and ears are playing tricks on me? No, I thought not. And as you know, the Horse People have the reputation of making very poor slaves. Worse than the Sueni. If I were a farmer buying her, you wouldn't even get a hundred."

The salesman smiled, revealing a mouthful of furry yellow teeth.

"But you're *not* a farmer, are you, Lord Castor, sir? And his Lordship your master, if I may be allowed to say so, has always been prepared to pay most generously for his purchases. And you are surely buying on his behalf?"

"No, I have no instructions from him to buy slaves today. So it is not his money that I am risking here, but mine. And since I am only his secretary, my purse is very much lighter than his!"

Finally, a price of 180 heavy silver pieces was agreed: ninety as the "basic price", plus an additional ninety for Mara's virginity. This was to be taken on trust, since the buyer showed no interest in ascertaining it for himself.

Orcus was called over to confirm the price and seal the bill of sale, which he did without quibbling, though he was plainly dissatisfied. Mara would have fetched more in Trebenna, or in the City, but those much larger slave-markets were worlds away from this provincial nest. The slavers were nervous, and wanted to sell up and be gone.

Orcus gave her a parting smack on the rump.

"See, princess, we've arranged a royal palace for you: the number one address in Fanum Fortunae. You are such a lucky girl!"

And then Manasa realized who the old gentleman might be, and where Mara would be going.

XVII

THOMASIUS PLAYS WITH FIRE

✠ *The fortress of Cascantum.*

Thomasius twisted in the saddle, trying to make himself comfortable. How the Horse People could ride so well, and enjoy riding so much, even without a saddle, was a mystery to him. Or the Blood-Drinkers, on their shaggy little ponies.

He was an infantryman. Marching was not a problem. It took some learning, admittedly, as recruits soon found out. Thomasius could well remember the blisters from his first pair of studded marching sandals, the sores from having to carry so much gear, and the aching muscles. But a unit of experienced Citizen soldiers on the march was a wonderful thing to behold. In step, if their Sub-officer had ordered them to be, and reeking of sweat, garlic, and leather—the best method ever invented to project brute force against barbarians,

Yes, it was frightening to be ridden at by whooping savages on horseback. Yet as long as the men stayed in formation, each of them shielding the man to his left and protected by the shield of the man to his right, with the narrow area in-between as a killing ground for spear and sword, not too much could go wrong. Even if a man lost his sword, he knew how to kill with his knife, with the boss of his shield or the heavy edge, or if need be with his bare hands.

This was Thomasius's world, the only life he had known since he entered manhood.

Poncing about on a horse was not part of it. However, he needed to reach Fanum Fortunae quickly, and a mule, though more comfortable, was slower and less in keeping with a Citizen Sub-officer's dignity. So a horse it had to be.

The previous day, which was the day after Staff Officer Petronius had come to collect Corvo, to escort him to the Lord Commander, Thomasius himself had been called to the Presence in the map-room. And without his Company-commander, which was unprecedented.

Lord Commander Rhaetius was nothing like as big as Urtho, and much older, but he was still physically impressive. He would be a fearsome opponent, if you were unlucky enough to face him in battle.

He had come up through the ranks, to become a divisional commander, a military governor, and a Senator (though Thomasius doubted whether he'd ever spent much time sitting in the Senate). At heart, though, he was still an old-fashioned soldier. For instance, he was a believer in the tradition that a Sub-officer or a Company-commander should never command his men to do anything he couldn't or wasn't prepared to do himself, and that he should be better at doing it than most of his men were. Only that way could he be sure of their respect and loyalty.

Staff Officers, on the other hand, however elegantly turned out they were, were exempt from such expectations. Fortunately most of them went into the Senate after their spell in the Citizen Army, without endeavoring to become Lord Commander of a division.

Rhaetius was square-faced and heavily built. He had no time for niceties. After dismissing the other soldiers and officers present, he had commanded Thomasius to be "at ease" and then asked him which route he had taken to the map-room. Had he passed along the northern battlement? Had he walked past the execution platform?

Thomasius answered that he had.

And what had he seen there?

What Thomasius had seen there was disgusting. Impaled on thick wooden stakes were the dying remains of two naked human beings. They had once been men, but their male parts had been sliced off. Judging from the caked blood around their mouths, their tongues had also been ripped out. One of them was quiet, though still breathing; the other was shuddering and slobbering as the weight of his body forced it further down onto the wooden spike, which was coated in his blood and shit.

Thomasius had no appetite for such cruelties. He had carried out executions himself, as commander of a punishment detail, lopping off a man's head ceremoniously with a special long-sword—the infantryman's short-sword was for thrusting, not slashing—or cutting his throat, if there wasn't time for the fancy stuff. He had once supervised a crucifixion (he made sure the man didn't suffer for too long). But impaling was a vile form of execution, and reserved for barbarians. Except by Imperial Prerogative, Citizens and even slaves could not be punished in this manner.

Thomasius had naturally kept these thoughts to himself. What had he seen there? He had seen the impaled bodies of two barbarians, he answered.

"Barbarians? Yes, perhaps. *Scum*, certainly. They were slavers. I am sure that you remember, Sub-officer, the clear orders that I gave, to be announced immediately in every settlement within a day's ride of Cascantum?"

Thomasius remembered the orders well. There was to be no raiding for slaves this side of the Great River, that is, within the frontiers of the Empire, under penalty of death. Raiding beyond the River was still permitted, except among the Horse People, as was the purchase or bartering of slaves by agreement with chieftains of the Horse People, the Sueni, the Free People, and the lesser tribes.

"Those orders came directly from the General. No Citizen would dare to disobey them. I therefore assumed that these slavers were *not* Citizens, but themselves barbarians, and that the manner of their execution was therefore for me to determine. They didn't tell me anything to the contrary."

No, of course they didn't. Hard to correct such a misunderstanding if you haven't got a tongue.

"No, my Lord."

"My orders came from the General, and I obeyed them. I have served with Ogilo. I served under him as a Company-commander at the greatest battle of our times, when we held back the Blood-Drinkers. The combined armies of East and West, under his command, and it was still a close-run thing. He knew that if he made a mistake, the world would be dark for a hundred years." He paused. "That was greatness. So when the General gives me a command, I carry it out."

"Yes, my Lord."

Thomasius had heard these tales of the battle often before from veterans. By chance he had not been present on the great battlefield under the walls of Neopolis, capital of the East—he had already finished his training as an infantryman, but because he was a persuasive speaker (for a soldier) he had been seconded for recruiting duties in the Province.

Victory had never been a possibility—the odds against the Citizens were far too great. Since they couldn't face the Blood-Drinker host in open battle, they built earthworks. Wave after wave of the Blood-Drinkers crashed against them, but the lines held. When they had picked the land dry like locusts and had no more provender for their horses, the Blood-Drinkers disappeared back across the Great River and into the northern mists.

That was the story that everyone knew. However, there was another, darker, story. Ogilo should never have been given command of both Imperial armies, he was much too young, but the two Emperors, the fathers of Maximillus and Theodore, were nincompoops, and the senior commanders were running scared. The priests of the Slave cult (Sol rot them!) had proclaimed loudly that the Blood-Drinkers were a punishment from their god, a scourge for the backs of men for rejecting the call to worship Him unconditionally. Only Ogilo had been willing to make a stand against the demons, and he had seized his chance. A quarter of his troops were left dead or dying on the battlefield, but after a week he had saved the Empire. And the rulers in East and West had hated and feared him ever since.

Rhaetius rambled on, boasting about his own role in the battle, as old soldiers tended to. Finally, just when Thomasius was wondering why he had been called to the Presence, the Lord Commander told him what he wanted of him. Slavers, like those scum impaled on the stakes, had been raiding in the frontier lands, not only beyond the River but also within the borders of the West. Among the Horse People, for instance. And they had been snatching the wives or children of priests or chieftains, to turn the tribes against the Empire.

The old man who had been brought in was such a chieftain. His name was Corvo; his daughter's name was Mara. Citizen patrols had covered the borderlands southeast of the River, but she had not been among the captives they had recovered. Looking southwest, there was a small slave-market in Fanum Fortunae. Though it was unlikely, perhaps some of the captives had been taken there? If they could be found, and returned to their own people, it might be helpful. The girl's father was only a minor clan chieftain, but her grandfather was in the High Council of the Horse People.

Thomasius must leave at first light.

Asking for permission to speak, Thomasius had explained that his Company-commander had given him additional duties as a punishment for insubordination...

"Yes, yes, that is Decius! Typical! But let that gentleman be my concern, Sub-officer. Do this well, and you will be advanced to Company-commander the next time a position falls vacant."

Thomasius was so astonished that he saluted spontaneously.

"My Lord!"

But then the Lord Commander's voice had dropped almost to a whisper.

"No, don't be so pleased. That promotion may happen sooner than you think. Or wish. Small parties of Blood-Drinkers have already crossed the River. Raiders were seen near Fanum Fortunae. I hope that they *were* only raiders, but if they were scouts or outriders the horde will not be far behind. The Lord Governor is in a panic, of course, and has asked for reinforcements. I've sent him cavalry, not regular troops—I can't afford to weaken the border. Lord Memmius and I must try to secure the country between here and Fanum. Find out what you can, and come back. You may soon be needed here."

"Should this girl's father not accompany me, my Lord? How shall I recognize her?"

"Don't be an idiot, man. She's a blonde horsey-girl. She's had the first bleeding, but her hair is still in plaits. If you find her, tread carefully. My secretary will give you heavy silver for your expenses and some gold pieces to buy her with. I'll expect a bill of sale."

"And if the owner won't sell, my Lord?"

"You can't force the owner to sell her. Not in Fanum. The military have no jurisdiction there, and the Lord Governor will give you no support."

"No, my Lord."

Everyone knew that the Lord Commander was Ogilo's man, and a Green; Faustus Pomponius Atticus, the Lord Governor, was a notorious Blue.

"If you come back without her, be sure to bring the gold pieces with you! Oh, and one last thing, Sub-officer: before you turn in for the night, you'll go to the signaling station and give them this message"—he handed Thomasius a small piece of parchment—"to be sent to the General. Stay until they've done it, and then destroy the parchment." He paused. "Our two *barbarians* did say something, before their tongues were removed, and the General ought to be told."

Thomasius had gone to the signaling station as instructed, after it became dark. It was on a high turret of the fortress. Fire signaling worked much better at night-time. A team of highly trained signals personnel were responsible for three separate fire-beacons, which were spaced out in a line, and could be raised and lowered at will. When lit, the beacons were visible to watchers at the next signaling station, and so on again and again down a long chain of stations reaching all the way to the City.

Each beacon represented a third of the letters of the alphabet; *which* letter was determined by the number of times that that particular beacon was raised and then lowered. "A" was thus the first beacon, raised only once; "B" was the first beacon raised and lowered twice; and so on for all the other letters. The timing of the raising and lowering had to be just right, hence the need for the signalers to be so carefully trained.

Only simple messages could be sent, often in shortened form: "I-M-P(erator) D-E-A-D", for instance. If the message contained sensitive information, it might be in a pre-arranged code. Signalers, who had their own corps within the Citizen Army and strict rules of practice, were not allowed on pain of death to record a message, only to send it on to the next signaling station.

That hadn't stopped the signalers from moaning at Thomasius for bringing them extra work. They'd been pretty busy, they said, with messages going backwards and forwards between Cascantum and Fanum.

The fire-beacon system worked well, and before the end of the night the Lord Commander's message would have crossed the Gap to Fanum Fortunae before being passed down through the length of the Province along the Great Provincial Road and then across the central mountains to the City. Whatever its content was, the General would know it by dawn.

Thomasius himself took much longer to get to Fanum, even though he had been able to requisition a fairly reasonable horse from the fortress stables. He had had to wait while they fitted it with leather and metal hoof-boots; only the horses used by the barbarian cavalrymen had permanent horseshoes.

The road across the Gap was excellent, with a good surface and distance markers at fixed intervals. But it was boring. This was still the plain—with dull grasslands rather than lush farms like those in the Province or the Valley—and there were few settlements along the road, only the occasional shack or stall offering travelers a limited range of overpriced refreshments. There were no inns, because on such a good road Fanum was easily within a day's ride.

Thomasius saw only a couple of watchtowers or signaling stations, which now seemed to be empty. Had they been abandoned? Normally, the road would be busy, but Thomasius encountered only a handful of other travelers, riding in the other direction. There were fires burning on the horizon. He didn't like the look of that.

The message had covered the same distance much more quickly than he could, before heading on to its final destination—if it had been passed on while the signaling stations were still occupied, that is. Had it been the last message to leave Cascantum? It had consisted of a single word, which Thomasius didn't understand but the General surely would: C-H-A-R-I-S-S-A. Wasn't there a suburb of Trebenna with that name? Or was it Chaerissa?

He had burned the parchment when the signalers were finished.

XVIII

FLORIANUS SEES AN OPPORTUNITY TO

CHANGE THE COURSE OF HISTORY, BUT

ALSO IMAGINES HIS OWN HEAD ON A SPIKE

�֎ *The Imperial Palace.*

"There are other parts of you, eunuch, that could still be cut off. 'No' is not a word in our vocabulary."

"There is no reason to shout, Quintus. The High Chamberlain knows that this is in his interests, too."

Senator Naevius had also made a restraining gesture with his hand, which was unnecessary—there was sufficient power and authority in his voice alone. Not for nothing was he the unchallenged leader of the largest faction in the Senate. Majestic in appearance and gracious in his movements, he was how an Emperor *should* be, Florianus couldn't help thinking, but cold and ruthless.

His son was good-looking, too—it must run in the family—but more in the style of a self-confident gangster: athletic build, and a handsome, sensual face, with proud, cruel eyes and a cynically curling, full-lipped mouth. Technically he was a Senator, but there had never been any question of Quintus Naevius participating in debates. His stage was out on the streets; and his debates were carried out with knives and iron-studded clubs.

Although they were in the antechamber to his office, and there were Imperial Guardsmen in attendance, and Quintus's entourage of thugs had been held back at the gate, Florianus still felt intimidated, as he always did when the Naevii came calling. Julian had announced them in a sweaty flurry of excitement, before Quintus Naevius pushed him to one side. Now Florianus must re-establish the authority of the court over these aggressive visitors.

"Sir," he said, addressing his remarks to the Senator, "there can be no instant access to the Presence of his Imperial Majesty. Today is not a day of audience. A private audience must be applied for in writing, allowing several days for the application to be processed. And it is not I who will approve or reject it, but the Lord General."

"Fuck the Lord General!"

"No, Quintus, be patient, there are...*procedures* that must be followed. This is what chamberlains are for! We must respect the etiquette of the court. But"—and he turned his iron-gray eyes from his son to Florianus—"you realize that Ogilo will not be eager to grant us access to the Emperor. Nor do I wish to apply to *that man* in person. He is my sister's bastard—"

The Guardsmen shifted perceptibly, tapping their spears on the mosaic floor. Their commander spoke.

"Sir, we can't allow the use of that word to describe his Lordship the General."

"Why not? It is on record that he *is* her bastard child. His father abused the hospitality of my family and robbed us of our honor. And I lost a sister because of that man."

The officer made a show of catching the High Chamberlain's eye. Should they be removed? Florianus's gesture of response was silent but equally clear: No. Not yet. Let them speak first.

Naevius was unruffled.

"Detain us if you wish, my Lord Chamberlain. Put us in chains, even. But if you do, not one of you will ever leave this Palace alive. You may control what happens within these walls, but who is master of the streets outside? Even your precious General is only here on our tolerance. Or has he withdrawn all his divisions from the frontiers, to police the City without my noticing it? I think not."

"We're done here, father. Fuck them all!"

"No, Quintus, we are not done yet." He turned again to Florianus. "Or are we, my Lord?"

Florianus did his best to sound dignified, firm, but polite all at the same time.

"I must ask you not to use that word again, sir, to refer to the General. If you agree to that, we can continue this discussion."

"As you wish. Not using the *word* won't make the *fact* go away. But it is not the reason why we are here, merely the reason why we wish an audience with the Emperor without first having to speak to his, er... *protector*?"

"There is one possibility, sir: if his Imperial Majesty considers your matter to be of direct interest to him, we may assume that he would demand—*demand*, I say, not *request*—your immediate attendance on his person. His Lordship the General would need to be informed, and he would be entitled to attend the meeting. He would be unlikely to try to forbid it if the matter were of sufficient importance, and was not a threat or challenge to his own authority. However, I will need to know the *content* of the matter, if I am to convey that information to his Imperial Majesty."

Quintus pushed himself forward.

"It's quite easy, eunuch. The Placidi have offered him a whore. A whore for the Emperor's bed! Does Maximillus even know about it?"

"Quintus…"

"A fucking southern bitch as Empress? Decent people won't stand for it. She won't get to the Palace, though. Not in one piece."

Florianus thought: how do they *know*?

The Senator's voice interrupted his thoughts.

"I must apologize, my Lord. My son has taken this much too personally. But he is correct in one respect: people will not accept a southern Empress. The war against the south has not been forgotten. And in Sybaris they still subscribe to the old, unreformed heresy of the East, with all its disgusting practices. That in itself is an affront to those of us who worship the Slave as he *should* be worshiped."

Florianus had never been interested in religious controversies, and had always been puzzled by the obscure theological arguments that lay behind the schism in the Slave cult. Western followers had broken away from the "Greater Worship" that was the state religion in the East (Sol was still the official cult of the West). Their "Lesser Worship", however, had found little favor in the more conservative southern provinces.

Although he *didn't*, he told Naevius: "I understand, sir."

"Would the General really attempt to impose this girl on us as Empress? I have never held him to be stupid. How would he secure the support of the Senate? Not only Blues, but many White and Green Senators would also find the marriage difficult to stomach."

There he had a point: the Placidi were loathed by almost everyone, if only for their enormous wealth.

"Votes in the Senate, sir, are not always easy to predict."

"What I meant when I said that my son took this *personally* is this: he has a charming and beautiful daughter, Naevia, whom I was hoping to present at court. If his Imperial Majesty is looking for a bride, wouldn't my granddaughter be a far more suitable match? It is an option that ought to be considered. And a discussion from which his Majesty himself should not be excluded."

At the back of his mind, a voice was whispering to him: something else is going on here. The Placidi and the Naevii are heading towards a collision, and someone wants it so! Who had the most to gain? It came in a flash: *Ogilo*, of course!

The General couldn't directly refuse the offer made by Gnaeus Placidus without enraging the Reds, could he? But he wouldn't want to accept it, either. If a counter-offer came from the Naevii, he could play them off against each other and gain time. Time which he might need, if assorted barbarians were about to hurl themselves against the Empire. Let Reds and Blues keep each other in check. Greens and Whites would support the General…

Eunuchs were supposed to stay in the shadows, whispering, plotting, spinning webs of intrigue. Not for them the great stage of public affairs. Nobody expected them to shape the course of major events. It was not their role to change the world, so that people for generations to come would talk about them. But Florianus had often had such a dream—the dream of being *respected*, of being something more than just an incomplete man.

Here was such a chance. If he held his nerve, he could make a decision that might change the history of the West.

If the General had planned this, he would want Naevius to speak to the Emperor, and he wouldn't intervene. At their meeting a few days before in the small audience chamber, he had said "we". Ogilo was now in an urgent conference of military commanders. If he *hadn't* intended this, he would rush out of the meeting immediately to be at the audience with Naevius. That was the way to find out!

"What is your answer, my Lord Chamberlain?"

Florianus took a quick breath, and drew himself up to his full, admittedly unimpressive, height.

"This concerns his Imperial Majesty's possible marriage. It cannot *not* interest him. I shall take full responsibility for disturbing his Majesty. I will lead you to him, sir, you and your son."

For the first time, Senator Naevius looked at him with something resembling respect.

"That was a wise decision, and one that you will not regret. Whatever the outcome will be, know that in future you can rely upon the friendship of the House of Naevius."

Florianus tittered, slipping back into the role of the foolish eunuch.

"I sincerely hope so, sir! His Majesty doesn't much like being disturbed. We'll take the slower route through the outer corridors, and I'll send one of the Guardsmen on ahead to warn his Majesty's attendants.

If his Majesty refuses to see us, I can help you no further." He giggled again. "And the next time that you see *me*, it will be my head on a spike!"

He took the Naevii, escorted by a detachment of white-cloaked Guardsmen, by the slowest route he could possibly think of. Letting Quintus Naevius into the Presence without a substantial number of guards for the Emperor was out of the question. Even though he had been made to leave his weapons behind—all *four* of them, a Guardsman had told Florianus: a sword, an evil-looking dagger, a bludgeon, and a metal knuckleduster!—Quintus was a violent, choleric man, who had killed or maimed other thugs in street battles and was capable of killing with his bare hands if he wanted to.

With whispered instructions, Florianus also sent Julian to find Ogilo and inform him what was going on. He should then come as quickly as he could to the Emperor's private rooms, to tell his master whether he thought the General was on his way to break up the audience with the Naevii or not.

Florianus's mind was buzzing. He was taking an immense risk. If the General had *not* intended this, the eunuch's head would not be on a stake the same or the following day, but it would be advisable for Florianus to make arrangements to spend the rest of his life somewhere else, and as far from the City as possible.

He realized how the General might have set it up. He had insisted on letting Julian stay at their meeting, knowing that he would soon go rushing off to the people most likely to pay him generously for such interesting news. The Naevii must have loaded him down with silver! Silver, of course, not gold—if Julian were seen spending gold pieces, it would be rather obvious what had happened.

His Imperial Majesty was not particularly happy to see them.

Maximillus was wearing neither the purple robe of state nor the pearl diadem. Had he been sleeping? Pasty-faced as always, his cheeks were puffy, which didn't go well with his otherwise narrow, foxy features. His eyes, too close together but usually bright and gleaming, like jewels embedded in a pale tree-trunk, were bleary. His robe of golden silk embroidered with black and red thread was badly crumpled, as if it had been doubling as a night-gown.

Maybe he had been drinking, and was sleeping it off? He was barely more than a child, but he was the Emperor—who was there to tell him what to do? Florianus still could, in small and harmless matters. Otherwise, only the General could clip his wings, and he seldom had the time (or the inclination) to talk to the boy.

The little group now facing him can hardly have given the Emperor much cause for pleasure. The High Chamberlain he knew and accepted.

When they had entered, Florianus had prostrated himself at the Imperial feet, which he noticed were both unshod and unwashed, and fervently kissed the hem of the Imperial gown. He referred to himself as "your slave" when addressing the Emperor, and avoided eye-contact. The disturbance of his Imperial Majesty's leisure might yet be forgiven.

Senator Naevius, on the other hand, would not have been a welcome visitor. Stern, humorless, conservative, he was the father-in-law that you thanked the gods you didn't have! He spoke to the Emperor as one Citizen to another, and managed only a stiff bow. A junior Senator would never have dared not to make the full obeisance, but Naevius had considerable power in the City, and the loyalty of the Blues was very uncertain. Maximillus would know that, despite all provocation, he needed to be careful with this man.

And then there was the Senator's vicious son, Quintus, who created an atmosphere of potential violence wherever he went. Maximillus was unlikely to send the Guardsmen away while Quintus Naevius was still anywhere near him. They held him at a distance from the Imperial person—his father would do the talking, so there was no need for Quintus to come any closer.

Marcus Naevius spoke with dignity, but with clearly suppressed anger. Florianus had to admire his rhetorical skill, polished in year after year of debates in the Senate.

After the opening pleasantries, he addressed the subject of the offer from the Placidi. The proposed marriage to the Placidus girl would cause outrage in the City, and infuriate almost every member of the Senate, except for the small number of Reds. The girl was widely known to be plain and dull-spirited, he said, and might not even be a virgin. The offer was an affront to the Imperial dignity, and in countenancing such a grotesque misalliance the General could only be pursuing some sinister political intrigue of his own…

Maximillus briefly pretended to be surprised, as Florianus in a private audience had advised him to do, should the news of the Placidian offer break before any official announcement. The General had told him *not* to speak to the Emperor, and of course Florianus had done just that—as the General would have expected him to.

The Emperor had never seen Julia Placida, and confessed that he had no idea what she was like.

"Why has she not been presented at court? Why has she been kept from us? Is she really so ugly? Or deformed, perhaps? Are any vital parts missing?"

Florianus turned occasionally to glance at the door. If he was right, the General would not come to the audience, although he had doubtless been told by now. He *must* be right! The other possibility, that the Naevii were mounting an unexpected and unwanted challenge to the General's plans, was too awful to think about.

Now the Emperor raised the topic of Julia Placida's virginity.

"Can't she be tested?"

"Of course, your Majesty, there are formal procedures. The girl would be examined by the High Priest of Sol and the High Priestess of Luna, by your humble slave, in his capacity as High Chamberlain—"

Maximillus smirked. "I'd like to be present, too. After all, if I'm supposed to marry her…"

From behind him, Florianus heard Quintus call out, "Let me test her!" Speaking out of turn like this, and uninvited, was an unheard of insolence in the Imperial Presence. Both Florianus and Senator Naevius turned to rebuke him, and in that very moment Julian slid into the room past the Guardsmen, a smug expression on his face. He nodded to his master, and mouthed a silent "No". The General would not be coming! The gods be praised!

With a great show of dignity, Naevius advised against the ritual examination.

"Priests and doctors can be bribed. For it to be convincing, the examination would have to be witnessed. And the Placidi would never allow the girl to be humiliated like that in public. She is, after all, from a Senatorial family."

Maximillus put on the bored, petulant face that Florianus knew so well.

"What a pity. Then no Julia Placida…"

Naevius advanced a step towards the Emperor.

"But there is a further option, your Majesty. There is another young lady from a Senatorial family, a girl of great beauty and of spotless virtue"—actually, Florianus had received somewhat different reports from his informants on the question of her virtue—"my own granddaughter, Naevia. She has her father's good looks and her mother's modesty of character"—good that it wasn't the other way round, thought Florianus—"and she is waiting to be invited to court. She yearns to be admitted to the Presence."

"Oh, well, send her then! And she *is* a virgin? Let's take *her*, then. Make the arrangements, Chamberlain. The General will need to be told, and the Senate will doubtless want to vote on it."

Naevius was beaming.

"Only the Reds will vote against it, your Majesty! She is a delightful girl. She will make your Majesty deeply happy, I promise you, and will give you many children: fine, strong sons, and beautiful daughters."

This was now going too fast in the other direction. Florianus was sure that the General had set up this confrontation between two ambitious families, with the intention of causing a stand-off that would gain him time. If so, Florianus must now win that time for him. His moment had come, the moment for a flabby eunuch to step out on to the world stage and, incomplete as he was, help to shape the future of the Empire.

It would be easier not to argue with the formidable Senator Naevius, but to address himself to the Emperor, whom he knew how to manipulate.

"Your Majesty, may your slave speak?"

"Of course, Chamberlain. I imagine that you have some practical advice, from one virile man to another, on how I should, um, pleasure my bride on the wedding night?"

That was an invitation to the complete men to laugh at him. As they did. Let them, he thought.

"Your Majesty, there are now *two* Senatorial virgins eager for your embrace. But perhaps there are even more? Your Majesty should be given the opportunity to choose his own bride, from a selection of candidates."

"Yes?"

The Emperor was showing interest, but even without turning round Florianus could sense that Senator Naevius was now very displeased with him. So much for the undying friendship of the House of Naevius!

"There is an ancient tradition that fell into abeyance before the time of your grandfather. It is called the 'bride-show'. The loveliest virgins from our most distinguished families are invited to present themselves at court. There is a prescribed ritual. Each tries to show herself to her best advantage, seeking only to please your Majesty. Because your Majesty, and your Majesty alone, will be the judge!"

This suggestion met with the Emperor's unqualified approval. It sounded like great fun! The General would have to agree, naturally. And why shouldn't he? (Florianus was also confident that he would, especially when he found out how long it would take to organize the elaborate ceremony.)

They were soon dismissed from the Presence, so that Maximillus could go back to bed. Florianus once again made the deep prostration, and touched the hem of the Imperial nightdress.

Outside in the corridor, Senator Naevius rounded on him angrily.

"Are you a complete fool? The Imperial assent to my granddaughter had already been given. Why did you have to come up with this stupid ritual?"

Quintus Naevius said only: "You're a dead man, eunuch!"

Florianus adopted the emollient tone usually expected of senior court officials.

"Please consider it carefully, sir, and you will see that I am right. If your granddaughter were chosen too precipitately, there would be opposition from within the Senate, and perhaps from the Army and the provinces, too. And there could be resentment among some of the other noble families, whose daughters were given no chance to shine at court."

"True…"

"But at a public ceremony, if your charming granddaughter is seen by everybody to win, and to win fairly, there will be popular support for her to become our next Empress. And competing against the dull Julia Placida, and against a handful of plain daughters of Senatorial colleagues of yours, who will be hand-picked for the occasion—"

"Capito's daughter Anthemia, for instance."

"Precisely, sir, you understand exactly what I mean! Without wishing to be rude to the young lady, I can safely say that his Imperial Majesty will *not* find the Lady Anthemia much to his taste. And then there is the Lady Cornelia, the daughter of Cornelius Rufus—"

Quintus sniggered.

"Another Red slut."

"—who is also widely renowned for her plainness. I've already made a short-list of suitably feeble candidates. Against such drab competition, your beautiful granddaughter is *bound* to win, isn't she?"

"Of course she will."

Quintus Naevius was more enthusiastic than his father.

"I know my daughter—she can't lose! And she'll even suck his dick, if that's what it takes."

XIX

AULUS ENTERTAINS TWO YOUNG LADIES,

WHILE HIS UNCLE INSPECTS THE SEWERS

✠ *The house of Senator Lucius Pomponius Atticus, in the City.*

Lucius Atticus had not been very happy. He told his nephew that he had taken shameless advantage of Davus. The secretary had been forced to keep to his bed that day with back pain, and Aulus had then entertained in the Senator's home two young people whose families were the Senator's political enemies.

"Davus himself is in no way to blame. Nor do I apportion any blame to the gatekeeper. Servo is slow at the best of times, and he probably barely understood the arguments that you advanced for countermanding my orders. Strangely, none of the other slaves saw your visitors…"

Aulus was used to his uncle's rebukes and admonitions, which tended to be in the vein of "more in sorrow than in anger".

"I have spoken to Servo, uncle, and…well…I have *apologized*. I am glad that you haven't punished him. It is I who deserve the punishment."

The Senator's eyes widened in surprise.

"Apologizing to slaves? Begging to be punished? Sol in the bright heavens! What a way to talk! Don't tell me that you've joined the Slave cult! Have your parents infected you with their religious nonsense after all?"

And they had both laughed.

Aulus had prepared himself for this conversation very carefully. He now did what his uncle would have least expected him to do: he reminded his uncle of the ultimatum that he had set him.

"Aulus, I don't know what to make of this. Have you had a complete change of character? Are you going to devote the rest of your life to sobriety, good works, and clean living?"

"No, uncle, but I took your ultimatum to heart."

"Come, come, *ultimatum* was the wrong word. I was never going to enforce it! But we old politicians have our silly way of expressing ourselves. It was advice. It was a request. It was a little push. And on your parents' behalf. I couldn't ignore what your mother wrote to me, could I now?"

Aulus explained why Sextus Placidus and Fannia had visited him that day.

"I know that you don't approve of either of them, uncle."

"Well..."

"But Sextus and I share an interest in poetry. A *serious* interest."

"I'm happy to hear that there is *something* that you take seriously, Aulus. Even if your interest has not yet borne much fruit in the form of... completed verses."

"But study must come before practice, uncle. In any discipline. And Sextus is an accomplished poet."

His uncle sniffed.

"I leave that for *you* to judge, my boy. This is not an area of life that I am overly familiar with."

Aulus took a deep breath.

"The waywardness of his outward behavior merely reflects the inner turmoil of creativity that he is experiencing!"

This time the sniff was a snort.

"And the Lady Fannia? What kind of inner turmoil explains her... I really don't know what word to use, *waywardness* hardly expresses it."

"She is his muse, uncle, his inspiration."

It had hurt him to put it in words. Unfortunately it was true, he realized.

But then came the essential move. Dissolute as both of them might seem, Sextus Placidus and the Lady Fannia were remarkably expert in all matters social. They knew every young person of noble family in the City, and many others in Trebenna, Sybaris, and even in the East, and whether they were of good or bad character. They would be his guides and advisors in the search for a suitable partner! Who better than Sextus Placidus and Fannia to warn him which girl was debauched (Aulus had preferred the expression "*too* experienced")? And who better than them to tell him which girls were boring (Aulus had said "pure")?

Amazingly, the Senator had swallowed the bait. Sextus would make recommendations, and Fannia (without Sextus, though) would escort the young ladies to the Senator's house and chaperone them at their meetings with Aulus.

"Excellent, young man! I can now report to your mother that the matter has been taken in hand. There is no need to introduce these young ladies to me, until you have discovered an outstandingly promising candidate. Unless of course you feel the need at some stage to consult a man of greater experience..."

Aulus had gratefully acknowledged this kind offer of help, although he doubted that his uncle in his long and distinguished life had gathered more experience in *that* area than Aulus already had in his short and undistinguished one.

And so it happened that one day very soon afterwards Fannia presented herself at the entrance to the Senator's house for Servo's uncritical perusal. She was accompanied by her cousin, the Lady Cornelia. An auspicious afternoon had been chosen for the visit. The Senator was attending yet another Senatorial committee meeting, this time to discuss (at length) the renovation of one of the City's ancient sewers. The members of the committee would then be embarking on a visit of inspection, which could take many hours to conclude. Finally, there would be a visit to a bath-house, for reasons of necessity rather than pleasure.

After a round of embraces, with Cornelia's embrace with Aulus being noticeably stiff and chilly, they began to make polite social conversation. At first, Fannia had to do most of the talking, as Cornelia was exceptionally shy.

Aulus had never really looked at her closely, and he was not quite as revolted as he had expected to be. She didn't *look* older than he was. She kept moving her veil with her hand, to shield part of her face, but it was only shyness (or embarrassment, Fannia later suggested), because she had no visible blemishes.

Her face was plain, not because her features were ugly, but because she refused to allow any emotions to play across them. Sol, she'll be frigid in bed! Was she really obsessed with him? She was showing no signs of it. He was slightly nonplussed by the fact that she was wearing no makeup. Admittedly she had no need to, because her complexion was flawless, but it was hardly what was expected of young ladies in society. Fannia, in contrast, was wearing enough makeup for two.

Similarly, although Cornelia was tall and slim, with limbs that might well be beautifully shaped under the drab, unrevealing gown that she had chosen to wear that day, her movements were stiff and ungainly. Aulus couldn't imagine her writhing sensually in the ecstasies of passion.

Her answers were brief, until the subject of religion was broached by Fannia (who was fast running out of topics of conversation). Her cousin immediately asked Aulus: was he a follower of the True Faith, as she was?

Aulus asked her to be more specific. There were numerous religions and cults in the eastern and western halves of the Empire whose adherents would describe their own belief as the only "true" one, and denounce all others as superstition or heresy.

She was, of course, a follower of Our Lord the Slave—none of the other religions made such a fetish of sexual purity as *they* did—but it was the older form that she favored, the "Greater Worship" of the East, as most southerners did.

And Aulus?

"No, I am still a seeker after truth," he replied (best not to make his religious skepticism too obvious to her), "but my parents adhere to the Western form of your religion, and my uncle to the worship of Lord Sol, so I live surrounded by religious influences."

Not quite what she was hoping for, but the best that he could manage.

"Then you haven't found the path of righteousness yet?"

He gave her as sweet a smile as he could muster.

"Perhaps you can open my eyes to, er, *revelations* that I have missed so far?"

And then the dam broke. There was no stopping her! With flashing eyes, she told him that the Slave was *of* God, not *with* him, as the deluded Western followers of the "Lesser Worship" propagated. That was the fundamental difference, from which sprang all the ridiculous lies and heresies of the Westerners. Poor Aulus had been denied the chance to experience the wondrousness, the sheer beauty, the *purity* (that word again!) of the true religion. But she would gladly be his guide, accompanying him step by step and holding his trembling hand on the upward journey into the glorious Presence of the Oneness of the Slave!

Cornelia became positively animated, her face glowing sweetly and her body moving instinctively to emphasize the points as she made them. Aulus had soon given up trying to follow the tedious religious rigmarole, but now, and against his will, he found himself almost charmed by her girlish enthusiasm.

And she looked much prettier too. On the scale from one to ten that he and Sextus applied to their female acquaintances (and on which Fannia, to his mind, represented the perfect score), Cornelia had leapt in barely a few moments from a dolorous three, or at best a dull four, to a serviceable six, and maybe even a promising seven.

And who would ever believe it? Aulus could even imagine *doing it* with her. Perhaps he could be *her* guide, in matters of the flesh, while she was instructing him in matters of the spirit? It wasn't a completely unpleasing thought.

Fannia turned the conversation to the subject of matrimony, on which she knew her cousin had strong feelings. (What young girl didn't?) Indeed, said Cornelia, it was the ultimate goal to which every woman should aspire. And, remarkably, her faith upheld the values of those upright Citizens of earlier days, before the rot of decadence set in, who pronounced that ideally neither the person nor the name of a virtuous wife should ever leave the marital home.

Yes, yes, said Fannia, but wasn't it an awful pain that young people were given so little say in the choice of their future husband or wife? She, of course, had no intention of marrying, and who in any case would be interested in a penniless girl from the Fannii, a family that wasn't even represented in the Senate? She loved only one man—Sextus—and she would never stop loving him, with her whole *body* (she shuddered dramatically) as well as her soul, even if he was forced to marry another.

She looked pointedly at Cornelia (and fortunately not at Aulus, whose little boat of emotions had just been tossed onto the jagged rocks of despair).

"It's not *your* fault, Cornelia, I know that. And Sextus has as little wish to marry *you* as you have to marry *him*! But your father has decided, hasn't he? You poor girl!"

A moment before, Cornelia had blushed at the mention of physical intimacy. Now she looked thoroughly downcast.

"I would never knowingly cause you pain, cousin. But what can I do? He is so anxious for me to get married at last. Sextus would not be the perfect choice, but he's from a Red Senatorial family."

"It's a pity that there is no other candidate! If your father is so desperate to get you off his hands—"

"He thinks that I'm unmarriageable."

"—then he won't worry about religion or politics, will he? Provided it's a Senator's son." She eyed her cousin slyly. "Do you know, Aulus is in the same position as you are, more or less."

"Really? Whom is *he* being forced to marry?"

That was awkward! Details like that hadn't been worked out in advance, and Aulus wasn't good at thinking on his feet. But Fannia was.

"Keep this to yourself! They haven't told him officially, but there is one name that has been mentioned…"

Which name was that? Aulus was agog to know who it was that Fannia had arranged for him in her imagination.

Cornelia was also eager to know.

"Who is it?"

"The Lady Livia Ogulnia. *Her* name has been mentioned in connection with Aulus."

"No! *No!*"

Well, her name had definitely been mentioned now! So that at least was no lie. And what an excellent choice it was. Livia Ogulnia, daughter of a Green Senator and niece of the pompous Terebinthian, had been at the center of an enormous scandal. While visiting her country cousins in an obscure corner of the Province, she had been seen participating in some gross night-time ritual, dancing, scantily dressed, around a so-called fire of fertility in the company of several strapping farmers' sons, who were also as good as naked.

Soon after this shocking occurrence, Livia Ogulnia had disappeared, first socially, and then literally.

It was rumored that her distraught parents were searching frantically for a husband to unload her onto. It should if possible be a gullible young man from a Green, preferably Senatorial, family. More important than that, however, was that whatever poor fool they did find for her, he must be willing to take on the hefty Provincial baby that might now be growing in her belly.

"Yes, poor Aulus." And Fannia flashed him a fake-pitying look that was entirely for Cornelia's benefit. "Poor Aulus. He's always been too nice, too willing to sacrifice himself for others." Then she brightened up. "Never mind! It's *your* problem that we must concentrate on now. Sextus and I will give it our full attention." She paused very slightly, with exquisite timing. "And maybe *Aulus* can be of help too."

He was only too willing to help, though not so happy that Fannia could imagine him in the role of the simpleton who was going to rescue Livia Ogulnia and her unborn child.

"Yes, of course, anything. Anything at all."

"And now, cousin, I think we ought to be going. We don't want to outstay our welcome, do we? And there was no particular reason for you to see the Senator, was there?"

There wasn't. Senator Lucius Atticus should be the last person to find out that his nephew wanted to marry one of the enemy. (Although it would all be a pretence.) The seed had presumably now been sown in Cornelia's mind.

She gave Aulus a much warmer embrace than she had given him when they arrived.

As the two young ladies left, one of them turned to give Aulus a lingering look of genuine heartfelt feeling. Unfortunately, it wasn't Fannia.

XX

MARA IS TOLD THAT SHE IS ONLY GOOD

ENOUGH FOR THE KITCHEN

 *The house of Lord Governor Senator Faustus Pomponius Atticus, in Fanum Fortunae.*

Mara was provided with clothes, of a sort: a scratchy tunic made out of what once might have been sacking for vegetables. Then Castor led her through the streets of the city to the "royal palace" that Orcus had spoken of, the "number one address in Fanum Fortunae", whatever that meant.

Mara stared, turning her head from side to side, as they negotiated squares, wide streets, and alleyways. She had never seen a proper city before. The shacks and booths of Cascantum were nothing compared with this!

The air in the narrower streets was fetid. And there were so many people, jostling, shoving, breathing in each other's faces. How could they choose to live so disgustingly? Some stared at her, and a few made unpleasant comments. She heard the word "cunt" several times. One man said, "She'll soon wear *him* out!"

The old man had untied her bonds. She could easily have run away from him, but where would she run to? She would soon get lost in this horrible place. They would chase after her, and quickly catch her, and what then? Whips? Branding-irons?

Once or twice she stumbled. The alleyways were muddy, but the wider streets were paved with cobblestones of different sizes, worn down and polished smooth by many years of being walked on. Mara was used to feeling earth under her feet. The long march with the slavers had not been too difficult for her, but now she slipped and slithered on the cobblestones.

The old man told her that his name was Castor. He said that he was secretary to the Lord Governor, Senator Faustus Pomponius Atticus, a very important man indeed. It was to the Lord Governor's house, on the outskirts of the city, that they were now going.

"You are Lord Castor?"

"No, just Castor."

"But the man at the market said *Lord* Castor."

Castor laughed.

"He was being ironic!"

Mara wasn't sure what "ironic" meant.

"So you are not a lord?"

"No, child, I was once a slave, just like you, until my master freed me. If you ever speak to the Senator—no, if he ever deigns to speak to *you*, and you need to answer, because you must never address him directly—or the Lady Pomponia his wife, you must say 'Your Lordship', or 'Your Ladyship'. But when you speak to me you can call me 'Castor'. Unless you're trying to wheedle something out of me—then you should say 'Master', or 'Sir'. Or even 'Lord Castor'! Now do you understand what 'ironic' means?"

"Not really."

"I wish I could explain it to you in the Tongue of the Horse People, but my knowledge of your language isn't sufficient. But you can give me lessons, starting tomorrow even. I'm a quick learner!"

Mara was surprised.

"You want me to be your teacher?"

He chuckled, but didn't answer her. Finally they reached the gate of a large house.

"This is the Lord Governor's mansion!"

Mara wasn't impressed. Maybe it was bigger than other people's houses, but it was smaller than the open plain, or the hills, or the forest. She had been in houses, of a sort, in Cascantum. They were smaller than this, but they were all places that trapped you, confined you. The air wasn't good. There was no view.

The Horse People lived in tents, which could be huge, semi-permanent affairs, if you were a chieftain, with separate areas curtained off for different purposes or for different members of the family. But the air was always fresh. And there was always a view. Even the horses were not locked into rooms.

Castor was greeted by a large, unpleasant-looking man carrying a spear. The great lord Faustus had a slave just to stand by the door? He spoke politely to Castor, in the Citizens' Tongue, though with the heavy, ugly accent of the Sueni.

Mara looked for signs of branding or mutilation, and to her relief saw none. Nor did the man have any obvious tattoos. Mara wasn't worried about tattoos. Among the Horse People only slaves had them. Yet a warrior captured in battle could also be made a slave—there was no dishonor in that. It could happen to anyone.

Inside the house, the corridors and rooms were dark and gloomy, despite the lamps and decorations. Why did they willingly live like this when there was daylight outside? Castor beckoned to a tall young man to approach.

"Mara, this is Leon, the footman. You will go with him to the kitchen, where Tania the head cook will look after you. Be polite to them, and do what they tell you."

He gave Leon the bill of sale, and told him to show it to Phoenix, the steward. Mara should be washed, given new clothes, and fed. If she caused any trouble, Castor would deal with it himself.

Mara had absolutely no intention of causing trouble.

The washing was a strange business. It took place in a special room, with water-troughs sunk into the floor. The kitchen-maid who had been told to take her there stripped off Mara's sacking tunic and rubbed her body down with a wet cloth, giggling as she touched Mara's breasts and the parts between her legs. Then she pushed her into one of the troughs. To Mara's surprise, it contained warm water. It felt unnatural.

The girl laughed.

"Horsey-girl never had a hot bath? You can go in the cold tub if you like, but don't think I'm getting in there with you!"

She took off her own tunic, and climbed into the water too. She was much darker than Mara, with very smooth skin, slim legs and no body hair. She rubbed at her again with a different cloth, which reminded Mara of how her mother or a slave used to wash her in the stream, before she was old enough to wash herself. But that water had been cold, and they had rubbed her fiercely, until her skin was red. This girl rubbed her very gently, and the water was so warm that she could have slept in it.

"Your skin's so rough!"

"And your skin's so smooth. You are not from the north, are you?"

The kitchen-maid's name was Lelia, and she was from Sybaris, she said. She had been a slave since her childhood, and had been trained as a lady's maid. She shouldn't be working in the kitchen, she complained, she should really be serving in the house, but the Mistress wouldn't have her there because of her scars.

Lelia's skin was smooth, but on one side of her face it was rougher, and furrowed and discolored, from a burning accident.

After the accident, her previous owner had sold her, cheaply, to the House of Faustus Atticus.

Lelia told Mara to get out of the water. She dried her with a long, rough cloth like a horse-blanket.

"There's other stuff we do in the bath-house. It can be fun. I'd like to show you, but we haven't got time for that now. Did you like it when I put my hand between your legs?" Mara didn't know what to say. "Oh, never mind. You know, I came here with Leon once"—she giggled—"but don't you tell anyone!"

Next, she fetched a long tunic for Mara, like the one that she herself had been wearing. Mara put it on, but it didn't fit well, so Lelia fetched another one. They had a distinctive pattern on the left breast.

"That's the badge of the master."

"So there's no branding?"

She hadn't seen any such brand-mark on Lelia's body, except for the scarring on her face.

"No, of course not! They don't do that kind of thing here. Though the mistress—"

"Yes?"

"Enough talk! You'll find out everything for yourself, Mara Horse-lady. Now it's time for food!"

Lelia took her back to the kitchen, made her sit at a wooden trestle-table in the corner, away from where the cooks were working, and brought her soup and a hunk of bread; then, because Mara was so hungry, more soup and another hunk of bread. The bread was fresh from the oven, and the soup tasted good.

While she was eating, Tania the head cook returned, with two men. Mara had already seen her briefly. She was a fleshy woman, with rolls of fat on her thighs and upper arms, and a hard face.

The older of the two men was carrying her bill of sale. He was dressed in a tunic like the ones that Lelia and Mara were wearing. He was a slave, like them. But around his neck was a chain with a medallion hanging from it. He didn't speak to her, but Mara guessed that he must be Phoenix, the steward.

The younger man wore different and much finer clothes. He was handsome and dark-skinned, even darker than Lelia, with his black hair dressed in curls and ringlets. He was small and slim, with delicate features, like a girl's, and small hands. He had a permanent knowing smile on his face, not at all like the frown on the face of Phoenix, or the head cook's scowl, and seemed quite interested in Mara.

Tania called her over to them, then spoke to the younger man.

"This is the girl that Castor bought. A useless barbarian trollop. He must be losing his wits."

The steward coughed.

"Let us not be disrespectful, Tania. He is now a free man. He can spend his money as he chooses."

With a graceful movement, the younger man reached out his arm towards her and, with his hand under her chin, turned her head first to one side, then to the other.

"Hmm, I don't know. She's a pretty thing—for a barbarian. And the price was not insubstantial."

He looked her directly in the face, and the twinkle in his eyes gave her courage to speak.

"Are you the master?"

Tania stepped forward. Smack!

"That's for speaking out of turn. You might as well learn it now, from me. It'll save you more pain later. No, he's not the master. And he's not the mistress either!"

The steward spoke: "This gentleman is a house-guest, who was simply curious to take a look at you. Your master, your *owner*, is Castor, who before me was steward here. Now of course he is secretary to our master, the Lord Governor Senator Faustus Pomponius Atticus." His voice was dry and disinterested. "Our mistress is his wife, the Lady Pomponia Godslave."

Mara was puzzled. "God-Slave?"

Tania smacked her again, then drew back her hand for a further blow. The younger man restrained her.

"No, don't punish her. How can she possibly know things like that?"

"Well, Victor, in this house she'll need to find out, won't she? The sooner she finds out the better. Why don't *you* explain it to her?"

Phoenix intervened.

"It is not the duty of our master's guests to train the slaves under his roof. Mind your rudeness, Tania."

But Victor only smiled.

"No, no, she has a point. Tania and I have known each other for a long time, haven't we? Besides, my dear, the pigeon pie that you served us last night would excuse tenfold any rudeness that I could ever imagine."

The cook simpered, making cow-eyes at him. There was some kind of understanding between them.

"It was specially for you. I know it's your favorite."

"Humor me, Phoenix. Let me explain it to her—if such peculiar things *can* be explained." He turned to Mara. "It's like this: the gracious Lady Pomponia is a follower of The Slave. The Slave Religion."

Mara asked timidly, "Is she a slave?"

"No, of course she isn't! And it doesn't stop her beating her servants. The followers give themselves cult names. The more humble the name, the more important you are. You don't have that north of the River, do you?"

Mara moved her head from side to side, as she had observed the Citizens did when they meant "no".

"So, God*slave*: that means she's rich."

Tania looked alarmed.

"Shh! Not so loud!"

"And then they have their priests, the Slave Men. It's a good job: they don't have to pay tax like the rest of us. They hang around the rich old ladies. Where the money is, of course. The more important ones call themselves Godservant or Godchattel. However, if your name is God-seeker or Godfollower, Godfriend, Godlover, well, then you're just a nobody."

"Don't talk like that!"

"Don't worry, Tania. To your dear mistress, I am simply Victor God-searcher, a fervent believer now returned to the true path after a life of pagan licentiousness."

Mara wasn't sure what "licentiousness" meant, and was scared to ask.

"Victor, be careful what you say. You never know, the mistress might encourage her to join in the worship."

"No, she won't do that. She doesn't want to have any young women there. *Real* women, Tania, women like you. Women whose parts aren't dried up like prunes."

"Derya is a follower, though."

He laughed.

"Derya! Is that a woman? Only a brave man would want to go there. But this one's got some juice between her legs!"

Tania took a sudden step towards Mara.

"Which reminds me."

With an unexpected movement she pushed Mara down onto the wooden bench.

"Open your knees!"

As Mara hesitantly did so, the cook slipped a hand under her tunic and between her thighs. Close to tears, Mara struggled only half-heartedly.

"Keep still, girl, or it'll really hurt! Ah, as I thought! You've been *ridden*, haven't you? Castor paid good money for a virgin, it says so in the bill of sale, and they sold him a little slut! The old fool—he didn't examine you, did he? No, of course not! So who was it that broke down *your* gate? One of the slavers? Or maybe it was someone from your family? A nice hairy uncle, perhaps, poking you open."

"No, I've never… *done it*."

Tania snorted in disbelief, but Victor smiled.

"Oh, I believe her." And to Mara: "How long have you been *riding*, then? Horses, I mean."

"Since I was weaned. Because that is the way of our people."

He turned to Phoenix, the steward.

"And there you have it! That is the explanation. She hasn't *been* ridden. She's been riding. It was a horse that got between her legs! Lucky horse."

Tania was not over-impressed.

"Who knows? I don't care—it isn't my money. But Castor paid extra for her virginity—"

Phoenix peered at the bill of sale that he was holding.

"It constituted half the total price."

"More fool him! It's not as though *he'll* be popping her cherry, will he?"

For some reason, this was funny. Tania laughed at her own joke, if that was what it was, Phoenix smiled, and Victor sniggered. It was a cruel laugh, which seemed out of place—he was otherwise so charming.

The steward was the first to return to seriousness.

"Castor must have had a motive for buying her. She isn't for his bed, that's obvious I think, so there must be some some other reason."

Victor was intrigued.

"I wonder what that might be? Strange that Castor of all people should buy her, and at such expense. It's hard to think why, given her new master's well-known *predilections*. It would be interesting to find out."

"She may belong to Castor," the steward announced, "but if she is to remain in this house, eating and sleeping under the Senator's roof, and wearing his badge on her chest, the Senator will have to be told, and the mistress, too. And she could do some work around the house, to pay for all the food she'll be consuming."

"Oh, yes?" Tania said. "And what exactly did you have in mind for her, if I might ask? Lady's maid?"

"Maybe as a household maid? She speaks the Citizens' Tongue."

"Yes, but she moves like a boy—a *clumsy* boy. Besides, look how coarse her skin is."

The steward sighed.

"That is true, she is hardly pleasing on the eye…"

"She's as hairy as a barbarian pony too"—which was a gross exaggeration—"so the mistress won't want to look at her more than once. If she won't tolerate Lelia, she won't want this thing anywhere near her either. And she can't be used for waiting at table, can she? Her stink would repel our guests. But she can serve here in the kitchen, or in the store-room, or as a privy-cleaner. Phoenix, it's *your* decision."

"The kitchen, then. But why not the stables? After all, she's from the Horse People. She must know a lot about horses."

Victor now joined in the conversation.

"That might not be a good idea, steward. We want to keep our little horsey friend nice and safe, just where she is. Give her the run of the stables, and—who knows?—at the first chance she might be off and away. And who would be fast enough to catch her?" He looked at Mara. "I'm right, aren't I?"

He was. Give me a horse, Mara thought, and I'll be gone from this bad place, and never look back.

XXI

MANASA GETS TO WATCH A GAME OF

DICE, THE OUTCOME OF WHICH IS

OF NO SMALL CONCERN TO HER

✠ *In Fanum Fortunae.*

To her disgust, Manasa had not been bought until almost the end of the day. They had priced her too high. Lots of men came and peered at her, and a few enquired. She was too expensive, though. There was only one Senator in Fanum Fortunae, and his secretary had already been and gone, taking Mara with him. Rich merchants—did Fanum have any rich merchants?—had not been much in evidence. And Manasa was not destined to be a toy for a shopkeeper or craftsman.

The slavers' best hope of selling her (even at a more reasonable price) would be to someone from the Citizen Army, such as a wealthy Staff Officer, or a Sub-officer willing to blow his savings. Fanum wasn't a military town; indeed there was only a small garrison stationed there to protect the Lord Governor, and for ceremonial duties, but soldiers did come down from Cascantum on leave, or as couriers, or on other business.

And so that was how Manasa came to be sold, shortly before sundown.

Unfortunately, the buyer was not a handsome Staff Officer, smelling of violets and perfumed hair-oil, nor a sensible, hardworking Sub-officer, but a monstrous-looking cavalryman, who was still wearing his riding leathers and stank of horse- and human sweat.

The man was slightly drunk. He was quite taken with Manasa, pawing at her and telling her in a thick Sueni accent that she was a "handsome piece of horseflesh" and that he was going to "give her one", "do her", "nail her good and proper", and so on, once he got her back to the inn.

Manasa had no liking for the Sueni. Based on their reputation, but also on her past experience of them, she regarded them as being both primitive and two-faced. They had sold out to the Citizens, but they had learned few of the Citizens' manners or skills.

She was also worried about what might happen at the inn. He was huge, but heavily built and muscular rather than just overweight. When he came at her, she would need all her wiles and skillfulness to avoid being badly torn and bruised. Even if he only collapsed on top of her, after battering her black and blue, it would be like being crushed under the dead-weight of a Sybarite bull.

However, when it did finally occur, and after he had had the decency to order some food for her (and wine for himself), and had waited surprisingly patiently until she had eaten, consuming a large quantity of wine while he was waiting, it was over almost before she had noticed it. He did the deed, most unimaginatively, and then turned over and fell asleep, snoring.

Snoring hardly described it. He groaned and shuddered like a deep-sea monster all night. When he turned over in his sleep, Manasa had trouble not being pushed out of the narrow bed. She considered switching to the floor, but it was even filthier than the bedclothes were, and she heard animals scampering about during the night.

Outside the inn they had passed some of his men, who were lodged in cheaper accommodation but had come to "sign off". Seeing Manasa, they had made obscene comments, as soldiers were wont to do, and had tried to fondle her breasts, whose charms were barely hidden by the rags she had been given by the slave-merchants. All this happened while their Troop-commander—his name was Urtho—was giving instructions for the following day.

One of the Sueni cavalrymen, who introduced himself as Turgulo, even made a timid play for Manasa. If she got bored with the big guy, which would happen soon enough, believe me it would, he told her (though the old man wasn't too bad, as Troop-commanders went), well, she wouldn't have trouble finding *him*, and he would give her a *really* good time (so long as Urtho didn't get to know about it).

They would be in Fanum, he said, for a week if not longer. The Lord Governor had imagined seeing a filthy Blood-Drinker, probably lurking under the bed, and had crapped himself on the spot. *They* had been sent to sort things out! Of course there weren't any fucking Blood-Drinkers south of the River, or even any of the Free People, for that matter, but if there were, well, let them beware!

He could teach her a thing or two, Turgulo assured her. Oh, yes! From the northern mountains to the Sybarite Sea, Sueni men were famous for their skills in love-making.

Manasa—again from experience—knew this to be completely untrue.

She also doubted whether this little troop of swampies would be likely to put the fear into any intruders that they happened to bump into. Any encounters that these troopers had with real live Blood-Drinkers would be over in seconds. Only the finest Divisions of the Citizen Army would have even the faintest chance of holding the Blood-Drinkers once they had crossed the River in large numbers.

Why did men delude themselves so much? Wasn't it easier to get through life if you looked the truth in the eye?

The next morning, Urtho had a massive hangover. Before they got up, he mounted Manasa again, but even more perfunctorily, as though it was expected of him and he didn't want to be rude. So much for the love-making skills of the Sueni! Then he ordered breakfast.

The dumpy Sueni maid who brought it took in the scene at a glance, then glared rudely at Manasa—at inns, it was the maids who were supposed to provide this kind of service, for a small fee of course. Noticing this, Urtho shouted at her and threw a heavy lead tankard across the room.

His hangover stayed with him for hours, to judge from his behavior. He talked to himself, muttering, snarling, and growling in his own tongue in such a way that Manasa, whose knowledge of it was excellent, had trouble following him. Was he angry with himself for wasting his money on her? That's what it sounded like.

When the sun was high, Urtho left the inn (he said) to see to his men. In the meantime, Manasa could clear up and clean the room. After having a tankard thrown at her, the maid had understandably not bothered to return. But he didn't want any maids sniffing around anyway.

Above all, she must clean and polish his gear. She knew how to do the saddle, didn't she? She did indeed. (Military saddles were too valuable to be left in the stables of an inn, so Urtho's saddle had spent the night at the food of their bed.)

If she did it well, he promised, he'd buy her some better clothes and take her with him that evening—they'd have some proper fun, oh yes! Manasa wasn't sure whether Urtho's idea of "proper fun" was something for a girl to look forward to, or not.

He came back with clean undergarments, a tunic, and some sandals for her. All of them were oversize. Had he been thinking of himself when he bought them?

The evening's "fun" proved to be a drinking and dicing party at a tavern in the next street, a hostelry that was even less appealing than the inn they were staying at. The other participants were all Citizen Army people, mostly Sueni like her new master.

Manasa's role was to fetch her master's drinks, and to allow him to fondle her and show her off to the other men, in order to make them envious ("She's an unbelievable fuck," he let them know). Above all, she was there to admire his skill at dice, about which he had boasted over breakfast.

However, the success that Urtho expected was slow in coming. He had very little money left to stake, after buying Manasa the day before on a drunken whim, and to be able to get into the game and stay in it he needed to win some cash early on. But the dice didn't roll as he wanted them to.

They were playing Doghead, a simple game favored by drunks, soldiers, children, and anyone else not inclined to be bothered with complicated rules. It had been agreed that only heavy silver could be staked—no Maximians.

In the classic form of the game, you played with six dice, putting a coin in the pot every time you threw a six. The more sixes, the more coins. Six sixes, or the Goat, was a terrible throw, but not as bad as the Dog, which was six ones, when you were required to double whatever amount was already on the table. Towards the end of a game, that could be really nasty—unless you went on to win in the end. When someone threw the Goddess, where each of the dice showed a different number, they scooped the pot.

Urtho threw a Goddess in the second game, but it was only the third round, so he didn't win much. Otherwise, he threw lots of sixes, his money slowly draining off into the kitty, which was being eyed intently by two brothers named Gorgo and Gorgias.

Urtho was convinced that he would triumph eventually, but he was rapidly running out of stake-money. Whenever players dropped out because they had no more money left, they were replaced by others. But Urtho was unwilling to give up. The more he drank, the more determined he seemed to become to hold out until the final great victory, which he probably imagined would come after an immensely long game of thirty or more rounds, with lots of sixes, which would end when somebody threw a Goddess—that somebody being him!

Players came and went. Gorgo won big, and dropped out to enjoy his winnings. He was replaced by the innkeeper himself, which was not a good sign, because innkeepers seldom lost in their own taverns (though nobody ever accused them of cheating).

Gorgias also won, and left the table. The new player was a Citizen Sub-officer, a quiet, middle-aged man, whom Urtho immediately took offence to, for reasons that Manasa didn't understand. Urtho needled his new opponent constantly.

"Where's your dirty horsey friend, then? You still hanging out with granddad? You need to learn their fucking lingo! I hope the Blood-Drinkers got her."

Then he threw a Dog. The pot was full, so he couldn't double it with the handful of coins that he still had left in his purse, but the other players let him stake his silver Sueni bracelet instead. It was clunky, and valuable.

The pot continued to grow. It was now a small fortune waiting to be scooped up with a Goddess.

Two rounds later, unbelievably, Urtho threw another Dog. He raged and cursed. Would he now have the courtesy to hand over his last few coins and drop out of the game? No, there was far too much at stake. He suggested adding Manasa to the pot; after a brief discussion, the other players agreed.

Manasa should have been outraged. She looked around the table. Unless Urtho was truly beloved of the gods (something for which she had seen no evidence so far), one of the other men sitting there would soon be her new master. None of them were young. None of them were very good-looking. But, unpromising as they were, at that moment they all seemed more attractive to her than the drunken Sueni cavalryman.

A few sixes were thrown. The innkeeper whispered to Manasa that he was looking forward to what the two of them would be doing later on, after he'd won the pot.

Urtho heard him, and was furious.

"Shut up, you cunt! You haven't won yet!"

In the background, two of the innkeeper's doormen positioned them-selves to move quickly if Urtho should dare to make a lunge at their boss. Though threatening in appearance, they were smaller than the cavalry-man was, but Manasa knew that men like that were skilled in every kind of street fighting nastiness, and could throw or incapacitate men much bigger than themselves.

Urtho and the innkeeper glared at each other.

"Fuck you."

"No, fuck *you*."

"We'll see, my friend, we'll see."

And see they both did, five rounds later, when the Sub-officer, whose name was Thomasius, threw a Goddess.

XXII

FLORIANUS FINDS OUT WHAT SENATOR

GAIUS PLACIDUS KEEPS IN HIS CELLAR

�֍ *The Imperial Palace, and then the house of Senator Gaius Julius Placidus.*

Florianus had been anticipating a visit. He was sitting quietly at his desk, dealing with a backlog of orders and commissions that had accumulated in the past few days, when the expected messengers from the Placidi arrived.

He had just commuted the punishment order for the thieving assistant cook. The stupid man would not now have his right hand removed, and then be sold; instead, he would receive forty lashes from a whip of customary weight (without the added refinements of the metal-studded scourge, for instance) and be demoted, so that he no longer had free access to the treasures of the pantry. (Florianus had made enquiries, and learned that the man was a promising cook—it would be a pity to lose such a talent permanently.)

Julian showed the two visitors in, announced them, and then stayed, hovering in the background, with an exaggerated expression of concern on his face. Was he curious, or did he really think that he could be of further use, if the situation turned unpleasant? Florianus doubted very much whether Julian would be much help. The men were not courtiers.

They both had the front of the head shaved, and wore their hair long at the back, a look that was popular with thugs and gangsters. Ignoring niceties, one of them told Florianus that he was to come with them, because there was someone who wanted to speak to him.

"Do I have any choice?"

The hour was late, and the streets outside the Palace were fraught with danger even before sunset. But Florianus had known that he would be sent for. The Naevii had made their move; now it was the turn of the Placidi.

No, you have no choice, they said. One of the men did all the talking, but they stood side by side, like great ugly twins, filling the central space of the room with their threatening presence.

Fear was no stranger. Eunuchs spent a lot of their lives being frightened—an imperial palace was always a frightening place, especially the imperial apartments and the women's quarters, where favorites could quickly fall from grace, and the risk of being poisoned was ever present. To get rid of a hated rival, deadly powders could be added to their food, or snake venom, or (if the death was to be slow and painful) ground glass mixed with chopped human hair.

In this case, however, Florianus wasn't frightened at all. The Placidi would not kill him—yet. They knew that it was not the eunuch on his own initiative who had thwarted their offer of Julia Placida to be the bride of the Emperor. He didn't have the power to do so, and probably not the courage either. If their offer had therefore come up against a serious obstacle, it can only have been through some decision by the General, or through a whim of the Emperor himself.

On the other hand, he was still in a position to help them, since he would be the master of ceremonies at the bride-show.

He would happily go with them, he said, if they could ensure his safety? The streets, as they well knew, were controlled by Quintus Naevius and his friends.

"Not a problem," he was told. "We have a small escort waiting outside the Kitchen Gate."

A good choice! There was always a coming and going of slaves and contractors around the outer entrance to the kitchens, where deliveries of flour, spices, fruit, or fresh fish might arrive at any time of the day or night.

Julian made as if to accompany them.

"No, your man stays here."

That was a good sign. If they had intended an abduction, they wouldn't have left such an obvious witness behind. Unless Julian was part of the plot. He had been paid by the Naevii; could the Placidi have bought him as well?

The escort was unflatteringly small, but they assured him that there would be no danger.

"You see, there's a fight going on over in the Market Quarter. Some of our boys went to one of their taverns and wrote 'Fuck Naevius' on the outside wall. In nice big letters. It's turned into quite a battle. That's where they'll all be now."

They brought Florianus to the house of Gaius Placidus, a ramshackle old building in the heart of the slums. His brother owned a large and luxurious villa beyond the walls of the City, as befitted one of the most influential members of the Senate. Gaius, despite his fabulous wealth, obviously felt no need for that kind of ostentation.

The door was opened by a hulking gatekeeper, which was nothing unusual: gatekeepers were normally chosen for their sheer size, and Florianus had never seen one who didn't tower over him. The gatekeeper then passed the eunuch on to a footman, who escorted him through a sequence of gloomy, barely-lit and almost unfurnished rooms, and finally into the presence of his master.

Senator Gaius Julius Placidus remained seated behind a bulky, ornately carved wooden table that was covered with parchments. He allowed Florianus to wait, standing fidgeting like a naughty schoolboy, before looking up from the document he was reading and giving him his famous one-eyed stare.

Small children were often told frightening tales about the "wizard", but Gaius Placidus was not physically impressive. He was scrawny, with a pockmarked face, thin lips, and a slight muscular deformity that made it difficult for him to look at anyone face-on without his body being turned slightly to the side. Instead, he would stand face-on, but stare with his head turned, so that you normally saw only one of his eyes.

Those eyes, whichever of them was fixed on you, were huge pools of blackness, with nothing behind them: no indication of character, or kindness, or humor, just darkness, as though the man himself were somewhere else in spirit—or as if a different being had taken over the body of Gaius Placidus for its own sinister purposes.

Unlike his brother, the Senator never took part in Senatorial debates, and was seldom seen in public, and even then never before dark. Perhaps he was ashamed of his unattractive appearance—though Florianus doubted it. He noticed that Placidus had a tattoo on his forearm, but couldn't make out what it was.

"So, now I have time for you, eunuch. It was wise of you to accept my invitation."

The voice was quiet. Florianus had to strain to follow what he was saying. Again he asked: "Did I have any choice?"

The Senator laughed softly, an ugly, subdued sound that made Florianus think of a beast gorging contentedly on its prey.

"No. My men had orders to take you by force if necessary. But then they would have *bruised* you a little. And they would have killed your man."

"Oh, there would have been no need for that, sir. He is easily bought."

"I know that. But why waste money?"

And the Senator laughed again, his eye drawing Florianus in and seeming to invite him to share in the laughter.

He resisted the temptation.

"I am here now, sir, and at your service."

"Yes, I know that you are here, and that you are at my service. And I expect that *you* know why I sent for you."

"I can imagine, sir, that it concerns the offer of your ward, Julia Placida, as a bride for his Imperial Majesty."

The Senator made a tut-tutting sound.

"Dear me, I am disappointed by your lack of acuity. I always assumed that eunuchs compensated for the removal of their testes by increasing the power of their brains. Or maybe you merely expressed yourself sloppily?"

"Sir?"

"It does *not* concern the offer that my brother made to the General. That offer stands. Nothing more needs to be said, or unsaid. No, it concerns what has happened *since*."

"The offer made by the Naevii?"

"Indeed." The Senator pursed his thin lips together. "*That*."

"Please believe me: we had no choice but to humor them."

Florianus explained how the Naevii controlled the City—which was true. Also, how they could overrun the Palace at any time, killing the Emperor and seizing the throne for themselves. This, however, was not necessarily true.

The truth was that they would have to kill the General, which would bring down upon their heads the wrath of the Citizen Army; also, that the conservative supporters of the Naevii yearned for security, and the safety of their property, not civil discord and anarchy. In any case, they had no obvious candidate for Emperor: old Naevius wanted control rather than direct power, and the loutish Quintus would not be acceptable to the Senate or to the Army.

From the point of view of the Naevii, an illegitimate successor, or, even worse, a clash of contenders, would be disastrous. It would be an open invitation to the hated heretics of the East to intervene, in the name of revenge for the murder of their own Emperor's cousin.

But if Florianus hoped that the Senator would accept his explanation unconditionally, he was mistaken.

"Eunuch, you are only telling me what I already know, and only *part* of what I know. But I didn't have you brought here for that."

Could the Senator read minds? Florianus shivered. The house was cold as well as dark.

"No, sir."

"As you say, the Naevii already have physical control of the City. And as you know, we are not from here, we are from the south—our power lies elsewhere. Even so, we *can* effect changes here, but slowly, and not always openly. We use influence, we use money, and sometimes we use…certain other methods. But not brute force. We can't block Senator Naevius directly, *and nor can you*. We understand that. We don't blame you for anything."

Florianus gave inward thanks to all the gods, wherever they might be.

"The Emperor won't allow the bride-show to be canceled; he is looking forward to it far too much. I can advise him, sir, but I can't *tell* him which bride to choose."

The Senator responded with unexpected friendliness.

"Of course you can't! We must all tread carefully—but that includes the General too. Old Naevius hates him, and the General would be crazy to allow that pack of rats to establish themselves in the Palace. But I have heard that Ogilo made an agreement with my brother, and I assume that at the right moment he will honor that agreement. And that you will also play your part by whispering in the imperial ear when that moment comes."

"Of course, sir."

"Then let the bride-show go ahead. We have nothing to fear from it. My niece is a charming young lady, unlike the child of the repulsive Quintus Naevius. My brother has tabled a motion for the next meeting of the Senate, 'On the future marriage of his Imperial Majesty' or some such wording. Let us see what happens."

"Sir, there is no hurry!"

"Not true. The sooner that Naevius is taught a lesson, the better. This should be resolved quickly, don't you agree? Good. I see that we understand each other. And so there is no need for further discussion? Our business for the day is over, then. You are free to leave, you'll be happy to know! I see that you are shivering. Personally, I never feel the cold."

Despite his feeling of relief, Florianus was far from content. Caught as he now was between the expectations of the two most powerful families in the Empire, he was about as happy as a man being pulled apart by two huge dray-horses.

The Senator informed him that his men would escort Florianus safely back to the Palace.

"Though before you go," he added, "let me show you something."

A slave bearing a torch led them down a narrow flight of stairs into the cellar. There was a long corridor, with rooms to left and right, but with closed doors that were secured with heavy padlocks. On the doors were arcane symbols. Florianus, who out of curiosity had delved occasionally into such matters, recognized several of them. One of them was the sign of the demon Abraxas, eater of souls.

The corridor turned sharply to the left, and the torch spluttered in a draught as the Senator pointed to a open door.

"This way."

The three men entered the room, which was murkily lit but surprisingly large. There was a row of tables, with nothing on them but straps and chains. A secret torture chamber?

Florianus was close to panicking. Had he miscalculated after all?

As they walked the length of the room, Florianus saw that there was something on the last of the tables. It was all that was left of a human being, still strapped down even though most of its skin, flesh, and organs had been removed. The skull grinned. Surrounding the tattered skeleton, dark stains were visible on the wood of the table.

Florianus felt queasy, and had a strong urge to sit down.

"Are you not feeling well?"

"The air is close in here, Senator. I didn't realize that you, umm, had a…"

"A torture chamber? Oh no, this is not a torture chamber! Surely you have seen real torture chambers in the Palace?" Florianus had indeed seen them, and seen them in use, too. "You do me an injustice. I am a seeker after knowledge, not some thug who gets drunk on the pain that he inflicts on others."

"I recognized the signs of arcana on the doors. Your Excellency seeks particular forms of knowledge that are denied to most mortals."

"Very true! And the greatest mystery of all, my Lord Chamberlain, is the human body. Why does the blood flow? What enables us to see, or to hear? Why do we breathe? How can we find out, except by looking more closely? Normally, we glimpse the inner parts of a man's body only when the man is being done to death. The executioner tears off limbs or cuts organs out of the victim's body and burns them in front of his eyes. Or he forces him, or his children, to eat them. A vulgar, messy spectacle, always the same crude butchering, and we learn nothing from it. But how do those organs function? To know that, we must look inside the *living* body, and look at our leisure. That is the kind of knowledge that I seek."

Florianus realized what he meant, and shuddered. He pointed to the remains on the table.

"Who was that?"

The Senator shrugged.

"Who knows? I forget. And who cares? There is not much left of him, is there? Or of *her*. What you see here represents many days of hard work on my part! Chamberlain, I am honoring you by showing you this. You are squeamish, yes, but you have the intelligence and learning to realize the significance of my work. I expect no praise or appreciation."

"This was a person, with a name…"

Yes, but it would be a person of no significance. It might be a condemned criminal, supplied by arrangement with the executioners. Or his assistants would bring him material that they had acquired (he never asked them how). Occasionally he would place an order for a particular person, someone of no importance, but who was *in the way*, and therefore need to be rendered inactive.

"And I have to admit a small personal weakness: it makes my work more interesting if I know who it is, there on the table in front of me. If they have enough education, I even try to explain to them what I am doing, before the pain clouds their consciousness."

Florianus was now trembling.

"May we please go upstairs again? I am having some difficulty breathing. I believe that I need to sit down."

"Of course. This way please. I am sorry that there was so little left for you to see after all. Maybe I promised too much. This must be very boring for you. And I am sorry that you are not feeling very well. Still, since we are going past them, look, let me show you my vats, over there on the left. But that is only discarded material, for disposal. I am moving out of here, you know. I have important business elsewhere."

Florianus saw a row of large earthenware jars. In the first were small pieces of jellyfish, or squid. He looked closer. They were eye-balls.

He didn't care to look in the other jars.

XXIII

MARA MEETS A BOY WHO LOOKS LIKE

A GIRL, GIVES HER MASTER A LESSON,

AND SWEARS A SOLEMN OATH

✠ *The house of Lord Governor Senator Faustus Pomponius Atticus, in Fanum Fortunae.*

After Phoenix and Victor had gone, Lelia showed Mara what her future kitchen duties might be: chopping vegetables, for example. Mara was good at that. She knew how to handle a knife without cutting herself or injuring someone accidentally. A knife might also be a handy acquisition, she thought, if she could find a way of smuggling one out of the kitchen. But Tania supervised the kitchen staff closely; she made a note of which person was using which knife, and she reclaimed it when the slave's duty came to an end.

Afterwards, the kitchen-maid took Mara to the quarters of her master, Castor.

"Why did he buy you? He's never touched a girl in his life! He's the only man in the house who keeps his fingers to himself, when girls are around. Except for the master. And that's only because the mistress would cut his bits off if he…you know?" She stopped and looked at Mara. "Or maybe you don't know? You're the famous virgin, of course!"

"I don't know why he bought me."

"He must have had a reason. You were expensive enough. Maybe he wants to give your virginity to someone as a present? But I didn't know he had friends like that. They're usually boring old professors and lawyers."

"He wants me to be his teacher. He can speak our Tongue, quite well, but he isn't satisfied. He wants me to teach him, though I don't know why."

Lelia looked thoughtful.

"How interesting! And how unusual…"

Lelia left her at the door to Castor's room, after telling Mara always to come to her if she needed help, or wanted a shoulder to cry on, or had something interesting to share.

She wished her good luck with the lessons. Maybe Mara could instruct her, too? In return, Lelia would teach her some Old Sybarite, "the ancient tongue of the sorcerers—very useful for casting spells and placing curses".

Mara tapped on the door and, hearing a sound from within, entered. She had barely crossed the threshold when she was almost knocked down by a raging demon that threw itself at her, shouting "I hate you! Go away!"

Then Castor was there, pulling the demon off her—it was a girl, no, it was a boy who *looked* like a girl. Mara had never seen such a creature before. It was even wearing makeup!

"Phrygillus, I can't have you attacking everyone who comes near me. If you don't stop it, I'll have to sell you. And that would break my heart."

Upon which the boy-girl burst into tears, and fell sobbing at its master's feet.

Castor introduced her to Phrygillus, his "little assistant". Now she understood the remarks about Castor that had been made in the kitchen, and by Lelia. There were boy-lovers among the Horse People, but these were mostly young, unmarried warriors who formed blood-brotherhoods with each other. If one of them married, he might even share his wife with his friend. The wife would accept it as her duty, the friend would feel honored, and no-one would take it amiss.

Sometimes it was an older man and a youth, but a youth who had already begun to grow hair on his body. The older man would instruct him in hunting and fighting, and everything else that manliness required.

But a hairless boy painted like a girl at a festival? What was the point of that? The world of the Citizens was indeed peculiar!

Castor reassured the boy that his place in his master's affections was safe. He had important work to do, he said, for which he needed to improve his knowledge of the Tongue of the Horse People. Mara would be helping him. That was why he had bought her. That was the *only* reason.

The boy stopped sniffling.

"And wouldn't it be nice for you to have a big sister? Someone to look after you, and cuddle up with you at night, when I'm not there?"

Mara was less than enthusiastic about that idea. The nights on the march when she and Manasa had cuddled up together had kept them both warm. And had kept her spirit from going to a dark place. But this little creature might be a biter and scratcher, or even a bed-pisser, and in a few years he might want to do things to her.

She didn't say anything, though. She was a slave now, and must learn to take what was thrown at her, until she had a chance to escape. She had expected a fate far worse than having to bed down with a painted boy.

"Now, give Mara a kiss, and say sorry for hurting her."

And the boy did so. Despite his dark coloring, he had gorgeous, violet-blue eyes.

"Can we be friends?" she asked him.

He nodded, looking very serious.

"'Friend' is *alaphā* in the Tongue. Am I right?"

Oh dear, the lessons had already started. This was not going to be easy.

"Yes, but only if the friend is a girl." She pointed at Phrygillus. "A boy is *alaphé*."

"So, my little finch, you are my *alaphé*!"

"Yes, but if someone is *a bit more* than a friend, he is *anaré* if he is a boy, and *anarā* if she is a girl."

"Then you are my *anaré*!"

"No, we don't say 'the' or 'my'. *Anaré* is not a thing, it is what you are with someone. *Alaphé* means that you are good with someone; *anaré*, that you are…very close with them."

Mara was surprised that she could explain the Tongue so well. She had only ever used it; she had never talked about it.

Castor wouldn't give up.

"You are *anaré*. And I am *anaré* too!"

This was also wrong. Two young warriors could be *anaré* for each other, but not an old man and a boy who looked like a girl. That was silly. *Anaré* was between equals, and included trust and taking responsibility for each other. She had to be careful. She wanted to correct Castor, but there was no polite word in the Tongue to describe the relationship that he had with Phrygillus.

"*Anaré* is only used for young men, who hunt together and share their weapons." Then she had an idea. "He is your *seflar*: it means 'treasure'. And you are his *seflarôn*: the owner of the treasure."

"Yes, I like that—he *is* my treasure. Now, little *seflar*, go to the kitchen. Let them spoil you, but before you return ask them what I can have for a late supper. Can you do that?"

The boy nodded, and slipped away.

Castor sighed.

"The Tongue of the Horse People is harder than I thought. And it seems to have little in common with the Citizens' Tongue. But you must teach me more."

"Yes, Lord Castor!"

He looked at her intently, and then laughed.

"That was irony, wasn't it? You see, you're learning!"

There was no more teaching, however. He asked her about her clan, the Speaking Bird, and her father. She told him about her grandfather, too: although he was very old, his voice was still a respected one in the High Council of the Horse People. When he spoke, men were silent. Then they talked about how she had been betrayed and abducted.

"They thought I was a princess. They were looking for a princess. How could that be? There are no princesses among the Horse People."

That was very interesting, he said. But he showed even more interest when she mentioned the name "Issachar".

"Who spoke that name?"

"One of the other girls, Manasa. She said that now I belonged to Issachar of Maritima."

"Really? Did the slavers say that name, too?"

"One of them, Orcus, did, but they told him to shut up. Who is Issachar?"

Castor told her that this was something she didn't need to know, and, besides, she would sleep better if she didn't.

Phrygillus returned from the kitchen, looking petted and spoilt. He sat down happily at his master's feet, gazing up at Mara, and listened to their talking. Suddenly Mara looked down in surprise: he was snoring! For a small boy, he made a great deal of noise.

"He is sleeping. Good! He doesn't need to hear this. Mara, I bought you for a special reason, but not quite the reason that you think. There is somebody that I want you to meet, when he returns from Cascantum. He asked me to look out for you, or someone like you, and he will be interested to hear your story. So will his master. In the meantime, trust no-one and talk to no-one, except me, about any of these matters. Even Phrygillus. He is only a child: he has no control over his tongue."

Mara told him that she had already confided in Lelia.

"She wants to be my friend."

"She is an intelligent young woman. Because of her face, though, she is trapped in the kitchen. That makes her bitter, and desperate. She might sell information, if somebody came asking to buy it."

And she told him how Tania, Phoenix, and the house-guest, Victor, had talked about her.

"Victor is a trader in luxuries—including slaves."

Mara was shocked.

"But he was so charming, and good-looking!"

"Hush, you'll wake the child. Victor deals in spices, silks, gemstones, and in very expensive house-slaves from Sybaris and the East—not kidnapped Sueni women and horsey princesses! And he's wormed his way into the favor of Lady Pomponia. That's all I know about him. But I don't trust him. He's been asking too many questions among the slaves. Including questions about me. I have avoided speaking to him so far. Keep away from him, Mara. He will be leaving soon."

Mara promised to do so. It was a pity, because he was such a handsome man, even if he was a slave-trader, and he had such a sweet smile and twinkle in his eye...

Then, ruefully, she remembered the conversation she had had that night in the forest, with Manasa. People weren't always what they looked like. Had she forgotten her discovery so soon? She hoped not. But she also hoped that Victor was truly as nice as he seemed.

Phrygillus snored again, very loudly. He was now curled up like a puppy.

"Perhaps he should be put to bed?"

Castor looked down at the boy tenderly.

"He is all I have. He is my *seflar*—you see, I remember the word! But I won't be here forever to look after him. I don't want anything bad to happen to him. And I don't want him to be broken, so that he can never grow up into a proper man."

"I don't understand."

"Because he is such a beautiful creature, there are men who desire to possess him. They would do things to him, very cruel things, without kindness. I've never done that. Yes, I spoil him. I kiss him. I cuddle with him. I drink in his beauty with my eyes, every day, and it makes me happy to be alive. As he grows up, perhaps he'll learn to love me in return. Perhaps he won't. I'm just a foolish old man." His voice hardened. "Mara, listen. I've probably saved your life—one day, you'll understand what I mean—and so there is something that I want *you* to do for *me*."

He asked her, should anything happen to him, to look after Phrygillus while he was still a child. Mara said "yes" immediately, but that wasn't enough for him. He made her swear a solemn and binding oath, after the manner of the Horse People, pledging on the spirits of her ancestors, the honor of her clan, and the secret name of the God Who Cannot Be Named (how did Castor know such things?) to love and protect Phrygillus as best she could. If she broke her oath, may She with the Talons come and tear out her heart. She swore the oath.

Looking down at the spoilt child, who was now muttering in his sleep, Mara wondered what she could be letting herself in for.

XXIV

FLORIANUS GOES WHERE EUNUCHS

ARE NOT SUPPOSED TO GO

✠ *The Senate Chamber.*

In attending a meeting of the Senate, Florianus was taking a calculated risk. The sessions were open, but only to those of Senatorial rank—meaning serving Senators, and their eligible sons, who were supposed to attend in order to learn what would later be expected of them. They were also open to those high officials and ministers of state who needed to interact with the Senate or bring it instructions in the name of the Emperor.

However important his position in the Palace hierarchy might be, the attendance of a eunuch chamberlain at Senate meetings wouldn't be regarded as necessary or seemly. It was not in keeping with the dignity of the Senate for castrati to be seen listening to its deliberations.

If he were discovered, Florianus wouldn't be lynched, but he would be subjected to a humiliating eviction from the Senate Chamber. Most of the Senators knew him; his presence there was accepted, and none of them would deliberately expose him; but he was expected to remain in the background, and to be *discreet*.

That said, there were always plenty of non-Senators in evidence. There was the permanent Senatorial staff of scribes and clerks, and each Senator was entitled to bring a slave or freedman secretary with him. It was in the rows of uncomfortable wooden seating at the side of the Senate Chamber occupied by these underlings that Florianus, wrapped in a rough woolen cloak, had hidden himself.

It wasn't the first time he had attended a session of the Senate. The grand new Senate Chamber, replacing the one burnt down during the Years of Chaos, had been built adjoining the Imperial Palace. This symbolized very neatly the way that the Senate had become completely dependent upon the Throne—its glory days were over. And the closeness to the Palace made it easy for Florianus to slip into meetings without arousing unwanted interest.

Altogether there were hundreds of Senators in the Western half of the Empire, but most of them at any given time were absent from the City, either because they were living on their estates or because they had been excused their Senatorial duties and were serving, in the provinces or on the frontier, in some civil or military function. And many who *were* in the City were too old, sick, or lazy to attend meetings.

Those who did attend were the politically ambitious, the self-important, the snobs, and the windbags. (A less cynical person might have said "those with a sense of civic responsibility".) The quorum was a modest fifty. Attendance was never much over a hundred, and that ninety or so were present today was a good showing. But then again, the main item on the agenda was of great interest to everyone, and not least to Florianus.

Those ninety were being remarkably undisciplined and restless, and it took some time for the chairman, the City Prefect Lentulus, to call them to order. He stood facing them, standing beside the ornate throne reserved for the Emperor as First Citizen (on those few occasions when his Majesty deigned to address the Senate), next to which a more modest magistrate's stool had been placed for the chairman himself to use during the debates. Behind the throne stood two Imperial Guardsmen in their white cloaks.

It took some time, because Lentulus was notoriously doddery and incompetent—the Naevii had used all their influence to ensure that the City Prefect would be a weakling, unwilling or unable to use his police to control their gangs. They had made one concession: Lentulus was a White, and so very co-operative in rearranging the agenda at short notice, or in supplying Florianus with confidential information.

How pathetic he was! Florianus longed for someone to crack a whip and bring the noisy wretches to heel. He had experienced better-behaved schoolchildren. Earlier "strong men" who had wielded power in the days of weak Emperors had not been shy to march into the Senate Chamber with a troop of soldiers and "invite" the Senators to support or oppose a particular motion.

That was not the style of the General, though. Ogilo preferred the outward show of constitutionality to be maintained. Was this respect for centuries-old procedures because he himself was half a barbarian? Florianus had far less respect for the Senate. They had only one truly important function, which was to confirm the accession of a new Emperor. Otherwise, they should do what they were told.

The delicate balance of votes within the Senate added to its ineffectiveness even further, since no single faction could regularly command a majority.

The largest faction was that of the Blues, led by Senator Marcus Naevius.

Then came the Greens, the supporters of the General, led by Appianus Terebinthian from the Province and by Lucius Atticus from the City.

The Greens were in uneasy alliance with the Whites, the followers of the Maximian Dynasty, an alliance that Florianus had helped to forge. In matters on which Whites and Greens could be brought to agree they would usually hope to win the vote, but only by a narrow margin. It helped if a small number of Blues or Reds could be induced, by arguments or bribery, to vote with them, or to abstain.

The smallest faction, the Reds, representing the interests of the great landowners of the South, was led by Cornelius Rufus and Gnaeus Placidus.

Reds and Blues loathed each other: for reasons of history (the Sybarite War), of geography and culture, and of religious belief (the southerners adhered to the "Greater Worship" of the Slave, the Blues of the City to the reformed "Lesser Worship"). When they *did* vote together, which happened only seldom, the result was stalemate in the Senate.

Florianus peered across at the Senators on their marble benches. Some of them had already unpacked parcels of refreshments. The Founding Fathers would be turning in their graves! The General would also not be amused. Two elderly Senators at the back were sleeping, nodding and wheezing happily. They were probably senile, but unwilling to give up their membership because of the generous expenses that they could claim.

There were about thirty Blues, eighteen or twenty Whites, perhaps twenty-five Greens, and fifteen or so Reds—the usual balance. The first motion would not be contested, but then things might become more interesting. A strategy had been put in place, however, and the key players carefully briefed. Florianus, the author of that strategy, was there to observe, and trusted that everything would proceed as planned.

Having at last achieved a measure of quiet in the Chamber, the Prefect addressed the Senators using the age-old formula of greeting, which was in an archaic form of the Citizens' Tongue that no-one had spoken for more than two hundred years. Even Florianus, who had scholarly interests, found the text difficult to follow.

Then the Prefect offered the customary thanks to Sol, invoking His protection and guidance. The noise started up again, with jeers and catcalls from Senators who were followers of the Slave. Except for the

Whites and a few Greens, there were no Senators who were believers in the state religion of the West.

Lentulus called for silence, to no effect. This situation had been anticipated, and Lentulus knew what to do. He signaled to the two Guardsmen, who thumped on the marble floor with their spears. Then he shouted out that this show of disrespect, if reported to him, would displease the Emperor greatly. Which produced the desired result: the Maximians were closely identified with the worship of Sol, and no Senator wanted to be accused of scorning the Emperor.

Now Lentulus announced the first motion, "On the future marriage of his Imperial Majesty". He invited the tabler of the motion, Senator Gnaeus Julius Placidus, to explain its content.

Gnaeus Placidus was assisted to his feet by the Senators sitting either side of him. The effort involved in this covered his face in a sheen of sweat. While he spoke, his neighbors continued to hold him upright. He was immensely fat. Looking at him, Florianus always thought that it was as if for once a whole pig had been inflated, rather than just a pig's bladder. It would be so easy to laugh at him, but no-one did, and there was silence as he spoke.

Placidus was a fine debater, with the skills of a brilliant lawyer and a gift for crushing opponents with sarcasm and witty invective. He was also known for his cruelty and ruthlessness, as well as for his great wealth. No-one wanted him as a personal enemy.

There would be no debate on this issue, so there was no need for him to display his rhetorical brilliance. Both Reds and Blues were strongly in favor of the motion, and the White and Green Senators had been asked to support it. His Imperial Majesty, now that he was entering the first years of the full glory of his manhood, was humbly beseeched by his loyal Senate to take to himself a wife, who would offer him the delights and comforts of matrimony, stand at his side on occasions of state, and, by bearing his children, provide for the succession, thereby ensuring the safe continuation of the incomparable dynasty established by his magnificent grandfather, Maximus the Great. And so on and so forth.

Nobody would vote against *that*!

Convention required that the members be invited to speak on the motion in order of seniority, which meant that the faction leaders would be among those who would be asked to speak first.

Marcus Naevius, the longest-serving member of the Senate and the leader of the largest faction, indicated his support, as did Cornelius Rufus for the Reds, Terebinthian for the Greens, and Lentulus's equally doddery brother Lentulus Pulcher for the Whites.

After a respectable number of elderly Senators had voiced their support for the motion, Lentulus the Prefect asked for a vote by acclamation. "Yea" produced a huge shout from all sides; not a single voice shouted "nay".

That was the easy part.

Gnaeus Placidus rose once again with strenuous effort to propose the second motion, which was in three sections:

> —section one suggested that his Imperial Majesty should be aided in his search for a suitable Empress by a bride-show, to be organized by those directly responsible for his household (Florianus ducked his head slightly, in case anyone should look in his direction);
> —part two stipulated that the bride-show should be in public and should take place immediately, but no later than the new moon;
> —part three proposed that the candidates should be (in descending order of age): Cornelia, daughter of Senator Gaius Cornelius Rufus; Anthemia, daughter of Senator Marcus Anthemius Capito; Julia Placida, daughter of Senator Publius Julius Placidus of revered memory; and Naevia, daughter of Senator Quintus Naevius (there was laughter at the mention of Quintus Naevius as a Senator—he hadn't been seen at a meeting of the Senate for ten years or more).

Once again the members of the Senate, in order of seniority, were invited to express their views.

Florianus twisted uncomfortably on the wooden bench. In the name of all the gods, this could take all day! He had forgotten to bring a cushion.

Senator Marcus Naevius supported all three points of the second motion. It would, however, be unseemly for him to comment on the candidature of his granddaughter (there was polite applause).

Senator Cornelius Rufus reassured the previous speaker across the factional divide that the candidature of his granddaughter was wholly acceptable. Naturally he could not comment on the suitability of his own daughter, whose name had been put forward by Senatorial colleagues unrelated to him (further polite applause).

Florianus was suffering. An older member asked the Prefect for permission to answer a call of nature. And now the great Appianus Terebinthian rose to his feet. He adopted the pose expected of an orator who was about to deliver a major speech. Florianus groaned.

"Esteemed colleagues, faced as we are with a motion of some complexity, on the three parts of which we may be called upon to vote separately, or on all three parts taken together, our Honored Chairman not yet having clarified the procedure to be followed..."

Like Marcus Naevius, he cut a majestic figure, but while Naevius looked the part of the stern Imperator, Terebinthian was more the great statesman, florid in appearance and gesture, the folds of his toga arranged with the same care given to the preparation of his speech.

He would, he declared, comment on the three parts of the motion in reverse order, concluding with the question of the suitability of the bride-show as a method for selecting a wife who would, after all, be co-regent with her husband and the mother of his son and successor. He would take into consideration the arguments for and against the bride-show, as well as its historical origins, its congruence with established social and religious practices, and questions of precedent and constitutionality.

Terebinthian usually formulated his major speeches with an eye both to publication and to posterity. This was going to be a big one! Yet despite the prospect that faced him of having to sit through a massively long showpiece of classical oratory, Florianus had to admire what the man was doing.

The most difficult part—elaborating on why the bride-show should *not* take place immediately—would be tucked cleverly inside the far less controversial topics of who the candidates should be and whether the bride-show itself was a suitable procedure. On this latter point, Terebinthian would conclude his speech with a mind-numbing catalog of the precedents for the bride-show—he was strong on legal precedent—producing a general mood of agreement (or at least of "Let's get this over with!") and creating a false impression of consensus.

What a clever fox! But this was what the General wanted from the Senate: that the bride-show should be delayed for as long as possible. Not much help could be expected from Lentulus Pulcher, speaking for the Whites—he was an ineffective orator—so it was Terebinthian who would have make the arguments and swing the vote. If Whites and Greens voted as one, and a couple of Reds or Blues failed to see why things needed to be rushed, the vote would pass.

Terebinthian enumerated the four candidates, praising their qualities in broad and unspecific terms: their virtue, breeding, and modesty, their beauty, their known loyalty, their likely fecundity.

"How is one to choose from amongst so many paragons of their sex? Fortunately, it will not be up to us; it will be the joyful task, and rightfully so, of his Imperial Majesty to make the selection. And he will have an abundance of charming ladies from whom to make his choice. Four, no less. Now four, gentlemen, is a magical number. There are the four seasons, the four winds, the four humors of the body, and the four temperaments. Many of you are followers of the Slave, whose life and death have been recorded in the Four Chronicles; or worshipers of Sol, with His four attributes: the chariot, the fiery crown, the thunderbolt, and the sword. Also fourfold are the stages of a man's life, namely the innocence of childhood, the energy of youth, the responsibilities of adulthood, and the wisdom of age. There are four social classes: nobles, commoners, slaves, and foreigners. And our ancestors in their wisdom gave our great city four main gates, not three or five. *Four is a good number!* Many of us support one of the four teams of the hippodrome. And we Senators have formed ourselves into four factions, too. Our four young ladies have been proposed by members of those factions, and you might therefore expect each faction to be represented by a candidate. But what do we see? The smallest faction is represented by *two* candidates, the largest by only one, and the second largest has no representation at all!"

At this point the Senator was forced to break off his speech by heckling from all sides. Why hadn't the Greens suggested someone, then? Why had the honorable Senator concurred in the wording of the motion? Why was he wasting everyone's time? Wasn't four also the number of boils on his backside? The number of his wife's lovers? The present number of his bastards?

The Guardsmen thumped with their spears.

"Order, order! The Senator must be allowed to continue. But may I remind him that he apparently intends to comment on all three parts of the motion, and that we wish to be finished by sunset. It would be a discourtesy to his Imperial Majesty to stretch this debate over several days. We are his loyal Senate, and he is waiting for our humble advice and support."

"Thank you, my Lord. And in that same spirit, may I say that these initial comments of mine on the third point of the motion immediately and directly affect what I wish to say about the second. Which is this. There is no Green candidate. In fairness, we should therefore be allowed to choose one, a process for which we shall need a certain period of time. A few small amendments should therefore be made to the second part of the motion. I would propose a period of two months minimum, allowing us to consult not only eminent colleagues who are present in this Chamber today but also those currently serving as provincial governors or frontier commanders. During that same period of two months, the colleagues of the Red faction may wish to consider reducing the number of their candidates from two to one!"

There were outraged shouts from the small band of Reds, and laughter from the Blues. Another clever move! Some of the Blue Senators might now vote to delay the bride-show, if only to anger the Reds.

Gnaeus Placidus raised a point of order, asking to be allowed to speak out of turn.

How did he justify the interruption of a colleague in mid-speech?

Very simple: that same colleague had, as a faction leader, approved the wording of the motion in advance, but was now calling it into question, an abuse of procedure for which he could be subjected to a vote of censure. However, if allowed to speak, Placidus would make a pertinent contribution that would resolve that problem and render a vote of censure unnecessary.

The Prefect gave him permission, but told him to be brief, and so Gnaeus staggered to his feet for the third time that day. Again he was held in position by his two neighbors, although he tried to make the classical rhetorical gestures once or twice to accompany his arguments.

Florianus saw that, like his brother, he had a mark or tattoo on his forearm.

"My colleague has spoken at some length, and very prettily. I shall, as instructed, be brief. Prettiness is an attractive quality in many things: in a race-horse of the hippodrome, in a woman, in a young boy. But it is redundant in other things: in a soldier, in an Emperor, or in an argument! The emphasis on the number four is irrelevant. There is no reason to tie the four candidates to the four *anythings*: winds, seasons, or city-gates. So why should they be tied to our factions? But I do appreciate that our colleagues of the Green party are disgruntled, though entirely through fault of their own. It was they who failed to name a candidate. Perhaps there are no Green virgins?" (Laughter) "Let us pass the second point of the second motion as it stands: the bride-show shall take place before the new moon. The High Priest of Sol and the High Priestess of Luna shall fix the exact date. Let no-one say that we followers of the Slave show no respect for the state religion! But it will be within that period of time: there is no good reason to wait any longer. The High Chamberlain shall organize it, and be held personally responsible for any delay. The Greens shall be permitted to name an additional candidate of their own choosing, but only if they hurry up, and by all means let the third point of the motion be amended accordingly."

A Green heckler shouted: "Unfair! Where are we supposed to find a girl so quickly?"

"May I respond to that, my Lord?" The Prefect nodded his assent. "There is an easy answer to your question, colleague. There is an unmarried young lady from an eminent Green family currently residing here in the City, in the home of her uncle. Rumor has it that she is in desperate need of a husband! I am speaking, of course, of the Lady Livia Ogulnia, the niece of our distinguished colleague Senator Terebinthian. She is reportedly no longer a virgin, which might cause his Imperial Majesty some offence, but if she really is the best that the Greens can manage, then better her than no Green candidate at all. I believe that answers the objection made by my colleague? ...Thank you for allowing me to raise the point, my Lord."

There was uproar. Terebinthian was humiliated, and the Greens were in complete disarray. Florianus saw his strategy collapsing before his eyes.

Senator Terebinthian was invited to conclude his speech, but declined, so they were spared an hour or more of legal and historical precedents for the bride-show. The debate continued, and many voices were heard, but the result was a foregone conclusion. The second motion was put to the vote by division (not acclamation or show of hands) with only one small amendment to the third part—that a fifth candidate might still be added, at the discretion of Senator Appianus Terebinthian.

The unholy alliance of Blues and Reds voted for the motion; their confrontation would come at the bride-show (and both sides seemed confident that their champion would win). The Whites opposed the motion. The Greens, visibly demoralized, mostly abstained. The motion was passed, by a large majority.

Florianus was thoroughly dismayed. The bride-show would be very soon—within days—and he would be in charge. There were two serious contenders, from powerful and dangerous families, only one of which could win. The chamberlain was caught between two savage, hungry beasts, one of which was going to lose its prey.

He wasn't happy—acting on the world stage was more difficult and frightening than he had expected.

Nor would the General be very pleased with him.

XXV

THOMASIUS BECOMES A MAN OF

PROPERTY, AT THE SECOND ATTEMPT

✠ *In Fanum Fortunae.*

The day didn't start well.

Thomasius had a thumping headache.

He had also slept badly, probably because he had been sharing the narrow bed with the Sybarite slave-girl that he'd won at dice the night before.

And when he had put his leg over her thigh, after discovering with his hand that she had delightfully soft skin, especially between her legs, and observing that she smelt very pleasant (certainly a lot better than the soldiers that he occasionally found himself sharing a bed with), she had slapped him hard across the face.

"Ow!"

"Soldier Boy: let's be clear about one thing. *I don't particularly like soldiers.* Now—go back to sleep. And try not to snore."

With which she turned her back on him, grunted, and made herself comfortable for the remaining hours of darkness.

He had never owned a slave before, and somehow he had the feeling that this wasn't how to do it. But he did what he was told. He did notice, though, that she allowed him to put his arm over her back in a loose hug. If he hadn't, he would at some later point have fallen off the bed.

She must have woken before him. When he opened his eyes, he found that she was gazing at him, her own gray-green eyes narrowed and serious. She was strikingly beautiful, despite her facial tattoos.

This impression was reinforced when she slipped sinuously off the bed, stripped off her undergarment, and, her back turned to him, washed her face, armpits and private parts with water from a basin in the corner of the room.

Maybe she sensed how he was enjoying watching her. She looked back at him over her shoulder.

"Stare as much as you like, soldier. You're not getting any of this!"

"I could have taken you in the night, if I'd wanted to."

"No doubt. And I could have cut your throat in the night, if I'd wanted to. But I didn't. We both made a wise choice."

"I *am* your master, you know."

"Can you prove it?"

He couldn't. He had no documents of sale, as she promptly reminded him. Urtho still had them, and he could come and claim his property any time that he liked.

"There were witnesses."

Witnesses could be bought and sold. More to the point: did he have any friends in Fanum? Urtho did. Lots of them. He had a whole troop of his men with him.

"And where is Soldier Boy's army?" she asked. "Am I missing something? Have you hidden them under the bed, perhaps?"

Thomasius tried a different approach.

"Do you want to go back to Urtho?"

At first she didn't answer, but looked at him thoughtfully.

"That's up to you, Soldier Boy."

Their eyes were now locked.

"My name isn't 'Soldier Boy'. My name is Thomasius."

She laughed, then looked away before smiling at him.

"That's the first intelligent thing you've said. *Thomasius*. Have you ordered breakfast yet? I'm hungry. My name is Manasa, by the way."

They went out to find a more promising place for breakfast than the Two Lions Inn. Despite its noble-sounding name, the hostelry was alive not with lions but with cockroaches. They had plenty of money to pay for food. In addition to the coins that Thomasius had been given for his expenses, there were his winnings from the previous night's gambling: almost two hundred heavy silver pieces, and a very nice silver bracelet, worth another thirty or forty. He also had a tiny leather bag of gold coins, though these were to buy the chieftain's daughter, Mara.

He still had to find her. This one was a dark southerner, a grown woman, not a blonde horsey-girl. But he was getting close. Through her, he might be able to locate Mara.

Over breakfast, he explained it to her. He told Manasa why he had come to Fanum Fortunae and how, after arriving in the city, he had gone straight to the slave-market. It was already empty, but in a nearby tavern he had found one of the slave-merchants, tucking into a hearty supper of grilled meat and roast vegetables. At first the man didn't want to be disturbed, but after a couple of free drinks, he became quite chatty.

Yes, there had been some horseys on sale, on commission. Slavers had brought them in. A total waste of time! Who wanted to buy that sort of shit?

Were there any young girls among them?

"Oh, I can see that you're a man of taste, sir! Come back tomorrow, and I can promise you a sweet little thing. From the Province, but quite dark-skinned, none of that blonde rubbish. A farmer's daughter. Her papi drank and gambled his land away and had to sell some of the kids. I tell you, she fucks like a goddess. I broke her in myself, so she's well oiled…"

She obviously wasn't a virgin. He was looking for a virgin.

A virgin? He wanted a virgin? There was no accounting for taste. Yes, there had been a horsey kid with a board round her neck. "Virgin", it said. Stupid cunts! Who wanted that horsey stuff?

He couldn't tell Thomasius who had bought the girl, though he thought it was some elderly guy, dressed like a Citizen, probably local.

"But the girl who was standing next to her: I know who bought *her*. She was a cracker! You can't help noticing that sort of merchandise."

(Manasa: "Did he really say that? 'A cracker'? Well, well.")

The man told Thomasius that she had been bought by an enormous Sueni cavalryman.

That could only be Urtho.

It had been easy to track him down, and to follow him to the inn. Thomasius watched the dice-game, but he had only joined in after Gorgo and Gorgias had dropped out. They were professional gamblers, and would be very hard to beat. You could see that the whole game was a set-up. The two brothers would fleece the innocent players, especially the naïve Sueni and the drunken soldiers, making them really hot for revenge. Then, after the pot had reached a certain size, they'd take their winnings and step aside to allow the innkeeper to reap the main harvest. Everything was pre-arranged.

But Grassica had taught him well. The dice were always loaded. You just had to work out which players knew that, watch how they threw the dice and how they landed, and learn the patterns. Of course you needed a bit of luck as well. Outplaying Urtho had been easy. He was just a big, noisy baby. Beating the innkeeper had been harder. The innkeeper wouldn't throw a Goddess to scoop the pot until it was really full. So you had to guess which round that was going to be—how greedy *was* he?— and then get in your own winning throw just before he made his move.

"Then it wasn't chance that brought us together? That's interesting to know! And all the time it was Mara you were looking for." She stared down at her now empty plate. "Then listen to me. Order some more of that baked sausage, and the fresh bread, buy me some clothes and sandals that actually fit me, and afterwards I'll make Soldier Boy a very happy man."

"Really?"

"No, not like that! Demons of Esbus, you men have only got one thing on your mind. Go away somewhere and do it with your hand! I said *very* happy. Look: I think I know who bought Mara, and in whose house that man lives. This is a very small city—it shouldn't be too hard to find out where he has taken her."

Returning to the Two Lions Inn, with Manasa now in newly purchased finery, they found that some unwelcome visitors were waiting for them. Urtho and two of his troopers had pushed their way past the innkeeper, broken open the door, and ransacked the room. They obviously hadn't found anything—Thomasius was far too experienced to leave either his valuables or his weapons in an unoccupied room in a cheap inn, even if that room was locked.

Urtho was not in a good mood. He should have come on his own, without involving his men. He was losing face in front of them—Thomasius was only half his size. Perhaps he had thought: if this man can fight as well as he rolls the dice…

"Let's make this quick, Citizen. You want your life? Good! I want my property back."

"Just stick him, boss, and take the girl."

"Shut up, you fucker!"

They had all been drinking, it seemed.

"What property are you talking about?"

"All of it. My bracelet. My money. And the girl."

Thomasius reached inside his tunic, brought out the bracelet, and threw it to Urtho, who failed to catch it cleanly. That was promising. He had indeed been drinking.

"Take it. I'm not a Sueni: I can't wear it. Your gods would punish me if I did."

"Clever boy. Now my money."

"And how much would that be?"

"Two hundred silver pieces! And *proper* silver!"

That was ridiculous. It was more than Thomasius had won, and most of that had come from the other players. Twenty or thirty would have been nearer the mark.

"No."

"What do you mean, no? How would you like three swords up your arse?"

Thomasius was good, and he had once been *very* good, but he wasn't good enough to beat all three of them, especially when he was weighed down by several bags of money. He hoped that Manasa would be sensible, and do something to distract them—or keep out of his way.

"You're all drunk. Without boasting, I can take any drunken swordsmen this side of the River, and two if I'm lucky. And I *am* lucky, as you may have noticed yesterday. One of you boys will definitely be getting my sword in his gizzard. Which one is it going to be? Maybe two of you." He paused, to allow them to think that through. "Oh, now I see! *This* is why you brought two of your men along with you, Urtho. Very clever. Well, let me guess—which of you two lads will be going first?"

Urtho roared in anger, but significantly he made no move.

His two troopers noticed that, and exchanged glances. Were they being used as sword-fodder? They too showed no inclination to launch an attack. They must have been thinking: why can't the boss fight his own battles? He's big enough.

Thomasius had been taught that every battle is won in the mind, sometimes even before the first sword is drawn. And that words can be more effective than arrows.

Urtho was shaking and sweating.

"Fuck you, you Citizen shit!"

But nothing happened. The swords remained sheathed. The moment had passed.

Thomasius had also been taught that the enemy who is red in the face, and shouting, and blustering, is not a man who needs to be feared. The truly dangerous enemy is the one who is cold, pale, fast, and silent.

"I'll make you an offer."

"I said: fuck you!"

"I'll only make it once, and it's the best you'll get."

"There are three of us, you bastard. What offer can *you* possibly make?"

Thomasius knew that he was almost there, so long as the two troopers held back. With drunks you could never be sure. Urtho still sounded fierce, but he was talking, and he was listening. The time for fighting had come, and now it had gone.

"Well, listen…"

He had won the girl fairly (which wasn't completely true). He had only won a hundred silver pieces (also not correct), but he would buy the girl from Urtho for that sum exactly, provided that Urtho brought him the deed of sale. What could be fairer than that?

Urtho puffed himself up.

"I think not. No deals. No talk. No offers. We'll take what we want. And if you get in my way, one Sub-officer less won't hurt the Empire." He turned to Manasa. "You say 'thank you' to the man for the new clothes, and then go through that door. *Move!*"

But it was only bluff. Manasa must have realized that, too, because she didn't move. Instead, she pouted theatrically.

"No. He won me, so *he's* my master now."

Urtho probably wasn't used to women talking to him like that. He shifted his weight like a thwarted bear.

"Then we'll do it my way."

He unsheathed his sword with a clumsy flourish; the two troopers did likewise, but more half-heartedly.

Even though the swords were out, Thomasius was almost certain that they wouldn't fight. It was time to end it.

"Stop!" He held out his hand in a gesture of authority. "Answer me this: what do you think will happen to you if you kill a Citizen Sub-officer in the course of his duty? Lord Commander Rhaetius won't be pleased with you."

"He'll never know. No-one is ever going to find the pieces. And as for *that* one"—he jerked his head toward Manasa—"I'll take her tongue out. Women are better that way."

Then they would be making a big, painful mistake—all three of them. Thomasius explained that he was in Fanum Fortunae to carry out a personal order from the Lord Commander. He was in daily contact with Cascantum by fire-beacon (not true, of course: he had no authorization, but the Sueni wouldn't know that). Half the people in the city had seen him, and half of *them* knew that he and Urtho had clashed at dice, or had heard Urtho bellowing about him in the street or at the inn.

The two troopers wouldn't be hard to identify either.

"Do you *want* to be impaled? Because that is what the Lord Commander now does to people who cross him. It's his new pastime. It's not a nice way to die. I'd take a sword any day."

The two troopers looked at each other and sheathed their swords. Urtho became still.

"A hundred silver pieces?"

"On my honor. A hundred silver pieces. Heavy silver, no Maximians. No more, no less. When you bring me the bill of sale."

"How do I know you won't run?"

"I won't. But post your men at the door if you don't trust me. *Outside* the room, though, please."

And so the matter was resolved. Urtho left, and Thomasius complimented the two troopers out of the room and into the corridor, but gave them some coppers for beer.

Then he shut the door. The lock was smashed, but the door could still be bolted from the inside. He breathed a huge sigh of relief, sat down on the bed, took out the bag with the silver coins, and started counting out a hundred pieces. They would wait for Urtho to return with the document. Then, for reasons of safety, they should seek new accommodation, perhaps further away from the city center. The search for Mara would have to wait until the following day.

"I like the way you did that. Good to see a man thinking with his brains just for once. Instead of his sword-arm, or his prick. Would you have fought them, or just handed me over?"

Thomasius, still counting the coins, was only half-listening to her.

"Fought them? Yes, probably."

Yes, he would have done. Not over the money, but over Manasa, because he needed her in order to find the horsey-girl—

"Good! I like to see men fighting over me!"

—and (he had to admit) because he wanted to keep her. He looked up from the coins.

"By the way, did I hear you say that I'm your master now?"

She snorted.

"True, you heard me say that. But it was a tactic, that's all, like the stuff you said. And it helped, didn't it? So don't raise your hopes."

XXVI

MARA IN THE HOUSE OF SENATOR

FAUSTUS POMPONIUS ATTICUS, LORD

GOVERNOR OF THE NORTH, AND

WHAT SHE EXPERIENCES THERE

✠ *The house of Lord Governor Senator Faustus Pomponius Atticus, in Fanum Fortunae.*

The whole household was made to line up in the courtyard outside Castor's room. There were sleepy-eyed footmen, and the huge gatekeeper, Tania the head cook, maids, and kitchen-maids. There were cleaners, stable-boys smelling wonderfully of horses (the smell of freedom!), litter-bearers, yawning and smelling of sweat, and several people whose function Mara couldn't even begin to guess.

Phoenix the steward walked up and down in front of them. It looked as if he wanted to address the assembled slaves, but couldn't find the right words.

Phrygillus wasn't there, though they could hear him screaming and wailing in the little storeroom that Tania had locked him in.

Lelia wasn't there either (or, if she was, Mara couldn't see her).

And Castor wasn't there—his body still lay inside the room, his head twisted round at an angle, and his throat cut.

At last Phoenix began.

"Listen! *Listen!* We must speak about this before the Master returns. The Mistress will soon be here, too. Derya is dressing her—she will remember to do it slowly, I hope, to give us time."

Several of the slaves shouted or called out something.

"No, one at a time! Tania?"

"Where is the Master?"

"He is taking his house-guest to the city gate. The southerner wanted to pray at the sanctuary of the Slave before setting off on his journey. The Master accompanied him."

"Will we all die?"

That was one of the maids. There was suddenly a deathly hush. Phoenix fumbled nervously with his tunic.

"I don't know. I'm not a lawyer. How should I know?"

It was Phrygillus who had found the body.

Just before dawn the boy had woken his master and complained that he needed to "go". Mara, sleeping outside the room on a pallet, had been woken and told to take the boy to the privy. He was too scared to go on his own in the dark.

Castor had warned her beforehand that this would happen. It happened nearly every night, in fact, and was a common joke in the household. Such a big lad, and frightened of the dark!

When it indeed happened, on Mara's second night in the house, Castor told her: "Now it's your turn to take him. Let him clean his own pretty bottom, though, he needs to learn that. Good thing that I bought you! Now I can get some sleep for once."

And he had turned over to do just that.

With only a small lamp to guide them, Mara and Phrygillus had made their way down corridors and across courtyards to the slaves' privy. It smelt horrible. Out on the plain, when you did a shit you would cover it with earth, and the wind and the smell of the grassland protected you from the stink. Human dung was vile. Horse-dung, on the other hand, was sweet and aromatic—she had often collected it for her father, and had traveled with him once to Cascantum to barter it for Citizen goods.

Having to shit in a room, though, an enclosed space with no fresh air, was not good. And they call *us* "barbarians"!

Phrygillus had begged her to hold his hand. He didn't want to be alone in the privy, even with a lamp, while he was doing his "poo-poo".

Mara was disgusted with him. Among the Horse People, a boy of his age would already be riding, and learning to look after a horse, not having his bottom wiped by his big sister! But she stayed with him, and helped him when he asked her to, despite what Castor had said. Afterwards, she felt a sudden small need of her own, and told him to wait for her outside. Even though he was only a child, she didn't want him staring at her. Yes, he could take the lamp; she could manage in the dark.

She had found him asleep when she groped her way out, his little body pressed against a plaster column, the lamp by his side. He looked so sweet that she had let him sleep for a while, but then she woke him, and they returned by the route by which they had come. He went back into his master's room, to slip into the warm bed with him, while she lay down again on her pallet.

And then his screaming had begun…

Phoenix was still talking, and trying to answer questions and keep the slaves calm, which was not easy.

"We'll all be crucified! When a master is murdered, they torture the slaves to find the murderer, and then they kill everyone! That's their law."

"I told you: I'm not a lawyer. But Castor was not a master; he was one of us."

"But he was a freedman, not a slave!"

"Didn't Maximus change that law?"

"Yes, yes!" From the reaction, this was something that they desperately wanted to hear. "Maximus abolished that law!"

"No, the Slave followers in the Senate did it!"

"Who cares who did it, so long as it was abolished!"

Phoenix held up his arms for silence.

"Again, I'm not a lawyer, but I do know this: if a magistrate comes, and they hold an enquiry, some of us will be tortured. Because a slave's evidence is always given under torture." Again there was a hush. "But the Master himself is a magistrate. Let us take hope from that! We are valuable. Would he torture and kill his own property?"

Leon, who was standing next to Mara, whispered: "No, he's too mean to damage anything he could sell."

"We need to help the Master. We must find the murderer ourselves."

One of the litter-bearers shouted: "It was the bum-boy!"

"Don't be so stupid. Can't you hear him crying?"

To Mara's horror, another voice called out: "It was the new one, the horsey-girl! She's a barbarian! They're all savages!"

Mara couldn't see who it was, but no-one else took up the cry, and Phoenix said, "No, it couldn't have been her. She was with the boy at the privy when it happened. He said so. Those were the only words I could get out of him." He turned to one of the footmen. "You—fetch me the weapon."

The footman went into Castor's room and came out holding a long, thin knife. Even from a distance Mara could see that it was covered with blood.

"It's a kitchen knife! Tania?"

Tania pushed forward to examine it more closely.

"Yes. It's the knife that Lelia always used. Look, there, in the bloodstains on the handle, you can see the marks of fingers. *Small* fingers."

"Where is Lelia?"

Lelia was nowhere to be found.

Lelia was the murderer!

But why should she murder Castor?

Someone said that she had been talking about running away, about going back to Sybaris. No, said one of the other kitchen-maids, she's not stupid, she wanted to escape across the River and join the barbarians. That would be much easier. She had been hoarding money for the journey.

Perhaps Castor had found out about her plans, and tried to stop her?

Then the Master arrived, attended by armed soldiers.

It was the first time that Mara had seen him. This was the great Lord Governor? A chieftain among the Horse People *looked* like a chieftain, but this man looked flabby and womanish beside the soldiers.

He took Phoenix aside, and they spoke to each other for a few moments. Then Phoenix stepped back, his arms folded modestly in front of him, and the Master addressed his household.

"Slaves! Fellow believers! This is a terrible crime. Castor served me loyally for many years, as a slave and then as a freedman. He didn't deserve to die like this. Although he never found his path to the Slave, even so, I ask you all to join me in prayer."

He fell clumsily to his knees, raised both his arms in a dramatic gesture, and gazed heavenwards. Most of the household slaves also dropped to their knees. Behind the Master, Phoenix made a signal with his hands and silently mouthed the word "Down!"

Mara thought he looked ridiculous, but she also knelt. Only the soldiers remained standing, as if the Master still had to be guarded from his own slaves, even while he was at prayer.

"O Lord, You who sit at the right hand of God in Paradise, hear this prayer of Your humble follower. Forgive this poor dead sinner Castor, who, blinded by false learning and intellectual pride, never found his way to Your bosom. Let his punishment in the beyond be tempered by Your mercy. Reward those who have taken You into their hearts, but destroy and extinguish Your enemies. Blessed be Your Name for all eternity!"

There were isolated shouts of "Blessed be Your Name!"

Phoenix helped the Master to his feet, and the slaves also got up.

"I am told that the identity of the killer is known: the kitchen-maid Lelia. She will be caught, and ruthlessly punished. As Governor and High Magistrate, I shall deal with this case myself. I can reassure you that, under the present circumstances, I have no intention of subjecting any of you to interrogation under torture"—cries of "Thank you, Master!" and "The Slave be praised!"—"All of you should therefore now go about your duties as you normally would. There will be regular morning prayers, led by my wife your lady mistress and by Sister Derya God-seeker. Full attendance is expected."

After the Master had left, the slaves scattered to see to their various tasks. Unless Tania gave her a job to do in the kitchen, Mara's duty would be to comfort poor Phrygillus.

The little boy had been released from the tiny storeroom, but he and Mara were given that same room to use until other arrangements could be made. Phrygillus had now stopped crying, out of sheer exhaustion. He had wet himself. Mara cleaned him up, cuddled and stroked him, called him *seflar*, her treasure, whispered to him in the Citizens' Tongue, and sang to him in her own. It was like comforting an injured foal, or a sick puppy. Finally, he fell asleep, a dead weight in her arms.

She had sworn a solemn oath to love and protect him. She would do so: her honor required it. Could a slave have honor? Yes, this one could! Also, she had no wish to meet She with the Talons any time soon.

Mara fell asleep too.

She was woken by Leon the footman shaking her.

"Wake up! And wake the boy! Hurry, the Master commands your attendance."

He propelled them through the house, allowing them only a brief stop at the privy on the way. The Master was not to be kept waiting.

When they arrived, Mara was surprised to find that it was not the Governor who was sitting on the gilded couch at the center of the room, but what could only be his wife, a fleshy, bad-tempered-looking woman wearing far too much makeup. Behind her, fanning her, was a thin, hard-faced woman of about the same age. The Master himself sat on a simple wooden chair to one side of the women. Phoenix was also present, clutching a scroll.

The Mistress stared at the two of them in disgust.

"Ugh, the creature! Doubtless the boy can be sold to some pervert. I am told that there is a market for such abominations. And this is what the girl looks like! Victor told me about her. Dreadful." She had looked at Mara while speaking, but now she turned to her husband. "I don't know why you bring these hairy barbarians into our home—don't you see enough of them in the course of your duties as Governor? The stables are the only place she could possibly work. We couldn't have her serving our guests. Not all of them are as tolerant and broad-minded as dear Victor."

"I didn't bring the girl into our home, my dear. Castor brought her. She belonged to him. Just as the boy did."

"Then dispose of them!"

The Governor coughed and looked uncomfortable.

"It isn't quite as easy as that, my dear. They were Castor's property, and they must be *disposed of* according to his wishes. He had no heir—"

"Of course not! And he owed everything to you anyway. Just sell them both. If it worries your conscience, you can donate the money to the sanctuary."

"Phoenix?"

The steward stepped forward with the scroll.

"There is a will, my Lady, which Castor changed yesterday. It was witnessed by his friend the lawyer Anicius—"

"That unbeliever!"

"—who may also have a copy of the document. Castor gave his own copy to me for safekeeping."

Lady Pomponia rounded on her husband.

"Faustus, this is nonsense. Whatever next? I can't believe it: a will made by a freedman! As his former master, *you* should inherit his property."

"No, my dear, it was his right to make such a will, and as High Magistrate I must be seen to respect it. I can't place myself above the law." The tone of his voice changed. "As you know, there are certain people, *enemies* even, who could find ways to use that against me. Causing trouble for me in the Senate. Phoenix, tell us what the will contains."

Phoenix coughed to clear his throat before proceeding.

"My Lord, if I may summarize the contents of this document, you are indeed the chief beneficiary of the will—"

"You see, I told you!" The Mistress looked at her husband triumphantly.

"—and will inherit his movable goods and his savings, a sum amounting to eleven hundred heavy silver pieces, to use as you see fit—"

"The sanctuary, of course! Let us have no further discussion about that." She paused. "But eleven hundred silver pieces: how did he obtain so much money?"

The governor shrugged his shoulders, but gave no answer, and Phoenix continued reading.

"—to use as you see fit, with the following two exceptions. Firstly, the boy Phrygillus is to become the property of your Lordship's son, young Master Faustus Pomponius Atticus; the deceased humbly requests your son not to sell the said boy, and to grant him his freedom within ten years. Secondly, the girl Mara, recently purchased, is likewise to become the property of Master Faustus, with the same requests humbly made to him with regard to sale and manumission of the said girl." He paused to catch breath. "The girl Mara is charged with guarding and protecting the boy Phrygillus when the time comes for him to be transported from

Fanum Fortunae to the City. The lawyer Anicius is instructed to inform Master Faustus Pomponius Atticus of these bequests."

Although she had only half-understood the text, thoughts rushed through Mara's mind. Who was this young Master Faustus? What sort of man was he? How far away was "the City"?

The Governor looked across to his wife. She had not interrupted during Phoenix's further description of the contents of the will.

"My dear?"

"It's ridiculous that a former slave is dictating to you. From the fiery pit where he is now burning for all eternity! Dictating to *you*, the Lord Governor!" She sighed, and her maid began to fan her even faster. "But at least the creature and the barbarian will be gone from this house. Then send them at once. Send them today! Why should *we* feed them? I have almost finished a letter to our son—they can carry it with them. Although what *he* will do with them the Slave only knows. But I have the consolation that your brother will not be pleased with such exotic additions to his household. For all his faults, Senator Lucius is a man with traditional values!"

Mara didn't know what to make of that. But maybe it would be better to leave this place, where her master had been murdered, her only friend was the suspected killer, and the mistress of the house hated her.

"I agree, my dear. But they can't travel on their own. One of the footmen will go with them. It'll need to be someone trustworthy, of course. He can deliver the letter. And one of the soldiers from my staff will go too, as their guard. We wouldn't want my son's property to be stolen, would we? Or to run away!"

"Then get them out of my sight, Faustus. Do what needs to be done. Derya and I have a prayer meeting to organize. The meeting will give me spiritual strength, and, guided by our Lord the Slave, I'll finish the letter afterwards. Then they can leave, before midday. I want them gone"

XXVII

MANASA AND THOMASIUS SEARCH FOR A

PRINCESS, AND ENCOUNTER A SHADOW

✠ *In Fanum Fortunae.*

She could do worse than Thomasius, she decided. He was polite and good-natured, and on their second night in an uncomfortable tavern bed, this time at the sign of the Eagle, he had made no further attempt to take his pleasure with her.

She would normally have allowed him to. He was legally her master, with rights to her body, just as every husband had rights to the body of his wife. She didn't have her monthly bleeding, and she wasn't pregnant. She hadn't been placed under a curse or a priestly ban, nor was it the feast of some god during which carnal activity was specifically forbidden. There were so many feasts of that kind, men were always complaining! But the encounter with Urtho had made her disinclined to allow any man to get too close to her. It wouldn't be for ever, no, but for the time being.

They *were* close, though, because this bed too was very narrow. Thomasius hugged her again, to avoid falling out. This time, his hands didn't roam elsewhere. She sensed that he was not very experienced, and maybe even shy with women. Many nice men were. She could handle him! And she would help him to find the horsey-girl.

She insisted, once again, that they should have a proper breakfast. She knew that he had enough money for a hundred or more hearty meals. And what better thing was there to spend money on than good food? She had the impression that food wasn't quite as important to him as it was to her. But then again, he had never been a slave, had he?

Their destination was the house of the Governor. Mara had been purchased by the Governor's secretary, so that was where she would be.

Finding the house proved to be easy, and gaining access was also easier than Manasa had expected.

Thomasius outranked the two young soldiers who were slouching outside the mansion. He puffed out his chest and bellowed at them. Weren't they supposed to be on guard duty? If they *were*, and *that* was how Citizen soldiers were now being trained, then the days of the Empire were surely numbered! Who was their commanding Sub-officer? Thomasius would want to have a word with him.

In the meantime, he wished to see his Lordship the Governor. On urgent business.

Manasa smiled inwardly. It wasn't entirely acting—he was taking it out on the two soldiers because he hadn't had a shag... How predictable men were! Discoveries like this always confirmed her in her confidence that, whatever life chose to throw at her, she could deal with it.

One of the soldiers found the courage to ask Thomasius the nature of his business with the Governor. There was more bellowing. How dare he? Who did they think he was? Having such a cushy posting had given them delusions of grandeur, but that could soon be rectified, oh yes: fearless men like themselves were urgently needed to hold the line against the Blood-Drinkers. In-between, though, Thomasius did let slip that he had a commission from Lord Commander Rhaetius to speak to the Lord Governor. The less courageous of the two soldiers said that he would fetch Togulus at once.

Who in Sol's name was Togulus?

The soldier returned with a hefty slave who was obviously the gate-keeper. In an ugly Sueni accent, Togulus asked the same question that the soldier had asked, and Thomasius gave the same answer, but without bellowing.

Esbus, how she hated the Dream People! She'd had enough of muscle-bound swampies recently to last her a lifetime.

Togulus informed them that Lord Governor Atticus had gone to another office of the Governorate, but would return in the late afternoon, at around the hour when the sun dipped. They could wait, or they could go away and come back later. They decided not to wait.

First they went for a walk through the city. Thomasius said that it was a delightful place, with some fine wine shops and several pleasant, er, hostelries. From the way he blushed he could only have meant brothels—he couldn't have been referring to the two inns that they'd stayed at. To Manasa, who had seen some of the world's greatest cities, Fanum Fortunae was no better than a dump, but she didn't say so. Was Thomasius naïve, or just lacking in knowledge of the world?

They lunched at what he said was one of his favorite wine shops, which served meat pies, and tasty sausages seasoned with herbs. The wine was acceptable, Manasa thought, and Thomasius had rather too much of it, so more sightseeing was out of the question, and he parked himself for a couple of hours on a bench in a shady corner in the garden behind the inn. She looked after his sword for him while he slept. He had kept it sharp. The thought came to her that she had had more than one master whom she would gladly have skewered with his own sword, given an opportunity like this!

When Thomasius woke, there was no longer any need for shade, and they returned to the Governor's house.

A different pair of soldiers were now on duty, but they were also youngsters, and to the eye of a Sub-officer just as unimpressive. Thomasius shouted at them much as he had shouted at the first pair. Once again, gatekeeper Togulus was fetched, and this time he escorted Thomasius into the house, after warning him that his Lordship was in a meeting, and that he might therefore have to be patient for a while.

Manasa ("the slave") was to remain outside.

As it turned out, Thomasius need hardly have bothered.

While Manasa stood waiting with the two soldiers, they made harmless attempts to impress her with their manliness. They were almost pitifully innocent compared to Urtho's troopers. The display that they put on was more of an attempt to regain some of the face that Thomasius had stripped them of than with any serious hope of seducing her. But they also retailed all the gossip of the house, giving her the very information that Thomasius was trying to obtain from the Lord Governor.

Old Flabbyguts (they said) was in even more of a state than he usually was. First there had been the Blood-Drinker scare, and now there had been a murder under his roof. Fortunately it hadn't been on *their* watch. Anyway, it was an inside job, and had nothing to do with the guards. His Lordship's secretary, a notorious chicken-fancier called Castor, had had his throat slit, apparently very professionally.

At this point Manasa, who had not been deriving much enjoyment from the soldiers' feeble line in chat, perked up and showed interest. Really? Had they caught anyone? My, they were *so* well-informed about everything. She batted her eyelashes at them.

No, they hadn't caught anyone.

First they thought it was the old guy's little sweetie, but the kid had been crying pitifully ever since. You couldn't fake that.

Then they said it was the slave he had just bought: some stupid horsey-girl. It was anybody's guess why he'd bought her, and it was logical enough that she might be the killer: those barbarians were capable of anything, weren't they? But it couldn't be her because she'd been in the privy all night with the shits. Those horseys only ate horsemeat and grass, so if you gave them proper food it fucked up their bowels like nobody's business!

So the horsey-girl was still there?

No, Lady Fuckface Godslave wouldn't have her in the house.

Manasa felt obliged to ask them who that charming lady might be?

Like most soldiers, the two boys were followers of Sol and the old gods, and had no great love for the Slave-worshipers, especially those of the more fanatical kind. The Governor's wife, Lady Pomponia, was just such an enthusiast. She hated backdoor warriors even more than she hated barbarians, so the horsey-girl and the bum-boy both had to go.

Had the lady of the house sold them?

No, they'd been sent to the City. The day before. Given to the son and heir as a wedding present. (How weird was that?) They'd never actually seen the young master, as he was known, but with parents like that he could only be a total shitbag. And the worst thing was: *they* could have gone too! But their Sub-officer didn't like them, sod him, because he was from the City, not the Province, so he'd picked two Citizen soldiers, Sempronius and Dexter, as the escort. Both of them arseholes, just like him.

It was so unfair. They could have looked in on their families on the way through the Province, both going and coming back, and had a couple of days' fun in the City as well.

They complained bitterly about their Sub-officer, throwing each other cues to well-worn anecdotes about how awful he was, and virtually ignoring Manasa. How about this? And what about that? And then there was the time when he... It was like watching circus clowns tossing each other colored balls.

It had grown dark and they were still in full flow when Thomasius came back out of the house.

"Attention!"

This time he ignored them. He told Manasa that they must go back to the inn and be prepared to leave early the next morning. Mara was on her way to the City, and already had a full day's start on them.

Yes, she knew that.

Oh! He was surprised to hear it, and to learn that she had obtained almost the same information as he had, and with far less trouble.

The Lord Governor had been rude, and uncommunicative. He had shown no wish to discuss matters of his household with a lackey of the Lord Commander's ("Yes, he actually used that word: lackey!"). The Lord Commander had no authority over him, the Lord Governor, or any jurisdiction in Fanum Fortunae. And no, he would *not* permit Thomasius to use the fire-beacon to contact his master.

Finally, the Lord Governor had admitted that Mara had belonged to his secretary, and had spent two nights under his roof.

"But I don't understand all this fuss about her. She was purchased perfectly legally. She was left, in her late master's will, to my son Faustus Pomponius Atticus Junior in the City, which is where she is now being taken. And you, Sub-officer, have already taken up enough of my time."

The steward of the household, Phoenix, had been more forthcoming. It was from him that Thomasius had obtained the two small pieces of information that Manasa didn't know: that Mara and the boy were being escorted not only by the two soldiers but also by a trusted footman, whose name was Leon; and that a search was on for the killer of the secretary, a kitchen-maid named Lelia, "a dark Sybarite girl, very pretty, but with bad burn-scars on one side of her face."

At which Manasa's heart had missed a beat.

"Are you alright?"

She lied: "Of course I am."

But she wasn't. It was something that she couldn't talk about, though—with anyone. She changed the subject.

"Phoenix—that's a funny name for a slave."

"He must have been his mistress's favorite pageboy when he was small, or his master's little sweetie. That's how you get that sort of name..."

Deeply sunk in their conversation, they must have missed a turning, causing them to wander around in the narrow alleyways looking for the inn. How strange to be lost in such a small town! There were very few people out on the streets, and Manasa had the feeling that they were being followed. Sometimes when they turned a corner she looked back and saw a shadow that *didn't* turn into a person, but disappeared back into the gloom.

Since Thomasius wasn't allowed to use the fire-beacon, they would have to set off and try to catch up with Mara and the others. He had a warrant from the Lord Commander—it would impress Sempronius and Dexter, who *were* ultimately under the Lord Commander's authority, far more than it had impressed the Lord Governor.

Mara and Phrygillus would be on mules, or in a wagon, and the three men definitely on mules. They would be in no huge hurry, once they were away from the Fanum area, where there were supposed to be Blood-Drinkers on the loose. The soldiers would be enjoying their unexpected leave. There were several inns along the road; they would be using them, rather than the government rest-houses, and taking their breakfasts late.

On horseback, Thomasius and Manasa should be able to overtake them within two days. He asked her: could she ride a horse?

Yes. She'd lived among the Horse People. She knew how to ride a horse, with or without a saddle.

Unfortunately, requisitioning a horse for Manasa wasn't a feasible plan. The Citizen soldiers who were guarding Senator Atticus had no horses; the Sueni cavalrymen, on the other hand, had plenty, but Urtho would just laugh at him—or worse. So he would have to hire one from an inn, or even buy one, and get it fitted with hoof-boots. A good horse cost more than a slave, but Thomasius still had plenty of the silver pieces, and the gold that he had been given to pay for Mara.

It would be inviting disaster to go clattering down the road in the darkness. (Manasa suspected that he wasn't a confident horseman—he was a foot-soldier, after all.) So they would get up very early, and he would look for a horse for her while she was having breakfast.

Suddenly they found themselves standing in front of the inn. The alleyway was dark, and very little light was showing from any of the buildings, although behind the heavy wooden door of the Eagle they would by now have lit lamps or torches and would be serving their guests with supper.

Again, there was that movement of shadow, this time very close. Manasa instinctively stepped to one side as the shadow slashed out with a flicker of bright metal. The trained soldier Thomasius saw it too, though he was slower. He dodged the sword-cut, but stumbled as he pulled out his own sword, and toppled awkwardly to his knees in the mud.

The shadow moved in on them again, cutting at Thomasius and catching his upper arm or his shoulder, Manasa couldn't see exactly. She heard his yelp of pain, though. The sword dropped from his hand.

The shadow pulled back. This was the dancing thrust-or-cut, retreat, thrust-or-cut, retreat, of an expert swordsman. A man who knew what he was doing.

She heard the shadow whisper: "Good!"

That single word saved the life of Thomasius. Because the word was spoken in Sybarite.

Hearing her own tongue, Manasa shouted out "*Arthaq na Esbon!*" ("Go to hell!"), sprang forward, and picked up her master's sword, even as the attacker slashed down at Thomasius, cutting deep into his body as the Sub-officer twisted sideways on the mud.

Again, the dancing step backwards.

Now Manasa could see the man, crouching down and preparing for a third and final blow. He was small, garbed in dark, tight-fitting clothing, and holding a curved Sybarite scimitar. It was a frightening weapon for slashing and for throat-cutting, but not so good for a direct thrust into the heart or the guts, which would already have left Thomasius dead or dying.

Moreover, she had surprised the attacker by shouting at him in his own Tongue. His concentration had slipped, and he had misjudged the distance for that second slashing cut, which could otherwise have been fatal.

He stood upright and looked at her, his eyes gleaming malevolently.

"*Arthaq na Esbon*? Go to hell? No, *you* will be there long before me."

She stood over Thomasius's body and brandished his sword.

"Then send me there, if you can!"

It was foolishness, but it was all that she could do. It would be easy for him, she knew that. She had no skill with a sword; only her courage. But then the door of the inn opened behind her, and there was angry shouting, and the flare of torches.

She caught a last glimpse of the smiling face of the attacker, as he raised his own sword in mocking salute before slipping away into the darker reaches of the alleyway.

She didn't recognize him. But she recognized the tattoo that he had on his forearm, and for the second time that day her heart missed a beat.

XXVIII

AULUS LOOKS FORWARD TO THE BRIDE-SHOW

✠ *The house of Senator Lucius Pomponius Atticus, in the City.*

Despite the cooler weather, Aulus had chosen to receive Sextus Placidus on the terrace. It had the advantage that it would be harder for anyone to spy or eavesdrop on them than if they were in the dining-room.

This time there would be no Sinica lurking in the background.

The alternative would have been Aulus's personal room. But this was not much more than a sleeping cubicle with an added desk and chair. (Hoping against hope, his uncle had imagined that he might use these to work on his poetic masterpieces.) He couldn't entertain Sextus there.

The poet had promised to recite the opening lines of his latest work. Aulus would be only the second person to have heard them. (Who had been the first? Fannia, no doubt.)

"It begins very dramatically, with the poet rushing to spend a night of delirious passion with his beloved:

Swiftly to horse! My heart was beating:
To be in your arms until first light!
The earth was cradled by the evening
And on the mountains hung the night...

Fannia *loves* it, by the way." (So she *had* been the first person he had read it to!)

"Really?"

"Yes, by and large. Though she did complain that I'd never come to see her on a horse. Ever. On a mule, though, which is a bit less dramatic, I suppose. And once, when I was feeling poorly, in a litter, which is not dramatic at all. You know how sarcastic she can be! But you need to understand that the horse-ride is a *metaphor*, for the urgency of my need to be with her, to be riding her, gripping her flanks, feeling the trembling of her loins..."

Aulus was most uncomfortable with the direction that their conversation was taking, and tried to change it.

"*Can* you ride, Sextus?"

"Of course I can! Just not too fast, thank you, and not a big stallion or anything like that."

"Yes, I can see that mules and litters might be more practical. You wouldn't want to turn up at your beloved's house with a broken neck, would you? But 'Swiftly to mule!' doesn't have the same ring to it."

Sextus looked displeased.

"As a fellow poet, Aulus, I would have expected better of you. You've fallen into that fallacy where you connect the writer's life with his work."

Aulus took a deep breath.

"No, but you have to admit that your poems are pretty personal, aren't they? Can you have it both ways, you know, write about your intimate life and *not* write about it, both at the same time? I mean, if this rushing-about-on-a-horse business isn't true, why should your reader believe all the rest of it? You know, about what you and your beloved get up to once you've arrived?"

Sextus blushed bright red. Aulus had badly overstepped the mark, and they both knew it. He really didn't want to speculate about what his friend got up to with Fannia, though if he had to, it was less painful if he could believe that Sextus was inventing most of it. Poetic licence, as it were.

"I'm sorry if you feel like that, Aulus. I *do* believe in artistic integrity…"

"Yes, of course. No, *I'm* sorry: I expressed myself badly! You know that I'm absolutely your greatest admirer? I think what I meant to say was that your work, um, kind of *hovers* on the boundary between reality and dream, crossing backwards and forwards. That's what makes your poems so exciting."

Sextus helped himself to another fig in honey.

"These are nice." The crisis was over. The god had been propitiated. "Does your uncle know I'm here?"

"Yes, he thinks you've come to give me some good advice on the choice of my future bride. But he's not there today—he's gone to the Senate. He almost lives there."

"Like my uncle Gnaeus. He's probably there as well. But uncle Gaius never goes. In fact, I imagine he only leaves the house after dark, you know, to drink blood and suck out bone-marrow and murder newborn babies. Stuff like that."

"They're talking about the bride-show, and how they're going to organize it."

"Really? I thought that that slimy little eunuch was in charge?"

"Florianus?"

"Yes. He must be a *huge* expert on women!"

They both sniggered.

"I wonder how my uncle Lucius likes working with a eunuch? He's very traditional. But I suppose he knows him quite well. They spend a lot of time together. They have to coordinate what the Greens and the Whites are doing."

"*My* uncles would have no problems. They hang around with all sorts of perverts. Poor Florianus might have problems with *them*, though."

"He'll be running it on the day. They need to fix the procedure in advance. It's at the Palace, so they have to get the protocol right. It's an *event*. There'll be bloody eunuchs and court officials scurrying around everywhere. Ambassadors from the East. Everyone genuflecting, kissing the Imperial booties. I hate that nonsense."

"But you're going, aren't you?"

"Oh yes, I wouldn't miss it for the world."

Sextus looked thoughtful.

"I'm almost hoping that Cornelia wins. Wouldn't that be a laugh? That would solve *my* little problem for a while, though it wouldn't help *you* very much. And my uncles would be livid if Julia didn't win. But she will. It's all been fixed. My little sister: I wonder what she looks like?"

"Better-looking than you, I hope!"

Sextus repeated that the bride-show was a foregone conclusion. His uncles had offered the Emperor his sister, on a plate, and Ogilo had said "yes" on his Majesty's behalf. Sextus was going to be the brother-in-law of an Emperor. Did you get a title for that? They would still have to go through the motions with other young lady candidates, but it was only to avoid upsetting all those proud Senators who had marriageable daughters.

"So it's just a formality."

Aulus wasn't convinced that it was a foregone conclusion that Julia Placida would win. That wasn't how Naevius and his friends saw it. They had supported the idea of a bride-show—because they expected to win it. And why shouldn't they? They were strong in the Senate. They controled the streets…

"Aulus, do you actually know Naevia?"

"No."

Sextus did. Well, he knew *about* her, and there were two good reasons why she wasn't going to win the contest. Firstly, she'd just come back from the East. She'd been to the court there, and been presented to Emperor Theodore. She'd been on the party circuit. Apparently there were lots of parties, and (according to a reliable source of information) she'd made a number of...*friends*. Sextus made it sound dirty. It *was* dirty.

People were frightened of Quintus Naevius. Her new *friends* would keep it to themselves, but it would only take one of them to talk, or one of his servants, and the whispers would soon spread. If they had already spread as far as Sextus, the eunuch Florianus was bound to have heard something.

And there was another reason why she wouldn't win: her hair.

"What about her hair?"

"They say it's red."

Oh.

Aulus knew what *that* meant. Redheads were from Esbus. Redheads had no soul—but they had claws. Redheads sucked all the strength out of a man, leaving him spent and flabby and unable to pleasure a woman properly ever again. He quoted some lines of popular doggerel on the subject:

> *"Red the hair on cunt and head:*
> *Touch it, and you'll soon be dead."*

"Yes, yes, the wisdom of the tavern. And not a piece of verse that I'd personally be proud of. But there must be some good reason why they say all that stuff about redheads."

"Oh dear. Well, that still leaves Anthemia." They groaned in unison. "Here, have some of these nuts."

They were still chatting when Senator Lucius Atticus returned to the house from the Senate.

If he was displeased to see Sextus Placidus under his roof, he didn't show it. Sextus for his part was charm and good manners personified. He had been on the brink of leaving, he said, but the Senator made him sit down again, and called for more wine.

He even invited Davus, who had accompanied him to the Senate, to join them, but the secretary excused himself. He had paid for a copy to be made of a rare scroll from the City archives, an account of constitutional events in the early history of the Citizen Republic, and a slave had brought this to him at the Senate. So, unless the Senator specifically needed him, he would prefer to withdraw to his room to enjoy this great treasure that he had so looked forward to. Permission was granted.

How could a freedman have afforded to have the copy made?

He had some modest savings, the Senator explained, augmented by the small presents with which his loyalty was occasionally rewarded. And he lived frugally. But copies from the archives were very expensive. What an admirable fellow he was! A good example to everyone! Most men in his position would be wasting their money on debauchery.

Aulus wondered whether that was aimed at Sextus and himself. But the Senator didn't follow it up.

After Beltran had served the three men with fresh wine, the Senator announced that he had some news for Aulus. There had been a fire-beacon message from his father.

A fire-beacon message? That could only be a matter of great urgency, and Aulus struggled to imagine what it might be.

"Has someone died? Has he finally disinherited and disowned me?"

"He has used his right to send messages by fire-beacon—*abused* his right, in my opinion—to send the following words: 'Two presents on their way.' Aulus, is that a code? Has Decimus recruited you as a secret agent?"

"Perhaps he means wedding gifts?"

So his parents had given their approval in advance for whichever person he had chosen as his bride? He found that *very* hard to believe.

As did Lucius Atticus. The Senator asked Sextus how the project to find his nephew a bride was actually progressing.

Most actively. Definitely. It wouldn't be long now. They had been running through a list of names at the very moment when the Senator arrived.

Had there not been a Lollia-something-or-other?

This time, Aulus had an answer prepared. No, Lollia was traveling in the East, and was being introduced to young noblemen in Neopolis and Maritima. It was unlikely that she would ever return. She was as good as married. It was Decimus who had recommended her name, but he had got it wrong.

"A pity. Decimus seldom makes mistakes. But I recall you saying that there were so many charming young women to choose from, and indeed, look: in two days from now his Imperial Majesty will be offered a choice of no less than *four*."

Was that a joke? Aulus didn't find the topic of arranged marriages terribly funny—especially when it concerned himself. Sextus was quicker to respond.

"If we didn't know you were joking, sir, we might almost think you were suggesting that we imitate his Imperial Majesty and arrange a bride-show for your nephew! Perhaps with the same four ladies?"

But the Senator didn't laugh.

"Julia Placida and Cornelia are both completely unsuitable for Aulus. He knows that. For political, not personal, reasons. I've actually heard nothing but praise of your sister—"

"I've never met her, sir."

"—and Cornelia comes from an excellent family. There is no personal bad feeling between Cornelius Rufus and myself. However, both those young women are from families on the wrong side of the Senatorial chamber. The Red side. An alliance with either of them would be out of the question."

Aulus caught his friend's eye. That strategy might just work, then. He would need to put on a great show of infatuation with Cornelia—assuming that she *wouldn't* be chosen by the Emperor, which seemed to him a reasonable assumption. (How would Maximillus appreciate being preached at about the "Greater" and the "Lesser Worship"?) His uncle would of course be infuriated when he found out, and he would declare his veto. There would be a massive row, but it would gain him the time that he needed.

"There is the daughter of Quintus Naevius, sir?"

The Senator snorted indignantly.

"Yes, and who is *she*, may I ask? She's the daughter of Quintus Naevius, that's who she is! Enough said. Would my nephew want to have a murderer as his father-in-law?" His voice darkened. "More to the point: would his Imperial Majesty?"

"Let us hope not, sir. And I say that not just because my name is Placidus!"

For the second time that day, Aulus found himself pointing out that there was also the Lady Anthemia.

"Ah, yes. Politically sound. Her father is a White Senator, as you know. A pleasant girl, but, as you might have noticed, Sol has bestowed on her neither beauty nor brains. Still, it's a wife you're looking for, not a mistress! Once she'd given you children, you wouldn't have to spend too much time with her—that isn't the purpose of marriage, is it? That's what most men would say. Though my own marriage was a very happy one, as you know."

"Yes, uncle."

"No, what worries me is how the *children* would turn out. The members of our family have always been rather handsome. Even your father and I were good-looking when we were young men."

Aulus reminded him: "I'm the ugly one, uncle. That's what they always say."

"Rubbish. There's nothing wrong with you. You just need to smarten up a bit!"

This was a favorite topic of the Senator's. When had Aulus last worn a toga? Did he realize that, seen from behind, he could be mistaken for a girl? Did the young women of today *really* appreciate the effeminate look that he and Sextus affected? And more along those lines.

"Yes, uncle. I'm sure you're right, uncle."

"Anyway, *your* bride must wait! Our next duty is to see that his Imperial Majesty chooses a wife, and chooses wisely. I have spent many hours today discussing the arrangements for the bride-show with my colleagues. It is a pity that all further responsibility for the event now lies with a Palace eunuch!"

"If I know my two uncles," Sextus said, "they will have spoken to him. And so will his master."

"The Emperor?"

"No, of course not, Aulus! His master is the General. It is Ogilo who will decide. Isn't that right, sir?"

At first there was no reply, and then the Senator said that it might not be so easy. The General would have given careful instructions, but Florianus would still have a difficult job to do. He would have to control a room full of dangerous, ambitious men, and without his master there to help him.

Yes, they had heard him correctly. The General would not be there. Because another, much longer, fire-beacon message had come at dawn: the Blood-Drinkers had crossed the River, in small numbers, but as scouts, not as raiders, and thousands more had assembled on the far bank. A huge host was gathering. The General was already on his way to the north.

XXIX

DECIMUS IS KEPT WAITING

✠ *From Fanum Fortunae to Cascantum, and back again.*

The first indication that something was wrong had been the fire in the distance. Decimus was unwilling to turn his horse away from the road to find out what it was—he was on a mission, he was on his own, and he was carrying money. He ignored the fire, and rode on.

There were no farms here. The area traversed by the road to Cascantum was barren grassland, part of the great plain that reached from the Amethyst Sea northwards to the Great River and far beyond, stretching out to the furthest horizon and into the icy lands of the Fish People. There were no farmers here, who might be burning off the brush and scrub, or lighting great bonfires to the Horned One, as they did in the Province— or having their little farmhouses burnt about their ears by marauders.

Was it a campfire? He had met no cavalry patrols on the road. In fact, he had seen hardly anyone on the road, and the watchtowers and signaling stations were eerily empty. The cavalry would, he hoped, be out scouring the plain for barbarian intruders. But it might not be *their* campfire. The thought made him reach down to make sure that the sword was still at his side.

Perhaps there had been a skirmish, and the victors were burning their dead. If so, the victors were barbarians: Citizens would carry the corpses of their fallen comrades back for proper burial. Even the Sueni would try to do that, so that their soothsayers could chant spells over the bodies to protect them on their journey into the Land of the Spirits.

As he approached Cascantum, he saw several more fires flaring in the distance, but no signs of battle. There were none of the "death pyramids" that the Blood-Drinkers liked to leave behind as grim mementos. Maybe the marauders had been from the lesser tribes like the Free People, or simply outlaws or renegades.

Surely they weren't from the Horse People? If they were, it would mean that his mission had already failed.

At Cascantum, the gates were closed. The battlements were fully manned, and not just with the usual lookouts and sentries. As Decimus neared the South Gate, it opened and a small troop of Sueni cavalry came out and went clattering past him—the first sign that he had observed of any military undertaking beyond the walls of the fortress.

The guards let him in, with a bad grace. He was obviously a Citizen, and a civilian, but they were nervous. When he told them that he had a message for Lord Commander Rhaetius, their section-commander shrugged. Both the Lord Commanders, Rhaetius and Memmius, had just that day left the fortress and were overseeing military operations involving units from their divisions.

No, he couldn't tell Decimus what or where those operations were, or how long they would last. Nor could he say when either of the Lord Commanders would be returning to Cascantum. In the meantime, two senior Staff Officers had been placed in command and he should try his luck with them.

Decimus groaned inwardly: why hadn't they left some sensible, experienced Company-commander in charge? And his worst fears were confirmed when he was allowed into the presence of Staff Officer Petronius of the Seventh Division.

Within minutes he had a strong urge to punch the patrician on his haughty nose. Petronius was an infuriating mixture of vanity and incompetence. In his privately tailored uniform, and wearing so much perfume that he was almost in danger of dissolving in it, he was like a military version of Aulus Atticus, but without the young master's harmlessness and basic goodness of heart.

Petronius declared that he had no inclination to waste his time on a freedman. *Anyone* could claim to be a messenger from the General. Why did he have no document of authorization? Why had no message been sent to warn of his impending arrival? No doubt because his arrival in Cascantum was not considered to be a matter of any importance! Oh, he had visited the Lord Governor in Fanum, had he? Then where was the forwarding note, the letter of recommendation?

Yes, of course he could wait for the Lord Commander, no problem there! Though he would have to organize and pay for his lodgings himself, and when Lord Rhaetius returned he could look forward to a sound flogging for wasting the Lord Commander's time.

And now "Acting Commander Petronius" had more urgent duties to attend to. (Did those duties include eating the fancy meal that had been brought into the room and laid out on an adjacent table during the short interview?)

Decimus had no choice but to go looking for accommodation. He left the fortress ("No luck then, mate?") and led his horse downhill into the grimy township of Cascantum. The hostelries were all depressingly dirty, even by the standards of the north, but eventually he found one where his horse would probably be safe—he tipped the ostler some Maximians in advance, and promised to pay him real silver when he left—and where the door to his room was sturdy and boltable.

Perhaps the man could also keep him informed about what was going on in Cascantum and around? He would gladly make it worth his while. He was, he told the ostler, a trader in amber, which was a very competitive business. His success depended entirely on contacts, on people coming and going, on knowing what the tribes were doing, how safe the roads were... This was the kind of information that he would gladly pay for.

The ostler grinned in happy anticipation of heavy silver, and busied himself with the horse.

Decimus had no wish to stay longer in Cascantum than was necessary. He hoped that his stay would be mercifully short. He wasn't a drinking man, the food in the inns was certain to be dreadful, and one look at the whores convinced him that his evenings would be long and lonely.

What he most liked doing was reading. In a great city, he could have looked for a public library, or introduced himself to someone with a private collection, like a merchant prince or a wealthy nobleman. Decimus enjoyed literature, famous speeches, and historical texts, and devoured whatever he could lay his hands on. But who had ever heard of a young amber trader with such interests? And Cascantum would have neither public nor private libraries.

The ostler fed him with tidbits of information, but several days passed before the man brought him the news that he had been waiting for—that Lord Commander Rhaetius was back in the fortress.

Decimus walked up to the South Gate and asked to see the Lord Commander. He was taken instead to the duty Sub-officer. At first, he feared that he would be laughed at again and sent away, but the Sub-officer, whose name was Grassica, had far more between his ears than the effete Petronius (and smelt more like a soldier, too, he couldn't help but notice), and Decimus was soon being escorted to the map-room and into the Presence.

He and Lord Commander Rhaetius had met before. Even without documentation, the Lord Commander accepted that Decimus had been sent north on the General's business, and they discussed the matter of the slavers' activities.

"Go to the northern battlements," Rhaetius told him. "You'll find the rotting remains of two that I caught, and *questioned*. It took a little while, but they gave me a name before their tongues were removed. The name was Issachar. I have already sent that information to your master."

Decimus wasn't surprised.

"Ah, you know who that man is, don't you?"

"Oh yes, my Lord, everyone does. But I know him particularly well. He bought and sold me. I was once his *possession*. That is a very intimate kind of knowledge, I would say, even though we never actually met."

"He's one of the richest men in the Empire, for Sol's sake! So why is he doing it? He doesn't need the money, surely?"

"No, he doesn't need the money, though he's not like Gnaeus Placidus: you don't see his wealth. But he is much more than just a slave-trader, my Lord. He has interests everywhere, and he sits in Maritima, like the spider at the center of a web…"

Rhaetius thumped on the map-table, scattering scrolls and the remains of a meal.

"Spiders can be caught! Spiders can be crushed!"

"Not this one, my Lord. He is protected by the Emperor in the East, and they say that he never leaves Maritima. He didn't come to the frontier, but someone did, and to carry out his instructions. Someone whom he trusts. You won't catch Issachar, but you might catch *that* man."

"And then?"

Decimus had not mentioned the unwritten instructions that the General had given him: to kill the man who was causing all the trouble, if he could find him. Issachar he would happily have killed, with or without instructions, at any time since that day he had first stood on the slavers' block in Trebenna, to be poked at and prodded by the curious, or even abused on the whim of some wealthy boy-lover. But now a different idea crossed his mind.

"Issachar has always worked for money, my Lord, but now he also trades in power and influence. Because when you have those, the money comes by itself. What is happening here is not about money. They're playing for much higher stakes. It's a power game, and Issachar is in league with someone else. Someone in the East, or in the West, with political ambitions. So if we could catch the man who is running this slaving operation for Issachar, and not just a few low-level slavers, we might learn more—"

"Bring me the man. I'll make him talk. I'll make him *sing*."

"—and the General might be able to use that to make a case in the Senate, against Issachar and whoever his powerful friends are."

"Then I'll have to leave the man alive, and let him keep his tongue! What a pity."

"But we need to catch him first, my Lord. In the meantime, my task has been completed, through your prompt action, and I should therefore return to the City, to report to my master."

The Lord Commander rubbed his chin thoughtfully.

"Yes, and no."

"Yes and no, my Lord?"

It seemed that there was a matter in which he could be of help, and without straying too far from the orders that he had been given. The Lord Commander told Decimus about the missing horsey-girl, and how he had sent a trusted Sub-officer named Thomasius to Fanum to look for her. They had probably passed each other on the road! If possible, Thomasius should buy her, so that she could be returned to her tribe. Her father was only a minor chieftain, but her grandfather Haimo was a big man in the Council of the Horse People.

"Because of her grandfather, she was an obvious target for the slavers. The Horse People now blame us for robbing her. But they can't tell one Citizen from another. If we could give this girl Mara back to them, with gifts, and an explanation, and perhaps a couple of wicked slavers for them to play with, it could be of great usefulness. We may soon need their help, or at least their neutrality. You see, a *situation* is developing with the Blood-Drinkers."

"The signaling stations were empty when I crossed the Gap, my Lord, and there were fires on the horizon."

"Lord Memmius and I have dealt with that, as best we could, using the troops that could be spared from Cascantum. Your master is on his way north with reinforcements. Until he arrives, there is nothing more that we can do. In the meantime, perhaps you could go to Fanum Fortunae on my behalf?"

He should look for Sub-officer Thomasius, help him in his search for the girl, and, if they found her, question her about how she was captured, and by whom. The slave-market in Fanum would be a good place to start.

"I have an agent in Fanum, my Lord, someone close to the Lord Governor."

Rhaetius laughed heartily.

"That Senatorial nincompoop! Well, don't expect any help from him. He won't even let you use the fire-beacon. You'll have to come back here to Cascantum if you have news to send to the City. You might prefer to do that anyway, since your master will soon be here in the north, with the reinforcements that we need."

Decimus told him that on his way through Fanum he had instructed his agent to make enquiries in the slave-market, so there might be some information already waiting for him that Thomasius wasn't aware of.

The Lord Commander offered him a military escort for the road to Fanum, but he declined.

"A special escort? There are too many people who wish us ill, my Lord. Better if we not draw too much attention to a modest amber trader."

That was the right decision. Back at the inn, he spoke for one last time with the ostler, and was offered new information—for a whole silver piece. A proper one, of course. Once the man had the coin safely in his hands, he told Decimus that someone had come looking for him. He had described his quarry very accurately, but named him as "Decimus".

"And that isn't the noble master's name, is it?"

No, it wasn't (or at least it wasn't the name that Decimus had given them at the inn).

Oh, then it was probably just a misunderstanding.

When Decimus asked him for a description of the man, he was no help at all. He wasn't local, the ostler said, and might have been a southerner. Or an easterner. He looked normal. He was normal size, normal age. He wasn't a Blood-Drinker, or one of those fabled slit-eyes from Sin.

Either the ostler's powers of perception were less highly developed that his greed, or he was playing both sides for silver.

Decimus left as quickly as he could, and (he believed) unobserved, and made good time to Fanum Fortunae. The return journey was uneventful, and there were no more fires to be seen, but Decimus was nervous.

Perhaps the problem with the Blood-Drinkers had indeed been solved, as the Lord Commander had said. But if their main host crossed the Great River, the whole of the north would be lost, and no number of reinforcements would be able to save it. The General was aware of that—and, whatever the Lord Commander believed, he was not marching northwards in order to offer them battle.

If they crossed the River, there was only one small hope for the Empire, and it was not a military option. It was something that even Lord Commander Rhaetius wouldn't know, but the General had confided in Decimus.

As a young man, Ogilo had been a hostage among the Blood-Drinkers, just as his father before him had been sent to the City as a hostage. While he lived amongst him, he had made the acquaintance of a young nobleman, Horkhon, the nephew of the Great King. Many years had passed since then. Ogilo had become the military ruler of the West; Horkhon had himself been chosen by the khans to be Great King of the Blood-Drinkers, the Widow-Maker, the Bringer of Death and Destroyer of Cities.

With huge hosts on the move, could the General reach out to the Great King, in the name of a brief hunting friendship, struck up in the northern wilderness more than half a lifetime ago?

Occasionally, Decimus glanced back across his shoulder, but no-one was openly following him. If someone was on his trail, they were keeping just out of sight, and they would need a fine horse to keep up with him. Either that, or they were much better than he realized.

XXX

FLORIANUS KNOWS WHAT HE IS EXPECTED

TO DO, AND TRIES TO DO IT

※ *The Imperial Palace.*

The day of the bride-show had begun awkwardly for Florianus. He was alarmed to hear that the roads around the Palace were in the hands of armed gangs under the direction of Quintus Naevius. The City Prefect had not kept his promise that the City would be peaceful and secure during the bride-show.

The only exception was the road from the villa of Gnaeus Placidus—the Placidi had enough armed thugs of their own, and hired gangsters, to keep that open.

The house of his brother Gaius, on the other hand, had already been seized and looted by the mob, and then torched. Looted, except that the house had been nearly empty, and some had been mightily disappointed not to find any evidence of demonic worship. There was nothing more sinister than a gloomy cellar. The owner was last seen leaving the City by the North Gate. That gate had not been heavily guarded by the Blues—for why should one of the Placidi want to go north?

Florianus was always unsettled by situations where not everything was under control, and therefore predictable. For this reason, he had felt it necessary to rehearse the procedures of the bride-show with his Imperial Majesty at some length. The Emperor would be at the center of an elaborate ceremony, yet he was still barely more than a child. And, it had to be admitted, a spoilt, willful, and capricious child.

His revered grandfather, who had the personality of a volcano, would have made most of it up as they went along, while still deferring intelligently at the right moments to the needs of protocol and the vanity of the high officials.

His Majesty's less revered father, who had the personality of a sea-slug, would have dozed through the event, allowing the High Chamberlain to guide him at every step.

His Majesty, however, had a more limited experience of court ritual, and had never shown much interest in it, provided that his immediate physical needs were not left unsatisfied. There was consequently the danger that he might behave unpredictably, but then afterwards be angered when his officials, obliged to change the procedure, were forced to improvise.

There was one problem that urgently needed to be discussed, and resolved.

Florianus would be directing the ceremony. He was a small man, and a eunuch. He knew that the noble Senators looked down on him both figuratively and literally; he had absolutely no illusions about that. In fact, he had learned that being ignored, despised, or underestimated could be a great advantage in games of power and intrigue. But how could he direct the bride-show from the front of the throne-room if nobody beyond the front row was able to see him?

With the exception of a few very decrepit Senators, and personages like the High Priest of Sol and the High Priestess of Luna, for whom chairs would have to be provided, those attending the bride-show, including the candidates themselves, would be expected to stand. Only that way could all those of rank who wished or had the right to attend be accommodated. Florianus would be one of the smallest people in the room.

He would look ridiculous standing on a makeshift podium, and a rostrum would be inappropriate to his position—he was not a magistrate, a general, a preacher, or an orator. The easiest solution would be for him to stand on the Imperial dais, but modestly to one side, so as not to obscure his Majesty's view, or people's view of his Majesty. The dais was only a single step higher than the floor of the throne-room, but that slight elevation had great symbolic meaning. Naturally he had no *right* to be on the dais without his Majesty's express permission. This matter had therefore to be settled in advance.

After a brief discussion—actually, less a discussion than a lecture from Florianus about the protocol requirements of the event—his Majesty yawned, not once but twice, and agreed to everything. He and Florianus had always been close, he giggled, why, the eunuch had even wiped his bottom for him when he was a child. (That was true, and Florianus remembered that the need for wiping had continued for much longer than would be expected of most children, in fact almost up to the age when his Majesty began ejaculating in his sleep, the slimy results of which also had to be cleaned up.) So why, he said, shouldn't his beloved Florianus be on the dais with him during the ceremony?

In any case, who would care? When people saw a fat little eunuch up there on the dais, no-one was going to take him to be a Co-Emperor, were they, or mistake him for the General? Ha ha ha. (No, I am *not* fat, Florianus said to himself, I am definitely not *fat*.)

To make it abundantly clear, though, that the eunuch's customary position was not such an elevated one, a plain but comfortable chair for him would be placed below and to one side of the dais. On the low dais itself were therefore only the Imperial throne and, next to it, a magistrate's stool of office, which was used by the General (as Imperial Guardian) when he participated in the audience, or on the occasions when he took the audience in his Majesty's name. For this particular event, the throne would be moved forward, closer to the front edge of the dais, so that his Majesty could get a better look at the four candidates.

Other matters were more briskly dealt with. In what formation were the members of the audience to stand? Florianus had rejected the proposal that they should be allowed to group themselves according to their political allegiance. No, this was not going to be a session of the Senate; nor should it be like a race-meeting at the hippodrome. If they were bunched together in their factions, there was more likely to be fighting. (Men standing alone would be far less inclined to provoke a fight than those standing surrounded by their friends.)

Florianus had agreed that all those attending should be dressed in a manner befitting their status, the Senators in togas, for example. There were to be no cloaks or neckerchiefs in factional colors. It was too late to go back on the concession that had already been made that the four young lady candidates would be allowed to dress in white, red, and blue.

But if the day of the bride-show had begun awkwardly for Florianus, it began quite catastrophically for one of the footmen.

The disaster occurred as he and his colleagues were engaged in fetching in the chairs that would be needed, sweeping the floor, replacing burnt-out torches with new ones, and suchlike menial tasks. Florianus was in the process of rehearsing with his Majesty the moves for the Imperial entry and exit—the throne-room would be so crowded that a slightly different procedure from normal would have to be followed.

A pigeon, disturbed by one of the sweepers, flapped upwards in a rush of wings and took indignant flight just over the head of the Emperor. The Sublime Presence slipped, tripped over its robe, and fell flat on its Imperial face.

It was really funny. In fact, it couldn't have been funnier if they had rehearsed it. The footman laughed. (So did the High Chamberlain, but, being more practiced in dealing with such situations, he laughed inwardly.)

Florianus hastened to help the Emperor, but Maximillus, clambering back onto his feet and pushing him away, screamed with rage and beckoned to the Imperial Guards.

"Take that thing away!" he shouted, pointing at the now cowering footman. "Bring it back after the ceremony—without its face! I want to hear it laugh again. *If it can.*"

As the foolish man was dragged away, struggling and wailing, the Emperor repeated his previous movement across the dais, but without falling over this time. It would pay not to make such a mistake during the bride-show, in front of the whole of the Senate. Maximillus had enough animal intelligence to know that.

The torturers would start skinning the footman's face towards the end of the ceremony, rather than risk doing it straight away and having him die on them. Florianus would use one of the intervals to slip out and bribe them to smother the poor man and do the cutting afterwards (he had made such arrangements several times before).

The footman would then have "died under the knife", they would say, of shock or loss of blood. This was plausible: the Palace torturers were far less skilful in their work than their colleagues in Sybaris, or the East. And his Majesty, who was quickly bored, would be distracted by the more interesting events of the day.

But he was unlikely to be distracted by his new bride-to-be.

The General had given Florianus explicit orders. He had also told his Majesty that Emperors did not usually pick their brides: a certain behavior, a certain *acquiescence*, was accordingly expected of him. He could continue to enjoy the favors of the most beautiful women in the Empire, who would be brought or cajoled to his bed, or placed in it for him, whoever happened to become Empress. What mattered now was that he did his proper duty in the choice of his bride.

The intended outcome of the bride-show was that *no* candidate should be found suitable. To calm the feelings of the disappointed ladies and their supporters, it would be announced that the ceremony would be repeated at a later date, after his Majesty had been given further instruction, by the High Priest and Priestess, to acquaint him better with the institution and responsibilities of matrimony. Today's four contenders would in no way be regarded as having "failed", or having earned dishonor, or having disqualified themselves from participation in a second bride-show.

The desired result would have been guaranteed by the presence of his Majesty's Guardian during the bride-show, seated on the dais within arm's reach of the Emperor, but the security of the Empire was of greater urgency. After all, if nothing were done to counter the incursions of the Blood-Drinkers, soon there would be no Empire, Emperor or Empress left to worry about.

In the General's absence, the High Chamberlain must do his best to direct his Majesty towards the right decision, but obviously he couldn't force him in the way that his Guardian could. If, overwhelmed by feelings of duty (or of lust), his Majesty stamped his booted foot and insisted that he needed a bride—though why should he?—the only acceptable candidate was Anthemia, the White contender.

None of the others were to be chosen under any circumstances, although in theory Cornelia would be the least obnoxious choice, since her father had no strong power base, followed by Julia Placida, because her uncles' power base was so far from the City. However, choosing a Red over the Blue, or the Blue over the two Reds, could provoke an uprising or even a civil war.

As anticipated, no young representative of the Greens had been proposed, although malicious gossip had spread the word that the scandalous (and by now probably huge-bellied) Livia Ogulnia might yet be appearing; so the list of candidates remained at four. But in what order should they be presented to the Emperor? The Senate had decided that it should be "by age", but had not ruled on whether that meant *oldest* first (Cornelia, Anthemia, Julia Placida, and finally Naevia) or *youngest* (Naevia, followed by Julia Placida, Anthemia, and Cornelia).

The Placidi had objected to both suggestions. By neither of these arrangements would Julia Placida be last (the position that they favored).

The Naevii objected to the second proposal, which would mean Naevia going first.

The High Priest of Sol stepped in and declared that lots should be drawn, which (under his officious but scrupulous supervision) produced the following result: Anthemia, Julia Placida, Naevia, Cornelia.

This order still separated the two Reds, but neither of the two main candidates would have to go first or last, and so, after much complaining, their spokesmen accepted the new proposal.

As Florianus saw it, the Placidi probably thought that, with the virtuous (but boring) Cornelia appearing right after the whoreish Naevia, this would remind the Emperor of the advantages offered by his choosing as Empress a woman of impeccable reputation (but also of attractive appearance and personality).

The Naevii were doubtless content to have Naevia coming *after* Julia Placida, and followed only by the charmless Cornelia.

Now footmen were lighting the torches, and other footmen were directing the audience, mostly Senators and sons of Senators, to where they should stand. A special area in front of the dais was reserved for the four candidates, and their parents or guardians. Imperial Guardsmen lined the sides of the throne-room, with two small contingents standing to left and right of the dais.

Florianus, who knew all the Senators by sight, could confirm that the footmen were doing their job properly and that the audience was now thoroughly mixed. He wasn't quite so familiar with the Senators' various sons, although they were expected to attend sessions of the Senate as part of their training to become members themselves, but he recognized two who *never* attended the Senate: young Sextus Placidus, the debauched poet, and his friend Atticus, another wastrel and good-for-nothing.

Good mixing there, he said to himself: a Red and a Blue standing together. Or maybe not. He knew that both young men had quarrelled with their families, Sextus with his awful uncles, and Atticus with his father. He lived with his uncle, Lucius Atticus, who was a Green. Did that make young Atticus a Green, too?

Florianus, who enjoyed literature, had read some of the poems produced by Sextus Placidus. He had been irritated by the juvenile erotic yearning (a theme he himself had no time for, of course), the outworn images, and the clumsy structures. The poems were truly undistinguished—but they were no better or worse than what anyone else was writing. The Golden Age of Poetry was long gone; the Age they lived in was not even Silver, but an Age of Brass. Sad times indeed.

Neither of the young men had any known interest in politics. They had presumably come to ogle the four women, and to show off their foppish clothes. Even at a distance, Florianus could see that they were dolled up like cockerels: young Atticus in a riot of colors, Sextus Placidus in a rich Sybarite tunic picked out with gold and silver thread. They were probably both drenched in perfume. Some of the Senators standing near them were glaring at them in angry disapproval.

Who cared what the Senators thought? But the young men should be careful not to upstage his Imperial Majesty with their fancy outfits. Maximillus expected always to be the center of interest, and adoration. He had already shown his spitefulness once today.

There was a sudden blast of trumpets. A court official proclaimed the arrival of his Imperial Lord and Majesty Maximillus, First Citizen and Imperator in the West, Chief Servant of Sol, son of Maximus, second of that name, grandson of Maximus, first of that name and Restorer of the Empire, may all his slaves do him obeisance!

And Maximillus managed to climb onto the dais and place himself on the throne without stumbling.

There was naturally no room for everyone to do the full genuflection. Florianus, who had enough space, prostrated himself at full length, and a few of the Senators in the front row did the same. Everyone else bowed or knelt, some with more enthusiasam than others. These obsequious rituals had never fully caught on in the West.

Although from where he was stretched out Florianus couldn't actually see him, he imagined that Senator Naevius had not even stooped slightly.

If Gnaeus Placidus had prostrated himself, it would be hard to get him up off the floor.

The four young ladies had been informed that they would be excused the prostration, in order that their elaborately arranged dresses and coiffures not be put into disarray.

The ceremony would begin with prayers and a benediction, led by the High Priest of Sol, though first he invited the High Priestess of Luna, his Imperial Majesty, and the City Prefect to join him in lighting the lamp.

A majority of the Senators were followers of the Slave cult. As a sop to their sensibilities, the High Priest had been told to do without the usual animal sacrifices, and you might imagine that this show of tact would be respected, but no. Though they didn't in the Sublime Presence have the courage to mock the charming pagan ritual openly, the Senators chattered and made facetious comments. Florianus had soon had enough of this disrespectful behavior. He caught the eye of the Commander of the Guard, and the Guardsmen thumped the butts of their spears loudly on the floor for silence.

The High Priest beseeched glorious Sol to shine his light onto all those present, but in particular to illuminate with his blessed rays that follower of his who must choose wisely in a matter of concern to all. O Sol, lighten the burden of your servant Maximillus!

After a few further prayers and invocations, the bride-show began. Florianus climbed onto the dais and invited the first candidate, the Lady Anthemia, daughter of the honorable Senator Marcus Anthemius Capito, to come forward. Then he stepped down onto the floor of the throne-room, so as not to obstruct his Majesty's view.

Florianus stood slightly to one side of the Senator's daughter. He would ask each of the candidates in turn the same list of pre-arranged questions. They would have their answers prepared, but were not permitted to make speeches. At any time, however, his Majesty could interrupt with questions of his own.

What the High Chamberlain asked and what the girls answered was of no import, and unless everyone spoke up very loudly, or they climbed onto the dais, most of the audience in the back rows would in any case hear nothing of what was being said.

All that counted was that the Emperor be seen to be offered a choice of candidates, and seen to make the right choice—which would be to choose no-one.

Anthemia's parents hovered excitedly behind her. One could see where the horse-face came from—from both of them. Her father and her mother had surprisingly similar features. Had Capito married his cousin, or had he for some perverse reason chosen a wife who looked like himself? Anthemia had a dumpy figure. The pasty color of her skin was not flattered by her simple but elegant white gown. It also became apparent that she was sweating heavily, giving her face an unattractive glow like wet ivory.

Why should any man want to mount this creature? It wasn't a question that Florianus was well equipped to answer, but it had always intrigued him to know what "complete" men found desirable in a woman. Given that women were acknowledged to be inferior to men, a view that all religions preached and all philosophers supported, except for a few eccentrics, there would have to be something very special about a woman to make her attractive to a man of any discernment.

But Anthemia's responses to the High Chamberlain's questions gave no indication that she possessed that special something, the nectar that might lure the bee. Her interests were what would be expected of any aristocratic young lady (the other candidates would almost certainly give similar responses): weaving, embroidery, charitable works, supporting her mother in arranging her father's social calendar and his entertaining, and similar worthy activities.

Did she understand that as Empress she would have many ritual duties to perform, including participation in religious ceremonies in honor of Lord Sol and the older gods? Would that for any reason be a problem for her?

That was an easy question for Anthemia to answer. Since the days of the great Maximus her family had been loyal supporters of the Maximian Dynasty and followers of Sol. And everyone knew that.

There were mutterings from some of the Senators in the audience. The other candidates were all followers of the Slave. How would *they* answer that question? Did its inclusion mean that the bride-show had been set up so as to favor the White candidate?

Did the Lady Anthemia realize that the substantial costs of the wedding would be borne by her family, as was traditional?

Of course she did—and in the background her father nodded wildly to express his willingness. Those costs might be enormous, but the father of the new Empress would soon be able to recoup them once he had been appointed to a position like Lord Governor of one of the wealthy southern territories.

Was she pure?

Yes, she had been keeping herself for this wonderful man, her husband-to-be. She had maintained her body as a shrine for the worship of Love and the celebration of her eternal union with her glorious husband.

There was tittering among the audience, most of whom were rather less familiar with the excesses of court sycophancy than the High Chamberlain was. Anthemia had been schooled to produce this nonsense— she couldn't possibly believe it—but the honeyed words sliding off her tongue to describe the unworthy creature on the dais seemed not so much wrong, as downright tasteless.

Was she fecund?

Yes, definitely, her mother and grandmother had been extremely fertile, although tragically some of the children had died young. All the women in her family were wide-hipped and capable of bearing many sons.

Was she prepared to devote her whole life and all her waking hours to the service of her lord, loving and comforting him, nursing him in sickness, supporting him in the dark hours of hard decisions and heavy responsibilities? (For Sol's sake, she's not marrying the General, just a dull, spoilt brat!)

She gazed right past Florianus to meet the eyes of the Emperor, and as she did so her own eyes took on a misty sheen of loving adoration. Oh yes, a thousand times yes! If chosen, she would live only for him, fulfilling his every need, doing everything that he asked of her.

Florianus couldn't imagine that his Imperial Majesty *would* ask very much of her, at least physically. Though perhaps he would ask her to keep her mouth shut?

Without even needing to turn round to look at his master, he knew that Maximillus was taking no interest in Anthemia. And why should he? Everything had been decided in advance, and he was acquiescing. Good! If he could maintain this indifference, it would make it so much easier to announce that *none* of the candidates had been chosen.

Now it was the turn of Julia Placida. Although Florianus saw her obese uncle, standing in the second row but overshadowed by his hefty attendants and bodyguards, there was no sign of the girl herself. She could only have traveled to the Palace under her uncle's protection, so she must be there in the throne-room somewhere.

Florianus stepped up onto the dais again and called out the name of the second candidate, the Lady Julia Placida, daughter of the honorable Senator Publius Julius Placidus of revered memory and niece of the honorable Senator Gnaeus Julius Placidus.

There was a slight movement among the figures surrounding Gnaeus Placidus, and then a small girl in a long, rose-colored gown appeared between two of the Senators in the front row, the florid Terebinthian and a tall White Senator named Terentius Ager. She was dwarfed by them.

Florianus asked her to step forward, but she didn't move.

Julia Placida was like an expensive children's doll. Her face was a perfect oval, and her features were exquisite: large, dark brown eyes, a small, slightly petulant mouth, and flawless skin. How could she be a Placidus? For a moment, Florianus imagined the wizard uncle conjuring up a seductive female demon from the realm of Esbus, the kind that slid into the dreams of complete men on hot summer nights to suck on their genitals until they awoke in shock. But Julia's beauty was human and fragile, and Florianus could see that she was desperately nervous.

He asked her once again to step forward, and this time she did. Although the length of her gown, which covered her feet, obscured her movement, Florianus, who had spent years in the women's quarters dressing and undressing women, knew at once why she had wished to stay back among the audience, and maybe the reason for her nervousness: she was a cripple. One leg was shorter than the other.

Ah, the gods never bestow such unbelievable beauty on a mortal being without holding *something* back!

But an Empress, like an Emperor, had to be unblemished by any physical handicap or deformity. On occasion, ambitious cousins or younger brothers had been deliberately mutilated to bar their way to the throne. Putting forward a candidate who, however beautiful she was, was a cripple… that was a massive insult to the Emperor—or a huge gamble by the Placidi.

Perhaps no-one else had noticed her limp. Florianus began to ask her the same questions that he had posed to Anthemia.

Her interests were harmless, her daily routine irreproachable.

Yes, she would perform her ritual duties as Empress conscientiously and respectfully. (Florianus cast a quick glance at her uncle, but the expression on his face gave nothing away.)

Yes, her uncle Gnaeus would meet all the costs of the wedding. (And it would hardly bankrupt him, Florianus told himself.)

Was she pure?

Yes, she was still a virgin. No man had broken down her gate of honor and entered the halls of her chastity. And she was pure in mind as well as body.

Was she fecund?

How could she know that? But she hoped to be the mother of many sons, and she was prepared to devote her life to her lord and master.

Florianus was fascinated by her answers—not by what she said, which was banal, but by the loveliness of her voice.

He declared that the second presentation was over. Julia Placida smiled sweetly and stepped carefully back into the audience. Had anyone else noticed the hesitancy in her movement, and realized what caused it? Maybe not.

The High Chamberlain climbed back onto the dais and shouted that there would now be a short interval before the turn of the remaining candidates. The audience relaxed and became noisy, but no-one risked losing their place by leaving the throne-room.

Florianus heard a loud whisper from behind him: the Emperor was calling his name. He crouched beside the throne to note his master's wishes.

"Your slave awaits his Majesty's command."

The Emperor was agitated. Something about the Placidus girl had aroused his interest, unfortunately. Was it her innocence? Her delicate beauty? Maximillus enjoyed breaking things.

"She's a juicy little item. Just like a doll. But she's a cripple! What does fat Placidus think he's doing?"

So he *had* noticed.

"Perhaps she's only injured her ankle, your Majesty, or it's some minor affliction. But his Excellency the General has in any case advised strongly against choosing any of these candidates."

"I know that! Don't be stupid, of course I can't marry her. But I can *play* with her, can't I? Send her to me tonight. She can share my wine. We'll get her drunk! I want to watch her getting fucked. Your man Julian can do it."

Florianus explained how unwise that would be. Her family was the richest in the Empire. They were the greatest landowners in the West. If anything shameful happened to their niece, they would make war against the Maximian Dynasty. They would send Sybarite assassins. Nobody was safe against *them*.

"But keep her at court by all means, your Majesty, as a hostage for their good behavior. Arrange a marriage for her, perhaps with some great nobleman from the East. Her uncles will be flattered."

The Emperor had become still, but he looked displeased that a toy was being withheld from him.

"Make the interval short, then! Since I can't marry any of them, this is all a waste of time. I really thought it was going to be more fun. Let's *make* it more fun!"

Remaining on the dais, Florianus called for silence and announced the third presentation, that of the Lady Naevia, daughter of the honorable Senator Quintus Naevius. Scanning the audience, he soon spotted the tall figure of Marcus Naevius. Surprisingly, his son Quintus was standing beside him.

The Naeviii must be very confident that they had everything under control, if Quintus Naevius had abandoned his post on the streets outside the Palace!

But where was the girl? Florianus had never seen her—she had spent the last few years in the East, apparently—and he wasn't sure what to look for, though he had heard some disquieting rumors.

He called for the Lady Naevia to now present herself.

Again, there was a rustling and a movement among the audience, and a young girl stepped forward to stand in front of the dais. As she did so, some of those nearest to her gasped, and other members of the audience who were standing further back craned their heads forward to get a better look at her. There were shouts, and Florianus saw several people making the sign to avert the Evil Eye.

"Redhead!"

It was true. Naevia had streaked, dark-red hair the color of half-dried blood. She was definitely a child of Esbus. Where did that coloring come from? Florianus laughed at the thought that some brave, flaming-haired adventurer had cuckolded Quintus Naevius. (Inwardly, because no man who said such a thing out loud could expect to live for very long afterwards.)

She wore a pale blue gown of the flimsiest material, cut low to show off her breasts. She was slim and, though lacking her grandfather's height, was somewhat taller than Florianus. She wasn't beautiful—her nose was slightly too long, and her chin slightly too pointed—but the life and intelligence that played across her face gave it beauty.

She stood proudly in front of Florianus, fixed him uncomfortably with warm brown eyes, and said, "Ask me your questions, Chamberlain." And although she was the youngest of the four candidates, she gave a woman's answers, not a girl's.

What were her interests? Her interests were whatever she happened to find interesting, and that could change from day to day, as the world around her changed. No, she had no particular interest in weaving or embroidery. Were those skills really regarded as a vital qualification for being an Empress? If so, she would gladly learn them. But she would strive to share and understand the interests of her husband, as a good wife should.

She would likewise fulfil whatever ritual duties were expected of her in public, but hope and trust that her right to honor her own god in private would be respected. Her religion was not that of the state, but the worship of the Blessed Slave as widely practised among all classes in the City. It was an acceptable answer to a difficult question.

Yes, her father would stand guarantor for the costs of the wedding. He was not the richest man in the world (that was a dig at the Placidi), but all members of the House of Naevius had been brought up to be aware of what was required of them by the centuries-old traditions of the City.

That too was an excellent answer, which would appeal to Senators of all factions. Florianus noticed how Marcus Naevius was nodding his approval of his granddaughter's performance.

Was she pure? Because only a virgin could be taken to the bed of his Imperial Majesty.

Before she could answer, there were bursts of laughter from around the room, some of it good-natured, but also less friendly shouts of "red-head!" and "witch!" Then Florianus heard a clear voice from the back of the throne-room shout "whore!" Everyone swiveled round. Who had had the insolence to use that word?

Depending on who you supported, the timing was awkward—or well-chosen. Yet Naevia remained calm.

"I am unmarried. And I am a maid, as tradition and duty require me to be. But it is for my husband to be the judge of that, in the court-room of our wedding night, and not some drunken loudmouth hiding at the back of a hall." Just as Anthemia had done, she looked straight past Florianus to the Emperor. "I appeal to his Majesty himself, to decide what his wishes are, and to follow his desire."

And then she stepped onto the dais.

"Get down!" Florianus hissed. "Get down at once!"

But she ignored him—she had eyes only for the Emperor—and Maximillus waved for the High Chamberlain to cease his objections. He beckoned her to come forward, goggling at her in fascination, but seemingly unable to speak.

Florianus dared to step onto the dais beside her.

"Lady Naevia, there are still two questions for you to answer. The first of those questions is: are you fecund?"

Naevia's hands went to her gown and pulled at a hidden string or bow. The gown fell off her body, landing in a pool around her feet. She stepped carefully out of the heap of cloth and stood naked in front of the Emperor.

"This is what I am. Look at it." She opened her arms wide in a gesture of offering herself to him. "If this field is well-ploughed, I promise there will be a good harvest."

There was immediate uproar. The final question was never asked. Maximillus stared at her body, transfixed, taking in the perfect breasts and the fiery tuft of hair at her crotch. She turned round slowly, allowing him to view her from behind. She had the slim, lithe body of an athletic boy, but the soft ripeness of a young goddess. The throne-room now fell silent, in shock and amazement, as her nakedness was exposed for everyone to admire.

Finally Maximillus spoke, hoarse with excitement, and his words were addressed to Florianus.

"This is the one—this is the one that I want! But cover her up! My Empress shouldn't be seen like that!"

Florianus remonstrated with him, whispering as loudly as he dared.

"There is still another candidate, your Majesty. The General won't approve of this. This isn't what we discussed—"

"Fuck the General! Fuck your other candidate! And fuck you! I don't want you here. Take off your chain of office. You are dismissed."

As slaves rushed forward to help Naevia back into her gown, the Emperor turned his back on his High Chamberlain and walked across the dais away from him. Everyone in the throne-room saw him do it—it was like a scene from a drama—and knew what it meant.

Florianus had wanted his moment on the great stage of life, and now that he had it, the stage had suddenly tilted, throwing him off into obscurity. Despite the terror that gripped him by the throat, he tried to take in what he saw happening around him. The world that he was accustomed to, a world in which he had been a successful player, had suddenly changed. Yet even in his panic, as he felt his enemies closing in on him, he knew that every detail of information that he now gained could be helpful: a single chance observation might give him a better hope of survival.

He saw Senator Naevius, grandfather of the future Empress and leader of the most powerful faction in the Senate, stride forward to speak to the Emperor. Stepping past the High Chamberlain, he looked at him only briefly, as you might acknowledge the dog excrement that you had avoided treading in.

And why should the Senator pay him more attention that that? The balance of power in the West had shifted, and he, Florianus, had not been part of it. If anything, he had tried to prevent it from happening.

He saw Julian, of all people, talking to Quintus Naevius, laughing, gesticulating to make a point. They were standing close together, as though they knew each other well. Perhaps they *did* know each other well. Had Julian been told that this would happen? Had he helped to plan it?

He saw Cornelia, the forgotten fourth candidate, now in tears, with her parents standing beside her in stiff embarrassment. But someone was talking to her, and trying to comfort her—young Atticus, of all people! What could *that* mean?

He saw the other young man, Sextus Placidus, rushing backwards and forwards, searching for someone: his sister? The sister he had never met before. What did he want to say to her? But she was gone. Where to? Had someone taken her? The Imperial Guardsmen controlled the corridors and gates of the Palace, and an armed mob controlled the streets outside. For anyone named Placidus, there would be no easy passage without a small army of bodyguards. How could she survive without them?

He feared for Julia Placida when he saw Gnaeus Placidus being assisted away from the bride-show by two attendants, surrounded by just such a small army, but without his niece. Suddenly, the Senator swung round in the grip of the two men and, across the tumult and confusion of the throne-room, looked directly at Florianus. There was no expression on his face, though perhaps his eyes had narrowed. Then he turned away and was helped out of the room. He hadn't said anything, but it hadn't been necessary. Florianus had received the message very clearly.

His world was in ruins. Was there any way that the General would ever forgive him? Ogilo would respond somehow to what had happened, but Florianus would not be included in his plans. He had failed him—his usefulness was over. Why should he protect him against the powerful men who would now prefer to see him dead? His life was as good as forfeit. The only question was: whose killers would get to him first? Or would they graciously allow him to take his own life?

In the excitement, he had completely forgotten about the wretched footman.

XXXI

DECIMUS FINDS A BODY, MEETS A MEMBER OF THE ORDER OF THE FULL MOON, AND GETS TO KNOW A SLAVE WHO DOESN'T LIKE COCKROACHES

✠ *In Fanum Fortunae.*

About halfway to Fanum, the horse slipped and nearly threw its rider. Decimus had been scanning the country to left and right of the road, which was easy, since it was flat and there were few trees, and he hadn't paid attention to what was beneath the horse's feet. Now he turned the horse and rode back to look at what had caused it almost to fall.

There was a puddle of blood beside the road, and what might have been entrails. There were more smears of blood leading away from the road, a kind of trail as though a body had been dragged through the low grass towards a clump of bushes. He rode over to investigate.

There was no danger: if there had been a group of men hiding there, or horses, he would have heard them. If it was a single robber, he was confident that he could deal with him.

What he found was the naked body of a dead Citizen soldier, staked out on the ground. Items of his uniform were scattered about, also chicken bones, crusts of bread, and other leftovers from a meal. The man's head was missing, and he had been disembowelled and mutilated.

It was a Blood-Drinker ritual. They had been here and had taken their time with this prisoner, killing him slowly to capture his soul and enjoying their food while they did it. Perhaps he had killed one of them. Now his head would be burned along with the body of his victim, somewhere safely away from the road, and the spirit of the soldier would be enslaved to the spirit of the dead Blood-Drinker in the afterlife.

There were no other bodies. Why had the soldier been on his own? Had he been a courier?

Decimus rode on, now even more watchful than before. When he reached Fanum he reported what he had seen to the guards at the gate, and then went directly to the house of the Lord Governor. He asked to speak to Castor, and was astounded to be told (by the steward Phoenix) that the secretary was dead, murdered two days earlier by a kitchen-maid, who was now on the run.

Furthermore, Castor had been behaving very strangely. For example, he had bought himself a blonde horsey-girl, a clumsy barbarian creature by the name of Mara. Why would he do that? Everybody knew about the secretary's "inclinations", and that they didn't involve young girls.

Decimus congratulated himself on finding the girl, but celebrated too soon. Mara, the steward continued, was now on her way to the City, along with Castor's pretty-boy. Castor had left them both to young master Aulus. Which could only be described as most peculiar behavior.

Leon had gone with them. And two soldiers, to make sure they didn't run away or get stolen.

Did Decimus wish to see the Lord Governor, too?

No, there was no need to disturb him.

Decimus turned to go, and was already leagues away in his thoughts, riding down the Great Provincial Road, aiming to overtake them before the road forked after it crossed the old bridge over the River of the Valley. If he didn't catch up with them, he would have to gamble on their following the same route southwards that he had taken on his journey north: the long road down the length of the Province. The soldiers would have been told to choose that, rather than the left fork, which led to the Stone Gates Pass and through the Riverlands to Trebenna, with a boat from there—quicker and easier, yes, but much more expensive.

Phoenix called him back.

Did Decimus know that someone else had come looking for the horsey-girl, only yesterday? A Sub-officer named Thomasius, with a Sybarite slave-girl in tow.

Because they came from Lord Commander Rhaetius, the Lord Governor had given them no joy, and Phoenix wasn't sure where they had gone. Down the road in pursuit? Maybe, although it had already been dark. Still, if they had hurried, they might already have found the girl. As a Sub-officer, Thomasius could have ordered the two soldiers to hand the girl over to him. Or had he just gone back to Cascantum, to report to the Lord Commander?

Phoenix *did* know where they had been staying in Fanum—first at the Two Lions, and then at the Eagle, or was it the other way round?—because Thomasius had made a joke about it, saying that the slave-girl was picky about inns and didn't like cockroaches. Where did she get such airs and graces from?

Personally, he would have recommended the Stork, where even the girls were clean (it was said), but that place cost serious money. Probably more than a Sub-officer would want to pay. (And he had a woman with him anyway.)

Decimus went to the Two Lions first. Thomasius and the girl might well be gone, but perhaps he could find out which direction they had taken, whether they had gone north to Cascantum or south to the City. And if they had found Mara, they might have brought her back to the inn.

They weren't there, and the innkeeper was far from friendly. Indeed, he abused Decimus as the helper, collaborator, and co-conspirator of the wretch who had brought marauding Sueni cavalrymen into his respectable establishment. He showed Decimus where everything had happened. First the swampies had pushed him and his man aside. Then they had broken down the door and ransacked the room, damaging the furnishings in the process. And finally the savages had got their swords out and had a drunken free-for-all.

Weren't soldiers supposed to protect the honest Citizenry from rampaging barbarians, rather than doing the rampaging themselves? And the miserable Sub-officer (may the Great Mother take him!) had laughed about it, and added insult to injury by only offering him a few silver pieces as compensation.

Those silver pieces were probably more than the "damage" was worth, Decimus reflected. In such a dump, how could you tell what was damaged and what wasn't? All the furniture was falling apart anyway. But he kept those thoughts to himself.

Then he went to the Eagle, and it was there that he found Thomasius and the slave-girl.

At first she didn't want to let him into the room, and when she finally did, it was only after he had explained to her at great length through the door exactly who he was. Even then she stood over Thomasius protectively, like a bitch defending her puppies. She had the Sub-officer's sword in her hand, and the manner in which she held it suggested not so much a high level of expertise as that she would use the sword if forced to.

Thomasius, lying battered and dazed in the narrow bed, was not in good shape. He had taken a slicing cut to the upper arm and a deeper wound to his haunches. A doctor had come, the girl said—Thomasius had money—and had stitched the wounds and bandaged them up. He had left them some herbs to be made into a soothing draught, and would soon be back to check on his patient's progress (and collect another payment).

Although he had lost a lot of blood, the Sub-officer wouldn't die. Citizen infantrymen often took such wounds, the doctor had observed, pointing out to her the numerous scars on Thomasius's body from old fights. But the deeper wound would be slow in healing. He wouldn't be able to sit without discomfort for a long time, and riding was out of the question.

"Who did this to him?"

"A Sybarite, like myself. The man spoke in our Tongue, and I answered him. He was smaller than you, and darker. He had a tattoo on his forearm. Like a star, but it's not: it's a starfish."

"A starfish?"

"Every Sybarite knows what that means."

Decimus did too. If it was true, it was the most important thing he had found out since coming to the North.

They had almost forgotten Thomasius, who was now wide-awake and irritable.

"*You* may know, but I don't, so tell me! I'm the guy who got cut up by the bastard, not you. And give me some wine." Groaning, he tried to raise himself on one elbow, but quickly gave up. "Oh, for Sol's sake, wine, I said!"

Instead of wine, the girl brought him the herbal draught.

"Here, O lord and master! *This* delicious drink is what the doctor recommended, not wine."

And she forced him to drink some of it. From the expression he made, it can't have tasted very good.

"Sol's bollocks, this is dreadful! Oh, this is Manasa, by the way. My slave. Even if she doesn't behave like it."

He asked again about the tattoo, and Decimus told him: it was the sign of a fellowship—not a *brotherhood*, because there were women who bore the mark too—called the Cause. They were committed to restoring Sybaris to its former greatness, and undoing the defeat of the south in the Sybarite War.

"The starfish stands for the power that their navies once had on the sea, just as the armies of the Citizen Republic were unbeaten on the land."

Thomasius grunted.

"Oh, well, that's alright then. If that's what makes them happy, let them get on with it, I say! No skin off *my* nose. Southerners don't like northerners, we all know that. And I'm in a secret brotherhood, too: the Order of the Full Moon. Sub-officers only, no-one else allowed. We do a lot of drinking, once a month, you know, when there's a full moon, obviously. All good fun. Except you have to drink urine the first time round, when you're initiated. Oops, that last bit's secret, forget I said it!"

"No, it's *not* alright. the Cause is not that kind of secret society." He turned to the slave-girl. "You're a Sybarite, Manasa, that was your name, right?—*you* tell him."

She was unwilling at first, and when she spoke she seemed to shrink into herself, becoming still, and her voice quieter.

"What you said is true. But it is not only because of the wars, or because of religion. It's an old, deep hatred. Those who carry the mark have sworn a blood oath. Many of them work in the shadows. They are skillful in the use of instruments of death, and they always strike out of the darkness, to catch their victim when he is relaxed, or drunk, or unsuspecting—when he is off his guard."

"Like the man who was waiting for you outside the inn."

Thomasius nodded.

"Maybe he was the one who killed Castor, too?"

"Perhaps. Castor was my agent, supplying me with information. That was reason enough for him to be killed. And why should a kitchen-maid do it?"

Manasa touched her master's hand, but spoke to Decimus.

"It was not the kitchen-maid who did that killing. It can't have been her. I am sure of that." She spoke with quiet emphasis, her voice still only a whisper. "These men are evil. They choose to kill from the dark-ness, because that creates fear. But they are not the worst. They are only the extended arm of their masters, the Sleepless Ones, who use them just as they also use poison, spells, and dark sendings."

"The Sleepless Ones? Do they have names? Do you know who they are?"

"No-one in Sybaris will name them."

"Why not?"

"Because they're devils. Wizards. Creatures of the Lord of Esbus." She shuddered. "Beside *them*, that man who waited for us in the darkness is truly nothing to be feared."

Sub-officer Thomasius didn't seem like a man who was easily pan-icked, and he was certainly no coward—the scars on his body were proof of that—but Decimus thought that he now looked distinctly uncomfort-able.

"Will he come back to try again?"

Manasa shook her head.

"No. He failed. He will have to do penance for that before he is permitted to try again. Those are their rules. But they may give him another task."

"Well, Sol be praised, that's a relief! At least we won't have to worry about *him* for a while."

Manasa looked at him coolly.

"Not about *him*. Possibly they will send another killer, though."

Decimus was curious how she knew so much about these matters. It was almost suspicious. She was a Sybarite. Was she involved in the Cause?

"Look, no tattoos!" She held up her arms. "Only the tattoos on my face, which the Horse People gave me. And, look again, no starfish! I'm not a follower of the Cause. I'm only a slave. Slaves do a lot of standing and waiting. We watch and we listen, and sometimes we learn things."

"I was a slave, too, Manasa, though not that kind of slave."

Decimus felt ashamed the moment he had said it, and wished he could take it back. She smiled scornfully.

"There is only one kind of slave. Either you're a slave, or you are free. Some day you can explain to me how you were a slave but also *not* a slave. A difficult trick, I would say."

"I'm sorry, Manasa."

Ignoring him, she turned to Thomasius. "And I'm sorry if all this slave-talk is boring you, dear master! But I have a lot of experience of being a slave. I tried to teach Mara, to prepare her for what it would be like for her. She only knew the plains, and freedom."

Decimus slapped his thigh.

"Mara! She is the one who is in danger now!"

Thomasius tried to prop himself up on his elbow again, this time with greater success.

"Why Mara? *I'm* the one they tried to kill."

"Don't you see? They found out that you were searching for her, and sent someone to stop you. And he *has* stopped you. For you, my friend, the search is over. The man who killed Castor that night may have looked for Mara too—"

Manasa interrupted him: "She was in the privy, the soldiers told me that! He waited for her, but he needed to kill her before the household woke and the slaves were up and about. He waited for as long as he dared. When she didn't come back from the privy, he left the house. Having the shits saved her life."

Decimus nodded.

"So Mara is on her way to the City now… And when she gets there, who knows what she might say? And whom she might talk to? She is the living proof of their dirty little plan. They know that we are looking for her, so they'll try to silence her."

Thomasius became agitated.

"Then we must go—at once!"

Manasa gave him a pitying look.

"Oh dear, not *you*, master. Not unless you have a litter at your disposal? And a team of litter-slaves? No, I thought not."

She was right: Thomasius was in no condition to go chasing after anyone. Decimus would have to pursue them on his own.

It would have been much better if he could have had Thomasius with him, to pull rank on the two soldiers and persuade them to hand over the horsey-girl. But the Sub-officer had no written authorization from the Lord General or any document of empowerment that he could sign over to Decimus, only a standard travel warrant enabling him to requisition horses or accommodation. How would the soldiers react to a freedman trying to give them orders? If they didn't cooperate, Decimus realized that he would have to take Mara from them by force—but he didn't say as much to Thomasius.

As it was, the Sub-officer would need to rest for a few days, and only then travel back to Cascantum, probably by cart. A litter would be incredibly expensive, and even a slow mule would be unbearably painful. There was also the danger of the larger wound breaking open again. He would have to be made comfortable in a tradesman's cart. Money was available to pay for this, and for a price the innkeeper would surely be willing to make the arrangements for him.

Word must be brought to Lord Commander Rhaetius, and as soon as possible, that Mara had been found—and not found. And also the information about the man with the starfish tattoo. Since Thomasius couldn't use the fire-beacon, the news would have to be delivered in person. There was only Manasa to do it.

Could she be trusted? Manasa must have somehow read his thoughts.

"Yes, you can trust me, my lord freedman. I could have run away several times these last few days, but I didn't. Now why was that, I wonder?"

Decimus didn't understand what she meant, but he didn't press her further.

She pointed out that she was the only one who had actually met Mara, and that she knew better than either of them what had happened to the horsey-girl. She would leave the following morning at daybreak, carrying with her nothing in writing, except an authorization from her master stating that she was traveling on his errand, and was not a runaway.

In Cascantum, she would seek out Sub-officer Grassica—this was Thomasius's suggestion, but it was immediately approved by Decimus, who had met the man—in the hope that he could bring her to the Lord Commander. In the meantime, she could stay in her master's quarters until he himself arrived.

Decimus would accompany her to the market square—the place of assembly for groups of travelers, as it had been the North Gate in the City—and negotiate for her to join a company of merchants and crafts-men. It might even contain other slaves who were traveling on their master's business. Admittedly, a female slave traveling on her own was an unusual sight, but Decimus would pretend that he was her owner and explain the situation to the leader of the caravan. It was only a short journey, but now that Blood-Drinkers had crossed the River it could turn out to be a very dangerous one.

Then Decimus would ride in the other direction, down the Great Provincial Road, in pursuit of Mara.

XXXII

MARA ON THE GREAT PROVINCIAL

ROAD, AND NOT ALONE

✠ *The road to the south.*

Nobody had asked her, naturally, and the arrangements for the journey were not at all to Mara's liking.

Where was "the City"? How far away was it? It didn't really matter. Among the Horse People, if you wanted to go somewhere you swung yourself onto your horse and rode until you got there.

That was how Mara would have done it. A strong horse could have carried both her and Phrygillus, though he would have had to cling on and would have needed something to cushion his soft little bottom. They would have had to stop slightly more often to allow the *seflar*—as she had found herself calling him—to recover from the rigors of the journey, but it wouldn't have taken them long to get to this "City" place, however far away it was. There was nowhere in the world that the Horse People couldn't ride to.

Leon and the two soldiers were fully-grown men and they would have ridden horses too.

To her great surprise, she and the boy had been loaded onto a wagon, pulled by an old dray-horse. A wagon! Mara would rather have walked. Wagons were for transporting horse-dung, and only if you had a great quantity of it. Among the Horse People, even pregnant women rode horses.

More surprising still was that Leon, a fully-grown man, was in the wagon with them. Was it because he was a slave? Among the Horse People, anyone, even a slave, who was told to ride in a wagon would die of shame.

No, he explained to her, that wasn't the reason. It was because the Lord Governor was so mean. The two soldiers would be riding mules (which didn't surprise Mara at all, since she knew what bad horsemen the Citizens were), and mules cost money. No, not the animals themselves—they belonged to the Governorate—but the fodder that every inn along the Great Provincial Road would be charging them. If the Lord Governor had been able to, he would have put all five of them in the wagon!

And so there was no mule for Leon, who had been degraded to wagon-driver.

She asked him: did he know how to ride? (Among the Horse People, that would be a tremendously rude question to ask a man, likely to lead to the spilling of blood, but Leon was from the south.) Yes, of course he did. Where he came from, the nobility were proud of their horses, and as a slave-boy he had often been in the stables, looking after his former master's favorites.

She remembered: Victor too was from the south. Mara was sure that he must be a fine horseman. He looked so elegant and self-assured.

The two soldiers were crude, unpleasant people. Sempronius was large and clumsy. He grunted a lot, and made it clear to anyone who was prepared to listen to him that he hated barbarians (like Mara), southerners (like Leon), and little faggot boys (like Phrygillus). He was elderly, with bad skin and dried scabs, which he picked at like a hungry bird. Didn't he ever wash?

Sempronius was looking forward to retirement—or he *would* be, he said, if he had any hope of getting a decent retirement settlement. But that wasn't going to happen, and he didn't have any savings worth mentioning. Unless there was soon a change of Emperor, and the new guy handed out a big donative to the troops, Sempronius had nothing much to look forward to.

The street gangs in the City often recruited ex-soldiers. That might be a good idea to follow up, he said. Perhaps he could sign up with that guy Quintus Naevius? Quintus Naevius hated southerners too.

Dexter was smaller, younger, and much quicker-witted than Sempronius. He was also cleaner. He showed a lot of interest in Mara, or in any other young woman who came near him, though not in a manner that Mara liked. He didn't actually say anything to her about what he wanted from her, but he leered and, when any opportunity arose, brushed against her "accidentally".

While Sempronius was rude to Leon, he ignored Mara. He didn't hit her or shout at her, as he hit and shouted at his mule. And when he noticed Dexter making sly advances to Mara, he reminded him that she was property that had to be delivered to the Lord Governor's son—*intact*.

Mara sat with Leon on the driver's seat, while Phrygillus dozed on blankets behind them. They spent the short first day of their journey traveling southwards on a wonderful road. She had seen roads before, but she had to admit that, if you were unfortunate enough to live in a world where wagons were necessary, the building of such a road was a great achievement. Here was something *good* that could be said about the Citizens!

On the other hand, no-one would ever claim that the Citizens knew how to ride. Mara had to laugh at how uncomfortable both the soldiers looked, perched on their mules. What would they look like on proper horses?

They passed by watchtowers and what Leon referred to as "signaling stations", whatever that might mean, and crossed a great bridge over a river. Mara was convinced that this was the same bridge she had crossed with the slave caravan on her way to the slave-market at Fanum, but it looked different seen from the back of a wagon. After the bridge the road forked, and they took the right-hand branch.

"This is the main road," Leon told her.

Either side of the road there was now farmland, quite unlike the grasslands that Mara knew and loved. Men had *tamed* this land. It was pretty, but she wasn't sure whether that was a good thing or not.

By evening they had reached an inn and the two soldiers went inside "to make arrangements". Some time went by. They heard shouting, and then the soldiers came out again and said that everyone could settle down for the night. The soldiers would sleep inside; the three slaves would sleep outside on the wagon.

Mara was delighted by this news, but Phrygillus cried piteously: it would be so cold, and dark, and there would be wolves, and bogeymen. For his age, he was a very childish boy, Mara thought. The Horse People also believed in bad spirits, but if you made the right signs and said the right spells no harm would come to you.

Nor was Leon very happy. He went inside the inn to fetch their supper, and came back with the food—a dirty basket containing stale bread, moldy cheese, and apples, and three lead tankards of watery beer. He was fuming with anger, and it wasn't just because of the food.

The soldiers had forced him to hand over the little purse that his master had entrusted to him, full of heavy silver pieces to pay the expenses of the journey. They had indeed made arrangements with the innkeeper, but not in accordance with the instructions that Leon had been given.

They wanted to steal the Lord Governor's money, he said, which was why the three of them were sleeping outside, and not in a comfortable room inside the inn. The soldiers had a room for themselves, though, and had even tried to requisition it instead of paying for it! But there was another guest staying at the inn, an elderly official called Plancus, who had asked them whether they were traveling on government business. When they said "yes", he invited them to show him the warrant.

"Well, they couldn't, could they? Because there is no warrant. Private business is private business—the master's very correct about that sort of thing."

Plancus was attended by a servant, and two hired thugs, so the soldiers had backed down. They only got the second-best room, and they were asked to pay for it.

"I don't like sleeping on a wagon. I want to sleep in a bed!"

"Well, get used to it, little man, because they won't be paying for a room for us anywhere. Or spending much on our food." He pointed contemptuously at the bread and cheese. "Sempronius is saving for his retirement. The other one just wants some money to spend on whores." He spat out what he was eating. "Look—even the apples are wormy."

It was much the same the following evening. Once again, the three slaves were left to sleep on the wagon, while the soldiers tried to commandeer the best room in the inn, "because they were on state business". However, there were several officers and a government courier also using the inn, and so once again the room had to be paid for in full.

The next day the two soldiers were extremely bad-tempered, and quarreled constantly. Sempronius complained that the younger man had wasted "their" money on a maid. What did that mean? Mara didn't understand why they needed a maid, and tended to agree with Sempronius that it was a waste of money.

But she understood what the argument was about when Dexter responded.

"Oh yes? Are you jealous, then? If you're so horny, why don't you fuck the horsey-girl? Or the bum-boy?"

Fortunately, Phrygillus didn't hear him, or, if did, he didn't understand exactly what the soldier meant—Mara was thoroughly alarmed, though. And the boy definitely heard how Sempronius reacted, because it would have been impossible not to. The older man bellowed with rage, so vigorously that he almost fell off his mule.

After that, he and Dexter didn't speak to each other again for a while, until they made camp beside the road for a midday rest, when it was necessary to discuss the practical arrangements for the evening.

Why not, Sempronius suggested, since the weather was so good, camp out that night (and save the money that would otherwise have been spent on a room)? He had used the road many times, in the days when he was a military courier. They would soon be passing by a large village, and Leon could fetch them some food.

They could camp further down the road, where there was a ruined watchtower, which would give them shelter. Beyond the watchtower was a fine meadow where they could pasture the mules and the drayhorse, and on the far side of the meadow was a wooded hill with a stream running off it that had good drinking water. Or so Sempronius remembered it.

Dexter agreed that it would be worth a try, and once again the soldiers were speaking to each other.

Mara was happy at the thought of sleeping outdoors. Predictably, Phrygillus was very unhappy indeed, but before he could start crying Mara promised that she would look after him and would tell him stories when he settled down to go to sleep. The Horse People had so many stories about the stars, and how they got their names. Did he know that? Mara would tell him about how the Horse with the Golden Mane came to the Great Meadow in the Sky—that was a lovely story.

When they reached the village, Leon was sent to buy the provisions, and Mara was allowed to go with him. She had come to like him, even though on the first evening he too had made an approach to her, once Phrygillus had fallen asleep.

He knew that she was a virgin, he had said, pointing at her plaits. But did she know that there were still things that a man and a woman could do, if they were really fond of each other…?

Well, yes, she had thought to herself, she wasn't *un*fond of him.

"Like what?"

On that invitation, he had taken her hand and placed it under his tunic on something that was rather like a muscle, both hard and fleshy, while prompting her to stroke him. In fact, he would show her how to do it…

She knew that young men and boys among the Horse People sometimes played with each other like this, when they were sleeping out on the grasslands at night, far from the camp. But she wasn't a young man, she was a girl. She was a chieftain's daughter, and she wasn't betrothed yet, so it wasn't right.

She had told him that, and he had apologized and then slipped away to be alone for a few moments. They hadn't spoken about it since.

In the village, no-one stared at them or said anything unfriendly, but Mara had the feeling that they were being watched. She told Leon, who laughed. This was a main road, with strangers passing through every day. Why should the villagers be particularly curious about *them*?

Perhaps the local girls had taken a liking to his southern good looks? Or the local boys fancied a ride on a horsey-girl? He winked at her. Mara didn't think it was funny.

With the silver piece that Sempronius had begrudgingly given them, they bought slightly better and much fresher food than they had been eating at the inns, and had change left over. With all the stress and worry of the journey to cope with, Phrygillus now had an attack of the runs, and it would be good for everybody if he could eat and sleep well that night.

The ruined watchtower and the meadow were as Sempronius had described them. The two mules and the drayhorse were put out to pasture, a fire was lit, and Leon busied himself cutting up and preparing the food for their evening meal. The soldiers had already chosen the best spots for sleeping and spread blankets on the ground. Leon brought them their food, and they scoffed it down greedily.

Phrygillus announced that he had to "go".

Dexter laughed.

"By all means: go somewhere and 'go', but don't do it here!"

Mara was told to take him somewhere where the soldiers couldn't see, hear, or smell what the little faggot was doing. She knew that she had no choice. Phrygillus wouldn't go alone—it would soon be growing dark, and he was terrified of being on his own at night.

Mara offered to take him across the meadow and over to the woodland. That would be far enough, and on the way back he could say "goodnight" to the mules and stroke the dray-horse.

It wasn't difficult finding their way. Phrygillus didn't want to go too far into the woods: far enough to be on his own, yes, but still close enough for him to be able to see Mara.

When they reached the trees, instead of doing what he had said urgently needed to be done, Phrygillus demanded a story. And he didn't need to "go" anymore, he said.

Had he been lying? Did he just want to get away from the soldiers? Yes, he admitted. He didn't like them, and he was frightened of the younger one, who had touched him. Only his master was allowed to touch him *there*.

Mara expected him to start weeping, but he didn't. So they sat down and made themselves comfortable. It was a beautiful evening, and they were in no hurry. Mara told him the story about the Horse with the Golden Mane. He asked for another one, and she told him about the Princess who was turned into a beautiful mare. All the animals came to worship her, even the lions and the wolves.

That last detail about the wolves was a mistake.

"Are there any wolves here? Have you got a knife?"

No, there weren't any wolves, she said. She didn't tell him, but she didn't have a knife. There was only the blunt knife that Leon used for chopping up the food, and Leon had that. In any case, what use would a knife be against a pack of wolves? Besides, they should now be getting back while they still could. The light had almost gone.

"Are you sure there aren't any wolves?"

She told him to "go" before they set off, and he said that he didn't need to.

"No, you do it, please. Quickly! You can find a place over there behind that tree. But don't fall in the stream!"

Mara didn't want to have to walk out to the woods again with him, later that night, when it might be really dark and cold.

"I don't need to go, really I don't."

An owl hooted.

"Did you hear that? That's an owl. It's telling all the other owls that the woods are safe tonight. It's a signal. Remember, I'm a country girl—I know all that stuff!"

It was complete nonsense, but how should Phrygillus know that? Rather gingerly he went off to do his business behind the tree.

She called after him to clean his own bottom with some leaves. And he could wash himself in the little stream, if he was careful not to fall in.

Several times while she was waiting for him, Mara was startled by what sounded like someone moving in the bushes nearby, but there was no-one there. Then she heard the sounds again, but from opposite directions all at once, and this time it was indeed Phrygillus returning from his mission, and a figure approaching from the meadow: Leon, carrying a long wooden club.

Mara wasn't frightened in the dark, but it somehow reassured her to see the club in his hands.

Phrygillus became quite agitated.

"Why have you got that, Leon? Are there wolves?"

"No, I've been for a walk and I didn't see a single one! Nor any lions or bears! I just thought I'd escort you back. The food is ready, and the others have already eaten. And gone to bed! They're snoring and farting. A long walk, even in the dusk, is more fun that having to listen to that." He laughed. "By the way, they didn't leave very much of the food for us, but I knew they wouldn't, so I held some of it back deliberately."

Phrygillus was still agitated. He stared past them into the darkness behind Leon. He could hear something.

"What's that, Mara? That rustling sound?"

Leon laughed.

"Not a wolf, I promise you. But perhaps a man-eating goat? Or a savage pigeon?"

Phrygillus was trembling.

Again, there was the rustling sound. This time, Mara heard it too.

"Listen, Leon, there is something there. Or somebody."

Leon swung around sharply and brandished the club.

"Come out and show yourself! Now!"

A cloaked figure stepped out of the night, and drew aside the hood that was covering its face.

It was Lelia.

Leon lowered the club, but made no move towards her.

"Is this how you greet an old friend, Leon? Is this how you greet a *lover*? You've seen me in the dark before, haven't you? Why be so frightened?"

"What are you doing here? How did you find us?"

"I followed you. I had a horse."

"You know that they're searching for you? They say that you murdered Castor!"

"Why should I do that? The old man never did me any harm."

"But it was your kitchen knife that killed him."

"Yes, someone killed him, using my knife. And why not? It was the sharpest in the kitchen. But that's why I ran—because of the knife. I was hiding in the house. I heard everything. I was going to give myself up, but when I heard them shouting about the knife... I mean, someone stole it, but could I prove that? Leon, I need to talk to you. Do you honestly believe that I murdered him?"

"No."

She turned to Mara.

"Do *you* believe it, horsey-girl? And what about you, little finch? Quite right, of course I didn't kill him! I ran, I hid, and I watched the house, hoping that you would come out. But then there were the soldiers. I saw you all leave, going south. So I stole a horse in Fanum, and followed you."

"Have you spoken to the soldiers?"

"No, not yet, I had to speak to you first. But now that I know you believe me, let's talk to them. We need to go back to Fanum."

"Why?"

"*Because I know who killed Castor.* And I have to tell the Lord Governor. But I can't go on my own—I need protection. We all have to go back."

"The soldiers are sleeping."

"Then we'll wake them."

The little group picked their way carefully across the meadow towards the looming shape of the watchtower. It was now much darker, and it was eerily silent, except for the sound of their breathing. The two mules and the dray-horse were very still, perhaps because they had been joined by another horse, a great black stallion.

"His name is Demon," Lelia whispered to Mara as they walked past.

Mara longed to throw herself onto the horse's back. How could Lelia, the kitchen-maid, the southerner, the lover of bath-houses, know how to ride such a majestic animal?

Inside the watchtower, the fire was still burning and making spitting and crackling noises. The light that it gave off illuminated the room intermittently, making it difficult to see clearly.

Sempronius and Dexter lay on their blankets, but stretched out awkwardly, as if they had both been frozen suddenly in the middle of a nightmare. The light flared up. Dexter's eyes were wide open, but the gash across his throat gaped even wider. Not as wide, though, as the knife-cut that had ended the life of Sempronius. Mara saw that the blankets were wet with blood.

Phrygillus took longer to understand what his eyes were showing him; then he screamed in shock. Leon cursed and raised his club.

"What is this, Lelia? You said they were sleeping. Did *you* do this?"

Who else could it have been? There was only one black stallion out on the meadow.

Lelia was now clutching a long, thin knife. Mara held the boy close.

"It's sad, Leon, but I don't think we can wake them anymore."

"*You* did this!"

Her eyes gleamed even brighter than the knife.

"I only did one of them."

And then another voice, from the shadows: "But she learns quickly."

A larger, shrouded figure stepped out from behind her. Mara gasped— it was Victor. He was dressed in black, and holding a curved sword.

Lelia smiled at him.

"I have a good teacher. But the soldier's throat was tougher than Castor's. Master, may I finish this?"

"You may."

What followed only took seconds, but it haunted Mara's dreams for a long time afterwards. And in her waking moments, she would go over it in her mind again and again: what might have happened, what almost happened…

Without looking at him, Lelia stabbed ferociously at Leon. Not looking gave her the advantage of surprise, but it robbed her blow of its accuracy: by chance, her knife caught in his wooden club. As he jerked the club, the knife flew out of her hand. Momentarily, Lelia was defence-less.

Instead of killing Mara and Phrygillus at his leisure, while Lelia dealt with the footman, Victor was now forced to attack Leon. His sword hacked deep into the slave's body.

He shouted in satisfaction, ugly words in an unfamiliar tongue.

Lelia picked up her knife and skewered it deep into Leon's middle. She too was muttering incomprehensibly.

Leon croaked, "Run, Mara, run!"

The two weapons were both hooked fast into Leon's body, for a second or maybe for two. And those two seconds were enough. Without looking back, Mara ran.

She scooped up Phrygillus and bundled him out onto the meadow. Every horse she had ever known understood the whistle that meant "We ride!" This one was no exception. He was ready for her when she threw herself onto his back, hauled little Phrygillus after her, and jabbed her heels into the stallion's flanks.

The southerners charged at the horse, but they were too late.

Mara thrilled at the feeling of the night air rushing past her. She was riding a superb horse, she was free again, and even the kicking, squawk-ing boy clinging on behind her couldn't spoil that moment.

Would they follow her on the mules? Just let them try! She almost laughed at the thought. But they could soon be after her with fresh horses, or other killers might be.

What reason did they have to kill Castor? Or for killing Leon? And why should they want *her* to die?

This world of the Citizens was cruel and horrible. There was only one place for her to go. She gazed up at the sky, and then turned the horse north. Yes, she told him, you're "horse" now. She patted him. *My* horse. No more nonsense about demons. (But let my enemies think that you're one.)

Though she hardly knew the way, it was time to go home. Even though a traitor would be waiting for her there—the unknown man who had betrayed her to the slavers.

And what the Horse People would make of Phrygillus was anybody's guess.

THE FACTIONS
IN THE SENATE

The Whites: Supporters of the Emperor and of the Maximian Dynasty; especially strong among the military; followers of the state religion of Sol; faction leader: Lentulus Pulcher

The Greens: Supporters of Ogilo, "the General"; strong among the wealthy merchants of Trebenna and the nobility of the Province (followers of the old northern gods); the "Peace Party"; faction leaders: Appianus Terebinthian and Lucius Pomponius Atticus

The Blues: The party of the old aristocracy of the City; followers of the Western or "Lesser Worship" of the Slave cult; faction leader: Marcus Naevius

The Reds: The party of the great landowners of Sybaris and the south; followers of the Eastern or "Greater Worship" of the Slave cult; the "War Party"; faction leaders: Gnaeus Julius Placidus and Gaius Cornelius Rufus

NAMES

IN THE CITY

Maximillus, Emperor in the West, son of †Emperor Maximus the Younger and grandson of †Emperor Maximus the Great

Ogilo, "the General", Master of Horse & Foot, Imperial Guardian and military ruler of the West

Florianus the eunuch, High Chamberlain

Julian, assistant to Florianus

Senator **Lentulus**, City Prefect and chairman of the Senate (a White)

Senator **Lentulus Pulcher**, his brother (a White)

Senator **Terentius Ager** (a White)

Senator **Lucius Pomponius Atticus** (a Green)

Davus, his freedman secretary

Sinica, a slave-girl

Beltran, a footman

Servo, a gatekeeper

Aulus Atticus (Faustus Pomponius Atticus Junior), son of Senator Faustus Pomponius Atticus and nephew of Senator Lucius Pomponius Atticus

Decimus, Aulus's freedman

Senator **Appianus Terebinthian** (a Green)

Senator **Marcus Naevius**, brother of †Naevia Senior (the mother of Ogilo) (a Blue)

Senator **Quintus Naevius** (a Blue)

Naevia, his daughter

Senator **Gnaeus Julius Placidus** (a Red)

Senator **Gaius Julius Placidus**, his brother (a Red)

Sextus Placidus, son of †Senator Publius Julius Placidus, nephew of Senators Gaius and Gnaeus Julius Placidus, and brother of Julia Placida

Julia Placida, daughter of †Senator Publius Julius Placidus, niece of Senators Gaius and Gnaeus Julius Placidus, and sister of Sextus Placidus

Senator **Gaius Cornelius Rufus** (a Red)

Cornelia, his daughter

www.ingramcontent.com/pod-product-compliance
Lightning Source LLC
Chambersburg PA
CBHW020803250626
47155CB00003B/1191